PRAISE FOR JOEL C. ROSENBERG

"Rosenberg's imagination is a tumultuous place where Middle Eastern geopolitics combine with devious minds. Authentic, fast-paced, and totally engrossing."

KYLE MILLS, #1 *New York Times* bestselling author of *Total Power*

"Rosenberg once again proves to be at the top of his game. . . . The plot is all too possible. Marcus Ryker is a perfect hero, right where we need him, at just the right time. *The Beirut Protocol* will take your breath away as Rosenberg marches to the brink of a war only Ryker can stop—if he can save himself first!"

ANDREWS & WILSON, bestselling authors of the Tier One, Sons of Valor, and Shepherds series

"Nobody builds tension and suspense like Rosenberg, who has quickly developed his hero Marcus Ryker into one of the most formidable action stars the genre has to offer. . . . Fast, twist-filled, and ripped-from-the-headlines, *The Beirut Protocol* soars with authenticity and will leave readers breathless. At this point, Rosenberg's stuff is pretty much mandatory reading for all lovers of high-octane thrillers."

RYAN STECK, *The Real Book Spy*

"A taut, brilliant thriller ripped right from today's headlines. Joel Rosenberg is masterful! *The Jerusalem Assassin* is an absolute home run."

BRAD THOR, #1 *New York Times* bestselling author of *Backlash*

"Gripping. . . . Readers will tear through the final pages to see whether Marcus can once again triumph over evil."

PUBLISHERS WEEKLY on *The Jerusalem Assassin*

"Joel C. Rosenberg continues to mix his unique blend of prophetic fiction and nonstop action unlike anyone else working today."

THE REAL BOOK SPY on *The Persian Gamble*

"Joel C. Rosenberg writes taut, intelligent thrillers that are as timely as they are well-written. Pairing a fast-paced plot with an impressive understanding of the inner workings in the corridors of power of the Russian government, *The Kremlin Conspiracy* is a stellar novel of riveting action and political intrigue."

MARK GREANEY, #1 *New York Times* bestselling author of *Agent in Place*

"*The Kremlin Conspiracy* is my first Joel C. Rosenberg novel, and I am absolutely blown away by how good this guy is. The story moves at a blistering pace, it's crackling with tension, and you won't put it down until you reach the end. Guaranteed. Simply masterful."

SEAN PARNELL, *New York Times* bestselling author of *Outlaw Platoon*

"Rosenberg cranks up the suspense, delivering his most stunning, high-stakes thriller yet."

PUBLISHERS WEEKLY on *The Kremlin Conspiracy*

"Joel Rosenberg has an uncanny talent for focusing his storytelling on real-world hot spots just as they are heating up. He has done it again in *The Kremlin Conspiracy*."

PORTER GOSS, former director of the Central Intelligence Agency

"Marcus Ryker rocks! Breakneck action, political brinksmanship, authentic scenarios, and sharply defined characters make Joel C. Rosenberg's *Kremlin Conspiracy* a full-throttle and frightening ride through tomorrow's headlines."

BRIGADIER GENERAL (U.S. ARMY, RETIRED) A.J. TATA,
national bestselling author of *Direct Fire*

"If you love the ABC drama *Designated Survivor* or are always looking for the next well-written novel about America and her fight against terrorism, you'll definitely want to pick up *Without Warning*."

BOOK REPORTER

"A compelling and complicated political thriller that includes an edge-of-your-seat climax impossible to put down."

MIDWEST BOOK REVIEW on *The First Hostage*

"Rosenberg has ripped a page from current headlines with a heart-stopping plot about the Islamic State."

PUBLISHERS WEEKLY on *The Third Target*

"If there were a *Forbes* 400 list of great current novelists, Joel Rosenberg would be among the top ten. . . . One of the most entertaining and intriguing authors of international political thrillers in the country. . . . His novels are un-put-downable."

STEVE FORBES, editor in chief, *Forbes* magazine

"[Joel Rosenberg] understands the grave dangers posed by Iran and Syria, and he's been a bold and courageous voice for true peace and security in the Middle East."

DANNY AYALON, former Israeli deputy foreign minister

"Joel has a particularly clear understanding of what is going on in today's Iran and Syria and the grave threat these two countries pose to the rest of the world."

REZA KAHLILI, former CIA operative in Iran and bestselling author of *A Time to Betray: The Astonishing Double Life of a CIA Agent inside the Revolutionary Guards of Iran*

"His novels seem to be ripped from the headlines—next year's headlines."

WASHINGTON TIMES

"Rip-roaring, heart-pounding, page-turning, high-octane, geopolitical thriller."

FORBES on *The Last Days*

"An action-packed, Clancyesque political thriller."

PUBLISHERS WEEKLY on *The Last Days*

"A wild, rocketing read. *The Last Jihad* is Tom Clancy writ large."

VINCE FLYNN, *New York Times* bestselling author of *Consent to Kill*

THE BEIRUT PROTOCOL

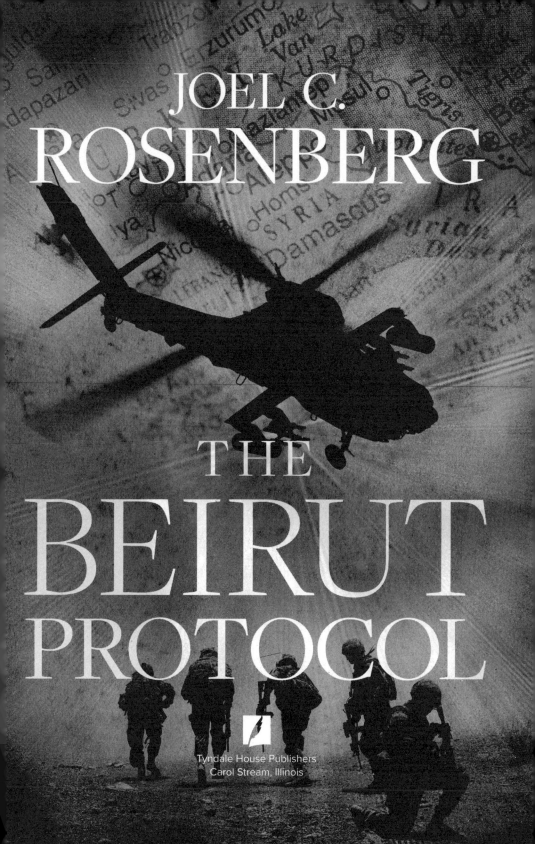

JOEL C. ROSENBERG

THE BEIRUT PROTOCOL

Tyndale House Publishers
Carol Stream, Illinois

Visit Tyndale online at tyndale.com.

Visit Joel C. Rosenberg's website at joelrosenberg.com.

TYNDALE and Tyndale's quill logo are registered trademarks of Tyndale House Ministries.

The Beirut Protocol

Designed by Dean H. Renninger

Scripture quotations are taken from the New American Standard Bible,® copyright © 1960, 1962, 1963, 1968, 1971, 1972, 1973, 1975, 1977, 1995 by The Lockman Foundation. Used by permission.

The Beirut Protocol is a work of fiction. Where real people, events, establishments, organizations, or locales appear, they are used fictitiously. All other elements of the novel are drawn from the author's imagination.

For information about special discounts for bulk purchases, please contact Tyndale House Publishers at csresponse@tyndale.com or call 1-855-277-9400.

ISBN 978-1-4964-3789-1 (hardcover)
ISBN 978-1-4964-5404-1 (International Trade Paper Edition)

Printed in the United States of America

27	26	25	24	23	22	21
7	6	5	4	3	2	1

To my wonderful and much-loved Lebanese brother-in-law, Dan,
who was born in Beirut and grew up there during the brutalities
of the civil war—may the people of Lebanon, your people,
know true peace and true freedom and true joy, and soon.

CAST OF CHARACTERS

Americans

Marcus Ryker—special operative, Central Intelligence Agency

Kailea Curtis—special agent, Diplomatic Security Service

Geoff Stone—special agent in charge, Diplomatic Security Service

Peter Hwang—special operative, Central Intelligence Agency

Jennifer Morris—officer, Central Intelligence Agency

Noah Daniels—officer, Central Intelligence Agency

Donny Callaghan—former commander, SEAL Team Six

Andrew Clarke—president of the United States

Carlos Hernandez—vice president of the United States

James Meyers—chairman of the Joint Chiefs of Staff

Richard Stephens—director of the Central Intelligence Agency

Martha Dell—deputy director of intelligence (DDI),
    Central Intelligence Agency

William McDermott—national security advisor

Margaret "Meg" Whitney—secretary of state

Robert Dayton—U.S. senator (D-Iowa)

Annie Stewart—senior foreign policy advisor to Senator Robert Dayton

Marjorie Ryker—Marcus's mother

Iranians

Grand Ayatollah Hossein Ansari—Supreme Leader of Iran

Yadollah Afshar—president of the Islamic Republic of Iran

Mahmoud Entezam—commander of the Iranian Revolutionary
  Guard Corps
Dr. Haydar Abbasi—director of Iran's ballistic missile program

Israelis

Reuven Eitan—prime minister of Israel
Shimon Levy—minister of defense
Asher Gilad—director of Mossad
Tomer Ben Ami—deputy director of the Shin Bet
Yonatan "Yoni" Golan—chief of staff (*Ramatkal*), Israeli Defense Force
Yossi Kidron—head of IDF's Northern Command
Yigal Mizrachi—IDF intelligence officer

Saudis

Faisal Mohammed—monarch of the Kingdom of Saudi Arabia
Abdulaziz bin Faisal—crown prince and minister of defense
Abdullah bin Rashid—director of the General Intelligence Directorate

Turks

Ahmet Mustafa—president of the Republic of Turkey
Hamdi Yaşar—producer, Al-Sawt satellite television network

Others

Abu Nakba—commander of the Kairos terror organization
Sheikh Ja'far ibn al-Hussaini—spiritual leader of Hezbollah
Amin al-Masri—deputy commander of Hezbollah's Radwan Unit
  (special forces)
Tanzeel al-Masri—member of Hezbollah's Radwan Unit
Zayan ibn Habib—member of Hezbollah's Radwan Unit
Abdel Rahman—member of Hezbollah's Radwan Unit
Kareem bin Mubarak—commander of Hezbollah's
  counterintelligence unit

*"There are things which a man is afraid
to tell even to himself, and every decent man has a number
of such things stored away in his mind."*
FYODOR DOSTOYEVSKY

PART
ONE

Marcus Ryker heard the whoosh of the incoming missile but never saw it coming.

What he did see was the lead Humvee disintegrating in a massive fireball. An instant later, the cool morning air erupted with the sound of automatic weapons fire.

"*Go back—go back!*" he yelled as burning wreckage rained down upon them.

Their driver tried to jam the vehicle into reverse. But it was too late. The vehicle behind them was already burning, hit by an anti-tank missile, and Marcus knew they were next.

"*Get out,*" he ordered his team. "*Everybody out—now!*"

Marcus grabbed his weapon and backpack and kicked open the front passenger door, then jumped out of the Humvee. Scanning the horizon, he spotted muzzle flashes coming from a grove of olive trees to the northeast. He raised his M4 carbine, positioned himself behind the engine block, and provided covering fire for his colleagues.

Kailea Curtis was the first to scramble out of the backseat. She grabbed their young Israeli counterpart by his jacket, yanked him out of the Humvee, and tossed him his Tavor assault rifle. "Find cover and radio for backup," she ordered.

Marcus's eyes locked on two masked men climbing through a breach in the security fence. They were thirty yards ahead to his right. Pivoting hard, he took aim, fired two bursts, and felled them both. Then he shouted for Kailea to move to the rear of the Humvee to cover their six.

"*Done,*" she shouted back, moving into position and beginning to lay down suppressive fire with her own M4.

Marcus ordered their young driver, no more than nineteen, to keep his head down and come out the passenger door. With dozens of rounds pelting their vehicle, it was far too risky to exit the exposed driver's side. There was no response.

Marcus finished loading the M203 grenade launcher attached beneath the regular barrel of his weapon. Spotting more muzzle flashes—these coming from an abandoned stone house on the top of a nearby ridge—he steadied his breathing, took aim, and squeezed the trigger. The 40mm grenade exploded from its tube, streaked across the ravine, and scored a direct hit. Flames poured out of the windows of the house, followed by thick black smoke. The muzzle flashes ceased.

Marcus repeated his order to the driver. The convoy had already been hit by two anti-tank missiles. The third was coming any second.

There was still no reply.

Finally Marcus turned and saw why. The young man was slumped over the steering wheel. The window beside him was shattered. Blood and brain matter were splattered all over the cab. Trained to be certain, Marcus leaned inside and felt for a pulse. There was none. Nor time to mourn.

"*Marcus,*" Kailea shouted, "*more tangos—eight o'clock.*"

Marcus looked over his left shoulder and counted no fewer than a dozen masked fighters racing through the ravine and advancing on their position. There was no question they were Hezbollah. The Iranian-backed terror group controlled the whole of southern Lebanon, the Lebanese regular army having long since ceded the frontier with Israel. As they reached the fence line, most of the fighters opened fire with AK-47s, while two carrying bolt cutters began to cut a second hole in the fence.

Marcus and Kailea returned fire, starting with a barrage of 40mm grenades. They took out two men. Most of the rest ran for cover, but one of them was preparing to use an RPG.

Marcus ordered a retreat. Both agents grabbed their backpacks off the ground and sprinted for the thick brush behind them. The grenade missed its mark, slicing just over their heads and exploding in the trees well beyond them. Five seconds later, though, the third anti-tank missile found its target. The explosion was deafening. The Humvee they had been riding in all morning was gone.

They found the young Israeli intel officer and took cover under the thick spring foliage, ignoring the roaring fires and billowing smoke. Marcus motioned for Kailea to take up a position facing the northeast. He ordered the Israeli officer to cover the northwest. Marcus himself aimed his M4 through the bramble directly to the north.

"Did you reach your guys?" Marcus asked in a hushed tone.

"Radio's not working," the Israeli replied.

"Broken?"

"No, sir—but I can't get through."

"Why not?"

"No idea, sir."

"Use mine," Marcus offered, fishing his radio out of his backpack and tossing it over.

But Marcus's radio didn't work either. Nor did Kailea's. The radios weren't the problem. They were fine. Hezbollah had to be jamming their signals.

Marcus checked his watch. It was only 9:17 in the morning. Yet already the temperature was soaring past ninety degrees. It was critical they connect with the IDF's Northern Command. They weren't going to make it to the bottom of the hour if they didn't get help fast.

"Send up a red star cluster," Marcus ordered Kailea, peering through the scope of his M4 and scanning for any signs of movement. "I'll cover us."

During the Vietnam War, American GIs would literally fire red flares into the sky to indicate to their commanders that they were under fire and needed immediate assistance. The flares also helped guide friendly forces to their position. In the modern era, "sending up a red star cluster" was simply code for calling in the cavalry.

Kailea set down her weapon, reached into her backpack, pulled out a device the size of an alarm clock radio, and powered it up. Designed and built exclusively for the U.S. military and known as a Blue Force Tracker, the handheld unit allowed her to almost instantaneously uplink their precise GPS coordinates along with a brief distress message via a secure military satellite to both American and Israeli commanders.

"Message sent," Kailea said a moment later, powering down the device and picking up her weapon.

Marcus continued scanning for tangos. He saw no one yet but had no doubt they were coming. Lots of them. Soon, he knew, this military service road, which ran for dozens of kilometers along the Israeli-Lebanese border, would be crawling with Hezbollah operatives. Feeling his heart rate spiking, he began silently counting down from fifty. It was an old trick he had learned in the Marines and used on the battlefields of Afghanistan and Iraq. As always, it worked like a charm. The adrenaline stopped pumping into his system. His breathing slowed. So did his pulse.

Marcus glanced to his right and could sense the fear in the young man—barely twenty—lying beside him. The Israeli officer's hands were shaking, as was his weapon, and Marcus knew why. This kid knew all too well the stories of the IDF soldiers who had been kidnapped on this border. And not just kidnapped but tortured without mercy. Butchered. Dismembered. Mutilated beyond recognition. For an Israeli, falling into the hands of a Hezbollah fighter was a fate worse than death.

Marcus turned back and peered once again through the reticle of his scope. Hezbollah was coming, fast and hard. If reinforcements did not arrive quickly, they would be overrun, and for all his moral revulsion at the notion of suicide, Marcus knew he'd sooner put a bullet into his own mouth than—

2

Marcus forced away such thoughts.

This was not the time to speculate about what *might* happen. He had to stay focused on what was happening right in front of him, in real time, and keep his team alive until backup could arrive.

Marcus wasn't worried about Special Agent Kailea Theresa Curtis. The woman was a pro. Though she'd never served in the military, she'd been a New York City beat cop before joining the State Department's Diplomatic Security Service, and she was as tough and smart as anyone he had ever worked with. Marcus had been most impressed watching her in a firefight in Jerusalem. Even while taking a bullet, she had never lost her cool. She had stayed in the hunt, returning fire, keeping her target pinned down until Marcus had been able to work around behind the guy and take him out.

She could have accepted a desk job after that. Indeed, she could have retired to a cushy private-sector position and a fat six-figure salary. Marcus would have been the first to applaud her for it. But Kailea was a warrior. She loved her country. She loved her job. She loved the DSS. She had been relentless about getting back into the field as rapidly as possible, and Marcus was glad to have her at his side now.

Yigal Mizrachi of the IDF's 869th was another story. Marcus had met him for the first time upon landing in Tel Aviv a mere twelve hours earlier. He had quickly become impressed with the kid's encyclopedic knowledge of the enemy and the terrain along Israel's northern border. But was the young Israeli officer really up for *this*?

Raised by a religious Jewish father who had made aliyah from Brooklyn in the 1960s and an even more religious mother who'd grown up in the Israeli port city of Rishon Leziyyon, Yigal was the baby of the Mizrachi family. The youngest of six brothers and two sisters, he was barely two years out of high school.

The kid was razor-sharp—borderline genius—and was fluent in Arabic and French, as well as Hebrew and English. It was no wonder, then, that Yigal had been recruited into *Isuf Kravi*, the IDF's combat intelligence unit, and assigned to Northern Command. There, he'd been assigned as an aide to the unit's commander and had worked hard to become a Hezbollah specialist. Still, Yigal had never seen war. Never been in a firefight. Never even been near one. So Marcus had no idea how the kid would handle himself under these conditions or if he could be trusted.

Marcus breathed a bit easier knowing that the message Kailea had just fired up the chain of command would set into motion events that could soon bring this nightmare to an end. Even now, he knew, Unit 669—Israel's elite combat rescue team—was spooling up and would soon be headed their way. So would a quick reaction force. In ten minutes, tops, the good guys would bring overwhelming firepower to bear on the enemy.

The question was, could they hold on for ten more minutes?

★

"Commander, you're going to want to see this."

The two-star U.S. Army general could hear the tension in the voice of his twenty-six-year-old duty officer. He stepped out of his office and moved quickly to the young aide's side. "What've you got?"

"We're getting a distress signal from the Israeli-Lebanese border, sir."

"We don't have any forces on that border."

"Nevertheless, sir—I've got reports of contact with the enemy and an urgent request for extraction."

★

Three fighters emerged from the east through the flames and billows of smoke.

Dressed in dark-green camo and full combat gear, they approached the remains of the last vehicle in the convoy.

Marcus motioned to his colleagues to hold their fire. He reached into his backpack and drew out a suppressor and attached it to the muzzle of his rifle. Then he waited—*ten seconds . . . fifteen . . . twenty*—until all three were obscured from the view of the rest of their cell. Then, accounting for the cross breeze coming from the Mediterranean just a few miles to the west, Marcus zeroed in on the exposed neck of the last fighter in line and took the shot.

A puff of pink mist filled the air. And before the man hit the ground, Marcus pivoted, found the neck of the next man, and squeezed the trigger again.

Both shots were nearly silent. Whatever incidental noise the suppressed rounds might have made was swallowed up in the roar of the raging fires. But the second tango didn't simply collapse to the ground. Rather, he stumbled forward several steps before falling and in so doing hit the lead fighter in the back of the leg.

Startled, the commander swung around fast, his weapon up, stunned to find his two colleagues sprawled on the ground. Pivoting toward the brush, the man searched desperately for a target to shoot back at, but he never got the chance. Marcus double-tapped him to the forehead and he went hurtling backward into the inferno of the second vehicle.

"Come on," Marcus said. "Time to go on offense."

He ejected a spent magazine, popped in a fresh one, and scrambled to his feet. Kailea did the same, as Yigal asked what he should do.

"Watch our backs and our gear," Marcus said, then led Kailea out of the brush.

He moved left, his weapon up, sweeping side to side, and reached the wreckage of the last vehicle in the line. Wincing from the acrid smoke in his eyes, he could see the burning bodies of the IDF soldiers trapped inside. He saw no movement. Heard no cries. Spotted no signs of life. The three men had surely been dead from the moment the missile hit their jeep. He certainly hoped so. At any rate, there was nothing he could do for them, so Marcus kept moving, peering through the smoke and the flames, hunting for the rest of the terrorist cell.

They were coming—all of them.

Marcus counted five masked men. They had made their way through the large hole in the fence and were coming up the ravine. There were two more out there somewhere, he knew—the ones who'd used the bolt cutters—though it was possible they had retreated back into Lebanese territory.

Marcus inched backward, careful to remain hidden by the burning jeep. Raising his left hand, he signaled to Kailea that he could see five targets, then motioned for her to take up a position near the wreckage of the first vehicle in the convoy. When she complied, he got down on his stomach, facing the east, tried to steady his breathing, and lay in wait.

3

It was 2:22 a.m. when the DSS watch officer took the call.

Not sure he had heard right, the officer asked the commander of the Joint Personnel Recovery Agency to repeat what he'd just said. When he realized the magnitude of what was unfolding, the officer spoke quickly. No, he hadn't received any direct word of DSS agents operating on the Israel-Lebanon border on an advance trip for the SecState. Yes, he would certainly work to confirm the information while also alerting his superiors.

A moment later, he was barking orders to his colleagues to try to establish contact with Special Agents Ryker and Curtis and to wake up the director. Meanwhile, he picked up another line and speed-dialed the national security advisor at home.

★

Neither Marcus nor Kailea was in uniform.

They certainly were not wearing helmets, flak jackets, or combat gear of any kind. They were not military, after all. They were DSS agents. Typically they would be in suits. But this was not a protective detail. The secretary of state wasn't arriving until the following day. This was an advance trip, so they were wearing street clothes.

Marcus wore black jeans and a black T-shirt, which was now soaked through. The heat thrown off by the three fires was unbearable, and between the smoke in his eyes and the sweat pouring off his forehead, it was becoming difficult to see. Mopping his soaked hair and beard, he reminded himself that at least he had the element of surprise.

Just then Marcus spotted two fighters coming around the corner. Reflexively switching from single shot to automatic, he opened fire. Two quick bursts and both men were down. Marcus charged forward around the back of the jeep, spotted another fighter, and unleashed two more bursts. This one, too, dropped to the ground. Marcus ejected the spent mag and reloaded as he continued his advance.

He swept his weapon from east to west but saw no one else. Then he heard an eruption of gunfire at the other end of the convoy.

Kailea was in trouble.

Marcus's first thought was to come all the way around the burning convoy and race forward along its northern side. That would give him the best chance of ambushing the fighters from the rear. Yet he quickly rejected the idea. To leave the cover of the burning convoy was too great a risk, exposing him to any Hezbollah sniper who might be hiding in the supposedly abandoned homes on the other side of the ravine.

So Marcus reversed course and worked his way up the southern side of the convoy. Suddenly two fighters came racing through the gap between the first and second vehicles. Had Marcus been another ten feet forward, they would have blindsided him and shot him in the back. As it happened, he saw them first and opened fire. The first man died instantly. The second was hit at least once, possibly twice, in the right shoulder or upper chest. He staggered forward several steps, dropped his AK-47, kept moving several more steps, and then collapsed.

Marcus pivoted to his left, lest anyone else was coming through the gap.

No one was there. He turned back to his right and found the man on the ground, covered in blood, writhing in pain. Marcus raised his weapon to finish him off but stopped himself.

The IDF was on the way. The Israelis would vastly prefer a live prisoner to another body to bury. And they, Marcus knew, could make this guy talk. In all probability, they'd get valuable intel out of him, then stash him away as leverage for some future prisoner exchange. Besides, the man was now unarmed. It would be murder—a war crime, no less—to kill him now.

Marcus kicked the weapon well out of the fighter's reach and scanned in every direction for Kailea. He was surprised and worried not to find any sign of her. On instinct, he wheeled around to see if anyone was behind him. No one was. All was clear. Yet he still saw no sign of his partner. Where was she? He couldn't call out for her. There were tangos out there, and the last thing he wanted to do was draw their attention. But what alternatives did he have? He couldn't radio her. Their handhelds still were not working—most likely being jammed.

Marcus preferred to go look for Kailea, but he knew he could not leave the wounded Hezbollah fighter unattended. So he picked up the man's rifle, popped out the magazine, and cleared the chamber of the additional round. Then he pointed the barrel of his M4 at the man's face and shouted at him to remove his mask. Though shaking, the man did not comply. Realizing he likely didn't speak English, Marcus motioned for him to remove the mask. Still there was no response.

Marcus was in no mood for games. He fired a single shot at the dirt, barely six inches from the man's head. This certainly got his attention. Except it was not a man. When the hood finally came off, Marcus found himself staring into the stricken eyes of a boy no more than fifteen years old.

4

"Get the choppers in the air—now."

It was 9:29 a.m.

Eleven minutes had gone by since they'd first received the distress call from the convoy, and Major General Yossi Kidron was livid with his staff that 669—the IDF's elite airborne combat search-and-rescue unit—was not already on the scene. "And get the drones up too."

"All of them?" asked a tactical officer.

"Yes, all of them—now. Let's go, people. What are you waiting for? We've got men in harm's way—move!"

As head of Northern Command, Kidron was in charge of securing the Blue Line, Israel's seventy-eight-kilometer-long border with Lebanon. It was bad enough to have already lost eight of his soldiers before 10 a.m. But he knew the situation could quickly get worse.

Not since the Second Lebanon War back in 2006 had so many Israelis been killed in this sector on a single day, much less in the span of just ten or fifteen minutes. Kidron knew he would soon be facing multiple official inquiries. One would certainly come from the top brass at the Kirya, Israel's equivalent of the Pentagon. A second would be mounted by the Defense Committee of the Knesset, Israel's parliament. These, however, would be nothing compared to the inevitable U.N. investigation and condemnations of his country at the Security Council in New York.

In the meantime, the piranhas in the media were going to eat him alive. And of course, in the next few hours he was going to have to personally inform eight sets of parents that they'd never see their sons again. It was the worst part of his job, and he dreaded the thought of it.

And yet if two American officials were also captured or killed by Hezbollah . . .

★

A massive explosion knocked Marcus off his feet.

An instant later came another explosion.

Rocks and branches and dirt rained down on him. Marcus began coughing violently. His ears were ringing. Wiping his eyes, he reached for his weapon and pulled it toward him.

As he fought to regain his bearings, a Hezbollah fighter suddenly entered his peripheral vision. The man was moving right to left, hurling grenades into the bushes close to where Yigal was hiding. His AK-47 blazed as the grenades detonated. Marcus raised his M4, switched to auto, and opened fire. The first burst went wide. The second did not. The man dropped to the ground a couple of yards from the edge of the brush.

Marcus wasn't sure why Yigal wasn't returning fire. Was he dead? Wounded? There was no movement in the bushes.

It was quiet for at least a minute, save the roaring of the vehicle fires off to Marcus's right. No one else was around. Marcus had lost count of the number of tangos he had felled, but seeing no one else coming, he began climbing back to his feet. Just then, however, the downed Hezbollah fighter tried to do the same. The man had dropped his Kalashnikov, which was now several feet away. Racked with pain, he was nevertheless groping toward it. Marcus could see blood gushing from his left leg and down his left arm. But then, without warning, the man changed tactics. Rolling onto his good side, he abandoned his quest for the AK-47. Instead, he drew a sidearm, raised it up, and took aim at Marcus's head.

Marcus did not hesitate. He unleashed another burst from the M4, riddling the man's head and chest with bullets. The pistol dropped to the ground and the guy finally ceased moving.

Getting to his feet, Marcus scanned the environment around him. Kailea was still nowhere to be found. Nor was Yigal. The only person he could see was the teenage Hezbollah fighter, who was now white as a sheet and frozen in terror. Marcus moved to his side and secured his hands and feet with flexicuffs, then headed toward the bushes, now ablaze from the grenades that had been lobbed into them.

Looking to the skies, Marcus neither saw nor heard any sign of IDF choppers. Reinforcements were coming. They had to be. But they weren't there yet, and Marcus knew he and his team were quickly running out of time.

He wiped blood and dirt off the dial of his watch. It was 9:32. They had to get moving, away from the convoy and all this carnage. They needed to retreat. It was not their job to hold off all the Hezbollah fighters that were still coming. Dozens of them. Maybe hundreds. It was time to head into the mountains and forests of northern Israel and hunker down until the coast was clear. But first he had to find his team.

Marcus resisted the temptation to call out to the Israeli by name. He had been trained better than that. Still, abandoning caution, he finally did call out, though not as loud as he might have.

"Hey, kid, you all right?

There was no reply. Weapon up, Marcus moved closer to the burning bushes and called out again.

"Kid, where are you?"

Still nothing.

Fearing the Israeli had been shot or blown to pieces by the last volley of grenades, Marcus shifted gears. Finding Kailea, he decided, had to be his top priority. They were partners, after all. They were responsible for watching each other's backs, and in the eighteen months they had worked together, in multiple countries and on multiple continents, they had certainly proven their loyalty to one another. *Find her,* Marcus told himself. *First he had to make sure she was healthy and safe. Then they could search for Yigal together.*

Then again, Marcus was increasingly convinced the kid had not survived the Hezbollah onslaught. There would be serious questions to answer back in Washington, not to mention Jerusalem. He shuddered to think of the firestorm that was coming. But that was tomorrow's trouble. Right now, he had to find Kailea.

Yet just as Marcus turned around, he found himself staring at a hooded fighter pointing a weapon at his face and about to pull the trigger.

5

Marcus's mind raced as he looked for a way out, but he saw none.

The man shouted something in Arabic. Marcus did not speak the language, but it did not take a rocket scientist to figure out what the guy was saying. Marcus dropped the M4. Slowly—*very slowly*—he removed his sidearm from his shoulder holster and tossed that to the ground as well. Then he raised his hands over his head as he simultaneously calculated the distance between him and the Hezbollah operative.

Two meters.

Six feet, give or take.

Close, but not close enough. There was no way he could make a move on this guy.

Marcus realized he was staring into the eyes of a cold-blooded killer. He had seen such eyes before. Too many times. He knew what men like this were made of. He knew what they were capable of. And no matter how much training he had received in the Marines or the Secret Service, he knew he could not turn the tables on men like this—not from such a distance. To attempt something would be suicide.

A thought flashed across his mind's eye.

Maybe that was the best thing.

To be taken captive by such a sick predator was a nightmare proposition. The stuff of horror films. Marcus would resolve not to betray his friends or his country. He'd do his best not to talk. And they would torture him without mercy. And he would break. No matter how hard he tried to resist, he would break. Eventually everyone broke. That was why the first rule in this business was simple.

Do not get caught.

That, Marcus told himself, was why he should make a move. If the guy's reaction time was too slow, there was also the possibility—however slim—that he could disarm him. More likely, this guy was jacked up on adrenaline and trigger-happy. If that were the case, the instant Marcus leaned forward, he would be shot between the eyes and be dead before he hit the ground.

Wasn't that the better way to go?

Just then, however, Marcus's eyes drifted down from the man's eyes to his hands. The hooded Hezbollah fighter was not holding a pistol but a military-grade Taser. Before Marcus could process another thought, the man lowered his aim from Marcus's face to his chest and fired.

The two probes hit Marcus in the chest. Fifty thousand volts of electricity surged through his body. His central nervous system shut down, and Marcus dropped to the ground.

★

Amin al-Masri stared at the twitching body.

The twenty-eight-year-old Shia Muslim had never seen an American before. Not in person. Nor had he expected to today. His mission had been simple: Capture an Israeli or two—alive and ideally unharmed. Transport them back to Beirut. Interrogate them. Then prepare to move them to the docks to ship them out of the country, far from the ubiquitous eyes of Israeli intelligence.

Now, however, it was beginning to dawn on the deputy commander of Hezbollah's elite Radwan Unit that he had hit the jackpot. True, he had not captured a single Israeli. But he had seized not just one but three Americans—two men and one woman. Aside from the burns they had suffered from being tased, all three were in mint condition—far better than he could have anticipated, in fact, given the intensity of the firefight they had endured.

The man lying at al-Masri's feet had blue eyes and sandy-blond hair, cut short with a touch of gray at the temples. There was no question in the young Hezbollah leader's mind that this man had been born and raised in the United States. He looked military—he clearly fought like someone with significant combat experience, probably Special Forces—yet he was wearing civilian clothes and had a beard. Most likely he was a federal agent of some sort, possibly Secret Service or DSS. He was tall, over six feet, and in excellent physical condition. Al-Masri guessed he was a shade under two hundred pounds, nearly all muscle with very little body fat.

His superiors were going to be ecstatic. They were also about to pay through the nose. Israelis were one thing. Americans were something else entirely. And if they were not about to give him his new asking price, al-Masri did not mind. These three were going to fetch a much higher price on the open market.

The Israelis might be crafty, but they were also stingy. They would not pay cash. They did not believe they had cash to burn. All the Israelis ever offered to get their people back were Palestinian prisoners—hundreds, even thousands of them. Yet al-Masri did not want Palestinian prisoners. They were of no use to him. Not for what he was trying to achieve. Worse, the Israelis would not offer a prisoner trade until they had tried everything else to get their people back. And even if a prisoner exchange did eventually happen, and al-Masri's superiors could find a way to monetize them, the Israelis would still never let it go. The Zionists would come hunting for al-Masri and his men. They would kill him and anyone and everyone else involved in the operation, even if it took them decades.

The Americans, on the other hand, were rich. And stupid. They did not exchange prisoners. They dropped off pallets of cash. By the planeload. And they did not seem to believe in vengeance. They paid top dollar to get their people returned, and they never looked back. If he could make a deal with the Americans, al-Masri knew he would not have to live the rest of his life looking over his shoulder. He could take his money and simply disappear forever. Yes, he would have to change his identity. Yes, he would have to say goodbye to everyone and everything he had ever known. But it could not be helped. He was running out of time. And this was the only option he could see.

6

Al-Masri ordered his men to bind the Americans' hands and feet.

Seconds later, they dragged all three paralyzed bodies to an opening not much larger than a manhole back on the streets of Beirut, the city of his youth. The opening was well concealed behind several boulders and beneath thick foliage.

Al-Masri was the first one in. Then his team lowered the prisoners into the tunnel, entered themselves, and sealed and locked the hatch above them.

Checking his watch, al-Masri ordered his men to double-time it back into Lebanese territory. He would bring up the rear. They had been far more successful than he could have possibly anticipated. But time was of the essence. The Israelis were coming. That much was certain.

How the IDF's sensors and ground-penetrating radar had missed this tunnel he had no idea. Nor did he care. Perhaps the IDF had been distracted by all the effort it had taken to find and destroy the many other tunnels along this border. But once the forces of the Northern Command discovered the

Americans were missing, they would quickly figure out they had not been handed through the breach in the fence and carried back into Lebanese territory. They would realize there was a tunnel nearby. They would find it. And they would flood it with fighters, water, or poison gas. If al-Masri and his men were still inside, they would all be history.

In truth, the young operative did not fear dying. What he feared most was failing. His superiors were counting on him to bring them a prize. They needed leverage for the next stage of the plan. The operation depended on getting the prisoners to the safe house in one piece, ideally before noon. So al-Masri directed his three largest fighters to choose a captive, sling him or her over their shoulders, and get moving.

The tunnel was cramped and claustrophobic despite the electric lights that had been hung every ten meters. It certainly wasn't wide enough for two men to walk side by side. Nor was it high enough to stand erect. That was a serious mistake made by Hezbollah's engineers because it significantly slowed their pace. Worse, the few fans did not allow proper ventilation. It was, therefore, ghastly hot, a fact that elicited no small amount of griping.

Al-Masri was in no mood to hear it. He ordered the men to shut up or take a bullet in the back. He expected the utmost in professionalism from his team.

Once underway, al-Masri did a quick head count and realized that one of them was missing. *"Where is Tanzeel?"* he shouted.

Everyone froze.

"Where is my brother?" he shouted again.

Nobody spoke.

Al-Masri, overcome by panic and rage, exploded. *"You left him there? You just left him? Are you insane? Do you know . . . ?"*

He could not finish the thought. There was no time and no point. There was nothing he could do about it now.

Tanzeel was lost.

7

"What do you mean, gone?"

"They've vanished, sir," replied the commander of the quick reaction force over an encrypted radio channel. "Disappeared. Nowhere to be found."

"Impossible."

"Nevertheless, sir—my men and I just arrived on scene. We've found eight KIA of our own and fifteen Hezbollah bodies. We've taken one prisoner, a kid, no more than fifteen or sixteen years old. Actually, he had already been stripped of his weapons and his hands and feet were bound in flexi-cuffs. On my command, we've opened fire on snipers shooting at us from some nearby homes, and we've begun blasting them with mortar rounds. But the two Americans and their handler—there's no trace of them, sir."

"Where'd they go?"

"No idea, sir. My men are scouring the area. We've found their backpacks. We've found the scorched remains of a BFT unit. There's blood and shell casings everywhere. But, sir, I think we have to consider the possibility they've been captured."

Yossi Kidron did not reply.

"Sir?" asked the on-scene commander. "Sir, can you hear me?"

Still the major general did not answer. A wave of panic was threatening to paralyze him. It wasn't just a crushing sense of fear. It was utter disorientation bordering on vertigo. Kidron had served in combat. He understood the fog of war. He was no stranger to fear. It had never threatened to shut him down. Not like this. Not ever. But suddenly everything had changed.

Thirty minutes earlier—if that—his country had been relatively peaceful and increasingly prosperous, steadily recovering from the devastating coronavirus pandemic that had crippled so much of the Israeli and global economy. Less than a century earlier, an independent Jewish state hadn't even existed. Now it was a rising regional power. Strategically allied with the world's only superpower and closer to Washington than ever, thanks to an unapologetically pro-Israel president in the White House. Energy independent, thanks to the discovery of trillions of cubic feet of natural gas offshore. Peace treaties with two of its Arab neighbors, Egypt and Jordan. A recent peace agreement with the United Arab Emirates. And on the verge of signing a historic peace treaty with Saudi Arabia, even if negotiations had been frozen for months due to the pandemic.

Yet now, in the mere blink of an eye, it was all at risk of falling apart. If Hezbollah really had seized not one but two Americans, together with an IDF soldier—and not just any soldier, but this particular soldier—then Israel was suddenly on the brink of all-out war with Lebanon. And not with the Lebanese army but with Hezbollah, Iran's most dangerous proxy.

Yossi Kidron had spent his entire life on the Lebanon border. He had grown up not far from Haifa on the Carmel mountain range, practically in the shadow of the Shia radicals who routinely threatened to storm across the border, kill every Jew they found, and seize the land they considered rightfully their own. Kidron had been drafted into the IDF at the tender age of eighteen and become a paratrooper. He could have just done his three-year mandatory stint and moved on with his life. Instead, he'd chosen the army as his career. Indeed, it was his life.

His father and all his uncles had fought in the First Lebanon War. "Operation Peace for Galilee" had begun on June 6, 1982. Everyone had expected it to last no more than a few weeks, but it had slogged on for eighteen brutal years, becoming a lethal quagmire, Israel's own Vietnam. Only on May 24, 2000, was the last Israeli soldier finally withdrawn. On that date, the Jewish state had unilaterally pulled back to the internationally recognized border. It was the hope of then–Prime Minister Ehud Barak that such a gesture of goodwill would lead to peace with the government in Beirut and decades of quiet along the border. Perhaps even a formal peace treaty one day.

It was not to be.

Even now, Kidron could vividly recall the morning of July 12, 2006. It was a Wednesday, hot and hazy. That was the day a Hezbollah cell had ambushed an IDF patrol along the border, killing three soldiers and capturing two more. Kidron had been in the resort city of Eilat on a weeklong leave, scuba diving in the Red Sea with a group of army buddies. He remembered eating falafel and drinking beer at a hole-in-the-wall restaurant near the beach when they heard the breaking news alert. They had stared at each other in disbelief as they listened to the prime minister explain what was happening in the north and order the IDF to retaliate and to get those boys back.

At that point, no one knew for sure if the captives were dead or alive. But Kidron could still remember the surging emotions as he tried to imagine what it would be like to fall into the hands of such a wicked and bloodthirsty enemy.

Kidron and his friends had not waited for word from their commander, ordering them back to the base to report for duty. Without hesitation, without even discussing the matter, they had jumped into his beat-up old Range Rover and raced back to the hostel where they'd been staying. They'd quickly packed their bags, piled back into the Range Rover, and sped north.

He remembered gearing up. He remembered boarding an armored personnel carrier and heading into his first live mission in enemy territory. And he remembered how ready Hezbollah had been for them. The land mines.

The tank traps. The rocket launchers. The sniper nests. And the carnage that had ensued.

How was it possible that the Israeli high command could have so disastrously miscalculated Sheikh Hassan Nasrallah's response? The generals in "the Pit"—the hardened subterranean war room deep underneath the IDF's headquarters in Tel Aviv—had expected Nasrallah to fold quickly and hand over the two prisoners. Instead, the Sheikh had gone crazy. He'd ordered his Hezbollah operatives to launch some 4,000 missiles at Israeli cities and towns, forcing more than a million Israelis living along the northern border into underground bomb shelters or to flee to friends and relatives in the center and south of the country.

When it was all over, 121 Israeli soldiers had been killed.

Nine of them were personal friends of Kidron's, including his best friend.

Beyond that, 44 Israeli civilians had died.

Some 2,000 were wounded.

And the "Second Lebanon War" had lasted only 34 days.

The next one, Kidron knew, would be longer and worse.

Unimaginably worse.

And it seemed it might already be starting.

8

If there was one thing Kidron knew, it was that everything had changed.

In the years since the end of the Second Lebanon War, Sheikh Hassan Nasrallah, the founder and spiritual leader of the most dangerous terror organization on the planet, had died of a massive coronary.

The funeral had been a sight to behold. More than two hundred thousand Hezbollah soldiers, draped in the movement's yellow flags and scarves, jammed the streets of Beirut, openly weeping, beating their chests, some slashing themselves until they were drenched in blood, all trying to catch a glimpse of the casket. After a thirty-day period of mourning throughout Lebanon, Iran, and much of Iraq, Nasrallah's replacement had been hand-chosen and announced by Iran's Supreme Leader.

Sheikh Ja'far ibn al-Hussaini had been only thirty-eight years old at the time. The man was not merely a Shia radical, Kidron knew. He was a lunatic, a follower of what the Mossad had dubbed "apocalyptic Islam." He had earned his doctorate in Islamic jurisprudence from the very seminary in Qom where Iran's Grand Ayatollah had once taught, the same religious training center from which Iran's president, Yadollah Afshar, had graduated. It was there that al-Hussaini had heard both men speak and began to get to know them. It was there he had written a bizarre dissertation titled "The Strategic Implications for Hezbollah of the Coming of the Hidden Imam."

Kidron had seen a copy of the 383-page tome that had been stolen from the seminary's archives by Mossad operatives. He had read it cover to cover four times in Arabic. In exhausting detail, and replete with citations from ancient and obscure Islamic poets and theologians, al-Hussaini had laid out a vision more chilling than anything Kidron had ever encountered before.

He had memorized the opening paragraph while preparing a detailed summary and analysis of the entire work for Mossad and IDF commanders.

The divine prophets were clear: the Hidden Imam will emerge from occultation in the End of Days, summon his army, and lead the forces of Islam to ultimate victory. The Lebanese people and the Party of God share a pivotal role with the whole of the Shia world in preparing the ground. However, time is fleeting. As such, the leadership in Beirut must urgently and diligently plan and prepare for this great event. There is no time to rest.

Al-Hussaini had spent the remainder of the dissertation laying out seven foundational principles. Kidron had highlighted the key points in his report.

1. The last days of human history have arrived.

2. The arrival and appearance of the Hidden Iman, also known as the Mahdi or the Twelfth Imam, is imminent.

3. When Imam al-Mahdi appears, he will in short order conquer and rule the entire earth.

4. The prophet Jesus will also return to earth as the Hidden Imam's lieutenant.

5. The prophet Jesus will require all Jews, Christians, and other "infidels" to convert to Islam or be executed at once.

6. The arrival of the Mahdi and the full establishment of the global Caliphate can be hastened if Muslims work to annihilate the Little Satan—Israel—and the Great Satan, the United States of America.

7. The people of Lebanon are to play a prophetic role in the establishment of the Caliphate. Therefore, the people must be prepared and must have in place the necessary weapons and alliances. The rewards for the faithful will be great. But for any who prove lazy and slothful, the fires of eternal judgment await.

Kidron, an atheist, found it astonishing that anyone could believe such nonsense, much less that someone who did could be appointed the head of anything, least of all Iran's most important paramilitary force.

Yet the more Kidron had studied al-Hussaini's life and thinking, the more worried he had become. The husband of three wives and the father of nine children, al-Hussaini was reportedly the most beloved of the Supreme Leader's myriad nephews. He wasn't Hezbollah's founder. He had, however, become its inheritor. He was far more loyal to the ayatollah than Nasrallah had been. He was also far more headstrong and rash than Nasrallah had been.

That, Kidron knew, was what made the man so unpredictable . . . and so dangerous.

9

Every murder required three elements: motive, means, and opportunity.

Kidron believed al-Hussaini's *motive* was clear. The crazed leader of Hezbollah was determined not simply to murder Israelis but to massacre them, not simply attack the world's only Jewish state but annihilate it.

That certainly made it all the more understandable why he was working so hard to build up the *means* to accomplish this nefarious mission. On the new leader's watch, Hezbollah had embarked on an unrestrained spending spree. They had assembled a massive arsenal of the most powerful, precise, and lethal short- and medium-range missiles the Iranians had ever developed. These were not unguided, homemade Qassam rockets like those Hamas fired from Gaza. These were far larger. These had guidance systems. They could do serious damage, inflict horrific casualties.

The Mossad estimated the total Hezbollah arsenal was upwards of 150,000 to 200,000 missiles. They were hidden in mosques. Hospitals. Schools. Barns. Warehouses. Even private homes. All aimed at Israeli population centers. There was no way to shoot down all the missiles, no matter how sophisticated Israel's air-defense system. Nor was it possible to take out the missiles and their launchers by superior airpower alone. Kidron and his colleagues had been war-gaming this scenario for years. They had concluded, however reluctantly, that a Third Lebanon War would require a full-scale ground invasion of Lebanon by thousands of tanks and APCs and tens of thousands of Israeli soldiers.

It had, therefore, become bedrock IDF doctrine to do everything possible to prevent such a war—to prevent giving Hezbollah the *opportunity* to pull Israel into a war. Even a limited IDF incursion into Lebanese territory could rapidly escalate. That, in turn, could severely damage Israel's economy, which was heavily dependent on exports. What was more, such an escalation ran the risk of seriously undermining—or at least significantly straining— ties with Washington, Israel's closest ally, and it also could scuttle any prospect of a peace deal with the Saudis.

All this was surging through Kidron's mind as he heard the commander of his quick reaction force practically yelling into his secure radio channel, *"Sir, what do you want to do?"*

Kidron forced himself to focus. He could not afford to think about what *might* happen. He had to remain intent on what *was* happening right then. There was no time to thoroughly process all the data. He was dealing with incomplete and possibly inaccurate information. But he had to decide right then and there what to do next. Whatever he decided—right or wrong—his entire career would be judged on the next words out of his mouth.

The clock was ticking, after all.

He did not have the luxury of waiting for a decision from the IDF chief of staff, much less the minister of defense or the PM. There was no time for briefings and deliberations. Every second that ticked by meant two Americans and an Israeli were being dragged deeper into Lebanese territory. This was his responsibility and his alone, Kidron told himself. It was his job to end this nightmare and end it fast, come what may.

"Sir, hello, are you there?" came the voice again over the encrypted radio.

Kidron glanced at the clock on the far wall of the war room. It was 9:41.

"We have no choice," he finally replied. "Initiate the Hannibal Protocol."

10

There was stunned silence at the other end of the line.

"Come again?" the QRF commander finally asked.

Kidron knew full well that what he was ordering was not simply controversial but might very well be illegal. But he did not care. The Hannibal Protocol had once been Israeli army doctrine for handling kidnappings and potential kidnappings of military personnel. The policy gave field commanders full authority to do everything in their power to prevent the seizure of Israeli soldiers by enemy forces. In the event that a kidnapping did take place, the protocol permitted commanders to use overwhelming firepower to stop would-be kidnappers from fleeing the area with their captives. It also authorized the use of extraordinary tactics to get those captives back. Such tactics included massive aerial bombardments of the area in which a kidnapping had occurred. In theory, this would slow down, disorient, and paralyze the enemy, and it would give IDF ground forces time to mobilize and mount an effective rescue.

The rationale was simple. The kidnapping of an Israeli soldier wasn't simply a tactical problem for Israeli generals. It was a strategic nightmare for the State of Israel. Not only could captive soldiers be tortured by the enemy to give up sensitive intelligence, but terror groups could also use captives as bargaining chips to force the release of scores of terrorists held in Israeli prisons.

In 1985, for example, the Israeli prime minister and his security cabinet had made an unbelievable deal. They agreed to release 1,150 Palestinian prisoners to get just three captured Israeli soldiers back.

In 2011, another Israeli prime minister and his government agreed to an even more astonishing deal. Israel released 1,027 Hamas prisoners to get back just *one* of its soldiers, a twenty-five-year-old corporal named Gilad Shalit who had been kidnapped in a Hamas raid along the Gaza border and held for more than five years.

Everyone knew Israel simply could not afford to release blood-drenched terrorists en masse every time a kidnapping occurred. Thus, the Hannibal Protocol gave IDF commanders a clear policy—don't ever allow such a situation to occur again. They were to use every means at their disposal to disrupt a kidnapping in process, even if that cost the lives of the Israeli soldiers being captured.

There was just one problem.

The Hannibal Protocol was no longer IDF policy.

Yet Kidron did not care. "Listen up, people," he said, his voice now calm and firm.

The general was no longer speaking merely to his field commander. He was demanding the full attention of every officer and staffer in the operations center.

"This is the most critical situation we've faced since the 2006 war, and we are thus left with no other choice," he continued. "I am activating the Hannibal Protocol. I want you to unleash everything we've got—and I mean everything. I'm ordering you to rain hellfire and brimstone on the savages who initiated this attack. Shut down all movement within twenty kilometers of the breached fence line. Cut off every path of escape. Then find these three and bring them back to Israel—dead or alive—or the next thing you're going to see is two Americans and one of our own, live from Beirut, bound, tortured, bleeding, and hanging from lampposts."

Kidron paused a moment and found himself staring at one of the soldiers under his command. The young man, evidently religious, was wearing a *kippah* and had just begun putting on *tefillin*—traditional Jewish phylacteries—when everyone had been ordered to stop what they were doing.

"You all know I'm not exactly the most religious guy in the army," Kidron conceded. "But for everyone who is, now might be a good time to send up a prayer."

★

A pair of F-16 Fighting Falcons were the first in the air.

From the moment they lifted off from Ramat David air base in northern Israel—in the heart of the Jezreel Valley, not far from ancient Megiddo, the biblical site known as Armageddon—the two fighter jets banked hard to the left. Their pilots then pushed their Pratt & Whitney engines to maximum thrust. Seconds later, they were penetrating Lebanese airspace and unleashing a salvo of air-to-ground missiles on four known Hezbollah sites not far from Avivim, the Israeli community closest to the breach in the fence line.

The shock and awe came hard and fast.

The first target—a command-and-control facility located in a farmhouse near the village of Aitaroun—was obliterated in a blinding flash and deafening roar.

The next two targets were weapons caches. Located in barns near the town of Maroun al-Ras, they, too, were suddenly consumed by massive balls of fire.

The fourth target was an apartment complex in Bint Jbeil. Israeli military intelligence had recently determined the complex served as housing for nearly two hundred Hezbollah fighters. Moments later, it was a burning crater, spewing smoke and ash.

The four strikes in such rapid succession destroyed the breezy calm of an otherwise-lovely spring morning. To the locals, the attacks came without warning or rationale of any kind. Word of the border raid had not yet made the news on either side of the fence. To many, the earsplitting, ground-rocking booms—one after another—felt like a series of earthquakes. Windows shattered. Bookcases, chandeliers, indeed whole ceilings, collapsed. Terrified masses were screaming and scrambling for cover wherever they could find it.

And this was just the beginning.

Eight more pairs of Israeli fighter jets soon streaked into Lebanese airspace, thus far unchallenged by Hezbollah's surface-to-air missiles or antiaircraft artillery fire. One by one, the Israeli jets took out power stations, bridges, electrical substations, and fuel depots in a twenty-kilometer semicircle from Avivim they dubbed "the zone." Additional waves of fighter jets were soon bombing major and even minor roads in and out of the zone, creating so many—and such large—craters that the roads became impassable. The IDF's hope was that this would cut off all possible escape routes for vehicles that might be trying to move the hostages northward.

Most traffic in the zone came screeching to a halt. Terrified drivers abandoned their vehicles, searching for shelter from the firestorm. Israeli drone operators hunted every truck, every car, every vehicle of any kind whose drivers were foolish enough to be on the move, especially those trying to come into or go out of the twenty-kilometer grid. With each vehicle identified, the operators zoomed in the high-resolution cameras to see if its passengers were carrying weapons. If they were, Kidron's rules of engagement were clear. The operators were authorized to fire. So fire they did, and every AGM-114 precision-guided Hellfire missile hit its mark.

On the ground, the QRF commander ordered his troops to direct mortar fire at the nearly two dozen houses located within sight of the breached section of border fence. All of them had been abandoned years earlier. No Lebanese citizen in his or her right mind wanted to live within a stone's throw of the "Zionist criminals." Fewer still wanted to be caught in the cross fire of the next war and be treated by Iran as human shields. Still, the IDF knew that all the structures were frequently used by Hezbollah scouts and other operatives.

Throughout northern Israel, roads soon became clogged with mile after mile of flatbed tractor trailers transporting Israeli battle tanks known as the Merkava—Hebrew for "chariot"—to the front. Also clogging the roads were hundreds of buses transporting thousands of active-duty combat soldiers who would soon be pouring over the border.

It was now ten o'clock.

Marcus Ryker, Kailea Curtis, and Yigal Mizrachi had been missing for the better part of thirty minutes, and the head of the IDF's Northern Command was pulling out all the stops in the effort to get them back.

11

Amin al-Masri knew the moment the bombs began falling.

Neither he nor his men could hear the Israeli fighter jets streaking over-head. They could, however, hear—and certainly feel—the IAF's handiwork. The entire tunnel began shaking violently. Shards of rock rained down on them and their prisoners. The lights flickered. Clouds of dust filled the air.

To his horror, al-Masri realized there was no way back. Furious at the incompetence of his men and with himself for not having kept his eyes on Tanzeel, he nevertheless ordered his men to run and run hard. They would all be dead if they did not begin moving again.

As more bombs fell outside, it became increasingly difficult to see, fur-ther slowing the pace of the fighters. To be fair, the men had no idea where they were going, what was ahead of them, or where the turns were. They had never been in the tunnel before and had only studied the map for a few moments during their briefing the previous day. But al-Masri did not care. Nor did he listen to them when they asked for water breaks. Instead, he unleashed a torrent of obscenities and drove them onward without mercy. With no margin for error, they had to press forward and pick up the pace, he told them. But the bombs kept falling and precious time was being lost.

The tunnel went on for well over a kilometer. Hunched over and operating in the near dark, it took them almost two hours before they reached the end. They heard and felt several sections behind them collapsing. Finally, however, they reached a wooden ladder and a metal hatch built into the roof of the tunnel.

The lead operative unlocked and opened the hatch, only to find himself staring down the barrels of a dozen submachine guns. It was not the Israelis who were waiting for them, however. It was fellow members of the Radwan Unit.

Drenched with sweat and gasping for fresh air, al-Masri was the last man up the ladder and through the hatch. He found the prisoners still unconscious and lying side by side on the bare concrete floor. His men were chugging bottles of water or pouring them over their heads, trying to wash the dust out of their eyes and cool down their overheated bodies. The Radwan fighters soon brought ice-cold bottles of grape juice and trays of freshly baked pita, grilled shawarma, and bowls of hummus and olives.

As his ravenous men wolfed down the food, al-Masri waved off their entreaties to join them and instead ascended another wooden ladder through another hatch until he pushed aside a rug and climbed into a small, dark room. The shade on the single window was drawn, but he could still see a simple cot, a wooden desk and chair, and a shelf of old books. He closed the hatch and replaced the rug. Then he dusted himself off, walked over to the window, pushed aside the shade, and peered into the Lebanese countryside.

They had done it. They had survived. They had reached their safe house—the basement of a mosque in the town of Aitaroun—just kilometers from the Israeli border. But they had also made critical mistakes, al-Masri told himself as he listened to the continuous explosions nearby and felt the ground shake again and again. And he had only himself to blame. He had lost too many men in the raid. Some of them had been friends since childhood. And then there was Tanzeel. The thought of his brother in the hands of the Zionists made him physically ill. The thought of having to explain this to their mother made it worse.

Al-Masri replaced the shade and walked to the door. Unholstering his sidearm, he slowly turned the knob and opened the door ever so slightly. He scanned the sanctuary, but there was no one there, not even the imam to whom he paid a small fee for the use of the mosque. He opened the door farther and eased into the room, his .45 up and ready.

He checked the office. It was clear. He checked the bathrooms and the vestibule. They, too, were clear. He briefly peered out of several more windows but found no one in the courtyard nor in the narrow streets that passed in front of and behind the mosque.

Beginning to breathe a bit easier, he holstered his weapon, removed his filthy boots, performed his ritual washings, and went back into the sanctuary and bowed toward Mecca. There was not much time for prayer or reflection. The rest of his men would be coming along soon. They certainly were not staying there. They could not. The Israelis were coming. Maybe not through the destroyed tunnel. But they were coming, al-Masri knew. They had to keep moving.

12

Reuven Eitan was livid.

Until now, the sixty-four-year-old Israeli premier's morning had been uncharacteristically quiet. There were no public events on his schedule. No one was coming to visit him that day. He had even slept in. For the first time in months, he had not bothered to set an alarm clock. He and his wife had enjoyed a simple breakfast of grapefruit and coffee, read the morning papers, and daydreamed together about what their lives could look like once he was out of office. Afterward, Eitan had showered, shaved, and dressed to go to Shabbat services.

Now he was being told that some idiot general had decided to invade Lebanon. How was that possible? How exactly could an Israeli general start a war without authorization from the prime minister and the security cabinet?

It had been just after 10 a.m. when the bizarre and infuriating call had come in from the Kirya. The PM and his wife had been getting into the motorcade, preparing to depart their official residence for the Great Synagogue on King George Street, when his security detail rushed him back inside to the secure communications center. On the line were two of his most trusted advisors. Shimon Levy was the country's minister of defense and one of his closest friends and most important political allies. Lieutenant General Yonatan "Yoni" Golan was Israel's *Ramatkal*—the IDF's chief of staff. Golan was a fine officer and a thirty-two-year veteran of the Israeli Defense Force. But he had been the chief of staff for less than a year, and Eitan did not know him well.

"How in the world could this have happened?" the prime minister erupted after Levy had briefed him on the events unfolding in the north. *"You're telling me a firefight has been underway on the Lebanon border for almost forty-five minutes and I'm just hearing about it now? Are you two out of your minds?"*

"I take full responsibility for that," the defense minister replied in a calm, nondefensive tone he wrongly hoped would douse the flames. "It's been a fast-moving situation. To be honest, I thought we could contain it quickly and—"

"And what?" the PM bellowed.

"Well, I—"

"Well, what? Spit it out, Shimon."

"I didn't want to disturb you on one of your rare days off, Ruvi," Levy replied, using the PM's nickname.

"That's lunacy," Eitan shouted into the phone. *"Absolute insanity—you should have called me immediately."*

Levy had nothing to say. Neither did Golan. So Eitan fired more questions at them.

"Wasn't there any sign Hezbollah was planning such an attack?"

The general took that one. "None at all, sir."

"You're saying this was an utterly unprovoked and wholly unexpected act?"

"Absolutely," Golan said. "My men are reviewing all of the intelligence now, but I can tell you categorically we've seen nothing in recent days suggesting the possibility of an attack. No warning. No hints. Nothing out of the ordinary whatsoever. What's also odd, sir, is that we have no indication that this attack was authorized or directed by the Nasser Unit, which is responsible for all Hezbollah operations south of the Litani River. Nor does it appear to be the work of Al-Talil, a unit specially trained at making infiltration attempts into Israel."

"Then who gave the order?" asked the PM.

"Sir, the initial indications suggest this was an operation conducted by a cell from the Radwan Unit, which is comprised of special operations forces."

"Haven't they conducted raids before?"

"No, sir," said the *Ramatkal*. "I'm not saying the fighters in the Radwan Unit aren't trained for invasive action. But we haven't seen them engage in such activities in years—not since the Second Lebanon War, at least."

"Then why now? Why today?"

"I'm afraid we don't have those answers—not yet, sir," Golan replied.

Defense Minister Levy shifted the conversation to what steps the IDF was taking to find and recover those who had been taken captive. "Prime Minister, as we speak, the entire sector—up to twenty kilometers from the site of the attack—is being bombed without pause or mercy," Levy noted. "Every known Hezbollah facility inside the zone is being destroyed. Every bridge is being taken out. As is every petrol station. And every vehicle moving north. At the same time, every road in or out of the sector is being bombed in the hopes of entirely disrupting—or at least slowing down—any and all efforts by the kidnappers to take the captives northward, deeper into Lebanese territory. We've also flooded the airspace in the zone with drones. We're intercepting and monitoring every phone call, text message, email, and radio signal. Believe me, Ruvi, we're doing everything humanly possible to get these three individuals back—alive, unharmed, and in short order."

Eitan was not impressed. To the contrary, the more his advisors tried to explain how hard they and their forces were working to rectify the situation, the more furious the prime minister became. And when they happened to mention, almost in passing, that the head of Northern Command had activated the Hannibal Protocol, the PM unleashed a blistering, expletive-laden diatribe that lasted several minutes. He declared yet again that they should have informed him of this *"unmitigated and far-reaching disaster"* from the beginning. *"And furthermore,"* he concluded, *"the Hannibal Protocol is not even IDF policy. It's years out of date and no longer part of the IDF's rules of engagement. Any general stupid and foolhardy enough to unilaterally activate Hannibal should be relieved of his duties immediately."*

When his rant had run its course, there was silence on the other end of the line for a long moment. But Eitan had more questions.

"How many did they take?" the prime minister asked, suddenly remembering that Levy had begun the call by saying Hezbollah had grabbed "several folks" along the border but had not actually provided any specifics.

"Three," said the *Ramatkal.*

Eitan exploded again. *"Three Israelis? Three Israeli soldiers? Three precious sons of the State and you wait forty-five minutes to tell me?"*

"Actually, Mr. Prime Minister, only one of them is an Israeli," General Golan clarified.

"I don't understand," said Eitan. "Then who are the other two?"

"Americans."

Eitan couldn't believe what he was hearing.

"Americans?"

"I'm afraid so," Golan replied.

"What Americans?"

The defense minister took that one. "Two DSS agents—they were doing an advance trip ahead of Secretary Whitney's arrival tomorrow," Levy said. "What's more, I'm afraid you know them, Ruvi." Levy paused a moment to let the thought sink in, then added, "They actually saved your life at the Jerusalem peace summit with the Saudis."

Eitan had been pacing around his office, talking into a headset. Now he felt like the wind had been knocked out of him. His legs felt weak, and he dropped into the chair behind his desk. "Who?" he asked, all the fire drained from his voice.

"Special Agent Marcus Ryker is one of the hostages," the defense minister replied. "Special Agent Kailea Curtis is the other."

"I don't believe it," Eitan said. "Are you absolutely certain?"

"I'm afraid I am, sir," Levy replied.

"This is a disaster," Eitan said. "Do you two understand just how serious . . . ?"

The prime minister's voice trailed off. He never finished his sentence. Nor did he need to.

Levy said nothing. Golan, too, remained silent.

"That's why your man activated Hannibal?" Eitan asked, his voice so quiet it was almost inaudible. "To get Ryker and Curtis back?"

"Well, sir, not entirely," Levy replied.

"Explain," said a baffled Eitan.

"Ruvi, it wasn't the capture of the two Americans alone that triggered Hannibal," Levy said. "General Kidron gave the order because of the Israeli."

"The Israeli? Why? Who's the Israeli?"

There was a long pause, and then Shimon Levy dropped the bombshell. "Your nephew."

13

All the blood drained from Eitan's face.

"My nephew?" he asked.

"Yes, sir."

"Yigal?"

"I'm afraid so," said Levy.

The prime minister's hands began trembling. For several moments, he said nothing.

"*Ruvi—Prime Minister—are you still there?*" Levy nearly shouted into the receiver.

"Yes, yes, I'm here," Eitan replied at last. "I don't understand how this could have happened."

"Yigal, as you know, is working for *Isuf Kravi*," Levy said.

"I know, but—"

"General Kidron assigned Yigal to be the security liaison for Secretary Whitney's visit to the border," the *Ramatkal* explained. "I spoke with Kidron just before coming on the call with you, Prime Minister. He's absolutely sickened by what's happened. As I said before, we had no intel whatsoever that Hezbollah was planning—or even contemplating—such a move."

There was another long silence as the prime minister tried to process what he was hearing. "Does Hezbollah know who they have?" he finally asked.

"We don't know, sir," the *Ramatkal* replied. "It's too soon to say. But again, this is why General Kidron took the actions he did. I spoke with him at length. The bottom line is that he didn't have the luxury of second-guessing himself. The instant he realized what was at stake, he knew that every second was precious. So he activated Hannibal on his own authority. He's ready to accept the consequences. But he stands by his decision. As do I."

"I do, too, Ruvi," added the defense minister. "I'd have done the same in the general's shoes. And so would you, and you know it."

The prime minister didn't reply. So Defense Minister Levy offered the PM the only piece of good news, such as it was. "Thus far, sir, neither Hezbollah nor the Lebanese army has retaliated against our incursion."

He went on to explain that the IDF's layered air-defense systems—from its Patriot antimissile batteries to Iron Dome and David's Sling—were all on high alert. Yet remarkably, not a single rocket or missile had been fired from Lebanese territory at the Jewish state. Nor did there appear to be any indications that Lebanese or Hezbollah rockets or missiles were being prepared for launch.

"That's a bit odd, isn't it?" Eitan asked. "If they're trying to lure us into a war?"

"It is, sir," Levy conceded. "And there's something else that's strange."

"What's that?"

"Well, sir, 8200 is picking up chatter from Hezbollah's communications networks indicating a great deal of internal confusion," the defense minister replied. Unit 8200 was the IDF's electronic eavesdropping division of military intelligence, roughly equivalent to the American National Security Agency. "We intercepted a message from a high-ranking Hezbollah general in Beirut to the commander of the Nasser Unit. He said the Sheikh did not authorize the attacks and was demanding to know who did and why."

"You're saying the attack was unplanned?"

"I can't say for certain. But it's possible."

"Could that just be spin, to slow down our response?"

"I don't think so," said General Golan. "That message is only nine minutes old. Hezbollah knows how aggressively we're treating the situation. They know our response is anything but slow. My guys say it's very possible that the Hezbollah high command was blindsided by this. For the moment, that's the only explanation they can come up with why they're not launching their missiles at us."

"You're saying Sheikh al-Hussaini didn't know his own men were about to start a war with us? I don't buy it. More likely the Sheikh is luring us into a public relations trap that could have devastating consequences internationally, making us look like the aggressor and providing hours—*days*—of coverage by European TV networks that hate us anyway."

Neither man had an explanation, yet both agreed that the situation was highly volatile and could change without warning. The young Sheikh could order his missile brigades to start firing everything they had at Israeli cities, town, villages, and kibbutzim at any moment, and then Israel would have little choice but to escalate into a full-scale war in southern Lebanon.

Reuven Eitan was now back on his feet and pacing around the room again. What bothered him most—amid a long and growing list of problems—was the sense that his hands were tied. Ultimately it was not Sheikh al-Hussaini who was forcing him to make decisions that could be ruinous for his country, to say nothing of his own political career. It was the mullahs in Tehran.

The Israeli people did not want another war. Nor could they afford one. Not after the recent economic devastation. Before the pandemic, unemployment in Israel had been under 4 percent. During the worst of the crisis, it spiked close to 30 percent. The stock market, which had been roaring, plunged to dangerous lows. Yes, the government had done an impressive job initially locking down the country and containing the plague. Since then, they'd done reasonably well in their efforts to reopen society and reboot the economy. With each passing month, there was more and more evidence that Israel was getting back on its feet. GDP growth was picking up steam. Unemployment was dropping. Eitan's poll numbers were strong. People saw him as delivering both peace and prosperity.

This could change everything.

Then again, what choice did he have? Two Americans and an Israeli—his own flesh and blood—had been kidnapped from the border. He was still as furious as he was dumbfounded that an IDF general would have the chutzpah to activate the Hannibal Protocol on his own authority. But he could hardly back down. Nothing would be worse than looking weak in the face of such a brazen act of war.

"What are our chances?" he asked as he continued pacing.

"Chances at what, sir?" asked the defense minister.

"Finding these three and getting them back in the next few hours."

For that, Levy deferred to the *Ramatkal*. "Sir, I wish I could promise you that we will get them all back alive," General Golan began. "But I can't—not in good faith. We're just using too much ordnance."

"That's the point of Hannibal, is it not?" Eitan asked.

"It is, sir," Golan replied. "That's the risk inherent in its design. We may be able to stop Hezbollah from moving their hostages north to Beirut, but we are also running a very high risk that we will inadvertently kill one or more of them in the process."

"Which is why Hannibal is no longer an active doctrine and should never have been ordered in the first place."

"Yes, sir," the *Ramatkal* replied.

"Nevertheless, we're stuck with it now," said the PM.

"Not necessarily," the defense minister interjected. "You can call it all off. Just give the word. It's your boy out there. The last thing we want is to see any harm come to him, least of all by friendly fire."

"Just give me a number," Eitan insisted. "What are the chances we get these three back by—I don't know—the end of the day if we stick with Hannibal?"

General Golan exhaled. "All things being equal, if we stick with what we're doing, I'd say we've got an 80 percent chance of getting them back by nightfall. Seventy-five, eighty."

"Then we have no choice, gentlemen," said the PM. "Stick with it, and send me updates on the hour."

"Very well, sir," said Levy.

And then the news took a turn for the worse.

14

"Prime Minister, I've just been handed a note," the *Ramatkal* said.

"What is it?"

"General Kidron's men have found a terror tunnel that was previously undetected."

"Where?"

"The opening is close to the breach in the fence line."

"And they're only finding it now?"

"Kidron says it was well hidden behind boulders and under a great deal of brush."

For the moment, Eitan did not reply.

But Levy did. "That would certainly explain why we've seen no evidence of the Americans or your nephew from any of our drones or other surveillance."

"Has General Kidron sent his men into the tunnel in pursuit?" Eitan asked.

"No, sir," said the *Ramatkal*.

"Why not? What's he waiting for?"

"It's too dangerous, sir. General Kidron has no idea who or what is down there. He's sending in a robot instead, one equipped with cameras, microphones, and sensors to pick up explosive material. It will feed everything it sees and hears back to us in the Pit."

"How long will it take for the robot to reach the end of the tunnel?"

"Too early to say, sir."

"Why?"

"We don't know how long the tunnel is or if it's even passable, given how many bombs we've dropped in the area."

Once again the prime minister felt himself becoming consumed by rage. He was sickened by the loss of his nephew. Mortified by the thought of having to inform the American president what had happened to two of his finest. Mortified still more by the thought of having to cancel the imminent visit by the U.S. secretary of state and the terrible message that would send Israel's enemies throughout the region.

The notion that the IDF had somehow missed this terror tunnel had Eitan seeing red. How was that possible? Wasn't the military spending hundreds of millions of shekels on ground-penetrating radar and other technologies to find these tunnels? They had already destroyed seven such tunnels on the Lebanon border and forty others on the Gaza border. How could they have possibly missed this one?

The implications went far beyond just these three kidnappings. Was it conceivable that Hezbollah had been infiltrating Israel's northern tier undetected in recent weeks or months? If so, how many cells were active inside Israel's borders? What kind of weapons did they have? What were their orders? How deep into the country had they gotten? Did they speak Hebrew? Did they have falsified Israeli IDs? On top of everything else, was the State of Israel about to face an unprecedented terror spree?

Despite the intel that Sheikh al-Hussaini had not ordered the attack, Eitan had little doubt that Hezbollah's spiritual leader was indeed responsible. Perhaps the Sheikh had learned that Hezbollah's communications systems—some of them, anyway—had been penetrated by 8200 and had decided to dribble out bits of disinformation specifically designed to reach Israeli intelligence and create confusion.

It was working.

Eitan wanted to order the entire Israeli Air Force into battle. He had the power to reduce the cities of Tyre and Sidon and Beirut to rubble with a single sentence. What's more, he wanted to order the targeted assassination of Sheikh Ja'far ibn al-Hussaini and his inner circle. Then again, why stop there? Surely al-Hussaini was too young and too inexperienced to be starting a war of his own accord. The orders had to be coming from Tehran. Eitan had no proof, no bits of damning intelligence, no smoking gun. But was there any other explanation?

Saudi intelligence was still reporting that the Grand Ayatollah was in poor health and probably in his last days. Perhaps, Eitan thought, the old man had decided to go out with a bang—one last war to bloody Israel's nose and sully its reputation and potentially scuttle its increasingly warm relations with the Gulf States.

Eitan pictured the three Israeli submarines lurking in the Persian Gulf, drifting silently along the Iranian coastline, just waiting for new orders. With a single command, he could end the wicked Iranian regime and melt down much of its capital. Condemnation of Israel would pour in from every direction. But who cared? Justice would have been served. The Iranian threat would be gone for good.

Yet none of that would bring home Yigal Mizrachi, Kailea Curtis, or Marcus Ryker. None of that would give him the moral high ground in the court of international opinion. To the contrary, it would kill innocent civilians and guarantee a massive new regional conflict Israel could not afford.

Eitan's entire body was trembling with anger. He knew what he wanted to do. Yet he had made rash, impulsive decisions before and always paid a steep price for them. Hard, bitter experience had taught him to contain and control his emotions. The decisions he made in the next few minutes could shape the course of history for a generation to come.

A war with Lebanon was the last thing Israel needed. With the help of the

White House—and despite numerous delays and distractions—the Jewish state was on the verge of a historic peace agreement with the Saudis. The relationship Eitan had forged with President Andrew Clarke, King Faisal Mohammed Al Saud, and Crown Prince Abdulaziz bin Faisal Al Saud— beginning with the summit in Jerusalem and in numerous secure phone calls and discreet correspondence over the course of the past eighteen months or so—was nothing short of miraculous. The satisfactory conclusion of such a comprehensive treaty had to remain paramount.

If Riyadh made peace with Jerusalem, the Bahrainis would likely soon follow. Then the Emiratis. Perhaps the Omanis would be next. Or maybe the Moroccans. Such breakthroughs would change the region and the world forever. This had been Eitan's primary foreign policy objective since the extraordinary visit of the Saudi monarch and his entourage and through complex and delicate yet encouraging rounds of shuttle diplomacy by Secretary Whitney ever since. Was it any wonder that Tehran and their Hezbollah thugs were trying to sabotage the effort?

Anger was not the right emotion, Eitan told himself. Anger was the product of feeling powerless, unable to choose his fate or chart his destiny. And there was no reason to be angry, he decided. This new crisis was an opportunity. By doing the unexpected, he could radically shift the political dynamic. By not overreacting—by keeping a cool head and staying focused on the big picture—perhaps he could turn this crisis to Israel's advantage.

Eitan finally stopped pacing. It was time to accept the fact that the three hostages were gone. Somehow—it no longer really mattered how or why— his sister's son and two Americans had been grabbed in a firefight, pulled into a tunnel, and likely dragged deep into enemy territory. The activation of the Hannibal Protocol had not helped. But nor had it hurt. It had not triggered the Third Lebanon War.

Not yet.

But it still could.

15

Marcus Ryker tried to open his eyes.

It took all his concentration. His eyelids were heavy, his thoughts foggy, his hands shaky, his mouth dry. They hadn't just tased him; they had drugged him with something. Something strong. Now he found himself tied—chained, to be more precise—to a wooden chair. He had been stripped naked, or nearly so. All he wore were his boxers. And there was a filthy rag stuffed in his mouth.

In the distance he heard a dog barking. He could also hear muffled voices in a nearby room. Whether the language was Arabic or Farsi he could not say. None of it was distinct.

A moment later he heard a series of distant explosions. He could feel the ground tremble beneath his feet, though the movement was slight. Every few minutes, a fighter jet streaked overhead. Yet he could not hear any small-arms fire. Nor could he pick up the high-pitched whine of incoming mortars and artillery shells or the rumbling of oncoming battle tanks and APCs.

Why not? How far from the border was he?

Wherever he was, the space was dark, steamy, fetid. As his eyes began to adjust, Marcus realized it was not pitch-black after all. Across the room, he could see specks of light seeping through and under what might be a door of some kind, but there simply was not enough illumination to provide any of the clarity or definition he craved.

Something rancid permeated the room. He could not identify the source of the odor, but the stench was exacerbated by the fact that the rag prevented him from breathing through his mouth, forcing him to breathe through his nose. Then again, Marcus realized, the rag might, in fact, be the source of the repulsive odor.

The room was broiling. It had to be a hundred degrees or more, Marcus concluded. The heat, plus the specks of light that he was now certain was sunlight, not from lamps, convinced him it was daytime. Whether it was the same day he had been captured he had no idea.

His boxers were soaked through with sweat. Rivulets of perspiration streaked down his back and arms and legs. His hair was wet and matted, and salty drips were sliding down his nose and ears and stinging his eyes. With his hands chained behind him, he had no way to wipe any of it away.

As he slowly came to, he began to wonder if he had been taken alone. Had Kailea made it? If so, where was she? What about Yigal? Had he been blown to smithereens? Had he been captured? Had he gotten away? Maybe they both had.

Marcus tried to remember the SERE training he'd undergone back at Camp Lejeune in the lush green fields near the North Carolina coast. For nineteen days, he and his fellow Marines had received a crash course in surviving, evading, resisting, and escaping behind enemy lines. But that had been a lifetime ago—nearly twenty years. In the state he was now in, dusting off those mental files was going to take some doing. Yet it had to be done.

He couldn't remember the name of his instructor or even his face. He did, however, have a vague recollection of the three-ring binder he and his colleagues had been given. And one thing was crystal clear in his mind—the acronym drilled into the Marines' heads from the first day of class.

SURVIVAL.

There were, they had been told, eight things they needed to do to make it. Marcus closed his eyes and tried to focus. Soon they came to him, one by one.

S—he needed to *size* up his situation, surroundings, physical condition, and gear.

U—he needed to *use* all of his senses to watch for danger.

R—he needed to *remember* who he was and where he was at all times.

V—he needed to *vanquish* his fear and any sense of panic.

I—he needed to *improvise* and be willing to adapt to every curve that was coming.

V—he needed to truly *value* living—a useful reminder, Marcus told himself.

A—he needed to do his best to *act* like the people around him as much as possible.

L—he needed to *live* by his wits and be prepared to use all his skills to survive.

There was no playbook for staying alive and getting free, his instructor had told him. Only principles. And he needed to start living by them.

Unable to see much of his current surroundings, Marcus tried to recall what had happened back on that dusty border road. He needed to reconstruct everything that had occurred. Not only would he need to be able to explain it all to his commanders back in Washington if he ever got out of this thing alive, but he also needed to sift for clues, for any detail—small or large—that might help him escape.

Escape.

That was now the name of the game. He had to start working on a plan to break free and run and keep running and never look back. He would head west, to the Mediterranean coast. Like every DSS agent, he had a contingency plan for every conceivable worst-case scenario. He and Kailea had developed theirs together. Since they were doing an advance trip in hostile territory along the Lebanon border, they had war-gamed what they would do if they ever came under fire, were captured by Hezbollah, and were somehow able to escape. It had seemed rather far-fetched the previous week. Now, amid the fog, he was trying to remember every detail.

A marina.

No, a port.

A beat-up old fishing trawler.

A guy named . . .

What was his name?

Marcus strained to remember but could not recall the name of the company or its owner. He and Kailea had used aliases and fake Spanish passports and a Gmail account and a Spanish bank app to contract with a small business in the Lebanese city of Tyre that handled deep-sea fishing charters. They had concocted a cover story about an engaged couple from Barcelona, fishing fanatics visiting Beirut on business. They'd paid in advance to have a boat ready to use with twenty-four hours' notice. Once they got out to sea, they'd planned to commandeer the vessel, use the satphone to contact the American Navy, and get picked up by a submarine or helicopter or whatever the Navy decided to dispatch.

But what was the name of that company? And their contact?

At the moment, it was still too fuzzy.

Then again, it might not even matter. An awful lot had to go right before he would ever set foot on the chartered yacht in the port of Tyre. First, he had to break free of a cell of Hezbollah jihadists, and that, he knew, was all but impossible.

16

Then another thought struck him.

In the unlikely chance that he could break free, how could he possibly devise a plan for all three of them to escape? Even if Kailea or Yigal or both were alive, were they in any condition—mentally or physically—to run? It was possible that they had been wounded during their capture. Maybe seriously. What then?

Focusing once again on that SERE manual, Marcus tried to recall the code of conduct he had been required to memorize. It had been years since he had recited it aloud. But to his surprise, the code began to come back to him, slowly at first and then in a rush, and his resolve grew as he silently mouthed the words.

I am an American, fighting in the forces which guard my country and our way of life. I am prepared to give my life in their defense.

I will never surrender of my own free will. If in command, I will never surrender the members of my command while they still have the means to resist.

If I am captured, I will continue to resist by all means available. I will make every effort to escape and aid others to escape. I will accept neither parole nor special favors from the enemy.

If I become a prisoner of war, I will keep faith with my fellow prisoners. I will give no information nor take part in any action which might be harmful to my comrades. If I am senior, I will take command. If not, I will obey lawful orders of those appointed over me and will back them in every way.

When questioned, should I become a prisoner of war, I am required to give name, rank, service number, and date of birth. I will evade answering further questions to the utmost of my ability. I will make no oral or written statements disloyal to my country and its allies or harmful to their cause.

I will never forget that I am an American, fighting for freedom, responsible for my actions, and dedicated to the principles which made my country free. I will trust in my God and in the United States of America.

For several minutes, Marcus thought about those last two sentences. The more he did, the more encouraged he felt. Closing his eyes, he bowed his head and said a silent prayer of thanks that the Lord had chosen to keep him alive. He asked for courage and the wisdom to know what to do next. Then he prayed for Kailea and Yigal, resolving in that moment that he would operate on the assumption that they were alive, unless or until he knew for certain that they were not. It occurred to him that if they were alive, they would likely have been taken by the same operatives. Thus, they might very well have been brought to the same place. Could it be their voices—or the voices of their interrogators—he was hearing in a nearby room?

In time, another section of the SERE manual came to mind. It had been an appendix, tucked away in the back, called something like "Having the Will to Survive" or "How to Maintain the Will to Live." Suddenly it was as if he were right back at Camp Lejeune, sitting in those classes, not just studying the manual but listening to his instructor—*Connolly,* he now recalled.

"If, God forbid, you are ever trapped behind enemy lines," Commander Connolly, an Alabama native, had told Marcus and the other Marines in his distinctive Southern drawl, "you have to know your capabilities and limitations. Keep a positive attitude. Develop a realistic plan. Learn to recognize and combat your fears. You have to anticipate injury, fatigue, illness, adverse environmental conditions, hunger, and isolation. Do not allow yourself to be overcome by fear, anxiety, guilt, boredom, depression, or anger. Be aware of signals of distress. Watch out for indecision, withdrawal, forgetfulness, carelessness. All these things lead to mistakes."

Someone had asked how a soldier might strengthen his will to survive after capture.

"Keep reciting the code of conduct," Connolly had insisted. "Say the Pledge of Allegiance every day, aloud if you can. Sing patriotic songs. If you stink at singing, do it anyway. If you're hiding in enemy territory and can't make a sound, recite the lines to yourself. And above all, think about what life is going to be like when you get back to freedom and how it's going to be when you're back in the companionship of family and friends and in the arms of the girl you love."

17

Marcus did not have time to think about his mom or sisters.

And certainly none to spend on the woman he had recently started seeing.

For the moment, there were far more pressing matters to focus on.

When he and Kailea had landed in Tel Aviv and been picked up at the airport by Yigal the night before, they had discussed their contingency plans during the two-hour drive northward. This was standard operating procedure for all American government employees operating in or near hostile areas. Marcus and Kailea hadn't shared the bulk of their own plans. Most of those details Yigal had no business knowing. But they had agreed on certain things.

First, Yigal would not be wearing an IDF uniform for their advance trip along the border. Rather, he would wear street clothes, like the Americans. If any or all of them were kidnapped, Yigal was under strict orders from the commander of his unit that he should under no circumstances admit to being an Israeli. Rather, he was to pretend to be an American—part of the

DSS team. Yigal's father had been born and raised in Brooklyn, and Yigal spoke fluent English with an unmistakably American and distinctly New York accent.

Second, Yigal had said he would go by the name Dan Case. He insisted that Marcus and Kailea never use his real name should the worst come to pass.

Third, they had all decided not to carry wallets or any form of civilian or military ID. If they were captured, their goal had to be to convince Hezbollah that they were all Americans, and they must not have anything on them that would prove otherwise. Yigal's operating theory was that an Israeli soldier would be subject to far harsher treatment by Shia radicals. Americans would be considered bigger fish to bargain with and thus would likely be treated at least marginally better. Marcus had not been hesitant to express his doubt that this would be the case. Nor had Kailea. Nevertheless, they had agreed to the ruse.

In return, Marcus had had only one request of the young Israeli.

"What's that?" Yigal had asked.

"I don't want you to use my name either," Marcus had replied.

"Why not?"

"If anything happens to us, I'm Tom Millner—remember that," Marcus had said, ignoring the question.

"Okay, but why?"

"Trust me," Kailea had interjected. "You don't want to know or be connected to anyone named Marcus Ryker. Not in Lebanon. Not in Hezbollah country. Got it?"

Marcus could see the young man didn't get it, but Yigal shrugged and nodded anyway. Neither Marcus nor Kailea was about to tell the young man exactly why the very mention of Marcus's name would be so dangerous. The reason was classified far above this kid's pay grade. More to the point, it would have created unnecessary fear in a young man who probably would never need to remember the name Tom Millner anyway.

At least that's what Marcus had thought as they'd driven up Highway 2, heading to Haifa. Now he prayed Yigal remembered not only the names Case and Millner but also the cover stories that were supposed to go with them.

18

An explosion of daylight suddenly filled the room.

Blinded, Marcus winced and turned away. He heard boots approaching. At least six sets of them. Maybe more. Then he felt something smash into his stomach. The force of the blow knocked most of the wind out of him. This was followed by savage blows upon his chest, back, and legs. When the beatings stopped, the rag was jerked out of his mouth and he was ordered to open his eyes and stand.

He complied, but someone grabbed the chains around his hands and jerked them above his head, hooking them to a winch of some kind. Then a motor began to whine. Marcus's arms were yanked higher and higher over his head until he was on his tiptoes and finally hanging in midair.

The door at the other end of the wide rectangular room was now wide-open. It was a garage door—three of them, actually—and Marcus realized that he was in an auto repair shop. He could see tools and diagnostic devices of various kinds hanging on the concrete walls. The floor, too, was concrete and covered with oil stains.

To his right, he saw a doorway to an office of some kind.

To his left . . .

Marcus froze. He blinked hard to make sure he was really awake, that he was actually seeing and not imagining what was next to him. But sure enough, to his immediate left was an Iranian-made surface-to-surface ballistic missile mounted on the back of a mobile launching vehicle about the size of an American fire truck. The solid-propellant missile was covered with black printing. Marcus could not read the words, but he was certainly familiar enough with Farsi to know that what he was looking at was the language of Iran. Almost ten meters long, this was not one of the clunky old unguided Zelzal-2 models from the late 1990s. This was a gleaming new Fateh-110 with a precision state-of-the-art guidance system and a range of upwards of three hundred kilometers—easily capable of hitting Jerusalem or Tel Aviv, Israel's two biggest and most populous urban areas.

Just then, someone jabbed a thick wooden truncheon into Marcus's ribs. The pain was intense, but he refused to give his captors the satisfaction of making a sound. Looking around, he noticed six hooded men, all sporting automatic rifles, taking up positions around the shop. The one who had hit him, however, was not hooded, and Marcus found himself staring at a young man no more than thirty years old, wearing green fatigues and a maroon beret. He was tall. Marcus pegged him at about his own height—six feet one—give or take an inch, and about his own weight, roughly 190 pounds. The man was broad-shouldered and muscular and clearly knew how to take care of himself. He sported a dark mustache and a scruffy, almost-patchy beard. In his hands was the truncheon. Yet what most captured Marcus's attention were the man's eyes. Brooding and gray, these were the eyes of a cold-blooded killer, the eyes of the man he'd first seen on the security road, the man who had sent fifty thousand volts into his chest.

"My name is Colonel Amin al-Masri," the man said in a husky, almost-raspy voice. "To whom do I have the pleasure of speaking?"

Marcus said nothing but stored away two new pieces of information.

First, if this guy was really a colonel—and there was no particular reason to think the man was inflating his résumé in front of his men—then this was a fairly high-ranking officer in the Hezbollah hierarchy. Second, if the man had just given his real name, then he wasn't Lebanese. *Al-Masri*, Marcus knew from his extremely limited Arabic, meant "the Egyptian."

"Let's start with your name," the colonel repeated in heavily accented English.

Still, Marcus did not speak.

"Okay—whom do you work for?"

Nothing.

"Obviously you are an American," the Egyptian continued. "Obviously you're doing advance work for someone in your government. But who?"

Silence.

"Who is coming to our border? And when?"

Marcus hung there from the winch mounted on the ceiling, head pounding, adrenaline surging, blood boiling. He felt a flash of anger in his eyes and saw the colonel's cold gray eyes react with anger as well. The man made a waving motion with his left hand, and one of his henchmen rushed to his side. He was carrying a bucket, which he set down under Marcus's feet. Using a bayonet attached to the end of his AK-47, the man speared a wet and dripping and filthy sponge from the bucket and proceeded to wipe it across Marcus's chest and feet. Then the man retreated into the shadows for a moment, only to return with what looked like jumper cables. The man attached one set of clamps to Marcus's toes and the other set to his bare, wet chest.

"Let me be perfectly clear," al-Masri said. "If you talk, you live. If not, you die. Take your pick. I really couldn't care less. I'm sure your colleagues would be more than happy to tell me what I need to know."

19

This was going from bad to worse.

Yet Marcus had also just picked up two more pieces of valuable intelligence. "Your colleagues" had to refer to Kailea and Yigal, which meant they were both still alive and very likely being held nearby. What's more, the Egyptian had neither spoken to them nor tortured them—not yet, anyway.

On al-Masri's command, guards closed and locked all three garage doors. What little breeze had wafted in was now gone. Once again sweat began to pour down his face. Marcus was becoming dehydrated. He tried to blink back the drips coming down his forehead, but it was no use. The salty discharge was stinging his eyes, but this was the least of his problems. He looked at the colonel and had no doubt this man had been thoroughly trained in the black art of sadism and took great pleasure in it.

"Don't fool yourself, American," al-Masri said. "You'll talk. The only question is how much pain you suffer before you tell me what I want to know."

When Marcus remained quiet, the colonel nodded to his sidekick, who reached over and flipped a switch. Electricity surged through the cables. Marcus's body went rigid, then began to shudder. His left arm started to spasm. Then his right knee and foot did too. He was hit by the stench of burnt hair.

The pain was absolutely brutal. But it had one side benefit. He was wide-awake now and thinking clearly. He gritted his teeth. He forced himself to remember that the IDF's quick reaction force had to have been just moments away from rescuing them back on that border road. That meant they knew he, Kailea, and Yigal had been captured, and the hunt for them was well underway.

Marcus knew the Israelis' capabilities. He knew their professionalism. He knew their commitment to getting their people back, no matter what it took. He had seen the Israelis in action over the years, and he had no doubt they were coming for them now.

His mission, he reminded himself, had to be twofold. First, he would not let his captors know who he really was under any circumstances. Second, he had to buy the three of them as much time as he possibly could. If Hezbollah was determined to kill them, there was nothing he could do to stop them. But he didn't believe they were going to kill him. The three of them were too big a prize. And that, he hoped, might just give him the time and leverage they would need to survive.

"Enough," al-Masri shouted.

The man flipped the switch. The electricity stopped flowing. The pain did not.

"Now let's try this again—what is your name?"

Marcus still refused to talk.

"I want your name, rank, and serial number—that's all," the Egyptian insisted. "Then we'll take you down and give you some cold water and something to eat."

Marcus knew this was only the beginning. The pain combined with the offer of food and water was designed to make him crack. Designed to test his breaking point. So he looked away and said nothing.

His mind raced. Hezbollah hadn't carried out a successful kidnapping on this border since 2006. They hadn't even attempted a kidnapping for years. Why now? There could only be one reason. Hezbollah's Sheikh, wherever he was—in some bunker near Beirut or the Bekaa Valley—wanted something. Needed something. So as much as they might brutalize him, Marcus was betting on the notion that they were going to keep him alive. All he had to do was hold on for a day. Maybe two. Then the IDF would do the rest. He could do that. He'd been trained to do that. So he braced himself for round two.

"Very well," al-Masri said.

Once again the Egyptian nodded to his subordinate. Once again the man hit the switch. Once again electrical current surged through the cables and into Marcus's body. Once again the pain was excruciating. And it wasn't just hair this time. Now he could smell his flesh burning.

"Stop," said al-Masri.

The cables grew limp. So did Marcus. But still he did not talk.

Al-Masri asked for the truncheon, then drove it into Marcus's right side again and again. This pain was different, in some ways worse than electrocution. Several of Marcus's ribs had been broken in an operation in the East China Sea. That had been more than eighteen months ago. The bones had long since healed. Yet Marcus knew it wouldn't take many more blows like this to break them again. And he found himself wondering if al-Masri already knew who he was.

"Again," al-Masri said. "And dial it up."

His assistant complied, and Marcus experienced electrocution on a level that he'd only heard of before from POWs or read about in books. Most of the muscles in his body began to spasm uncontrollably. The pain was so intense it was no longer possible to think or to reason, except to wonder if he was going to go into cardiac arrest.

"Enough," the Hezbollah commander shouted after another minute or so.

Again Marcus's body went limp. Remarkably, he had not blacked out. But he knew he was close.

"Look, American, you think you're a tough guy? Please. No one can hold out forever. Everyone breaks. Everyone. So just tell me your name, your rank, and your serial number before one of the others gives it to me and I simply decide to put a bullet through your head."

Marcus's vision was blurring. He could tell al-Masri was still standing there looking up at him, but he could no longer see his face clearly. So he looked blankly back at his tormentor and smiled.

That set al-Masri off. The colonel pushed his deputy aside and threw the switch himself. The leads sparked and smoked. Marcus's body shook and spasmed and then went rigid.

And then everything went dark again.

20

From inside the bedchamber rose a wail that pierced the eerie silence.

The wail became a shriek. A scream of utter despair. It did not seem human.

General Mahmoud Entezam had never heard anything like it. Yet the commander of the Iranian Revolutionary Guard Corps knew exactly what it meant. He looked up from the text messages pouring into his phone and stared down the empty hallway. The third door on the left was closed but not locked. Bracing himself for what was coming, he stood erect and smoothed out the creases in his uniform.

A moment later, Yadollah Afshar, president of the Islamic Republic, came rushing around the corner. Right behind him was Dr. Haydar Abbasi, a member of Iran's National Security Council and a recent addition to the Supreme Leader's inner circle. The three men converged in front of the door but said nothing. What was there to say? They had all known that this moment was coming. Indeed, they had expected it for well over a year. Somehow, the inevitable had been forestalled. But no longer.

General Entezam looked at Abbasi, then at President Afshar. The latter—wearing a crisp white shirt and freshly pressed French cuffs, his three-piece navy suit having just been immaculately tailored and newly dry-cleaned, his chartreuse silk tie in a classic Windsor knot—reached for the door handle, took a deep breath, and then turned the knob and entered first.

What Entezam witnessed at that moment took his breath away. The Supreme Leader's wife, Sayyida Farideh Ansari, shrouded in her black chador, had collapsed to the floor. She was weeping uncontrollably. Her entire body was shaking. She was gasping for air. Yet there was no one to help her. None of the men were permitted to touch her. Where was the doctor? Where were the nurses?

The IRGC commander picked up the receiver of the phone on the nightstand and barked a series of orders. Moments later, the Supreme Leader's medical team arrived, followed by his security detail. Two nurses rushed to the widow's side. They tried to pull her out of the room, but she began shrieking all the louder. She clutched at the bed, then at the body. More nurses arrived. It took five women to gain control of the hysterical widow. One jabbed her neck with a needle. Then they carried her away to another room to be cared for properly and discreetly.

The chief physician, an elderly man in his eighties, now entered the room. Asking the others to step away from the bed, he put on his stethoscope and examined the Supreme Leader. He checked for a heartbeat but found nothing. He lowered his head, his eyes welling with tears. It was finished.

The time of death was recorded as 1:47 in the afternoon in Tehran.

12:17 p.m. in Moscow and al-Quds.

5:17 a.m. in Washington.

Entezam couldn't help but stare at the Grand Ayatollah's gray, gaunt, cold, emaciated body. The man had always been a somewhat-frail, bespectacled figure. But the last eighteen months had been beyond cruel to the eighty-six-year-old Hossein Ansari. The pancreatic cancer that had seized his body had metastasized rapidly and ravaged every organ. The doctors had tried their best to manage his suffering, but there was only so much morphine a man could take.

All of Ansari's hair had fallen out. His beard, once thick and chest-length, was gone. Ghastly sores had broken out all over his body. The man was mostly covered by blankets. Yet the oozing, open blisters on his face and neck were visible. Worst of all, thought Entezam, was that Ansari's eyes were still open. The general had expected the nation's revered shepherd to slip away peacefully in the night. Instead, the man looked haunted.

Why? Entezam wondered. *Wasn't Ayatollah Ansari now resting in paradise? Wasn't he being attended to by the heavenly virgins the Holy Qur'an promised? Why, then, did he look so terrified? What exactly had he seen in his final moments?*

"Perhaps we could clear the room," the chief physician whispered to President Afshar. "The Supreme Leader's body must be prepared for burial."

Afshar nodded, then turned to his colleagues. "Come," he said quietly.

The president exited the bedroom, followed by Dr. Abbasi, after which General Entezam exited as well. Last came the security detail. The group headed down a long corridor and through two security checkpoints, finally reaching the Supreme Leader's private office. They were saluted by two armed guards in ceremonial uniforms standing to each side of a door that resembled the hatch of a submarine.

Once the three principals had entered and taken their seats on the thick Persian carpets, silk pillows, and cushions, the president insisted that they were not to be disturbed for any reason. A steward offered them tea, but Afshar waved him off. Then the hatch was closed and sealed. They were alone.

The magnitude of the moment was not lost on any of them. The last Supreme Leader to die had been the Grand Ayatollah Ruhollah Khomeini. That was June 3, 1989. Entezam remembered the date well. He had recently graduated from university and was then the youngest officer in the IRGC, just beginning his long and storied career. He remembered how he had wept—not because Khomeini was gone, but because at the time Entezam could not imagine a successor more unworthy than Hossein Ansari.

Over the years, Entezam had been promoted up the ranks of the

Revolutionary Guard Corps. The higher he rose, the closer he had the opportunity to observe the new Supreme Leader. Eventually the two had met and developed a cautious working relationship. In recent years, having risen to the role of commander of the IRGC, Entezam had begun meeting regularly with Ansari and was drawn into his personal orbit. Along the way, the general's view of the ayatollah had changed. Entezam had grown impressed with Ansari's spiritual depth, and even more with the man's strategic acumen and geopolitical instincts. Together, they had forged a rare and close alliance, dramatically advancing the Islamic Revolution and extending the reach of the regime. In this very room, in fact, they had mapped out strategies to seize effective control of four Arab capitals—Baghdad, Beirut, Damascus, and Sana'a. Here in this office they had praised Allah for the successes he had uniquely bestowed upon them, time after time.

Entezam had developed a deep love and warm affection for the old man. It was now as surreal as it was grievous to have to say goodbye to the Supreme Leader.

And with an acute, if nauseating, sense of irony, Entezam realized that he could not imagine someone more unworthy to replace Hossein Ansari than the man sitting across from him.

21

President Yadollah Afshar led them in prayer, then turned to his colleagues.

"I must go on television soon and address the nation," the president said solemnly. "We must activate plans for the state funeral. And of course, the assembly must move with all haste and discretion to anoint a worthy successor."

The first two sentences passed without notice. It was the last one that chilled Mahmoud Entezam to his core. Worried that the expression on his face might reveal the shock and horror he felt, Entezam fished through his briefcase and drew out a notepad and pen so he could make a list of actions that needed his attention. The most urgent, of course, didn't even require being written down. He needed to brief the man sitting across from him on the crisis unfolding in southern Lebanon. Yet he was suddenly having difficulty concentrating, so profound was his contempt for Yadollah Afshar.

It was no secret how long the late Supreme Leader and President Afshar had known each other or how fond they were of each other personally. The two men's friendship went back decades. While earning his doctorate in Islamic law and jurisprudence, Afshar had been a student of then-Professor

Ansari in the Shia seminary where Ansari had long taught in the city of Qom. Yet at Ansari's encouragement, Afshar had not entered the clergy. Instead, he had pursued a master's in public administration from the University of Tehran. Ansari had insisted that his disciple possessed a knack for leadership and could be very useful to the regime by serving in the highest levels of government. This counsel had both surprised and inspired Afshar and set into motion a remarkable career of public service.

In the years after graduate school, Afshar had served as Iran's deputy minister of the interior, then as minister. Later he'd been tapped to be the regime's minister of finance and still later, the nation's minister of foreign affairs. What almost no one beyond Entezam knew was that it was the Supreme Leader himself who had secretly encouraged his protégé to run for president.

Elections in the Islamic Republic of Iran were rigged from beginning to end. The public was led to believe that their votes mattered. The truth, however, was that any man the Supreme Leader wanted to serve in the presidency would, in the end, appear to be elected, no matter who the voters wanted to serve. To be sure, candidates went through the motions of campaigning. State newspapers and television and radio networks earnestly covered the would-be horse race. And the people were given a day off to go to the polls on Election Day to mark their ballots. Everyone played their parts convincingly. And why not? Most thought the elections were real.

Entezam knew better. One of the responsibilities of the IRGC commander was to ensure that the Supreme Leader's hand-chosen man was announced as winner on election night. Ever loyal to the Grand Ayatollah, Entezam had performed this duty not just once but twice. In two successive elections he had made certain that Yadollah Afshar emerged as head of the government. He'd done so despite how little he thought of the man. He'd done so because Afshar was so easy to contain and manipulate that Entezam had never seen him as a threat. The head of the IRGC had been perennially revolted by watching from the front row as Afshar had continued to ingratiate himself to his mentor and political patron. But Entezam had always consoled himself with the knowledge that one day Afshar would harmlessly pass from the political scene.

What horrified Entezam now was the notion that the Supreme Leader might have planned all along to reward his protégé by naming Afshar his successor. Entezam had no proof, yet there was something in Afshar's tone, his body language, his sense of calm, even his decision to come to this very room—the private personal study of the Supreme Leader—that suggested the man didn't simply *hope* to emerge as the assembly's first choice but actually *expected* it.

"General? General Entezam? Are you all right?"

The IRGC commander suddenly heard Abbasi calling his name and realized that he had zoned out for who knew how long.

"Please forgive me, Your Excellency—Dr. Abbasi—to both of you I profoundly apologize," Entezam stammered, realizing both men were staring at him with looks of great confusion and concern. "The death of our esteemed leader is not easy to bear."

"It is a difficult day, indeed," said the president.

"Can I get you anything?" Abbasi asked.

"No, no—I will be fine," Entezam demurred. "I just . . ."

His voice trailed off, and he was embarrassed to have lowered his guard before a man he considered his most serious enemy.

"Perhaps I should ring for the doctor," Abbasi suggested.

"Thank you, but I will be fine, I assure you," Entezam said.

"Very well," said President Afshar, returning to his checklist. "Then we ought to discuss the funeral. Today is Saturday. I think we should aim for Wednesday."

"Yes, that would be fine, Your Excellency, but before we get to such matters, we have another problem we must address," Entezam replied, trying to regather his thoughts.

"What could be more serious than the death of our leader?" Afshar asked.

"Well, Your Excellency, as I was arriving at the palace, I received an urgent message from our esteemed brother and ally in Lebanon, Sheikh al-Hussaini. I would have brought it to your attention immediately, but before I could, I heard the wail from inside the leader's bedroom and we all raced to his side."

"What is it?" Afshar pressed. "Is the Sheikh all right?"

"He is, but I'm afraid there's been an event on the Zionist border."

22

"What kind of event?" the president demanded.

"An attack, Your Excellency."

"Tell me."

"Apparently the Zionists opened fire on a Hezbollah unit near the security fence. From what I hear, Hezbollah forces returned fire and fought back valiantly. They destroyed three Zionist vehicles and killed many."

"How many?"

"I don't have a number yet. But I must tell you this—the Zionists have begun a blistering assault on the entire area. Bombing. Shelling. Ground forces and mechanized units have crossed the border. I hate to have to bring you such developments when we are all rocked by the Holy One's passing, but I felt you needed to know immediately."

"A war with the Zionists—now?" asked an indignant Afshar. "Did you authorize this? I certainly did not."

"No, of course not," Entezam said. "Why would I?"

"The timing could not be worse."

"I agree, Your Excellency, but Sheikh al-Hussaini insists that he did not authorize the attack. He said that he and his men were blindsided by this."

"That's preposterous."

"I'm simply relaying what he said."

Dumbfounded, the president looked over to Dr. Abbasi, who also looked aghast but said nothing, then back at Entezam. "Who fired first?" Afshar demanded. "The Zionists or the Hezbollah unit?"

"The Sheikh says it was the Zionists."

"Do you believe him?"

"Honestly, Your Excellency, I don't know what to believe."

"Why would Prime Minister Eitan order such an attack, especially now, while they are trying so hard to wrap up peace talks with the Saudis?"

"It makes no sense."

"Isn't Whitney, the U.S. secretary of state, heading to the region this weekend?"

"I believe so."

"Then why trigger a new war on the eve of her arrival?"

General Entezam paused a moment.

"What is it?" asked the president. "There's something troubling you."

"There is," the IRGC commander admitted. "Something doesn't smell right. The Zionists are sick, cruel, evil people. But as you suggest, they have no reason to launch a war right now."

"Maybe it's just a soldier or two that got trigger-happy."

Entezam shook his head. "I doubt it. Their forces are very disciplined, especially on that border. They know how many missiles we have supplied Hezbollah with, missiles aimed at their schools and hospitals and airports and population centers. And even if one soldier did go off and began shooting and a brief firefight erupted, why would the Zionists escalate matters? Why scramble fighter jets? Why send in ground forces? Unless . . ."

"Unless what?" the president asked.

"Unless Hezbollah grabbed hostages," Entezam said. "That's the only explanation for why the Zionists are going crazy."

"So you think the Sheikh's forces fired first."

"I'm starting to."

"And you think they ran an operation to grab some Zionist hostages?"

"Can you see another explanation for what's going on?"

"Not immediately, no. But why would the Sheikh take such an action without our authorization—without even discussing it with us?"

"I don't know."

"Then find out."

"I will, Your Excellency," said the general. "But we can't let it seem like there is any daylight between us and the Sheikh in this fight, can we?"

"Of course not," Afshar said. "Certainly not today of all days."

"Precisely," said Entezam. "I can make the Sheikh understand how deeply disappointed we are. But we still have Zionists pounding southern Lebanon. The Sheikh cannot unsheathe Hezbollah's missile force without our authorization. Usually that authorization would come from the Supreme Leader. Now it will have to come from you. What do I tell him? Should he stand down, or do you want him to go to war?"

"War is not in our best interest at the moment," the president said. "Don't we have enough on our plates? A state funeral to hold. A nation in mourning. The search for our next Supreme Leader. The upcoming test of our newest ICBM. The list goes on and on."

"All true," Entezam agreed. "But perhaps we should see this as an opportunity."

"How so?"

"Wouldn't the chance to drag the Zionists into a shooting war with an Arab state be useful?" Entezam asked. "Wouldn't the images of hundreds, maybe thousands, of dead Lebanese women and children inflame the Arab world against the Jews? Couldn't that light up the Palestinians? What if a Third Intifada were unleashed? What if Hamas and Islamic Jihad began firing rockets at Israel from the Gaza Strip? What if the Palestinians in Jordan began to turn out in the streets, demanding the king abrogate his wicked treaty with the Jews?"

Afshar considered, saying nothing.

"There is something else," the IRGC commander added.

"What's that?" asked the president.

"The more we can stoke the flames of Arab rage against the Zionists, the more pressure we can build against the Saudi royals to abandon their fool's errand and call off their peace talks with the Zionists once and for all."

"The Saudis have already crawled into bed with the Jewish dogs," Afshar said. "Why would they slink away now?"

"Perhaps the royals are rethinking that sick spectacle they put on in Jerusalem," Entezam replied. "They have already had their engagement party. Why else have they not consummated the relationship?"

"You think they're looking for a way out?"

"I do," Entezam confirmed. "And I would suggest that a bloody, messy, ugly, protracted war between the Zionists and Lebanon just might prove to be the straw that breaks the proverbial camel's back."

23

Kailea Curtis had no idea if it was day or night.

She had no idea where she was or how long she had been there. All she knew was that it was blistering hot and she could not remember the last time she had had something to drink.

She had awoken to find a cloth hood over her head. Sweat was pouring down her face and back. She felt claustrophobic. She was having trouble breathing. She could feel the adrenaline in her system spiking and knew she had to fight the fear.

Flashbacks began ripping through her mind. She could feel the M4 in her hands. She remembered firing three steady bursts. She could picture herself ejecting an empty magazine and preparing to reload. And then she saw herself being surrounded by hooded men—three of them—their Kalashnikovs raised and ready to fire. She saw a fourth man stepping toward her, holding a pistol in his hands. No, wait. It was not a pistol. It was a Taser. And that was the last thing she could remember until now.

There was no way, however, that she had merely been tased. She had to have been drugged as well. She had never done drugs. She rarely even drank. Her father had been a violent drunk, and she had vowed never to go down that path. She was not used to feeling drugged out or hungover, but that had to be what this was. Someone had given her a heavy dose of narcotics. The problem was they were wearing off and she could feel herself teetering on the precipice of panic.

Suddenly Marcus's face came to mind. It was distant and out of focus. He was saying something, but she could barely hear him. It was as if they were underwater. Still, she thought she could make it out if she concentrated. Most of it, anyway. *She'd been trained for this,* he was telling her. *You can do this. Fight the fear. Control the adrenaline. Channel it. Manage it. Let it sharpen your focus.*

Without even realizing it, she began counting down from fifty. It was a trick Marcus had taught her to slow her breathing and steady her nerves.

All stress is self-induced, she heard him saying. *It's in your mind. You don't need it. Lay it down. Panic is contagious. But so is calm. Stay calm. Do your work. Slow is smooth. Smooth is smart. Smart is straight. Straight is deadly.*

It was working. Her heart rate began dropping. Her breathing slowed. The claustrophobia began to fade.

She was sitting on a metal chair. Her hands were chained behind her back. Her feet were chained together too.

She could hear two people whispering. They were both men. But they were not speaking Arabic. They were speaking Russian. It struck her as odd, and she strained to hear what they were saying. She could not get all of it, but one of them was complaining he was hungry. The other was complaining their cell phones had been taken away.

Then she heard the roar of fighter jets and a series of explosions. They weren't exactly close, but neither were they so far away. Best of all, they were Pratt & Whitney engines. She would know them anywhere. Which meant they were American planes—or at least American built. Which meant they were almost certainly Israeli fighters. Which meant the Israelis were getting closer. That was a good sign. So, too, was the fact that no one had spoken directly to her. Nor had anyone laid a hand on her. Not yet, anyway.

Marcus was right. She could do this. She could endure almost anything they threw at her without giving away anything vital. She just needed to stall. After all, the good guys were coming. It was only a matter of time.

That led to another thought. Had she been the only one taken? What about Marcus? What about Yigal? Had they been able to retreat before she'd been overrun and captured? She hoped so. Marcus would make it his mission to come get her. He wouldn't rest until she was safe. She was sure of it. He'd probably demand to lead the rescue party. For an instant, that thought actually put a smile on her face.

Then it occurred to her that both men might have been killed in the raid. Yigal had been in the IDF less than two years. He was an intelligence analyst, for crying out loud, not a combat soldier. Did she really believe the young Israeli had safely eluded an entire Hezbollah raiding party if she hadn't? Not a chance. He was either dead or captured. If he had been captured, then maybe he was close by.

And what about Marcus? Was there any chance he had not fought to the bitter end? None, she knew. Nor was there any chance he had retreated to safety without her at his side. That meant Marcus, too, was dead or captured.

Which was it? Kailea wondered. And how could she find out?

Her thoughts were interrupted by the sound of heavy boots approaching. A moment later, she heard a metal key click in a metal lock. She heard a metal door turn on metal hinges. The boots were getting closer. Every muscle in her body tensed.

24

Someone was circling her.

She had no doubt it was a man. What would a woman be doing in a Hezbollah unit? He was moving around in a clockwise direction. He made two full revolutions, then stopped in front of her. All was quiet. The Russian speakers had fallen silent. Then the boots reversed course. The man began walking in the opposite direction. This time, however, he did not make it all the way around her. He stopped. Right behind her. She could hear him breathing. It was creepy, to put it mildly. Yet she was determined not to show him the fear rising within.

"My name is Colonel Amin al-Masri," the man whispered in heavily accented English. "Welcome to Lebanon."

The room was silent. But the stench of body odor hit her hard, and she feared she might gag.

"Let's start with your name."

Willing herself not to vomit, Kailea said nothing.

"Don't test me, little flower," the man said softly in her right ear, his voice even and controlled. "I have neither the time nor the patience."

The thug reached beneath the hood covering Kailea's face and caressed her cheek with his finger. Revulsed, she felt her entire body stiffen.

"The last thing I want to do is harm one so fair as you," he continued. "The others, perhaps, if they do not talk. But with you I am sure we can work something out—an arrangement—just between us."

The man paused. Then Kailea heard his boots begin circling her again. He circled once, then twice. She sensed that he had stopped directly in front of her. A moment later, she was certain of his location, for he had moved his face just inches from hers. The body odor was his. That much was certain. It took everything she had not to lose it all over the floor. But there was something else. Something that made her smile. His title and rank meant nothing to her. But what gave her a flash of hope was hearing that there were "others" in his custody. That had to be Marcus and Yigal. They were alive. And they weren't talking. Neither would she.

"All I want, for now, is your name," said al-Masri. "Is that too much to ask?"

Kailea remained silent.

"Don't you want me to be able to tell your superiors back in Washington whom I have in my possession?"

Nothing.

"Don't you want your family to know that you're still alive?"

Still nothing.

"Don't you know who I am?" he asked. "Don't you understand that I have the power to set you free, untouched, unharmed?"

His tone was becoming agitated. Kailea's smile broadened. She was messing with him. And it felt good.

"I grew up in a Shia neighborhood in Beirut," al-Masri told her. "Have you ever been to Beirut? Perhaps you have friends who have been there. Perhaps even some who have died there. Do you know any Marines?"

Al-Masri, she mused. *Al-Masri*. The Egyptian. That was a name she knew.

She'd read it before, she was sure, but in the utter darkness and this stifling heat she could not place it. Not yet.

"I have to admit," he continued, "when my men attacked that convoy, the last thing I expected them to bring back were Americans, and certainly not a woman and most definitely not one so lovely as this."

She heard him turn and grunt something to his men in Arabic. She had no idea what it was about, but the tone was curt. This was not a patient man. This was not a man used to having his orders defied. Especially not by a woman. Which meant he was going to snap. And soon.

A moment later, someone yanked the hood off her head. Kailea blinked and squinted as her eyes tried to adjust to the light being thrown by a single bulb hanging from the ceiling. She found herself facing the colonel, who was crouching, putting himself at eye level before her. Immediately she turned away and looked down at the floor. Yet she sensed he was smiling, even as he used the cloth hood to dab her face dry.

"Look at me," he said softly.

Kailea refused.

"Look. At. Me."

The tone was clipped and constrained. But the volcano was getting ready to blow.

"You understand that I could make your life most unpleasant, do you not?"

Through her peripheral vision, Kailea saw that she was in a storage room of some sort. There were wooden crates and cardboard boxes stacked along the walls around her. Off to her left were old car parts—rusty doors, what looked like carburetors—and boxes of tools. To her right she could see stacks of old tires. Then something else caught her eye. Behind the tires were rows of metal shelving. And on each of the shelves were stacked 122-millimeter Katyusha rockets. She raised her head to get a better look, but al-Masri suddenly took her face in his filthy, calloused hands and forced her to look him in the eye.

"The boy is talking, of course," he said, apparently referring to Yigal. "It wasn't hard. He's told me everything about you and your colleagues. But I need to hear it confirmed by you. Names. Ranks. Serial numbers. And the name of the bigwig you were doing an advance trip for. He's told us everything. But it's your job to confirm what I already know. And believe me, if the boy is lying to me—or if you do—it will not go well for any of you. Not well at all."

★

It had worked.

Nothing else had, until now.

Al-Masri was finally looking directly into this woman's eyes. They were milk-chocolate brown. Gorgeous. Alluring. And without a trace of fear. Al-Masri could not remember ever having met a more beautiful woman. He had certainly never enjoyed such close company with one.

He decided at that moment that he really would spare her everything he was planning for the other two. This one could prove useful, he thought. Very useful. She would fetch a price far higher than the others. Double, perhaps. Maybe even triple.

Then again, al-Masri mused, why even sell her? His superiors were only asking for one hostage. He now had three. But they didn't know that, did they? Not yet. Because he hadn't told them. Maybe he wouldn't. How could they miss her if they didn't even know she existed?

Al-Masri hadn't been lying when he'd told her he never expected to find a woman in that convoy, nor one as desirable as this. She was not glamorous. She would never walk the runways of Paris or Milan or land on the cover of magazines in the newsstands in New York or London. But he had never desired the anorexic skeletons of the model class. And he had never found a woman in Beirut or anywhere in Lebanon quite like this.

She was trim. Athletic. Without a trace of makeup. Without gaudy jewelry or the painted nails that he so despised. She was stunning. It was too bad she was not an Arab. Worse still, she was an American. His hostage. His slave.

And yet . . .

25

The Egyptian never saw it coming.

In a blinding fast move, the woman in chains reared back her head and just as suddenly shot forward, smashing her forehead into the center of his face.

Al-Masri heard the cartilage in his nose crack. Everyone in the room heard it. The force of the blow sent him flying backward. The back of his head snapped down hard against the concrete floor and blood began pouring both from his nose and the back of his skull. For several seconds, he couldn't see, couldn't think, couldn't move. Everything went black. But only for a moment. When he reopened his eyes, everything was blurry. The room was spinning.

Al-Masri heard the boots. He could see his men rushing toward him. Yet he held up his hand and cursed them in Arabic not to come one centimeter closer. Finding the hood lying on the floor to his right, he grabbed it and pressed it to his nose. A shock of immense pain jolted his body. Blood covered his face and shirt and much of the floor around him. He forced himself to his feet, staggered a bit, then stared at the woman who had, just a moment before, been the object of so much desire.

Then, still holding the hood to his nose to stanch the bleeding, al-Masri turned to Zayan, his most trusted aide, and growled at him in Arabic.

★

Kailea had no idea what the man had said.

Part of her hoped al-Masri had issued the command to kill her. But she doubted she was so lucky. Though determined not to show it, she was terrified by what this psychopath was about to do. Yet she knew it was nothing compared to what the Iranians were probably planning to do to all three of them once Hezbollah turned them over. She had no doubt that if she survived these few days, she would soon be transferred to Tehran. They all would be.

Left to their own devices, Hezbollah's leadership would likely try to make a deal to secure the release of thousands of jihadists held in Israeli prisons and at Guantánamo Bay. And at some point, she figured, Jerusalem and Washington would probably give in. The Iranians, however, would never make such a deal. They had no interest in making a trade. They were out to humiliate the Great Satan. They would torture the three of them in the most inhumane manner, extract every bit of intelligence they possibly could out of them, then hang them from cranes in the heart of the capital, leaving their naked bodies dangling there to decompose in the summer heat, to be gawked at by the people and picked apart by birds.

If she was doomed to die anyway, she preferred to die here and now.

Al-Masri's chief thug came toward her and towered over her. He motioned for the other guards to lift her to her feet. When they did, the man pulled out a hunting blade from a leather sheath on his belt and held it in front of Kailea's face.

This was it, she realized. She wasn't religious. Yet now she shut her eyes tightly and began repeating the Hail Mary. She didn't know what else to do.

The man, however, did not slit her throat. Rather, he cut away her black

T-shirt, soaked with sweat as it was. This caught her off guard. Her eyes went wide. To her shock, he put the blade away. But he was not finished. Instead, he unbuckled her belt, tossed it and the shirt aside, then unbuttoned her jeans and yanked them down to her ankles. He grabbed her head with both hands and forced her to look at him.

Kailea knew what was about to happen, and to her it was worse than death. Without another thought, she jumped up, yanked her knees toward her chest, and shot her chained feet forward as she fell back into the chair.

The force of the blow came hard and fast as her feet connected solidly with the man's groin, and he collapsed to the ground, squealing in pain.

★

"You whore!" al-Masri shrieked through gritted teeth.

Unleashing a torrent of obscenities, the Egyptian grabbed the wooden truncheon from Zayan and backhanded the woman across the face with all the force he could muster. Now it was her nose that everyone heard crack. Now it was her blood pouring down her face and body. Al-Masri watched her and the chair topple over, and now it was her head snapping hard against the concrete floor.

"Get her up," he snarled. *"Now."*

The men did as they were told. Yet the woman could barely sit upright.

"Hold her in place."

Again they obeyed their orders. Then they watched him take the truncheon, hold it up like a baseball bat, and smash it into her stomach.

The American doubled over and collapsed to the ground, gasping for air.

"Again," al-Masri shouted. *"Get her up."*

Once more Zayan and the others forced the woman to sit upright. This time al-Masri circled behind her. Raising the truncheon, he struck her repeatedly on the back and neck. When she again collapsed to the floor, again he ordered the guards to pick her up, and again the beatings commenced.

"Tell! Me! Your! Name!" al-Masri screamed, coming back around to face her, punctuating each word with another blow.

Still she would not talk. Still she refused to look at him. Instead, he noticed she was staring at his right hand. He could see she was waiting for the truncheon's next blow. He smiled, his face nearly as bloody as hers. Then, without warning, he balled up his left hand and drove his left fist into her right eye. The shock of the blow snapped her head back. Al-Masri dropped the truncheon, balled up his right fist, and drove it into her other eye. Again and again he struck her in the face until her entire body went limp.

And then al-Masri wheeled around and made for the boy.

26

General Entezam lit a cigarette and picked up his secure phone.

Incensed that the headstrong young leader of Hezbollah hadn't answered on the first ring, Entezam began cursing under his breath and pacing about his office. When the Sheikh finally picked up on the fifth ring, the commander of the Iranian Revolutionary Guard Corps exploded.

"How dare you?" he shouted into the receiver. *"First you order a raid against the Zionists without discussing it with me or the Supreme Leader, much less getting my authorization or his blessing. Then you take hostages without telling us who they are or how many you have. Only after you have sparked an entirely new regional war—one your patrons neither needed nor wanted—you have the gall to call and ask for our counsel. And if all that weren't egregious enough, you pick the worst possible day. Do you know what today is? Do you have any idea what's going on here right now?"*

Entezam was yelling so loudly he knew that even with the door closed, everyone on his floor could hear him. But he didn't care. It was time to remind Ja'far ibn al-Hussaini exactly what his place was and what it was not.

"The Supreme Leader is dead," he continued. *"Do you hear me? Do you understand what I am saying to you? Our beloved guide, the leader of our Revolution—your uncle—has just passed away. Today should be a day of mourning. It should be a day of remembrance, a day of honoring the man who accomplished more for the glory of Allah in his lifetime than you and I and all our sons combined ever will."*

There was silence on the other end of the line. The Sheikh was, no doubt, stunned by the news and by the tirade to which he was being subjected. But Entezam continued.

"You have no idea what you have done, Ja'far. I have warned you before, but you refused to listen. Your arrogance has completely blinded you. It has dulled your senses. It has created a recklessness that I will be forced to clean up after. Hezbollah is not now, it has never been, and it will never be an independent actor. Hezbollah is and always will be a wholly owned subsidiary of the Islamic Republic of Iran. Do you understand that?"

"Yes, General, I understand," came the reply.

"Do you?"

"Yes, I do, and I can guarantee you, General, that—"

"No, no, no—shut it—shut your mouth and listen to me, Ja'far. I don't want to hear a word from you beyond 'yes' or 'no.' I want no guarantees from you. I don't trust anything you say. And I can guarantee you this: if you had pulled such a stunt on any other day, the Supreme Leader and the war council would have authorized me not only to fire you but to put a bullet in your fat skull. Do you hear me?"

"Yes, General."

"You had better," Entezam said, no longer shouting, his temper beginning to come back under control. "As it happens, Ja'far, today is not any other day. There is no room for daylight between Tehran and Beirut. There is no benefit to the Islamic Republic to permit the appearance of any disagreement between us. Not today. Which means you have literally dodged a bullet. So listen to me very carefully. And take very precise notes. For this is what's going to happen next."

Entezam finished his cigarette and snuffed out the stub in an ashtray.

Then, as the Sheikh waited on the other end of the line, the general rummaged through his desk looking for another pack. Finding one, he ripped it open and lit another cigarette. He was now starting his third pack since breakfast, and the day was still young.

"First, you will wage war with the Zionists," he began upon exhaling. "You will unleash your missile force. You will target civilian populations, beginning with hospitals and schools—but do not target Ben Gurion airport. Not yet. Not unless or until I say so. Am I clear?"

"Yes, General."

"I hope so," Entezam said. "Second, you will engage the Zionist ground forces as well. Your objective is to bog the Zionists down in the southern tier of the country, inflict as many casualties as possible, and show that criminal Reuven Eitan that he and his country are going to pay a very heavy price for violating the sovereignty of the Lebanese people. Got all that?"

"I do."

"Good. One more thing."

"Yes, sir."

"Do you have hostages or not?"

"We are having trouble communicating with our unit," Ja'far replied.

"How is that possible?"

"Apparently the Zionists are jamming all of our communications."

"You still don't know whether your men have taken anyone captive or not?"

"We believe they have, but we don't have any details."

"*Get them,*" Entezam snapped. "*Quickly.*"

27

HEZBOLLAH HEADQUARTERS, BEIRUT, LEBANON

The Sheikh was not accustomed to such a dressing-down.

The only consolation was that Ja'far ibn al-Hussaini had taken the call in a secure chamber off the main war room. He had been alone. And he still was. Outside the door, two dozen of his most loyal generals and aides manned laptops and phone banks and were monitoring and coordinating every move of all Hezbollah operatives and outposts. Well, almost every move. At least none of them had overheard General Entezam's tirade or seen the look of horror on al-Hussaini's face.

He could not remember the last time he had felt such fear. It was not simply rare for him. It was unheard of. His sheer courage on the battlefield and his utter devotion to Allah and the Supreme Leader were the very reasons he had been chosen to succeed Hassan Nasrallah and lead the Party of God. At least seven other Hezbollah commanders were older and more experienced than he. Yet he and he alone had been the Grand Ayatollah's choice for leadership.

Now his mentor and patron, Hossein Ansari, was gone.

Now someone under his command, one of his own senior operatives, had gone rogue.

Now he and his men were going to war.

And he had no idea why.

If this were not enough, the commander of the Iranian Revolutionary Guard Corps—suddenly the most powerful man in Tehran—was furious with him, demanding he provide information that al-Hussaini neither had nor knew how to get, and point-blank threatening his life should he fail to obey Tehran's every command down to the smallest possible detail.

The Sheikh finally set the phone back in its receiver and turned to stare at the door of his compartment. What was he supposed to say to the men on the other side?

★

TEHRAN, IRAN

Dr. Haydar Abbasi knew full well the risk he was taking.

Still, he had no role in planning the funeral. It was not his responsibility to inform the nation about the death of the Supreme Leader. His superiors had no expectation that he was going to be back in his office working on the latest upgrades to Iran's ICBM program. The entire country was heading into a period of mourning. Government offices were going to be closed. All work on the rocket engines and guidance systems would grind to a halt. And besides, they had already made enormous progress over the past year.

Pulling into the parking lot behind his apartment complex, he shut down the engine of his Volkswagen Passat, closed and locked the doors, and headed up to his flat on the ninth floor. As was his habit, he closed all the curtains, switched on his radio to a station playing Persian love songs, turned up the volume, and unplugged his landline phone before entering the walk-through closet. There, he shoved aside a number of suitcases and various boxes filled with books and clothes and other household goods and lifted one of the floorboards. He found the satellite phone right where he'd left it, powered it up, dialed, and gave his clearance code when prompted by the voice on the other end. Then he relayed a single sentence to his handler.

"The leader is dead."

★

BEIRUT, LEBANON

The Sheikh opened the door and cleared his throat.

All activity in the war room came abruptly to a halt. All conversations ceased. Those on the phone apologized to their interlocutors, promised to call right back, and hung up.

When all eyes were upon him and a hush had settled over the room, al-Hussaini spoke in a calm and measured tone.

"Someone has broken the chain of command," he began. "I gave no order to any of our forces to engage the Zionists. Nor did any of my commanders. Can there be a greater breach of trust—a more serious violation of our protocols—than this? I can scarcely think of one."

The Sheikh scanned the war room, looked each officer in the eye. In each he saw concern. In none, however, did he see fear.

Spotting one of his generals sitting at his workstation before a bank of three computer monitors, he walked over and put a hand on the man's back, patting it gently. This commander, now in his midforties, was responsible for the Nasser Unit, overseeing all operations south of the Litani River. He was a legend in the hierarchy of the Hezbollah and revered among his men.

"Trust is all we have in this work," the Sheikh continued. "And trust is not something that comes with a man's rank. It comes with a man's faithfulness to his responsibilities. It is not granted. It is earned. When someone does his job day in and day out and can always be counted on to maintain the highest standards, then he earns our respect and our praise."

The Sheikh could see his men nodding in agreement.

"And yet when a unit leader commits treason against our party and against Allah, should not his superior be held accountable?"

At this, al-Hussaini reached under his robes, drew his sidearm, aimed it at the commander's head, and fired.

The man never saw it coming. His monitors splattered with blood and brain matter, he slumped to the floor as everyone in the room stared in shock.

"One of our units has gone rogue," the Sheikh explained. "This unit has taken hostages without authorization. And they have forced my hand and led us into war with the Zionists. I want to know who they are. I want to know where they are. I want to know who they are holding and why. And then I want them brought to justice. You have two hours. Get to it."

28

Prince Abdullah bin Rashid stared at the message.

His team had already confirmed it was from their deep-cover mole, a man the prince had code-named *Kabutar*—Farsi for "pigeon." There was no reason, therefore, for the chief of Saudi intelligence to doubt the message's authenticity. The death of the Saudi Kingdom's number one enemy, Iran's Grand Ayatollah Hossein Ansari, was hardly a surprise. It had long been expected, and it was long overdue.

There were, however, two key questions that Rashid was now going to be asked.

First, who was going to take Ansari's place?

And second, what was this going to mean for the kingdom and the region?

Rashid had no idea who was going to fill the Supreme Leader's shoes. Nor did he have much leverage to influence the course of events across the Gulf. The ideal outcome would be a moderate coming to power, particularly if he ended—or at least dialed down—Iran's financial and military support for the

Houthi rebels in Yemen, Hezbollah in Lebanon, and Hamas in Gaza and the West Bank. That was unlikely, Rashid knew. Yet even without a moderate in the post, a hard-line nationalist would suffice. What the region needed was someone who would shift the regime's priorities away from extending the Revolution, expanding Iran's nuclear and ICBM programs, and laying the groundwork for the coming of the Mahdi, and instead focus on rebuilding Iran's economy and reengaging with the international community.

Rashid's gut instinct, however, was that the role was not going to any of the prestigious clerics whose names had been bandied about in the media over the past couple of years. Such speculation about moderates and nationalists, he believed, had no basis in reality; it was merely wishful thinking and thus both illusory and dangerous. The man Rashid most expected to become Iran's next Grand Ayatollah was the man he most feared, a man who was neither a moderate nor a nationalist but a true believer in Shia apocalypticism. That man was Iran's current president.

Yadollah Afshar.

Picking up a secure phone on his desk, Rashid speed-dialed the private mobile phone of Crown Prince Abdulaziz bin Faisal Al Saud. As the country's chief executive officer, minister of defense, and heir to the throne—the man poised to rule the Saudi Kingdom for the next fifty years—there was no one who needed this information more.

"It's happening," Rashid told the crown prince. "Yes, I can be there in ten minutes."

★

SOUTHERN LEBANON

Al-Masri stared into the washroom mirror.

The sight of his broken nose and blood-drenched face and shirt enraged him anew. He wadded up some toilet paper and stuffed it in each nostril amid tremendous pain to stanch the bleeding. Then he splashed water on his face and neck and through his thick jet-black hair to clean himself up and cool himself down.

This thing had been far messier than he had planned. At sunup this morning, he had had thirty men under his command. Fifteen were now dead. And his younger brother Tanzeel was missing and without question had been captured by the Zionists. Al-Masri cursed himself. He should never have agreed to let Tanzeel come on the mission. He was smart and strong, but he was only seventeen and looked even younger.

Energized by his rage, al-Masri summoned Zayan and three more of his men and slipped out the side door of the auto repair complex and walked across a soccer field to an elementary school as the ground shook and the sound of Israeli bombs exploding echoed through the valley. There were no children in the school. They had all been sent home when the bombing had commenced. Indeed, there was no one to be seen outside in any direction.

When he reached the back of the school, al-Masri ordered Zayan to unlock the door. Inside were a half-dozen heavily armed men in the hallway. They saluted the Egyptian as he whisked past. He did not salute back.

Turning a corner, he headed down another long hallway and saw two more of his men standing post outside the door to the cafeteria. Both were armed with AK-47s and sidearms, both wore military fatigues and maroon berets, and both snapped a salute when al-Masri approached.

"Open it," he commanded, not deigning to return the gesture.

The taller one fished keys out of his pocket and unlocked the door, and they all entered.

The room was dark. The fluorescent lights hanging from the ceiling were turned off, and the windows had been covered with black tarps. Al-Masri ordered the lights back on. When they flickered to life, he saw that there were no tables or chairs. Instead, the room was filled with Zelzal missiles. Hundreds of them. A half dozen were mounted on launchers, pointed at a glass ceiling through which they could easily be fired.

That, however, was not why he had come. In the middle of the room was the youngest of the captives, barely twenty years old, if that. The boy was sitting on a wooden stool, his hands and feet bound in chains, his head covered in a black hood. He had already been stripped down to his boxer shorts. He was sweating profusely. His body was shaking uncontrollably.

Good, al-Masri thought. *This was going to be quicker than the other two.*

29

Al-Masri motioned to Zayan to remove the hood.

Immediately he saw the terror in the boy's eyes. "Do you know who I am?" he asked in English.

"No," the boy replied in English, shaking his head.

"Do you know what I want?"

Again the boy shook his head.

"It's simple," said al-Masri. "I want your name. I want to know who you work for. And I want your ID number. Tell me, and you live. Don't tell me, and you die."

It was likely he was going to spill his guts right there and then. *But why not have some fun first?* al-Masri thought. Grabbing the kid by the hair, he dragged him across the cafeteria and into the adjacent industrial kitchen. When he reached the double sink, he found a rubber stopper and put it into the drain of one of the sinks, then turned on the faucet full blast. It took a while to fill the sink to the top, and during that time, neither al-Masri nor the boy said a word. When the sink was full, the Egyptian turned off the faucet and forced the boy's head all the way down into the water. He held him there for almost a minute, then yanked him back out.

"I'll *talk*; I'll *talk*," the boy screamed.

But al-Masri didn't care. He forced the boy's head back down, counting to ten. Then twenty. Then thirty. Then forty. At fifty seconds, he yanked the boy out of the water and let him choke and sputter, but only for a moment. Then he pushed his head back into the water all over again.

Five. Ten. Fifteen. Twenty. There were fewer bubbles this time. He might not make it to thirty. So al-Masri yanked him out when he hit twenty-five.

The Egyptian had already decided that this was the one he was going to decapitate. They had three prisoners. They only needed one. He had intended on saving the girl and keeping her for himself. But no more. She would suffer for her crimes. But he wouldn't give her the satisfaction of killing her. The man, he'd concluded, was clearly the team leader. That meant he was important. Al-Masri would take great pleasure in torturing him. But he would also try to keep the man's face intact for as long as he could—at least until he got instructions from above.

The kid, however, he would personally behead. On video, so they could upload it to YouTube at the appropriate time. But first he would show the head to the boy's colleagues. That would force more information out of them, especially the woman. Then he'd pack the head on ice and ship it to the White House.

Al-Masri pictured the emotional impact this would have on the American people. This wasn't, after all, a veteran, battle-tested soldier being hacked to death in some camel-ridden Middle Eastern wasteland. This was a fresh-faced State Department employee on what was likely only his first or second trip to Israel, beheaded on the Internet for everyone to see. Beheading the older hostage wouldn't have the same effect. It had been done too many times before.

Truth be told, he now wanted to behead the woman. But he feared that might be too much for the American people and government to bear. Yes, he wanted to trigger widespread horror and revulsion. These were useful. Outrage was quite another matter. Butchering an American woman could create a martyr, a cause for which the American people might actually be willing to go to war. He had his orders, and they did not include triggering an American invasion of Lebanon. The chances of that really happening were slim, he believed. But it wasn't worth the risk.

The boy was perfect. But not yet. First, al-Masri needed to make him talk.

Again al-Masri forced the kid's head under the water, even as he was still coughing up water and gasping for air. Again al-Masri began counting. Yet on this round he did not even make it to twenty. The boy's body was writhing, convulsing, and then it shut down.

At this, al-Masri yanked his head up and threw his limp body to the floor. "Bring him back," he ordered.

Zayan dropped to the kitchen floor. Al-Masri watched as he checked the kid's pulse but found none. The American wasn't moving, wasn't breathing, so the deputy began administering CPR.

Al-Masri couldn't be bothered to watch, much less help. He'd been through this so many times, the whole thing simply bored him. But a beheading? That he had never done. Not himself. Not personally. Not yet. And the very thought of doing it for the first time, and on this particular operation, gave him something to look forward to.

Stepping out of the kitchen, he found an empty office. There, alone, he pulled from his pocket a pack of Hamra cigarettes and a lighter. Smoking was not exactly forbidden in Islam, but it was within Hezbollah. But al-Masri didn't care. He didn't have many vices. This was one. And he wasn't giving it up for the Sheikh. The hard part wasn't hiding it from his men. The hard part was finding boxes of the Syrian brand that he'd come to love. Lebanon had its own brand, of course, Cedars, and supposedly they weren't too bad. But the packaging infuriated him, trumpeting its "American blend." There was no way he was going to smoke an American cigarette.

It had been hours since he'd filled his lungs with the warm, sweet smoke. He considered this a small but just reward for all their hard work and good fortune thus far. And knowing it would be hours until he got another, he savored every drag.

When he finished and reentered the kitchen, he found that the kid had vomited all over the floor. One of his men was still mopping up the mess. His deputy was taking the boy's pulse. When he nodded, al-Masri motioned for Zayan and the guards to drag the boy back into the cafeteria and back over to the stool. They did as they were told. The boy was still gasping, still sucking in as much oxygen as he could, but he was alive.

"So are you ready to give me your name, or should we try that again?" the Egyptian asked with a smile, his teeth still covered in blood.

30

The Sikorsky UH-60 helicopter burst over the ridge and came into view.

It circled the base once before descending onto the landing pad.

Major General Yossi Kidron watched from the edge of the tarmac, then stepped forward to greet the two principals as they exited the Black Hawk. The first was Asher Gilad, head of the Mossad, Israel's foreign intelligence agency. Right behind him was Tomer Ben Ami, deputy director of the Shin Bet, Israel's equivalent of the American FBI. Neither man looked happy. Nor did their security details, all of whom were anxious to get their protectees out of harm's way.

"Is everything in order?" Gilad asked in Hebrew over the roar of the chopper's engines as they were hustled inside the secure facilities.

"Yes, sir."

"No one has talked to him yet?"

"No, sir," Kidron assured him as he led both men down several flights of stairs, past numerous armed guards, and through two sets of steel doors. "Okay, we're here, gentlemen. How do you want to do this?"

"Yossi, you and I will stay behind the glass," Gilad said. "Tomer has the most experience with interrogations. And his Arabic is better than mine. Okay?"

The Shin Bet deputy director nodded and handed his sidearm to Yossi for safekeeping.

★

Tomer waited several moments for the others to get into position.

Then he took a deep breath, motioned to the guards to open the door, and entered the interrogation room. Waiting for him was a young man chained to a metal chair, sitting behind a metal table, perspiring profusely.

"Good morning," Tomer said in Arabic. "Welcome to Israel."

The boy said nothing, yet his eyes darted around the room and toward the two-way glass, as if he expected more people to be coming through the two doors to the left and right of the table.

"Are you thirsty?" Tomer asked. "Has anyone given you something to eat or drink?"

No reply.

Tomer turned to the two-way glass and asked if he could get some water. A moment later, a guard entered and set two plastic cups on the table along with a liter bottle of water. Tomer poured them each a glass. The boy hesitated, but after Tomer took a sip, he drank all of his. Tomer poured him another, and this, too, he polished off quickly. A third time, Tomer filled the cup. This time, the boy took only a sip, then set it down. His hands were shaking. His right knee was bobbing up and down. And he didn't seem to know where to settle his eyes.

"My name is Tomer Ben Ami," the Shin Bet officer began. "What's yours?"

The boy said nothing but instead fixed his gaze on the cup sitting on the table in front of him.

"How long have you been a member of the Radwan Unit?"

This startled the boy, who briefly looked up, then back down at the cup.

"It would be better for you and for your family if you go ahead and answer my questions now rather than later," Tomer said. His tone was calm. But the message was menacing and was intended to be.

Still, the boy said nothing.

"Okay—let's try something else," Tomer said, leaning forward. "Your name is Tanzeel al-Masri."

The boy looked up immediately.

"You're seventeen years old. Your eighteenth birthday is coming up in July," Tomer continued. "You were born and raised in Beirut in a devout Shia family. Your mother is Lebanese, born and raised in Sidon. Your father is Egyptian, born in Alexandria, though he spent much of his life in the oil fields of Libya, where his father and brothers worked to provide for the family. You have six brothers and sisters. But today let's focus on your eldest brother, Amin."

Still nothing.

"Amin al-Masri, infamous deputy commander of the Radwan Unit," Tomer went on.

The boy was visibly astonished.

"Yes, Tanzeel, we know all about you and your brother. And we know all about your family's long devotion to Hezbollah. We know that your father, Marwan, before his untimely death, was close to Imad Mughniyah, the founder of Islamic Jihad and the number two man in Hezbollah, the man long known as *al-Hajj Radwan*. The unit in which you and your brother serve was named after him. What's more, we know that your father had American and Israeli blood on his hands. He helped Mughniyah torture and kill the CIA's station chief in Beirut in 1985. He helped mastermind the bombing of our embassy in Buenos Aires on March 17, 1992. The list goes on and on."

The radio receiver in Tomer's ear crackled to life. "Show him the pictures," said Asher Gilad from the other side of the glass.

Tomer reached into his leather jacket and pulled out six black-and-white five-by-seven photographs. He looked at each one for a moment, piquing Tanzeel's interest, then set them on the table.

The boy's eyes grew wider.

"Do you recognize these people?" Tomer asked.

Though Tanzeel did not speak, the answer was clearly yes.

"This one of your mother, Jabira, was taken as she walked home from the grocery store in Al-Dahiya. Remember Al-Dahiya, Tanzeel, those wretched, poverty-stricken suburbs on the south side of Beirut? You grew up in Haret

Hreik, did you not, Tanzeel? Of course you did. And your mother still lives there."

Tomer set the other photos on the table one by one.

"This is a cute one, isn't it? Little Hala. What is she, ten years old? How happy she looks at the Islamic girls' academy she attends. But I think this one is my favorite. Farez. The youngest of your clan. And your mother's pride and joy. What is he now, six? No, he just turned seven. He certainly loves to play soccer with his friends. Have you ever seen a more adorable little boy?"

Tomer was quiet a moment, letting the images and message sink in. But there was more.

"Let's see, here's a lovely drone photo of your apartment building," Tomer said. "Here's one of your front door. And one of your mother drinking tea on her balcony."

A minute passed.

Then two.

After three, Tomer spoke again. "Do you really think we don't know everything about you, Tanzeel, about your family, about your brother? Even as you and I sit here, Israeli forces are moving through the streets of Haret Hreik, disguised as Hezbollah commandos. By sundown, your mother and sweet Hala and adorable little Farez will not only be in our possession but in custody, here on Israeli soil. So long as no harm comes to the Americans your brother has captured—so long as he releases them all quickly and without any injuries whatsoever—your family will be safe. But if your brother acts, shall we say, imprudently . . . well, let's hope it does not come to that."

It was all a lie.

The photos had been taken months before. Both Tomer and Asher Gilad had implored their prime minister to authorize an operation to acquire the al-Masri family. Reuven Eitan, however, had refused to authorize anything of the sort, not even dispatching Mossad agents to place al-Masri's family under surveillance so they could grab them if the PM changed his mind.

Nevertheless, it all seemed most convincing to young Tanzeel. He was not ready to say anything. Not yet. Not now. It was too soon. He was too shell-shocked. But in time, Tanzeel would talk. Of this, Tomer had no doubt.

31

President Andrew Hartford Clarke left the Residence at 6:57 a.m. local time.

Surrounded by a beefed-up Secret Service detail, he took a private elevator down to the first floor, headed straight for the West Wing, and entered the Situation Room three minutes later. Every member of the National Security Council stood until the commander in chief took his seat.

It was not a full house.

Vice President Carlos Hernandez was there—at last—sitting directly to Clarke's right. A retired three-star vice admiral, Hernandez had been one of the highest-ranking Latinos ever to serve in the U.S. Navy before becoming the first Cuban-American elected vice president of the United States. Born in Miami to immigrants from Havana, Hernandez had played a game-changing role in securing Clarke's presidency, helping the political neophyte win a stunning 49 percent of the Hispanic vote, the most ever for a Republican ticket. Yet for much of the past eighteen months, Hernandez's contribution in the Clarke administration had been limited at best. Only fifty-seven, he'd already had two heart attacks since taking the VP's oath of office, then had been forced by his doctors to have a triple-bypass surgery, followed by many months of recovery. Rumor had it that Clarke had actively considered dropping him from the ticket prior to his reelection campaign. But the VP had stuck around and was finally back in the game and supposedly operating at or near full strength.

To Clarke's left was Margaret "Meg" Whitney, the sixty-one-year-old secretary of state he'd dubbed the Silver Fox. A two-term governor of New Mexico and former U.S. ambassador to the U.K., Whitney was a rising star in the administration, especially with growing speculation in the media that her months of painstaking negotiations and tireless shuttle diplomacy were about to bear fruit in the form of a history-making peace deal between Israel and the Kingdom of Saudi Arabia.

Also joining them around the conference table were National Security Advisor Bill McDermott; General James Meyers, the recently appointed chairman of the Joint Chiefs; and Richard Stephens, the sixty-six-year-old former senior senator from Arizona and chairman of the Senate Intelligence Committee who had been tapped by Clarke to serve as his director of Central Intelligence.

Missing were the director of national intelligence and the secretary of Homeland Security, both of whom were out of the country but flying back to Washington at that very hour. Also absent were the secretary of the treasury, the attorney general, and Defense Secretary Cal Foster, who had once served as the supreme allied commander of NATO and was arguably Clarke's closest friend and most trusted military advisor. The first two were on vacation but had been urgently recalled to D.C. and were currently en route. The last three were spread out across the country on various matters of government business but were also racing back to Washington.

"How in the world could this happen?" an angry Clarke began, flipping open the leather-bound copy of *The President's Daily Brief* waiting for him at the head of the table. The PDB was the U.S. intel community's top secret compilation of the day's most important matters, produced for the president's eyes, and those of the NSC, only.

"I'm afraid the answers aren't in there, Mr. President," the CIA director began.

"Why not?" the president asked.

"Events simply are moving too rapidly, sir," Stephens replied. "This morning's PDB was completed and printed before any of this began."

Clarke looked up in disbelief, then slammed his copy shut and shoved it aside. "Then tell me what you know."

Stephens took a deep breath to compose his thoughts. He knew all too well that the Central Intelligence Agency was on thin ice with the president. It had, after all, completely missed both the Kremlin's near invasion of the Baltics and the subsequent assassination of the Russian president, prime minister, and FSB chief. Langley had also botched two major extraction operations, the first of a high-level mole deep inside the Kremlin, and the second of an almost equally valuable mole operating close to the very top of the regime in North Korea.

True, the Agency had overseen two very significant successes since then. They had thwarted the transfer of five nuclear warheads from the DPRK to the Iranian regime. And they had effectively hunted down and stopped a terrorist cell in Jerusalem that was planning to blow up the American-sponsored peace summit there in December. The president, however, hadn't given much of the credit to Stephens or his senior team. To the contrary, he'd become enamored of the Agency's newest clandestine officer, Marcus Johannes Ryker, whom he credited as the mastermind of both operations.

For his part, Stephens could not have seen things more differently. Ryker was no hero. To the contrary, he was a maverick—dangerous, a rogue operator with a growing reputation for scoffing at the rules and ignoring laws and well-established Agency protocols to achieve his objectives. He was not a Langley man. He hadn't been trained at the Farm. Didn't know the Agency's culture. Barely knew any fellow CIA officers, much less had close ties inside the Company.

During the Moscow disaster, everyone in this room—the president included—had believed Ryker was a traitor to the country who should be hunted down and arrested, even taken out by force. How Ryker had flipped the script and rebranded himself a hero not only baffled but infuriated Stephens. Ryker had only been brought into the Agency as part of a secret plea bargain. He was supposed to be keeping quiet and out of the public eye. Instead, he seemed to find himself at the vortex of one dangerous operation after another. So far, each of his crazy moves had broken in his favor. But Stephens knew that any of them could easily have gone the other way and ended in total disaster.

Just as galling to the CIA director was that whatever so-called successes Ryker might have played a part in would never have come to pass without the assistance of hundreds of Agency personnel, financing, and assets. Yet the commander in chief kept giving all the credit to his new pet pupil.

And now this.

32

Stephens began his briefing.

"At approximately 9:15 this morning Israeli time—2:15 a.m. here in Washington—a Hezbollah terror unit cut through the security fence on the Blue Line and ambushed an IDF convoy," he began, flashing pictures he'd gotten from the Israelis on the wall monitors. "The attack was apparently unprovoked and came without warning. Neither we nor the Israelis picked up anything that would have suggested something was afoot. The ambush took place near an Israeli agricultural settlement, a moshav known as Avivim. In all, three vehicles were destroyed. Nine Israeli soldiers were killed. Several were shot execution-style. In the process, two Americans and one Israeli were seized by the terrorists. As best we can tell, they've been taken into Lebanese territory, but at present we have no idea where."

"Whoa, whoa, wait a minute," said Clarke. "I thought three Americans and no Israelis had been taken hostage."

"I realize that's what Bill told you when he called up to the Residence this morning," Stephens replied, glancing at National Security Advisor McDermott for confirmation. "That was the first report we received. But it turned out to be mistaken."

"You're certain that Agent Ryker is one of the captives?" Clarke pressed.

"I'm afraid so, sir."

"Has his family been notified?"

"No, sir, not yet."

"He's got a mom out in Colorado—near the Springs—right?"

"Monument."

"Right. I met her a while back."

"You did, sir."

"Any other family living?"

"Two sisters. Both married with kids."

"They've been through a lot these past couple of years," Clarke said. "Make sure whoever calls is someone they know, someone they trust. And let them know if there's anything they need, they've got it." The president turned to McDermott. "Bill, you know the family."

"Almost twenty years, sir."

"You must know someone."

"Yes, sir. Pete can take care of it."

"Who?"

"Dr. Peter Hwang," McDermott clarified. "He served with Ryker under my command back in the day. Ryker's closest friend. Now working for the Agency, though like Ryker, ostensibly for DSS."

"Perfect," Clarke said, turning back to Stephens.

The CIA director continued his briefing. "Sir, there's something I need to mention at this point, but it's unconfirmed and very delicate."

"What's that?"

"Well, sir, a source of ours recently informed us that an internal investigation by the IRGC—the Iranian Revolutionary Guard Corps—into the loss of their nuclear warheads in the East China Sea has pointed the finger of blame at Agent Ryker. It's not clear to us yet why they are singling out Ryker, since many other U.S., Israeli, and Saudi operatives were involved in that operation. Nevertheless, the source says the IRGC has put a $10 million bounty on Ryker's head."

"Ten million?" asked Clarke, visibly astonished.

"That's what we understand, sir."

"That's quite a bounty. Why am I just hearing about this now?"

"Well, sir, again, it's only the word of one source. We've been trying to verify it through other channels but thus far haven't been able to."

"Does Ryker know?"

"He does—Martha Dell briefed him soon after we received the report," Stephens replied, referring to the Agency's deputy director.

"Richard, are you thinking this attack on the border may be connected?" Whitney asked. "Is it possible this wasn't a random hit but that Ryker was targeted?"

This was precisely the question Stephens had feared in bringing up the subject. Still, his antipathy for Ryker notwithstanding, Stephens felt it was his duty to make sure the NSC had all the information at their disposal, to do with what they would.

"It's possible, Meg," he replied. "But it's too early to draw any conclusions. We simply don't have enough information yet."

"Look into it," the president ordered.

"We will, sir," Stephens assured him.

"Good—now who else is missing?"

"I'm afraid the other American is also one you've met, Mr. President—Ryker's partner, Kailea Curtis."

"She works for you?"

"No, sir, she's actually a special agent with DSS."

"Oh, right, Curtis—she's part of your detail, isn't she, Meg?" Clarke asked the secretary of state.

"My advance team, yes, sir," Whitney replied. "She's one of the most impressive agents on my team."

"Part of the team that saved our bacon in Jerusalem, wasn't she?"

"She was, indeed, sir. In fact, last month I presented her and several of her colleagues, including Ryker, the Award for Heroism at a ceremony we held at State."

"Is she married? Kids?"

"No, sir."

"Are her parents living?"

"Her father, I believe, and a sister."

"Where are they?"

"New York, sir—her dad's in Queens; her sister is out on Long Island somewhere."

"Have they been notified?"

"No, not yet—I'll have someone call them later today."

"Good—and same deal—make sure it's someone the family knows well, someone they trust, and see to it they've got everything they need."

"Absolutely, sir."

"And who's the Israeli?"

"Well, sir," Stephens replied, "that's where things get particularly complicated."

33

Stephens leaned forward in his seat.

"What I'm about to tell you all is highly classified and for this room only," he began. "The Israeli is an intelligence officer by the name of Yigal Mizrachi."

As the DCI flashed a picture of the young man up on the screens, Bill McDermott studied the face. The Israeli was young. No more than twenty or twenty-one. Dark features. Dark hair. Military cut. Brown eyes. Slight build. Clearly not a combat soldier. Wasn't likely to hold up in interrogation. Not for long, anyway. The knot in McDermott's stomach tightened. They had to find this kid and get him, Ryker, and Curtis out of harm's way and fast.

Stephens explained Yigal Mizrachi's role as a liaison to the DSS advance team and noted that he was an aide to the general in charge of the IDF's Northern Command. He mentioned that he was fluent in four languages, including Arabic.

Then he got to the main point.

"Mr. Mizrachi is also, I'm afraid, the nephew of the prime minister."

A hush came over the room.

"As you can see, we have a problem at several levels," Stephens continued. "If Hezbollah figures out that they've just nabbed Marcus Ryker, the first call they make isn't going to be here or the Pentagon. They're going to contact their friends in Iran and explain that they hold in their possession the number one man on the Revolutionary Guard's most-wanted list. If they were targeting Ryker, then that call has already been made, and this is going to escalate very, very fast."

This was the first time McDermott had heard of the bounty on Ryker's head, and he was growing more angry by the minute that Stephens hadn't deigned to inform the national security advisor—or even the secretary of state or the head of DSS, for that matter—that one of their men might be a particular target in that neighborhood. McDermott understood Stephens's decision not to inform the president unless or until the allegation had been confirmed. In his shoes, McDermott thought, he'd probably have done the same thing. Still, it was profoundly irresponsible for the director of the CIA to withhold information this volatile from those responsible for deciding whether to deploy Ryker on missions outside the United States.

Stephens continued his briefing. "So far as we know, no American woman has ever before been kidnapped by Hezbollah," the DCI noted. "As Secretary Whitney has noted, Agent Curtis is a fine, exemplary public servant. She cut her teeth as a beat cop for the NYPD. She's been tested under fire in the DSS. She's tough. Smart. Brave. A model agent, to be sure. Still, what Hezbollah operatives might do with her—*to* her—none of us can say, but I'm afraid we need to brace ourselves for the worst."

McDermott saw Whitney wince.

"And there's one more point, which hardly needs to be made, but let's be clear," Stephens concluded. "If Hezbollah figures out that they've grabbed a member of the Israeli prime minister's family, it will be the coup of the century. No matter how much Agents Ryker and Curtis will suffer, it'll be nothing compared to Mr. Mizrachi."

"Unless, of course, the Israelis are prepared to make Hezbollah an offer they can't refuse," Clarke noted.

Stephens shook his head. "I cannot imagine what Sheikh al-Hussaini—much less the mullahs in Tehran—would accept for such a prize."

"It's a nightmare," Whitney said.

"It is," Stephens agreed.

McDermott turned to the chairman of the Joint Chiefs. "General Meyers, what kind of contingencies do you have to find and rescue these three quickly? I think we're all agreed we cannot allow our people, much less Mr. Mizrachi, to be held and tortured by some of the most barbaric terrorists on the face of the planet."

"Agreed," said Meyer. "I've already ordered the commanders of SEAL Team Six and Delta to begin preparing options. In just a few hours—1300 local time—I've got a call scheduled with General Golan, the IDF's chief of staff. Yoni and I have known each other for years. He was with me at the Pentagon last month for a visit. We'll work together on this, and I guarantee you, if the intel guys can find them, we'll mount an operation to go get them."

"But time is short, am I right, General?" the president asked.

"Yes, sir, it is," Meyers confirmed. "If we can find them while they're still on Lebanese soil, then we've got a shot. But if, as Director Stephens is suggesting, they're going to be transferred to Iran—or even to Syria—then I would have to say that the military option will have been lost. There would have to be a negotiated diplomatic arrangement, if we're to get them back at all. Alive, at least."

Clarke recoiled at the notion of opening negotiations with Tehran. McDermott felt the same. They all did.

"Mr. President, there's another matter I need to bring up in this context," said the CIA director.

"What's that?"

"Sir, we've learned that Iran's Supreme Leader, Ayatollah Hossein Ansari, has passed away from cancer."

"What, just now?" Clarke asked.

"Within the last two hours," Stephens said. "The news hasn't been made public, but on my drive here from Langley, I took a call from Prince Abdullah bin Rashid."

"The Saudi spy chief."

"Yes, sir. The prince says they have two high-level sources deep inside Tehran, and both—independently of each other—have reported that the

Supreme Leader has died and that the regime is preparing to make an announcement tonight."

"This isn't really unexpected, right?" the president asked. "I mean, you've been telling us for more than a year, Richard, that the guy was suffering from cancer . . . uh . . ."

"Pancreatic."

". . . right, and that it was only a matter of time."

"True enough."

"Any reason to believe someone pushed him over the edge?" McDermott asked.

Clarke raised an eyebrow. "Foul play?"

"Is it possible?" McDermott prompted. "We'd heard repeatedly that he had no more than a few months to live. What if someone got tired of waiting?"

"I'll have my guys watch closely and ask the Saudis to as well," said Stephens. "But there's something else."

"What is it?"

"In the last hour, NSA has intercepted a number of messages going back and forth between Hezbollah's senior leadership and the IRGC. Apparently the Iranians are furious that Hezbollah is provoking a new war with the Israelis when all of Tehran is about to be consumed with a state funeral and the need to choose a successor. The Hezbollah guys, however—the ones close to the Sheikh—are pushing back. They're saying they had nothing to do with this and are trying to figure out how this thing erupted. What's even more strange is that the Israelis say they're also picking up chatter from Hezbollah field units suggesting a high degree of internal chaos. Nobody seems to know exactly how this thing got started, who ordered it, or why."

"I don't buy it," McDermott said.

General Meyers shook his head. "Neither do I. Sounds to me like a disinformation campaign. Far more likely, the Iranian Revolutionary Guard Corps secretly ordered Hezbollah to open up the Israeli front to distract from the death of the ayatollah."

"I agree," the president said. "This whole thing has Tehran written all over it."

34

The secretary of state agreed with the sentiment in the room.

It was Meg Whitney's job, however, to deal in facts, not suppositions. And there were more immediate concerns to deal with.

"Gentlemen, you all may be right, but I suggest we not draw any conclusions just yet," she cautioned. "We're in the very early hours of this crisis. Let's give Richard and his team more time to get to the bottom of it. Right now, two of my people are missing, and from what I hear, there's a serious battle underway over there that could set the whole of the Middle East on fire."

The president agreed and turned back to the chairman of the Joint Chiefs.

"General Meyers, what can you tell us on the military aspect of all this?"

"Well, Mr. President, just minutes after the attack, the Israelis launched an operation they call the Hannibal Protocol."

"What's that?"

"Sir, it's an aggressive saturation bombing campaign targeted where the kidnappings occurred, designed to bring all movement in the area to a halt and give IDF ground forces enough time to move in, find the hostages, and get them back, dead or alive," Meyers said. "Unfortunately, it didn't work. The IDF commander on the scene found the entrance to a previously undiscovered tunnel close to the breach in the fence line. The thinking now in IDF senior command is that amid all the chaos and confusion, Agents Ryker and Curtis and the PM's nephew were dragged into the tunnel and pulled deep into enemy territory. At that point, Prime Minister Eitan called off the Hannibal operation and ordered all Israeli forces to pull back behind the Blue Line."

"Why?"

"To signal a de-escalation in the hopes that cooler heads would prevail."

"And?" Clarke asked.

"Unfortunately, Hezbollah refused—or perhaps misread—the gesture. They've just unleashed a massive missile barrage against Israeli civilian population centers."

"Define 'massive,'" said the president.

Meyers looked down at the secure laptop on the conference table in front of him and scrolled through the latest data coming in from the National Military Command Center deep beneath the Pentagon. "Sir, in the last thirty minutes, we estimate that Hezbollah has fired more than a hundred Katyusha rockets into Israel. In addition, they've fired at least several dozen Zelzal missiles, which are significantly bigger and more powerful than the Katyushas. Since we've been gathered here, air-raid sirens have been going off nonstop across Israel's northern tier."

"Just like 2006," Secretary Whitney interjected. "Mr. President, that means that upwards of a million Israelis are currently hunkered in bomb shelters or fleeing southward, out of missile range. Half of those are children."

Though she did not say it, she appreciated the fact that the Israeli prime minister had tried to de-escalate. But she knew Reuven Eitan—had known him for more than twenty years, actually. They had certainly spent a great deal of time over the past year and a half or so working on this Israeli-Saudi peace agreement. If Israeli casualties were mounting, she knew Eitan would feel he had no choice but to retaliate. "General, how successful has the IDF been in shooting down these rockets and missiles?" she asked.

"Not that good," Meyers reported. "In the Gaza theater, the Israelis are typically able to shoot down something like 85 to 90 percent of the rockets shot at them. Preliminary reports—and, again, I underscore that it's very early—but the first reports suggest the IDF is shooting down only 50 to 60 percent of the missiles coming out of Lebanon."

"What's the problem?" Clarke asked. "I thought the Israelis had the best technology in the world."

"It's not the technology, sir. Hezbollah is firing so many missiles at once that the Israelis simply don't have enough interceptors in the theater to cope. CENTCOM just messaged me to say the Israelis are rushing more Patriot and Iron Dome batteries northward, but that's going to take time. Meanwhile, the damage to homes, hospitals, schools, synagogues, and factories is becoming extensive."

Meyers picked up a remote and changed the images displayed on the screens. Now they were seeing pictures of missiles and interceptors over the skies of Haifa and Kiryat Shmona, along with scenes of burning buildings.

"One of the few comforts, if I can put it that way," Meyers added, "is that it's Saturday, the Jewish Sabbath. The schools are closed. So are most businesses and public facilities. The synagogues are full, I'm told, but had this been a weekday, a workday, we'd be looking at some very serious casualty figures."

"And what's the situation in Gaza?" Whitney asked. "Have Hamas and Islamic Jihad begun firing their rockets as well?"

"Not yet," said Meyers. "But the Israelis are bracing themselves for that onslaught to begin soon."

35

"How come we've heard nothing directly from Prime Minister Eitan?"

It was the first time Vice President Hernandez had entered the conversation, Whitney noticed.

"I'm told the prime minister was in the process of placing the call here to the White House when the missile barrage began," CIA director Stephens replied. "At that point, he told his aides to schedule a call for later and ordered his security cabinet to convene in emergency session. Apparently Eitan is going to call up the reserves. He's already ordered air strikes against Hezbollah facilities all across Lebanon, including command-and-control centers in the Bekaa Valley. I'm told the security cabinet is even going to consider strikes as far north as Beirut. Eitan doesn't want to do it, but he may not have any choice—he insists Israel can't look weak in the face of such brazen and unprovoked attacks, or all of their deterrence in the region could begin to crumble."

Whitney shook her head, not out of surprise or even disagreement but with the weight of the diplomatic catastrophe that was falling in her lap.

"Who is giving you this intel?" Hernandez asked.

"Mossad chief Asher Gilad," replied Stephens. "Someone you know well."

"I do," said the VP. "Good man. We go back a long way, and I've always been able to trust him. So what do the Israelis need from us?"

"Several things," the DCI noted. "First and foremost, Gilad is asking, for understandable reasons, that the names of the three prisoners not be released to the public. He also wants the Pentagon—or State—to leak that three Americans have been taken, not an Israeli. Would you be open to that, Mr. President?"

Clarke looked around the room. Hernandez nodded immediately. When the others followed, the president signaled his assent.

"Great—I'll let them know," said Stephens. "Next, the Israelis would be grateful for a strong public statement condemning Hezbollah for this unprovoked act of war and fully supportive of Israel's moral responsibility to defend itself."

"Absolutely—and I'll call the Speaker and the Senate majority leader— we'll get congressional resolutions condemning Hezbollah as well," said Clarke. "What else?"

"Well, sir, Gilad said the prime minister is worried that a new war with Hezbollah—even one of self-defense—will scuttle the peace talks with the Saudis and set back all the progress Israel has been making with the Sunni Arab states, and especially the Gulf States, over the past several years. In fact, Gilad believes the orders for today's attacks are coming directly from the regime in Tehran. He says they are certainly aimed at deflecting atten- tion from the death of the ayatollah and what promises to be an intense and possibly messy bid among the leading contenders to replace the Supreme Leader. But they are almost just as certainly aimed at generating devastating anti-Israel coverage on Al-Sawt and other Arab TV networks and creating a tidal wave of rage against Israel throughout the Arab world and particularly in the kingdom."

"He's probably right," Clarke said.

"He may very well be."

"So what does he want?"

"Gilad said the prime minister would be exceedingly grateful if you would place an immediate call to King Faisal—along with a separate call to the crown prince—reminding them that we're all in this fight against the Iranians together and asking them to refrain from any public statement that would suggest that they are critical of Israel's response, much less thinking of backing away from the peace deal."

"Done," said Clarke, turning to his national security advisor. "Bill, get those calls set up immediately."

McDermott nodded and picked up a receiver from the bank of phones in front of him.

Clarke now looked at Whitney. "Meg, obviously you're not going to Israel tonight as planned," he began.

"Apparently not, sir."

"Go see the Saudis instead. Meet with the king and crown prince. Allay any of their concerns. Reinforce the message I'll deliver by phone in a few minutes. In fact, I'll want you listening in on that call."

"Got it, sir—will do," Whitney replied. "But perhaps I shouldn't stop there."

"What do you mean?"

"I should probably go see the Emiratis as well, and the Bahrainis—the Omanis, too. They're all going to be edgy, especially with the death of Iran's Supreme Leader and fears of more Iranian provocations as the hard-liners jockey to succeed the ayatollah."

"She's right, Mr. President," the VP noted. "And I'd add in stops in Doha, Amman, and Cairo while you're at it."

"And the Moroccans on the way home," said McDermott.

"Good, do it," said the president, turning again to Whitney. "I want you to make it crystal clear that I see this as an act of war—not by Israel but by Iran—and that we hold Tehran fully responsible."

"Yes, sir."

"Stress that we absolutely cannot let the mullahs in Tehran use this moment to divide us, as hard as they'll try," Clarke insisted. "Just the opposite. We need all of our allies to redouble their commitment to sticking together against the Iranian regime and to ratcheting up our campaign of maximum pressure."

"I'm on it, sir," Whitney assured him.

"And one more thing," said the president.

"What's that?"

"Tell every leader you talk to in the coming days—not just the Arabs but the Europeans and Asians as well—that for the sake of peace we all need to send Tehran a unified message," Clarke said. "As Iran chooses a new leader, they must choose a new path."

36

Marcus Ryker finally came to.

He was no longer hanging from the ceiling. Nor being electrocuted. He was still bound and gagged, but now he was lying in a fetal position, engulfed in utter darkness, and it felt as if the entire earth were shaking.

Was it the Israelis? Were their bombs dropping closer? Were their mechanized forces approaching? It took a few minutes, but such hopes proved a mirage. It finally dawned on Marcus that he was in the trunk of a vehicle, on the move over choppy terrain. The hum that filled his ears was a diesel engine that had seen better days. But where was he being taken?

Marcus was not blindfolded, yet though he strained to see even a single speck of light, there was none to be found. For some, that would have been terrifying. It certainly would have been for his late wife, Elena. She had always been scared of the dark.

Once when he and Elena had gone spelunking in high school, he had turned off his headlamp, pretending it had shorted out. Elena had freaked, and Marcus had nearly died laughing. It was not that he wanted to frighten her. Not really. Yet he remembered with great fondness how Elena had clung to him for comfort until he had "gotten the light to work again." Even now he could feel the warmth of her body against his, her breath on his neck, her hands holding his. And despite the searing pain of burns all over his chest and feet and the cramped darkness that surrounded him, Marcus found himself smiling. He had no idea where he was or what the future held. But he was not scared. He just felt . . . peaceful.

Marcus had never shied away from danger. To the contrary, he'd always been drawn to it—thrived on it. Jumping out of planes. Bungee jumping from bridges. Scuba diving in seas teeming with great whites. Rafting the most intense white-water rapids he could find. He had always loved adventure, loved testing the limits, loved pushing the envelope, and loved being with other people who loved it too.

True, as a kid, he had been an idiot. He'd taken crazy, unnecessary, foolish risks, and not just with his own life but with Elena's. Fortunately, God had been watching out for them. "Don't die, and don't get arrested," his mother had always said. And they hadn't. They had not died. They had not been arrested. Not on their adventures, anyway. Not while trying to suck the marrow out of life. They had walked away with memories Marcus would cherish for eternity, most of which he had never told to another soul.

His years in the Marines had taught him to push the boundaries even further, as for the first time in his life, he had had commanders who thought like he thought, wanted what he wanted. These were men who knew what the human body and mind were capable of, what the limits were, and how to take him there, all the way to the edge of death before backing him off just a smidge. He had thrived on it. All of it. The years he had spent on Parris Island and then on the battlefields of Kandahar and Fallujah and the mean streets of Baghdad and Mosul were some of the most difficult of his life, but also some of the most thrilling and rewarding. He had looked death square in the face and survived and worked to protect the lives of others in the process.

His years in the United States Secret Service had been far more stressful. He had enjoyed the training and the drills. But going into the job, he had never stopped to consider how much of the life of a Secret Service special agent was sheer boredom. Standing post in empty hallways. Rainy rooftops. Windswept tarmacs. Quiet stairwells. Waiting for something terrible to happen and praying it never did. And all the while spending so many nights on the road, away from home, alone in cold hotel beds, eating bad fast food and drinking lousy instant coffee.

Marcus had done it because he believed it was what God had called him to do. He hadn't always loved it. Elena certainly had not. Indeed, his time in the Secret Service had put stresses on their marriage they had not always been certain they could endure. But there was no point wallowing in regret. They had made their choices. They had made them in prayer. They had made them together, and he refused to look back.

Now he was back in the fight. He was being tested like he had never been tested before, and while he certainly wished he could have avoided being captured and tortured, he loved having a purpose. His mission was not simply to protect his country but to rescue Kailea and Yigal and get them back to freedom, back to their families and friends. If it cost him his life, so be it. He knew where he was going when he died. They, so far as he knew, did not.

In the darkness, Marcus found his thoughts drifting back to the SERE manual and specifically the appendix titled "The Will to Survive." He'd been giving a lot of thought to the section on the psychology of survival. But it occurred to him there had been a section after that, one on spiritual considerations. He didn't recall Commander Connolly or any of the guys in his training class spending any time discussing it. Yet while some of the details were still fuzzy, others were returning.

Marcus remembered his surprise at seeing an official U.S. government publication talk about anything spiritual. This was not something given to him by a chaplain, after all. These were official recommendations on how to survive in captivity. To be sure, some of the suggestions were vague, even superficial, instructing prisoners of war and those trapped behind enemy lines to take the time to "collect your thoughts and emotions. Identify your personal beliefs. Use self-control. Meditate. And remember past inner sources to help you overcome adversity."

Others, however, had struck him as particularly helpful. "Pray for your God's help, strength, wisdom, and rescue. Remember Scripture, verses, or hymns; repeat them to yourself and to your God. Forgive yourself for what you have done or said that was wrong, and forgive those who have failed you. Praise God and give thanks because God is bigger than your circumstances. Because God will see you through (no matter what happens). Because hope comes from a belief in heaven and/or an afterlife. Never lose hope. Never give up. If you're with others, encourage each other while waiting for rescue, and remember—your God loves you."

Marcus had only been twenty-two when he had read those words, and not especially strong in his faith. Yet even so many years later, he remembered how impactful these spiritual recommendations from the American military's most senior commanders had been. Upon finishing the SERE training, Marcus had sought out a chaplain and asked for a Bible. He had begun reading it as often as he could. He had even started attending a church service on base, and though he did not make it every Sunday, it was a practice he continued whenever possible when he was deployed overseas.

Marcus was starting to feel sleepy again. Still, he silently said a prayer for his colleagues and for his mother and sisters and their families. He prayed for Pete and Bill and the president and the NSC back in Washington. He prayed for Annie Stewart and Jenny Morris and for Nick Vinetti's widow and her children. His list was long, and the more he prayed, the drowsier he became. Nevertheless, he made himself recite Psalm 23, one of his favorite passages of Scripture, one that his mother had made him memorize after the death of his father. It seemed more apropos right now than ever before.

The Lord is my shepherd, I shall not want. He makes me lie down in green pastures; He leads me beside quiet waters. He restores my soul. . . . Even though I walk through the valley of the shadow of death, I fear no evil, for You are with me; Your rod and Your staff, they comfort me. . . .

And with those words echoing in his mind, and the steady hum of the diesel engine throbbing all around him, Marcus Johannes Ryker drifted back to sleep.

37

THE WHITE HOUSE

As requested, Bill McDermott placed a call to Riyadh.

It did not go well.

For starters, the national security advisor was told the royal family had just departed Riyadh for their summer palace in Jeddah and would not be available for several hours.

The next time he called, McDermott was told that His Majesty King Faisal Mohammed Al Saud had gone to bed with a head cold and, on the advice of his doctors, was not to be disturbed. Given the magnitude of the crisis unfolding in the Gulf, this struck McDermott as suspicious. When he asked to speak to the crown prince instead, he was told that Abdulaziz bin Faisal Al Saud, who also served as the nation's defense minister, was tied up in meetings with his top military advisors and would have to call him back.

Only when McDermott unleashed a torrent of expletives at his Saudi counterpart, demanding that the crown prince immediately take the call from the president of the United States, was he finally assured that His Royal Highness would return the call in five minutes.

It turned out to be twenty minutes, but the call eventually came.

President Clarke took it in the Oval, with Secretary Whitney and McDermott sitting nearby, both listening in on other phones while also taking notes. Clarke opened by asking about the king's health. The crown prince thanked him for his concern but said it was nothing to worry about. The comments were curt and perfunctory, and none of the Americans bought it. Something was seriously wrong with the octogenarian monarch. Why else would he not be available to speak, even briefly, with his number one ally?

"I want to thank you for the heads-up about the ayatollah's death," Clarke said, changing topics. "We still haven't been able to confirm it ourselves, and we have not picked up anything on Iranian state television or radio. But I'm grateful to you and your father for passing along the information you're obviously receiving from a very well-placed source."

"Ansari's death is a most disturbing development," the crown prince replied without acknowledging the president's gratitude. "The last thing this region needs is a succession crisis in Tehran."

"Who do you think the Iranians will appoint?"

"That's what my advisors and I were just discussing."

"And?"

"I have some thoughts, Mr. President, but I'm not prepared to share them at this time."

As the two men continued talking, McDermott caught Whitney's eye. This was not business as usual. The crown prince was being unusually distant, almost cold, toward the president. Whitney scribbled a note and slipped it to the NSA. McDermott nodded and passed it along to Clarke.

Maybe POTUS shouldn't bring up the Israelis now—just visiting HM and HRH in person, she had written, referring to "His Majesty," meaning the king, and "His Royal Highness," meaning the crown prince.

Clarke read the note, then nodded his agreement.

"Listen," he interjected in the next lull in the conversation, "I want to send Meg Whitney over there tonight to sit with you and your father and discuss all these issues in person. Can you receive her tomorrow?"

After an awkward pause, the crown prince agreed. The president thanked him and said the chief of protocol at State would be in touch with his Saudi counterpart within minutes to coordinate the details.

"Well," said Clarke after he had hung up the phone, "that could have gone better."

"It's not you, Mr. President," McDermott offered. "The king is obviously not well, and the Saudis are freaking out about Iran."

"What do you make of it, Meg?" Clarke asked.

"Well, Bill's right about one thing," she replied. "The health of the king is clearly worse than we thought. But that doesn't explain how cool Abdulaziz was toward you, Mr. President. And I don't think it's Iran."

"What then?"

"It's Lebanon, sir," she replied. "Iran and Hezbollah are playing a very dangerous but very shrewd game. They're trying to mobilize the Arab street against Israel and by extension against the Saudis."

"You think they're going to pull the plug on the peace talks?" the president asked.

"I'm afraid so, Mr. President. As of right now, I fear any hope of a treaty is over."

38

SOMEWHERE IN SOUTHERN LEBANON

When he woke up again, Marcus had no idea how much time had gone by.

Still engulfed by darkness, he strained to hear what was going in the outside world. There were no explosions. No fighter jets roaring through the skies. He certainly was not hearing gunfire or battle tanks. He didn't think there was any way the Israelis had stopped engaging the enemy. The only thing he could surmise was that he had been moved farther north, deeper into Lebanon. But where?

He heard no sounds of people—no voices, no boots, no radios or vehicles. But the longer he listened, he did begin to hear the sound of an occasional bird or two—gulls, in fact—and, however faintly, a low, dull roar. Could those be waves? Had the Egyptian and his men moved him to the coast? And if so, which one?

If he and the others had already been transported to Iran, then they would most likely have been taken to the capital, Tehran, a good 120 kilometers from the coast of the Caspian Sea and 650 kilometers from the shores of the Persian Gulf. Which meant it was unlikely they were in Iran.

Far more likely, they were still in Lebanon. Which meant they were somewhere along the Mediterranean coast. Tyre was one of the country's largest coastal cities and the closest to the Israeli border. But Marcus had not heard any traffic sounds. Perhaps they were in the suburbs. Or at a Hezbollah camp of some kind. Then again, thought Marcus, the Israelis would probably be bombing the heck out of known Hezbollah facilities. Which brought him back to his original question. Where exactly was he? And why?

Feeling around in the blackness as best he could, Marcus realized he was sitting on a wooden chair. His hands were shackled behind him. His feet were shackled as well. Yet he also realized that he was no longer stripped down to his boxers. He had no shoes or socks on, but he was wearing jeans and a T-shirt. It was hot. Immensely hot. His clothes were soaked with sweat. He stank. As did the room he was in. But the fact that he was clothed strengthened his conclusion that he had been moved.

That, however, raised a new question. Had they all been moved? Or just him? It was risky to move them at all. The vehicles could be spotted by drones or satellites. Then again, it did not make sense to keep them too close to the Israeli border. If al-Masri was smart, he would have moved Kailea to one location, Yigal to a second, and Marcus to a third. Why keep them all in one location? Why make it easier for the Israelis or the Americans to find them and rescue them?

Marcus's stomach growled. His mouth was dry. He flexed his fingers and rolled his neck, all of which felt stiff, and tried to get a sense of how long he had been in captivity. He remembered blacking out from the electrocutions. Then, he suspected, he'd been drugged again to get him clothed and transported without any prospect of him waking up and trying to resist. Was it still the same day? Or had several passed?

He wondered how Kailea was holding up. He wasn't really worried about her betraying her country or giving up secrets. He did worry about what these bastards were capable of doing to her whether she talked or not. And then there was Yigal. He was a good kid, but there was no question he was the weak link in the chain. If he talked, they were all going to die. And he was the most likely of the three of them to talk. He had no SERE training. He had no idea how to survive, evade, resist, or escape. His best chance—his only chance, really—was sticking to the story that he was an American. If al-Masri discovered Yigal was actually an Israeli, he would probably release his picture to mess with the Israeli government and people, like waving a trophy in front of the masses. Social media in Israel would light up. People—some, anyway—would recognize Yigal as the nephew of the prime minister. And if that got out, it was game over.

Marcus knew he had to escape from his chains. There was no point coming up with a game plan to get them all away from this place—wherever they were—and on to Tyre, and onto the fishing charter, if he could remember the name of the company or its owner, unless he could break free.

In the pitch-blackness, he began feeling around again, trying to determine exactly how he was secured. He discovered that his hands were not simply wrapped tightly in metal chains. At some point, they had also put metal handcuffs on him. That was smart. For even if he could slip out of one restraint—all but impossible under these conditions—he would still have to slip out of the other. And then there were his feet. Before, back in the auto repair shop, his ankles had merely been wrapped in chains, which had been bolted to the floor. Now, he realized, they had put him in manacles, which, best he could tell, were also locked down to the floor.

The floor. It was not concrete. It was metal. Not wearing socks, he could feel not just warm metal below him, but rust. That was interesting. And unexpected. It meant he wasn't being held in a prison cell, where the floor would likely be concrete. Nor was he being held in a mosque or a school of some kind, where the floors would more likely be wood or tile or even carpet. But metal? Rust? Marcus could only come up with one scenario for this. They were holding him in a shipping container, and an old one at that. Given their proximity to the Med, that made sense. But what did that mean? Were they going to transport him back to Iran on a container ship? Were they already at a port? He still did not hear any movement nearby. No trucks. No forklifts. Or cranes. Or horns.

Then a thought came to Marcus that should have occurred to him before. Why had Colonel Amin al-Masri given him his name? And why hadn't he kept his face covered? It was not to build trust. That was never going to happen, and al-Masri knew it. Why then? Marcus pondered the question from every angle. In the end, however, he could only come up with one reason. Al-Masri intended to extract as much information as possible out of Marcus and then kill him. Most likely he would keep Kailea and Yigal and leverage them to broker the release of thousands of Palestinian prisoners or to loot the American and Israeli governments for hundreds of millions of dollars. Marcus could not actually think of a time when the Israeli government had paid a cash ransom for any of its people, but then again, the nephew of the prime minister had never been taken hostage before.

But Marcus? He was a dead man. Why else would an experienced Hezbollah commander allow a hostage to see his face and hear his name unless he knew that hostage was never going to live long enough to make use of the information?

39

Marcus increasingly felt the burns across his chest and feet.

He felt the welts and bruises on his back, legs, and forearms where they had beaten him. The narcotics that had knocked him out so they could move him had been a blessing. They had dulled the worst of the pain the torture had inflicted and put him to sleep for hours, possibly days. Unfortunately, they were now wearing off.

Just then, a door burst open and light flooded the room.

Marcus squinted and turned away from the door. As his eyes began to adjust, his suspicions were confirmed. He was, in fact, in a rusty old shipping container that had been turned into a makeshift prison cell. At the other end, Marcus could see another chair, empty, and another set of manacles bolted to the floor. Against the wall to his right was a large blue plastic pail that Marcus guessed was supposed to be a toilet. That had to be where the stench was coming from.

Several men entered the container and surrounded him. Their faces were shrouded by black- and white-checkered kaffiyehs. Each wore green army fatigues. Each carried a Kalashnikov in his hands, a .45 in his holster, and a two-way radio on his belt. Given the light flooding in through the doorway, the men were essentially silhouettes. Marcus could see neither their eyes nor any other particulars. But it was just as well. They were not the main event.

As if on cue, a door opened somewhere behind him. One set of boots approached, then stopped. Marcus heard a leather holster being unbuttoned. He began counting silently. *Three, two, one . . .*

There it was.

The warm metal barrel of a 9mm pistol pressed against his temple. Not warm, actually—hot. The pistol had been fired. Recently. Indeed, only moments before. Why had he not heard the shot? Perhaps the gun had been silenced.

"Not one of you was carrying papers," said the voice behind him.

It was the voice of Colonel al-Masri, Marcus was certain.

"No driver's licenses," al-Masri continued. "No badges. No passports or credit cards. Nothing. But no matter. You cannot keep such secrets from me for much longer."

Suddenly Marcus found himself being unbolted from the floor and dragged out of the sweltering shipping container, across a courtyard, and into a cave in the side of a grassy hill. There, he was forced to sit on a metal chair and this time manacled to chains bolted into the bedrock. The cave was damp and certainly cooler than the container. What was more, Marcus could feel warm but refreshing salt-scented sea breezes entering the mouth of the cave. The sounds of gulls and waves were clearer now. They were not at a port. They were at a camp of some kind, though from what little he had seen while being dragged through the courtyard, it seemed to have been abandoned long before. The walls he had seen were chipping and badly in need of a fresh coat of paint. The grounds were overrun with weeds. Windows were cracked or missing glass altogether. And a Pepsi machine they had passed was covered with dust and grime and looked like it had not been touched, much less stocked, since before he was born.

The cave was dark and shadowy. There were no electric lights or fires.

The only light was natural and was coming in from the cave opening behind him, casting long shadows beyond him. Marcus guessed it was early evening, which suggested that he'd been unconscious for at least four or five hours.

Marcus heard movement behind him. More chains. More boots. The cocking of weapons. He was tempted to turn to see what was happening but thought better of it. Then the Egyptian came around from behind him, raised the 9mm to Marcus's forehead, and ordered him to shut his eyes. Marcus did as he was told. This was not a moment for theatrics, he told himself. Something was changing, and he wanted to live long enough to see what it was.

A full minute later, al-Masri ordered Marcus to open his eyes. Again Marcus complied. And immediately wished he hadn't. Sitting six feet in front of him, chained to metal chairs of their own, were the bloodied, bruised, beaten, burned bodies of Kailea Curtis and Yigal Mizrachi. They were both alive, though it looked to Marcus like they'd been through far worse than he.

Colonel al-Masri was now standing behind Kailea. She looked terrible. She, like Yigal, had been stripped to her undergarments. She had welts and bruises all over her body. Her nose looked broken. She was covered in blood. She was gagged but not blindfolded. Her eyes were swollen. One was turning black-and-blue. Nevertheless, the look Marcus saw in them was not fear but defiance, and from this he took encouragement. Kailea was still in the fight.

Yigal was a different story. His body was also covered with dried and oozing blood. His legs were a mess of welts and scars, as were his arms. Like Kailea, Yigal's eyes were also black-and-blue and swollen and caked with dried blood. But unlike Kailea, his eyes were also filled with sheer terror.

Marcus tensed. This was his fault. It had been his job to protect these two, to keep them out of harm's way, and he had failed.

"There's only so much the human body can take," al-Masri said. "Both of them cracked faster than you. In the end, they told me their names and yours. Now I need to see if they were telling me the truth."

At this, al-Masri pressed his pistol to the back of Kailea's head.

40

"Tell me her name—and tell me the truth," al-Masri said.

Marcus said nothing.

"Don't play games with me, American. I'm only going to give you one chance. If you don't give me the same name she gave me, I'll blow her brains out. Is that clear enough for you?"

Marcus watched as the man pulled back the hammer. Kailea closed her eyes. It was possible, of course, that the gun was not loaded. The Egyptian could be bluffing. But was Marcus really prepared to gamble with his partner's life?

Al-Masri glared at Marcus. The two men were not just looking into each other's eyes. They were staring into each other's souls. It was a high-stakes game of poker, and Marcus was determined not to lose.

Suddenly al-Masri shifted several steps to his left. Now he was standing directly behind the Israeli, pressing the barrel of the gun against Yigal's head, not Kailea's. Al-Masri did not say why, but there could only be one reason. The Hezbollah operative had initially calculated that a gun to a woman's head would cause Marcus to volunteer information immediately. Yet when Marcus had not flinched, when there was no look of panic or even concern in his eyes, al-Masri had recalculated, wondering if the prospect of seeing the boy's head blow apart in front of his eyes would cause the reaction for which he was hoping.

Marcus tried not to show it, but he knew Al-Masri was right. Kailea was a federal agent. No one should have to endure the kind of treatment she had at the hands of this monster and his henchmen, but she was aware of the risks inherent in her profession. But Yigal was an intelligence officer barely out of training. He was just a kid. What he had been through was unconscionable, and if their captors discovered his true identity, he would be subject to horrors Marcus couldn't even imagine.

In that instant, Marcus knew he had made a mistake. He felt a flash of fear behind his eyes. What's more, he knew al-Masri had seen it.

Marcus had blinked—and been caught.

"Three questions, three answers, no lies, or they both die," al-Masri said quietly.

Marcus steadied himself, knowing full well the man might kill them all no matter what he said.

"The woman," al-Masri prompted. "What's her name and her position?"

Marcus saw the Hezbollah operative press the barrel deeper into Yigal's temple. The man was a stone-cold killer. There was no point in dragging this out any further. The three of them had bought themselves as much time as they could. Unless the IDF helicopters arrived overhead and special forces operators fast-roped into the courtyard and burst into the cave at that second, it was time to start talking.

"Kailea," Marcus said.

"Kailea what?" barked al-Masri.

"Kailea Curtis."

"What does she do?"

"She's a special agent with the Diplomatic Security Service."

Al-Masri did not pull the trigger. Not yet anyway. Marcus silently prayed Kailea had given him the same answer. Almost before he could finish this thought, however, al-Masri stepped around Yigal, moved in front of Kailea, and pistol-whipped her until she was bloodied and unconscious. Then he stepped back behind Yigal and returned the gun to its original position.

"And this one?" al-Masri said.

Yigal Mizrachi's nearly naked body—bloodied and bruised—was shaking. Sweat was pouring down his face. This was the moment of truth. Had Yigal remembered to use his alias? Or had he blurted out his real name and real nationality?

When Marcus took a half beat too long to reply, al-Masri smiled. "Two American DSS agents touring the border I can understand," said the operative. "But babysitting a Zionist—why? What's the point? I cannot understand why you would drag a mere child into such a grown-up world."

At that moment, al-Masri stepped around Yigal and positioned himself between Marcus and the Israeli. The reason was obvious enough. Al-Masri didn't want Yigal to be able to communicate anything to Marcus with his eyes or any other part of his body.

Now Marcus had to choose. Did al-Masri really know Yigal's name? Nationality? If so, how long would it take him to discover the kid was the nephew of the Israeli prime minister? Perhaps al-Masri knew it already. Perhaps that was part of the test. Then again, maybe the man was bluffing, going on a hunch, hoping Marcus would confirm his suspicions.

It didn't really matter, Marcus decided. He was in no position to do anything other than stick to the plan. Yigal had an alias. A carefully constructed cover story. If he'd forgotten it—or been rattled—and given himself away, that was one thing. But Marcus was never going to give him away.

"His name is Daniel—well, we just call him Dan," Marcus finally replied.

"Dan what?"

"Case."

"That doesn't sound like a Zionist name."

"Because it's not."

"He's an American?"

"Of course—he works with Kailea and me."

"That's impossible," said al-Masri. "He's a Jew."

"Actually, he's a Catholic—not particularly devout, but who am I to judge?"

"You're a liar."

"Why would I lie when you're ready to shoot my friends and me in the head?"

"Very simple," al-Masri said. "You don't want me to think this child is a Zionist."

"I don't really even know what a Zionist is. I do security, Colonel, not politics. But if you're asking me if he's an Israeli, I'm afraid you're out of luck. Dan was born and raised in the good ole U.S. of A."

"Where?" sniffed al-Masri, growing visibly angry.

"New York. Brooklyn, I think, but it might have been Queens. I don't remember."

"And you're saying he works for you, for the two of you, at DSS?"

"I'm not *saying* he does," Marcus replied. "He does."

"Doing what?"

"Logistics. Communications. Look, he's been with us less than a year."

At that, al-Masri whipped around and smashed his pistol across Yigal's face, sending him flying out of his chair and crashing onto the cave floor. Blood poured down the Israeli's face, but he did not make a sound. Nor did he move.

Al-Masri turned back and shoved his gun into Marcus's face, pressing it into his forehead, right between his eyes.

"*I want your name and I want it now,*" he shouted, his face beet red. "*No lies or they both die.*"

"Tom," Marcus said calmly.

"*Tom what?*"

"Tom Millner."

"*No, no,*" screamed al-Masri. "*Your full name—all of it.*"

Marcus said nothing for a moment. Instead, he just glared into the eyes of the Egyptian. But seeing a man hell-bent on murder, Marcus finally spoke. "Thomas Harris Millner."

No sooner had the words come out of his mouth than Marcus saw the butt of the pistol coming at him. It hit him square in the mouth, and again everything went black.

41

Al-Masri exited the cave and strode through the courtyard.

With his bodyguards flanking him, he entered a set of connecting concrete bunkers, all of which were infested by rats and devoid of furniture or books or clothing or any signs of human civilization. Motioning for his men to stay put in one of the outer rooms, the Egyptian passed through a wooden door that was barely on its hinges, then through yet another door more securely fastened, until he finally came to a room that had once served as an office.

The floor was covered with broken glass from windows that had been smashed out long before. At the far end of the room was a weathered wooden desk that had seen better days. On it sat an olive-green backpack. Behind the desk was a rickety office chair whose springs had rusted and whose upholstery was ripped. On the wall was pinned a faded map of the Levant, with pencil markings noting the locations of other Hezbollah strongholds that, like this one, had been abandoned years before for better and more strategic facilities.

Al-Masri closed and locked the door behind him. Finally alone, he plunked down in the chair, lit a cigarette, took a long drag, and stared up at the water-stained ceiling. He glanced at his watch. He knew it was time to let his contacts know just how wildly he had succeeded and come to an agreement on next steps.

But first things first.

Al-Masri unzipped the backpack. The interior was filled with mobile phones. He counted and scrutinized each one to make sure he had them all. There were some things he could trust his men with. This was not one of them. None of them had any idea that they were not actually executing orders from the Sheikh. He had told them they were, and as loyal foot soldiers, they had believed him. It had been a lie, but a necessary one. Most likely none of them would have ever agreed to execute the mission if they truly understood what they were involved in. Which was why he hadn't told them.

Might one or more begin to suspect that something was amiss, given that they had not brought the hostages directly to Hezbollah's central command in Beirut, or even to one of its major bases in the Bekaa Valley, but to a facility that hadn't been used by the organization in more than ten years? Yes, it was possible. That was why he had ordered all the men to hand in their phones and agree to go "radio silent" until the operation was over. Now, as an insurance policy, al-Masri removed the SIM cards from the phones and smashed them with his boot.

All but one—his brother's. This he put in his pocket for safekeeping.

As he took another drag on his cigarette, his thoughts drifted to the Sheikh and his inner circle of sycophants and cowards. How he would love to be a fly on the wall of their war room. They had to be apoplectic. None of them had any idea what al-Masri had been planning. They certainly had not authorized this mission. Nor were they prepared for the blowback. But they had to be under tremendous pressure from their puppet masters in Tehran to explain themselves and produce whatever hostages the mullahs thought they now had in their possession. At this, al-Masri couldn't help but smile. It served them right.

Throughout the region and certainly throughout Zionist territory, Hezbollah, its suicide squadrons, and its missile force were feared. But al-Masri thought the truth was the Sheikh and the ayatollahs back in Iran were terrified of the Jews. Why else had they refused to engage the Zionists since 2006? Why had they done everything possible to avoid a Third Lebanon War? If the Sheikh and the Supreme Leader and all their minions with all their resources believed their own rhetoric, why had they not wiped Israel off the map already?

Left to their own devices, Hezbollah would never have opened fire on the Israelis. The border would still be quiet. The Shias of southern Lebanon would still be dirt-poor, and the criminal Zionists would still be getting filthy rich with each and every passing day.

Now al-Masri opened the desk drawer and pulled out a box. Inside was a brand-new satellite phone, the very one he had stashed there the week before when he had come to make all the necessary preparations.

Taking several more drags, he powered up the phone, then dialed a number from memory.

42

The call was answered on the third ring.

Al-Masri provided a nineteen-character code comprising both numbers and letters, speaking slowly and enunciating clearly. When he was finished, he listened as the person on the other end replied with another nineteen-character code. Convinced they were both members of the same organization, al-Masri began to speak. "Jackpot," he said in Arabic.

"We heard," came the reply. "Three Americans. No Israelis. Correct?"

Al-Masri was stunned. "How do you know that?"

"It's all over the news," came the reply.

"But how? I—"

"The U.S. State Department just put out a statement—it's the lead on all the networks. How could you not know?"

The question cut al-Masri to the heart. He could not afford to give these people the impression he did not know what he was doing, that he was not in control of every detail. Still, the Americans had been shrewd to announce that three of their people had been taken. It prevented him from acting like he only had one or two. He now had to account for all three.

"There's been no time," al-Masri replied. "We've been under fire and on the move."

"Well, you've certainly rattled the hornet's nest. The Zionists say they've already sent ten thousand ground forces and mechanized units into southern Lebanon. But reports say that number will likely double by tomorrow. Where are you now?"

"I can't say."

"This is a secure line."

"I'm not giving you operational details—that's the agreement."

"Just tell me if you're north of the Litani River."

"Why?"

"We're hearing that the Zionists are promising the Americans they won't go north of Litani, but they're going to search every house, every factory, every barn or building of any kind south of the river. Tell me they're not going to find you."

"They're not going to find us," al-Masri said.

It wasn't a lie. Not exactly. At the moment, al-Masri and his men were camped out north of the city of Tyre but just south of the Litani River. Soon, however, he would be taking them farther north. And he certainly had no intention of getting caught. Not with all that hung in the balance.

"Convince me," said the voice on the other end of the line.

"Listen, you either trust me or you don't."

"No, you listen to me. We've already paid you a fortune for this operation—you work for us, so you'll answer every question we ask."

"You paid for Israelis," al-Masri shot back. "I'm bringing you Americans—three of them—and the price just went up."

"Forget it—I'm not about to renegotiate in the middle of an operation."

"Do you want the Americans or not?"

"Of course."

"Then you'll pay me double."

"Have you lost your mind?"

"Maybe, maybe not—but I've got the Americans, and if you want them, you'll pay what I ask."

"Listen, Amin, if you renege on this deal . . ."

"Then what?"

"We will hunt you down—you and your family—every single one of you."

"I'm already a wanted man."

"You haven't seen anything yet."

"Enough," al-Masri said. "Ten million dollars—U.S.—wired to the accounts I gave you. Half now. The rest upon delivery."

"And if we say no?"

"Then I go to auction and sell to the highest bidder."

"Where are you going to go? No one's going to pay that kind of money—no one."

Al-Masri laughed. "Now who has lost his mind?" he sniffed. "You think the Iranians won't pay me $10 million for three American federal agents? Even Hezbollah would pay me the money. Every hour that goes by, the Sheikh is growing more desperate. He would fork over the money in a heartbeat. It's all coming from Tehran anyway."

There was a long pause.

"Ticktock, my friend," al-Masri said.

"Are they alive?" asked the man on the other end of the line.

"Of course."

"Are they well?"

"They've been better."

"But they'll live?"

"Probably—but they could use medical help, and sooner rather than later."

There was another pause. "Who exactly do you have?"

"Two men and a woman," al-Masri said.

"That much we know, you fool—I just told you it's all over the news. I need names. I need details. I need proof."

"Of course," said al-Masri. He spelled the names. "Check your email in about an hour. It'll take some time to upload. But I'll send you all the proof you'll need."

★

Hamdi Yaşar sat in his silver Mercedes, six blocks from his office.

These were not calls he could receive or make from the studios of the Al-Sawt television network. These were not calls he wanted to be making at all. He had implored his superiors that someone else should play the middleman, that things were far too sensitive for him to be directly involved. He had been overruled, told that precisely because these matters were so sensitive, they could not be left to lower-level operatives. Father needed someone he could implicitly trust, and there was no one he trusted more than Hamdi Yaşar.

Staring at the notes he'd just jotted down, he turned off one satphone, then immediately pulled another out of his briefcase and powered it up. He dialed a number from memory and went through a similar verification process that his man on the ground in southern Lebanon had just used, though the authorization codes themselves were entirely different. The process took almost three minutes.

He'd done this hundreds of times. He knew the phones were clean and secure. Yet with every second that ticked by, Yaşar feared the call was being intercepted by the NSA, fed into the supercomputers back at Fort Meade, routed to the Global Operations Center at Langley, and relayed in almost real time to a U.S. Air Force Predator drone pilot on some base out in Arizona. How long before some commander ordered a Hellfire missile strike on his car? How soon would Hamdi Yaşar find himself incinerated and hurled from this world into the next?

The founder of the Kairos terror network came on the line, his voice raspy yet full of anticipation. "Is it confirmed?" Abu Nakba asked in his classic modern Arabic, from his compound half a world away.

"It is indeed," Yaşar replied. Though a Turk, and a proud one at that, his Arabic was fluent, and it was the only language he and the founder ever used when they spoke.

"Three Americans?"

"Yes, Father—two men and a woman, all employees of the Diplomatic Security Service, just as all the reports are saying."

"Praise Allah—what a glorious day."

"Praise Allah."

"Does he have their names?"

"Yes," said Yaşar. "The two men are Thomas Millner and Daniel Case."

"And the woman?"

"Her name is Kailea Curtis."

"How do you spell the first name?"

"*K-a-i-l-e-a*."

"I have never heard of that name."

"Nor have we."

"She's really American?"

"Her parents are originally from India, but yes, we understand she was born and raised in the New York City area."

"Did your man send pictures and video proof?"

"He's about to, but there's something else."

"What?"

"He wants more money."

"How much more?"

"Ten million."

"For three American agents?"

"I told him he was crazy—that's twice what we had agreed."

"Surely you are joking, my son," said Abu Nakba, though he was not laughing. "Even at $20 million, this would be a bargain—a tremendous coup for Kairos. Especially after the disaster in Jerusalem. We need this. We need to remind Washington—and our investors—that Kairos is a force to be reckoned with. Make the deal. *Today.* And take custody of those three before your man changes his mind."

PART
TWO

43

SOMEWHERE IN SOUTHERN LEBANON

Marcus opened his eyes—or tried to.

He had not been sleeping. Al-Masri had pistol-whipped him until he had been knocked unconscious. Now both of his eyes were caked with sticky, partially coagulated blood. Turning his head as far as he could, he rubbed his right eye against his right shoulder. Then he turned the other direction and did the same with the left. Now he was squinting, trying to adjust to the fluorescent lights hanging from the ceiling as he realized two important facts.

The first was that he had been moved again. His hands and feet were still bound in iron manacles. Yet he was no longer being held in the cave or the old container. He was inside what looked like a walk-in freezer—the floors, ceiling, and walls of which were stainless steel.

The second was that Kailea and Yigal were with him. They, too, were bound, and they were right beside him—Kailea on his left, Yigal on his right. All three of them were chained to a large, dusty compressor unit that clearly hadn't worked for years. The freezer was not cold. To the contrary, it was quite warm and humid, with no fans running and thus little, if any, ventilation.

"*Hey, Ki—you okay?*" Marcus whispered, nudging her in the side. She was either asleep or unconscious.

It took a moment, but she began to stir.

"*Ki, look up,*" he whispered. "*It's me—Tommy boy.*"

Battered and bruised far worse than he was, Kailea finally cracked a smile. She hadn't opened her eyes yet. But she had recognized his voice and apparently remembered that he was using an alias.

"Millner?" she whispered back. "That really you, old man?"

"Yeah, it's me."

"It seems you haven't forgotten how to show a lady a good time."

Marcus recognized the line from the first Indiana Jones movie and smiled. "How're you holding up?" he asked.

"I've been better," she replied. She still hadn't opened her eyes.

He noticed more clearly her broken nose and a huge welt on her forehead.

"Good grief, Ki—what happened to you?"

"Ah, it's nothing. Just got into a little scrape—a little tussle—with our buddy the Egyptian. That's all."

Marcus couldn't help but smile again. He now understood who had broken al-Masri's nose and wished he had done it himself. "Last time I saw him, it looked like you gave as good as you got."

She didn't reply. Yet as she tried to sit up straighter—she was currently slumped against the wall of the freezer—she winced in pain. Marcus was grateful they had, at least, put a T-shirt on her. Seeing her up close, he noticed how badly her legs and arms had been beaten. They were almost completely black-and-blue, covered in welts and oozing blood in several places. In the end, she wasn't able to get herself into an upright position. Instead, she simply shifted from leaning against the stainless steel wall to leaning against him.

"Anything broken?" he asked. "Besides your nose."

"Feels like everything."

From the looks of her, Marcus was sure it did.

"Guess who has also graced us with his presence," Marcus suggested.

"Danny boy?" she replied.

"Yeah," he said, proud of her for remembering Yigal's alias.

"Is he awake?" she asked.

"No, but let's see what we can do."

Marcus proceeded to nudge the Israeli gently, seeing how badly he had been beaten as well. Yigal was not wearing a T-shirt. Only boxer shorts. And he was covered with horrific gashes and burn marks.

"Good morning, Mr. Case," he said softly. "Hello, Mr. Case—Danny, hey, time to rise and shine."

Yigal shifted slightly and moaned but did not wake up. Kailea asked if it was really morning. Marcus confessed he had no idea what time it was, what day it was, where they were, or how long they had been there. Now that he thought about it, though, given that they were in a freezer, he could probably rule out the notion that they were in the air. Given that he sensed no rocking motion, he was inclined to think they were not at sea. He guessed, therefore, that they were still in Lebanon.

All this Marcus said in a whisper. He had to assume al-Masri or his men were listening. Though he saw no evidence of microphones or cameras anywhere in the freezer, his training had taught him to be cautious. He knew Kailea would be too. He still wasn't entirely sure what to expect of Yigal, though Marcus had been incredibly impressed with the Israeli thus far. Despite unbelievable torture, the young man had stood his ground. He'd remembered his alias. He'd played the part of the American. He hadn't betrayed Marcus's real identity. And so far the Egyptian was buying it. It was an unexpected performance by Yigal, and it had saved his life. Probably Marcus's as well.

The key question now was how long Yigal could keep it up. Everyone broke eventually. *Everyone.* Yet based on what he'd seen of this guy's steely resolve, Marcus felt increasingly confident. That said, it was probably better to let him sleep for now.

Kailea began to stir again, drawing Marcus's attention. She winced as she tried to make herself somewhat more comfortable. Rather than trying to sit upright, she curled up beside him and rested her head in his lap. And mercifully, she soon drifted back to sleep.

Marcus was also drowsy. However, he decided to use the time to make a more careful survey of the freezer. It was spacious, roughly eight feet by twenty feet, maybe twenty-two feet, or about 175 square feet, give or take. There were several sets of metal shelves, all empty and dusty. At the end farthest from them were stacks of some two dozen cardboard boxes. The printing on them was in Arabic, which he could not read.

He saw no tools anywhere, nothing he might be able to use to unlock their manacles. And he saw only two openings to the outside. One contained a double set of exhaust fans, neither of which were running. Marcus guessed they did not work. The other was the door, located directly across from them. It had no handle. It did, however, have a safety release latch—a large plastic button on a short metal lever, designed to allow someone accidentally trapped in the freezer to open the thick, insulated door from the inside. Whether that worked or not, he could not say. Either way, he had to assume the door was padlocked on the other side and monitored by guards with AK-47s. None of it boded well.

And if this weren't bad enough, Marcus now realized that even if he could break them out of their chains—and get that door open and do it quietly, in the middle of the night when the guards happened to be asleep—neither Kailea nor Yigal was in any shape to run.

44

DOHA, QATAR

Hamdi Yaşar logged into his private Gmail account.

With so much breaking news, he had to get back to the Al-Sawt studios. During his calls with al-Masri and Abu Nakba, he had already received three text messages and had two missed calls from the network's vice president for foreign news coverage demanding to know where he was.

Despite all the Kairos work on his plate, Yaşar knew he had no choice. He had to go back. It was critical that he maintain his cover as an award-winning field producer for the most watched satellite station in the Arab-speaking world. He had repeatedly urged Abu Nakba to let him resign and focus his efforts on Kairos full-time. But Father had been insistent. There was no better way for Yaşar to talk to so many sources and travel so widely and be so effective at building up the fledgling terrorist network than being on the Al-Sawt payroll.

Still, if he was really going to wire so much money to his man in Lebanon, the Turk had to be sure.

Waiting for him were three new emails. Each was from al-Masri.

Opening the first, he found no message, only an attachment. It was encrypted, so Yaşar entered the prearranged passcode and found a nine-second video. The image was poor, but the point was made. It was a woman. She was alive but terribly beaten. Her face was bruised and swollen. But her voice was calm, if scratchy. She said her name was Kailea Curtis and that she was an employee of the U.S. State Department. She gave her DSS badge number and demanded to be released immediately. Most importantly, the time stamp was visible in the top left corner of the screen. The video had been made that very day.

The next two emails also contained attachments. Same passcodes. Similar videos, each less than ten seconds long. Both were men. Both had also been brutally beaten. The younger man's face was almost unrecognizable. The older seemed vaguely familiar. Both gave their names—Case and Millner—as well as their DSS badge numbers and more pathetic demands to be freed. The time stamps of the men's videos were consistent with the woman's.

Yaşar had no time to study the videos more carefully. Al-Masri was telling him the truth—that was all that concerned him. Satisfied, the Kairos operative completed the wire transfer to al-Masri's accounts, then drove back to the studio.

Once there, he apologized to everyone for being late and lied about why. Then he retreated to his office and hit the phones, looking for officials throughout the region who would be willing to go on camera to react to the new war in Lebanon and the death of Iran's Supreme Leader.

After a dozen conversations of varying lengths, Yaşar placed a call to the palace in Ankara, to the direct line of the spokesman for Turkish president Ahmet Mustafa. When the call went straight to voice mail, Yaşar dialed the man's mobile phone. When that did not work either, he called him at home.

His wife answered. Yaşar identified himself and apologized for intruding. It was no intrusion, she said and called for her husband.

"It's Hamdi. I just need a second."

"Good, because that's all you're going to get."

"Are you tracking all this? The region is really blowing up."

"I wasn't. It's a Saturday. I was about to take my family to Antalya for the weekend."

"I just need two minutes of your boss's time—a reaction, on the record or off."

"Can't do it."

"Why not?"

"He's not talking to anyone."

"He'll talk to me."

"Don't flatter yourself."

"Just ask him, okay?"

"Fine—but don't hold your breath."

Yaşar did not, but five minutes later, his satellite phone began buzzing like crazy. The number was blocked, but he had no doubt it was Ahmet Mustafa.

"Are you watching this?" Yaşar asked the Turkish president.

"Impressive, is it not?" Mustafa asked.

"It's unfolding just like you planned."

"Yes, although I never expected the Supreme Leader to die the same day as our attack."

"I know—it's crazy."

"I don't have much time. How many hostages?"

"Three."

"All alive? You're sure?"

"Positive—I just watched the videos."

"Three Israeli soldiers is better than we had dared imagine."

"Actually, it's better still."

"How?"

"They're not Israelis."

"What?"

"They're Americans—all of them."

There was a long pause.

"Sir?" Yaşar asked. "You still there?"

"It was supposed to be Israelis," said Mustafa.

"What can I say? We gambled and came up big."

"You don't understand. The last thing I need right now is a problem with the Americans."

"Sir, with respect, if you were worried about the Americans, you would never have come to Father in the first place. You would not have funded Kairos. And you certainly would not have supported—enthusiastically, I would remind you—the kind of operations we have been engaged in."

"But not right now," Mustafa snapped. "I've got Secretary Whitney coming to see me soon. This was supposed to be about the Israelis—drawing them into a war with Hezbollah, sandbagging the Saudis. Suddenly we're operating on a whole new level. And that's not what I am paying for."

"What do you want me to do about it now?" Yaşar asked. "I know we didn't target Americans. But we got them. What do you want Father to do with them?"

"I don't know," said the Turkish leader. "Give me some time. I need to think about this."

"Well, don't take long, sir. We've got to get them out of the country before Hezbollah figures out what's going on."

45

THE PRESIDENTIAL PALACE, TEHRAN, IRAN

It was now 6:36 p.m. in the Iranian capital.

Yadollah Afshar was set to address the nation in less than an hour.

Though his speech was substantially complete, the president of the Islamic Republic had retreated to his private study to polish the text. He had instructed his aides to hold all calls and refuse all visitors until the broadcast was over. He was both startled and somewhat annoyed, therefore, when his private mobile phone buzzed. Glancing at the number, however, he took the call.

"General, now is not a good time," he said without pleasantries.

"I apologize, Your Excellency, but there is one thing I need to tell you," said Mahmoud Entezam, pressing on though he had not been invited to do so. "You and I both know that the last thing this country needs is a lengthy and drawn-out succession process. Worse still would be a messy succession battle. The Supreme Leader, peace be upon him, was beloved and irreplaceable. He was a transformative leader who will be cherished for generations. And while the Assembly of Experts has a number of competent clerics from which to choose, we both know none of them are up to the challenges that lie before us."

"What exactly are you saying, General?" Afshar asked, careful to convey with his tone that he was pressed for time and determined not to sound too eager though he sensed, with no small measure of surprise, where Entezam was headed.

"Your Excellency, I am hesitant to take much more of your time," the commander of the IRGC continued. "I suggest we meet soon and discuss these matters in person and in private. But suffice it to say for now, I believe your country needs your unique set of skills and experience more than ever. And I want you to know that if you are willing, I am prepared to help you in every possible manner."

Though he was both stunned and electrified, Afshar nevertheless sounded noncommittal as he thanked Entezam and suggested they have tea the following evening. Then he hung up the phone and turned back to the sheaf of papers in his hands. He could not, however, concentrate on his remarks. He had just been given a game-changing pledge of support for a campaign he had told no one yet that he was about to wage.

Entezam's support was all the more surprising because the general had never seemed particularly warm toward him. Indeed, the Supreme Leader himself had cautioned Afshar not to get too close to Entezam or expect too much. The commander of the IRGC was a military man, not a theologian. He could be trusted to carry out complex military campaigns and special operations, but Entezam was not a Twelver. Nor did he have his own national political network that could prove useful to Hossein Ansari's successor.

And yet, Afshar now wondered, was it possible that both he and Ansari had misjudged the man?

Surely Entezam's loyalty—and that of the two hundred thousand or so Revolutionary Guards under his command—could prove exceedingly useful as Afshar began to execute a plan years in the making, a plan that if successful would make him the most powerful man in the whole of the Islamic world.

SOUTHERN LEBANON

Al-Masri sat alone in his makeshift office.

His aide brought him a hot cup of Turkish coffee, some pita, and a small tub of hummus. The Egyptian nodded his thanks, waited until the man was gone, then got down on his knees, faced Mecca, and said his prayers. Only then did he eat. The food, simple though it was, tasted sublime. Both the smell and taste of the unsweetened coffee were magical. Combined, the sustenance went a long way to reinvigorate his strength and lift his spirits.

Barely eight hours had elapsed since he had led his men into battle, and the more he thought about it, the less he could believe his good fortune. Yes, he had certainly lost men. More than he'd expected. And he'd lost his brother— that was true. But as ferociously as al-Masri hated the Zionists, he was confident they weren't going to torture Tanzeel. The boy would talk. That was certain. But he knew nothing of value. He'd be fed well. Given a comfortable bed. Be allowed to pray five times a day. And eventually he would be released in another prisoner swap. It wouldn't be so bad. Tanzeel would survive.

What's more, none of the surviving members of his team had any serious injuries. They had seized not one but three enemy combatants. All three were officials in the Great Satan's government. He had taken a risk by demanding more money. Yet Kairos had responded much faster than he had expected. They had, in fact, given him everything he had asked for, and the money had already been wired.

Kairos just had one request, and to this al-Masri had readily agreed.

Powering up the satellite phone again, he dialed the only number he knew for the Hezbollah war room in Beirut. When the call was answered, al-Masri disguised his voice and asked for the commander of the Al-Talil unit. The man was responsible for infiltrating Hezbollah operatives into northern Israel. Yet not in the six years he had been in the post had he ever actually done so. The commander, however, did not come on the line. An aide did instead. Knowing the call was untraceable, the Egyptian nevertheless delivered the message, as he had been instructed by Kairos.

"I am the man responsible for taking the hostages this morning," he began.

"Who is this?" the aide demanded.

"None of your business—just take notes and give them directly to the Sheikh."

"Not until you identify—"

"*Shut up, and do your job,*" al-Masri ordered.

There was now silence on the other end of the line.

"I led the raid," al-Masri continued. "I took hostages. And I'm more than willing to sell them to the Sheikh and let him take the credit for the raid and let him turn the captives over to our allies in Tehran. But I will set the terms, and I will not negotiate."

There was a long pause. "How many hostages do you have?" the aide finally asked.

"Three," al-Masri replied.

"Zionists?"

"No."

"No?" came the incredulous response.

"No," al-Masri repeated. "All of them are Americans."

"*Americans?*" came another stunned response.

"Yes—two men, one woman. All of them agents of the Diplomatic Security Service."

"They're alive?"

"For now."

"Wounded?"

"Of course."

"How badly?"

"If the Sheikh wants them to live, he's going to have to pay for them, and fast."

"How much?"

"Twenty million dollars, wired to a numbered account in Zurich."

There was another long pause.

"How do we know you're telling the truth, that you really have the hostages, that they're really alive?"

"Give me a secure email account."

"Why?"

"I will send you videos of the prisoners."

"Fine—anything else?"

"Yes, so listen carefully."

46

The best spies were women.

Richard Stephens not only believed this to be true, he'd made it his bed-rock policy from the moment he'd been tapped by the president to serve as director of Central Intelligence. The number of women serving as clandes-tine officers in the Agency had jumped by 32 percent over the past several years. The number of female analysts had jumped by an even more impres-sive 41 percent. Those recently hired in the science and technology direc-torate were fewer—only 19 percent so far—but Stephens was pushing his personnel division to recruit far more aggressively.

Women, in Stephens's view, generally processed and assessed mountains of data better than men. They had the patience and capacity for the very kinds of multitasking the Agency desperately needed. And, he'd always rea-soned, who was more likely to successfully approach and engage a target in a foreign country—most of whom were men—than a woman?

Far and away, Stephens regarded Dr. Martha Dell as his best hire. Now fifty-seven, Dell had grown up in the projects outside of Atlanta. She was responsible for helping gather secrets from all manner of foreign governments, but particularly from the enemies of the United States. She also made sure that the commander in chief and all senior policy makers in Congress and throughout the U.S. government had the most timely and accurate interpretation of those secrets as possible.

In Stephens's estimation, Dell had been born for Agency work. Graduating first in her class from Georgetown University in national security studies, she'd gone on to earn her master's degree in Russian-Sino relations from Oxford and not one but two PhDs from Stanford, both dealing with aspects of Chinese foreign and military policy. Fluent in Russian and Mandarin—as well as Arabic, which she'd picked up *after* finishing her postgraduate work—she'd been recruited to the CIA in her late twenties and spent six years in the field, running agents and training future spooks. Over the past two and a half decades, she'd served in a range of highly trusted Agency positions, all within the National Clandestine Service. Most recently, she had been promoted to the Agency's deputy director.

That, and she was a wonder to behold with a Glock 9mm.

At 11:17 a.m. Eastern time, Stephens and his security detail pulled into Langley after a long morning at the White House and headed to his spacious corner office on the seventh floor. A moment later, Dell entered through a side door, carrying a black leather notebook and a folder marked TOP SECRET in red. This she tossed onto Stephens's desk, then picked up a remote from his desk and turned on a bank of TV monitors on the far wall as she took a seat across from him.

"Tell me something I don't know," Stephens instructed his number two.

This was the director's standard opening line with everyone on his staff. As always, Dell was ready.

"The Iranian president is about to break the news of the Supreme Leader's death in a live address on state television," she replied, finding the right channel so they could watch the speech together. "Don't ask me who the Assembly of Experts is going to choose to replace Ayatollah Ansari. I have no idea. Nobody does."

"Fair enough," said Stephens. "What else?"

"The Israelis have taken out two more power plants, shutting down electricity for more than a million people in southern Lebanon," Dell noted. "I called you in the car but couldn't get through."

"I was on the phone with the Jordanian GID."

"And?"

"The pasha says the king wants us to pressure the Israelis to de-escalate this thing, and fast."

"He's worried it'll ignite a Palestinian explosion in the territories?"

"Exactly."

"Did they have any warning this was coming?"

"None," said Stephens.

"Doesn't that seem odd?"

"Very," Stephens agreed, turning to hand Dell her coffee in a large mug bearing the CIA seal. "What's going on with the ground campaign?"

"The Israelis are in the process of sending some ten thousand more combat troops into southern Lebanon and in the process mobilizing twenty-five thousand reservists to go in with them, though I suspect they'll actually end up sending in more."

"Battle tanks?"

"At least a hundred have crossed the border already, and two hundred more will within the hour. The Israelis are laying down withering artillery fire. They've launched hundreds of sorties and have hit dozens of known Hezbollah strongholds."

"How far north are they pushing?"

"We've seen no strikes above the Litani River."

"Nothing in the Bekaa Valley?"

"Not yet."

"Beirut?"

"No, thank God."

"And the hostages?"

"Nothing yet," said Dell. "But we've activated our assets. NSA is prioritizing all Hezbollah communications."

"And?"

"We're picking up the same confusion 8200 is—Hezbollah leadership isn't just fighting the Israelis; they're fighting each other. No one seems to know who authorized the initial attack or why. And no one seems to know where the hostages are or who actually grabbed them."

There was a knock on the door, and Stephens's executive assistant entered with mugs of freshly brewed coffee.

"You don't buy that, do you?" Stephens continued, nodding his thanks to his assistant before she turned and left the room.

"Honestly, I don't know what to believe," Dell replied. "The whole thing is odd."

"It's spin, Martha," Stephens said. "Propaganda. Agitprop. Fake news. Don't get distracted."

"What if it's not?"

Stephens took a sip of his coffee. "What are you saying, that a Hezbollah unit went rogue and launched an attack on their own?"

"It's possible."

"Anything's possible, but how likely? Why take such a risk? If a Hezbollah unit isn't acting under Sheikh al-Hussaini's orders, or under Tehran's, then whose? These aren't exactly the most creative strategists in the world. Someone has to be directing them. Someone has to be paying them. And it couldn't just be a Hezbollah commander on the take, right? He'd have to have the entire unit in on it. Who do you know that has the juice to flip an entire Hezbollah special forces unit and get them to start a full-blown war with Israel?"

"I don't know," Dell conceded. "But I'm working on it."

"Good. Now I've got something else for you."

47

"What do you need?" Dell asked.

"POTUS wants someone to call Ryker's mother and let her know what's happening."

"Let me guess. Pete Hwang."

"Yeah—how'd you know?"

"I had the same thought the moment I heard Ryker had been snagged," Dell said, taking a sip of coffee. "He'd be perfect."

"I'm not so sure."

"Why not?"

"I hardly know Hwang."

"Meaning you don't trust him."

"I don't trust anyone connected to Ryker."

"Hwang might be different."

"I doubt it," Stephens said.

Dell had anticipated this. She readily conceded that they needed answers to several questions. Could they trust Peter Hwang to carry out Agency orders? Just how much responsibility should they give him? He wasn't a Company man any more than Ryker was. He had, in fact, been drafted under unique—even bizarre—circumstances. What could they really expect from him?

Then again, Hwang had not been part of Ryker's eleventh-hour plea-bargain agreement with the president almost two years earlier. Rather, Hwang had been personally recruited by Ryker after Ryker joined the Agency. Yes, as director, Stephens had every right to overrule Ryker and let Hwang go, and Dell could see that her boss was inclined to do just that. Yet she pushed back.

Hwang, she explained, was a man in whom she saw real potential. It wasn't every day that one of the best cardiologists in the country entered the employ of the Central Intelligence Agency, least of all one of Korean ancestry who was fluent in the Korean language. Yes, the Tanch'ŏn operation had been a bust, but that was not Hwang's fault. In fact, he had served with bravery and distinction. Afterward, he could have left the Agency and gone back to medicine. Instead, he had stayed and was doing excellent work. He loved his country. He was proving loyal to the Agency, even while serving at DSS. And he could prove a useful link to Ryker.

This brought them back to the central question: Was Peter Hwang capable of discretion in the most sensitive of matters and missions, or was he beholden to Ryker? Given the two men's longtime association and deep, personal friendship, Stephens's working assumption was that the latter had to be true. That was certainly possible, Dell conceded. Yet it was a premise that should not be assumed. It ought to be tested.

Dell now made her case, and for a while, at least, Stephens listened without interrupting.

No clandestine officer in their employ, she argued, had become more important to the Agency's mission—or potentially more catastrophic to its fortunes—than Marcus Johannes Ryker. Dell was sympathetic to the fact that Stephens could not stand him and wanted to get rid of him. Yet she noted that for the time being, Ryker was the president's pet project, so they were stuck with him.

For good measure she added that for all the stress and chaos Ryker had injected into their carefully managed intelligence ecosystem, they had to admit—if only to themselves—that the man had racked up a rather lengthy list of accomplishments in the short time he had been with them. Among other things, Ryker was singularly responsible for identifying and bringing in "the Raven," the highest-ranking mole in the history of the Agency, a man who month after month was providing the most valuable intelligence they had ever seen, bar none, about the inner workings of the Kremlin at a time of breathtaking change and volatility inside the Russian regime.

"Maybe so," Stephens argued. "But that's Ryker. Why waste my time with Hwang?"

"Because Ryker brought us the Raven, and Hwang came to us with Ryker."

Stephens said nothing, just sipped his coffee.

"Look, sir, I'm no Ryker fan," Dell continued. "But when he was in trouble in Russia, who was the first person he turned to?"

"Not Hwang," Stephens noted. "He called Vinetti."

"Exactly," said Dell. "And when Vinetti was killed, who did he turn to next?"

Stephens did not reply. Nor did he need to.

"Sir, Ryker trusts Hwang, and this is not a man who trusts easily," Dell continued. "And perhaps there's cause for that. Ryker's father was killed when he was just a boy. His wife and only son were brutally murdered a few years ago. Ryker's closest friend, Nick Vinetti, is now dead. So is Ryker's pastor. Not to mention numerous other friends. Ryker's not close to McDermott, despite their years in the Marines together—"

"Perhaps because of them."

"Perhaps. As we both know, Bill is—how shall I put this delicately?—a strong cup of tea. And let's be frank—you and Ryker are certainly not close."

"Well, I did try to kill him," Stephens quipped.

"Fortunately, he doesn't actually know that."

"Sure he does," Stephens responded. "The guy's got a 146 IQ and a near-photographic memory. You think he hasn't done the math on what really happened on the Karelian Isthmus?"

"Fair enough, sir, but that just underscores my point."

"Which is?"

"You're never going to have his trust, sir. You can't earn it. You certainly can't buy it. But if Ryker is going to be truly effective for us, then we need a way to communicate with him, advise him—corral him, if you will. We need to understand him and anticipate his moves. In short, sir, we need a go-between—someone we can trust, someone he already trusts."

"Enough," Stephens said. "Get Hwang in here. Then we'll see."

48

HEZBOLLAH COMMAND BUNKER, BEIRUT, LEBANON

It was time to summon a killer.

Sheikh Ja'far ibn al-Hussaini picked up the phone on his desk and dialed his chief of staff, telling him exactly whom he wanted to speak to and that the matter was urgent. A moment later, there was a knock on the door of his private office.

"Come," said the Sheikh, sitting behind his desk and rereading the transcript of the call he had already read a half-dozen times.

When the door opened, in walked a tall, slim, muscular man in his forties with a thick black mustache, full beard, and bushy, unkempt eyebrows. He wore a black military uniform with red trim along with a black beret. His name was General Kareem bin Mubarak, and he was the commander of *Amn al-Muddad*, Hezbollah's counterintelligence unit.

The man clicked his heels and snapped a salute. The Sheikh told him to sit.

"General Mubarak, it is now 100 percent confirmed that we have a traitor in our ranks," the Sheikh began. "Furthermore, we know exactly who it is."

"I just heard about the call, but I thought the caller had not given his name," the general said.

"He didn't. But you can listen to the recording for yourself. It's a voice you will recognize immediately."

"Who?"

"Amin al-Masri."

"With the Radwan Unit? Impossible."

"I know it is difficult to believe," said the Sheikh, "but it's true. I don't know yet whom Amin is working for or why. What is clear is that he is responsible for launching the border raid without my approval. He and his men have captured three Americans. He has pushed us into a war with the Zionists. And now he is playing a game of extortion, trying to sell the prisoners to me or put them up for bid to other terrorist organizations the world over."

The Sheikh slid a thick brown folder marked *CLASSIFIED* across the desk and ordered Mubarak to open it. Inside were photos and biographical details of al-Masri and each of the men under his command.

"What do you need me to do, Your Holiness?" Mubarak asked after quickly leafing through the materials.

"I want you to find al-Masri, I want you to find his men and the prisoners, and I want you to bring them back to me—*alive*, if at all possible," the Sheikh replied. "And you must do this discreetly."

"Meaning what, Your Holiness?"

"Under no circumstances must the media or the public catch wind that we are hunting for these men," the Sheikh insisted. "It is imperative that we maintain the appearance to the Americans, to the Israelis, to Iran, to all of our allies and enemies, that this was our operation from beginning to end and that we are fully in control of the situation. Am I understood?"

"Absolutely, Your Holiness," General Mubarak replied. "You can count on me."

"I hope so," the Sheikh said coolly, leaning forward in his chair. "As you know, there is, suddenly, an opening for someone to take charge of the Nasser Unit."

Mubarak swallowed and nodded. Not that long before, he had been a witness when the Sheikh had drawn a pistol and blown out the brains of the previous commander of the Nasser Unit, the man responsible for all Hezbollah military operations south of the Litani River. Both the offer and the threat, therefore, could not have been clearer.

★

The moment Mubarak was dismissed, he headed straight back to his office.

Having served in the counterintelligence unit for nearly two decades—working his way up from a lowly case officer to the number two man in the unit and now, for the last three years, its head—Mubarak had been part of rooting out so many CIA and Mossad infiltrators and informants over the years that he had lost count. Yet never had he seen a Hezbollah officer as senior as Amin al-Masri go rogue.

It would have been impossible to believe if Mubarak had not donned headphones and listened to the recording of the phone call the Sheikh emailed to him. He listened to it twice, then a third time, and then a fourth.

The Sheikh was right. The voice was unmistakable, the evidence incontrovertible. Al-Masri actually had admitted to having captured the three Americans and was now trying to sell them to the Sheikh. For Mubarak, the big question was whether al-Masri was working alone or for someone else. Either way, he was playing the Sheikh for a fool. The fact that the Zionists had captured the man's younger brother made the picture even more confusing. Yet all those matters would have to wait.

The first priority of business, Mubarak decided, was dispatching a commando team to capture the rest of the al-Masri family. To resolve this thing as quickly as possible without paying a single Lebanese pound, Mubarak needed leverage on Amin, and he needed it fast. That meant going after his family. In the file were photos of his mother, Jabira, along with her home address on the south side of Beirut. There were also pictures of Amin and Tanzeel's siblings—including their ten-year-old sister, Hala, and seven-year-old brother, Farez, along with details about what schools they attended. All this Mubarak sent by encrypted email to one of his section leaders with the orders to grab any family members they could—alive—and discreetly take them to the Iranian embassy until further notice.

That completed, Mubarak transmitted photos of al-Masri to his entire force of intelligence operatives, spread out over the whole of Lebanon, with an order that he be arrested and brought to headquarters immediately. He offered a 150-million-pound reward—roughly 100,000 U.S. dollars—for whoever brought him in dead and a 300-million-pound reward if he was brought in alive. He sent the same notice to his colleagues on the general staff with orders from the Sheikh that the information be passed on immediately to the commanders at every roadblock and checkpoint across the country, as well as to units responsible for security at the airports and seaports. In none of his communications, however, did he explain why Amin al-Masri was the most wanted man in the country. That, he concluded, would have to wait.

One thing was missing, and it bothered Mubarak. No one at Hezbollah headquarters had received by email or text the video of the prisoners, the proof of life that al-Masri had promised to provide. But Mubarak couldn't wait. Whether Amin had really grabbed hostages or was just trying to bluff them, the man was engaged in a high-stakes game of blackmail with the most powerful terrorist group on the planet. Whatever the truth, Mubarak had his orders, and now so did his men.

The hunt for Amin al-Masri was on.

49

Bill McDermott should have been outside, enjoying a picture-perfect spring day.

Puffy white clouds drifted across a gorgeous azure sky. A warm gentle breeze was rolling in from the east. The South Lawn was a lush and vivid green after weeks of heavy rains. The Rose Garden was in full bloom, and there were still some late cherry blossoms visible, which reminded him of the puffs of pink cotton candy he used to get at carnivals, growing up in Pittsburgh.

The U.S. was finally getting back on her feet following the disaster of the global pandemic. A vaccine had been created and most of the country had been inoculated. The Dow had just hit another new record high the day before, the ninth record closing of the year. Oil prices were back up, breathing much-needed life into the U.S. drilling and fracking industries. Manufacturing was coming back online. The unemployment rate was steadily dropping. The Russians had backed off from their foolhardy threats to the Baltics. The North Koreans were not only quiet but had come back to the negotiating table. The Saudis and Israelis were tantalizingly close to delivering a peace deal for the ages. And if this weren't enough, the leader of the world's foremost state sponsor of terrorism was dead.

Yet the forty-seven-year-old U.S. national security advisor was not home with his wife and kids. He was stuck in his West Wing corner office, watching split-screen coverage of a Hezbollah missile barrage on northern Israel on one side and the president of Iran addressing his people on the other. The number of items on his to-do list was already more than he could count and growing by the minute. He knew he ought to be jotting down notes on the speech. And on the phone with Langley demanding an immediate assessment. And setting up a secure call between POTUS and the U.N. secretary-general. And coordinating talking points with Secretary Whitney, who would be wheels up to Riyadh by nightfall.

Yet McDermott found himself all but paralyzed with indecision on what to do next.

In every possible way, he was at the top of his game. He was happily married to a gorgeous and accomplished woman. He held an undergraduate degree in European history from Yale, an MBA from Wharton, and a master's in national security studies from Georgetown. He'd been a Wall Street whiz kid and made millions in the process. Now he was part of the inner circle of the world's most powerful man, working in the most prestigious real estate on the planet.

How was it possible he felt so powerless?

So much of his life had been consumed and shaped by war, and now, once again, war had come to rob, kill, and destroy. McDermott had started his military career near the bottom, a sergeant in the Twenty-Second Marine Expeditionary Unit. He'd wound up near the top, a colonel serving at the Pentagon. He'd been highly decorated during combat duty in Iraq and Afghanistan. It was in Kabul that he'd first met the men he'd come to dub "the Three Stooges"—Marcus Ryker, Peter Hwang, and Nicholas Vinetti—having been their commander in a unit known as the One-Six: First Battalion, Sixth Marines.

Serving as one of the few, the proud—like his father and brothers before him—had always been a dream of McDermott's. But somehow he had never imagined it coming at so heavy a price. How many hospitals had he been forced to visit because of combat injuries sustained by his Marine buddies? How many memorial services? How many grave sites? The losses continued to mount. Nick Vinetti was dead. Ryker and Hwang had been seriously wounded. Now Ryker had been taken captive. McDermott knew it was his responsibility, not just as NSA but as a friend, to get Ryker and his colleagues back. Yet he hadn't the foggiest notion of how.

The phone rang. It took several rings before McDermott snapped to and picked up. It was his executive assistant.

"Sir, I have Senator Dayton on line three. I told him that you could not be disturbed, but he—"

"No, no, that's fine," he said. "Put him through."

Yet McDermott was unprepared for the earful he was about to receive.

"Yes, Senator. I know, sir. . . . Yes, sir—mine, too. . . . Believe me, Senator, we're doing everything we possibly . . . Yes, of course, and I . . . Absolutely— I will, sir, and . . . Yes, Senator, I promise to call you the moment I hear anything—anything at all—on Marcus's whereabouts. . . . Yes, sir, and I'll be sure to let Annie know too."

★

HIGHWAY 50, MARYLAND

The silver Saab 9-5 Turbo raced across the Chesapeake Bay Bridge.

The windows were down, the sunroof was open, the Rolling Stones were blasting over the Bose speakers, and Pete Hwang was bound and determined to enjoy his first weekend off in months. With Annapolis in his rearview mirror, he checked his watch and the gas. Both were good. In another two hours and change, he would be parking at the yacht club, boarding the charter, and heading out into the Atlantic. It was just what the doctor had ordered.

Desperate to get away from Washington, Pete had not hesitated to say yes when several cardiologist buddies he had known for years had invited him for a bachelors' weekend in Ocean City. Like him, they were divorced, middle-aged, paying way too much alimony, and wondering how they had let the best years of their lives slip away. When they had promised him a weekend at a gorgeous beachside villa with a fully stocked bar and deep-sea fishing, he could hardly have said no.

The farther he drove beyond the Washington Beltway, the more the cares of the world seemed to lift off his shoulders. He loved the feel of the wind blowing through his hair. He loved the smell of the salt air and the chance to leave all the demands and pressures of his life at DSS well behind him. Though he was now fully healed from the rather serious wounds he had sustained in an operation in Tanch'ŏn, North Korea, Pete was grateful for a desk job. He did not want to be on the road or assigned to a protective detail.

When his cell phone rang, he glanced at the incoming number and recognized the government prefix immediately. Every muscle in his body tensed. He was tempted not to answer but reminded himself that he had taken an oath, and these days it was the one thing in his life he took seriously. He had disappointed too many people, his wife and children among them. He had no intention of shirking his duty to his country. So he took the call.

It was not, however, the DSS operations center in Arlington, Virginia. It was the seventh floor at Langley. On the line was the executive secretary to the director of the Central Intelligence Agency. The boss, she said, needed to see him, and no, it could not wait.

Pete hung up the phone. He exited at the next exchange, got back on Highway 50, and hit the accelerator, heading west.

50

HEZBOLLAH COMMAND BUNKER, BEIRUT, LEBANON

It was now the Sheikh's turn to go on live television.

Unlike the Iranian president, the leader of Hezbollah had never done this before. He disdained the media, preferring to operate in the shadows. It was not only safer, but he found it was far more effective. Yet now, one of his own men—an infidel worthy only of the fires of eternal damnation—had forced him into the klieg lights, and he was livid.

Worse, just moments before, his chief of counterintelligence, the estimable General Mubarak, had informed him that the commando team sent to capture al-Masri's family had come up empty. No one was in the flat, all the family's clothes were gone, and their safe had been cleared out. None of the neighbors had seen them leave or knew where they were. Apoplectic, the Sheikh had ordered Mubarak to check the manifests of every plane that had departed Beirut in the last week and find out where they had gone. But that search, too, had come up empty.

Ja'far ibn al-Hussaini was getting played by a shrewd operative. So far, Amin al-Masri was one step ahead of the organization that had trained and funded and nurtured him. It created a bloodlust in al-Hussaini that could not be quenched. For the moment, however, he had urgent and unpleasant business to focus on.

Grossly overweight, dressed in his trademark black robe and turban, and stroking his bushy gray beard, the spiritual leader of Hezbollah gritted his teeth as he stared through smudged spectacles and read from the teleprompter the text of the speech that had just arrived from Tehran.

"In the name of Allah, the All-Merciful, the All-Compassionate, praise be to the Lord of All Worlds, and peace be upon our Prophet, and upon the Promised One—Imam al-Mahdi—the Long-Awaited One, the Twelfth and Most Beloved Imam, and peace be upon his infallible household, upon his chosen companions, and upon all the prophets and messengers and martyrs who work tirelessly for the sake of building the glorious final Caliphate," al-Hussaini began his live broadcast on the Al-Sawt satellite television network.

"Dear brothers and sisters, today—the second of May—a great and glorious new battle has begun against the Zionist criminals and American crusaders," he continued. "And let me assure you, O loyal, steadfast, and brave warriors, this battle was spoken of long ago by our wise and holy prophets, peace be upon them. Make no mistake. This is no ordinary conflict. This battle was foretold in ages past. It is one that will most assuredly hasten the End of Days and the coming of the Promised One to rule and to reign from al-Quds, from a Palestine finally liberated and thoroughly cleansed from the cancerous tumor of the Zionist entity. And for this, we must give praise to Allah."

Al-Hussaini, sitting behind a wooden desk—the yellow flag of Hezbollah hanging as a backdrop—glanced down at the pages in his hands. Finding his place and making sure he was accurately transmitting every word, he adjusted his glasses, then looked back into the camera's lens.

"O warriors of jihad, remain ever faithful in your prayers," he continued. "Beseech Allah to destroy Israel—that wicked child of Satan—with all haste. Rejoice with me, for I can report that the Zionists are showing their weakness. In the face of our courage and overwhelming might, the filthy Jews have scampered back to their holes with their tails between their legs. They not only retreated. They were prepared to surrender. Why? Because these devils know whom we serve. They know we are the sons of the Twelfth Imam, children of the coming Caliphate—they know that we will eradicate Israel not only off the map but off the pages of history—and in this knowledge they shudder and rightfully so."

Al-Hussaini leaned forward in his chair.

"Now, with the entire Muslim world laughing at their cowardice, the Zionists are reentering the fight. Their soulless hordes are—right this moment, even as I speak—pouring over the border into the holy terrain of the proud and victorious Lebanese people. But fear not, little ones. There is no reason to worry. The Jews are being drawn into the trap we have carefully been setting for them for so long."

51

Al-Masri's men had been traumatized by the Iranian president's speech.

Yet after the shock of hearing that the Supreme Leader of the Shia world had died, they were electrified by the Sheikh's message, cheering every line he uttered.

Gathered in the courtyard under camouflage netting al-Masri had ordered them to hang to obscure themselves from the prying eyes of drones and satellites, the men huddled around a transistor radio as they drank coffee and slapped each other on the back, congratulating one another and reveling in their glorious success.

They still had no idea what they were really doing. Not a one of them could have conceived that the border raid they had executed that morning—and the war they had triggered with the Israelis—had actually been in direct defiance of the Sheikh and his patrons in Tehran. To a man, they were convinced that they were obeying the last dying wish of the Supreme Leader of the Islamic Republic. And the Sheikh's performance seemed to confirm that very point.

Al-Masri stood in the doorway to one of the abandoned bunkrooms. He enjoyed the sight of his men so deliriously happy. He enjoyed it almost as much as the sight of his three prisoners, chained to rusted flagpoles on the far end of the courtyard, bloodied and bruised and completely oblivious to what they were hearing on the radio.

Though he could never admit it to anyone, the Egyptian secretly wished he had thought of the whole thing himself. But the truth was it would never have occurred to him to give Hezbollah the credit for the operation. He certainly would never have thought of pretending to sell his hostages to the Sheikh, much less demanding the Sheikh broadcast his coup to the nation and the whole of the Islamic world. That had been pure Kairos from start to finish.

Al-Masri marveled at how effective the gambit had proven already. It was embarrassing the Little Satan, thus pouring gasoline on the war fires already raging with the Israelis. It was equally humiliating to the Great Satan, which had no idea what was really going on and was powerless to do anything about it anyway. And if any of his men had harbored the slightest doubts about why they were hiding out in an abandoned Hezbollah stronghold, not celebrating at Hezbollah headquarters in Beirut, the Sheikh's speech had erased them completely. Al-Hussaini was singing the praise of these very men before the entire world, gloating about their "great victory for Allah." Why would they have any reason to doubt him?

Still, al-Masri knew the truth. It was all a facade. In Beirut, the Sheikh knew the truth as well. At least he knew more of it than these men did. The Sheikh knew someone was playing him. He did not know who. He did not yet know why. And he was not going to take it lying down. Publicly he was playing along. Privately, however, al-Masri had no doubt the Sheikh was mobilizing his forty-five thousand Hezbollah fighters to hunt him down.

How long did he have to get these three Americans transferred out of the country and into the safekeeping of his Kairos patrons? Two days? Three? Certainly no more than a week, he calculated, and likely much less.

And then there was always the risk that one of his men had another mobile phone on him, one that he had not turned in, one that still gave him access to the outside world. Al-Masri was reasonably certain that wasn't the case, but he couldn't rule out the possibility. That would be a problem. A serious problem. These men were killers. That's what they'd been born to do. That's what they'd been trained to do. Al-Masri had trained them himself. But they didn't kill for just anyone. Certainly not for him. They killed for the Sheikh. They killed for Ja'far ibn al-Hussaini because they believed that al-Hussaini spoke for the Supreme Leader in Tehran, and the Supreme Leader—or whoever would soon replace him—spoke for God. Al-Masri's men listened to him because they believed he was the Sheikh's hand-chosen man to lead this unit. If they thought for a moment that he was leading them astray, that he was going rogue, they would not hesitate to slit his throat while he slept.

Such were the advantages, al-Masri mused, of men with no cell phones, no computers, and no Wi-Fi. No means whatsoever of communicating with the high command—or with anyone else in the world—except through him. For the moment, his men knew nothing but what he told them. It was critical that he keep it that way for as long as possible.

52

Annie Stewart closed the door behind her and tossed her keys on the counter.

With her boss out of town, she had enjoyed the rare opportunity to sleep in, have a late, lingering breakfast with her most nonpolitical of friends, and still get in her daily five-mile run through the nation's capital.

Annie adored Washington in the spring. The winter rains had passed. The trees and flowers were bursting with color. The world was quiet. And finally she was seeing someone romantically. It was all her girlfriends had wanted to talk about, and she had not minded a bit.

Still smiling, humming a little under her breath, Annie stepped into the washroom off the vestibule and turned on the faucet. After washing the perspiration from her hands, face, and arms, she removed her headband and pulled her hair back in a ponytail. Then she tossed both the towel and the headband into the laundry chute and headed to the living room. There, as was her habit, she scooped up the remote from the coffee table and clicked on the large flat-screen TV, which was set to CNN. Neither waiting nor caring to see what the headlines were, she turned on her heels and went into the kitchen, where she grabbed a cold bottle of water from the refrigerator.

By the time she returned to the living room, she was startled by the live image of the spiritual leader of Hezbollah speaking from some "undisclosed location." The Sheikh never did interviews. Or speeches. She could not think of a time he had ever previously addressed the Lebanese people.

Annie hadn't bothered to take her phone on her morning run. She certainly hadn't been listening to the radio. She'd simply been enjoying a much-needed day off from the intensity of life as a senior advisor to the ranking minority member on the Senate Intelligence Committee. She'd had no inkling that another war had broken out half a world away. Now she tried to make sense of Sheikh Ja'far ibn al-Hussaini's speech—being delivered in Arabic with simultaneous translation into English by a CNN translator—though it quickly became evident that she had already missed most of it.

". . . those who ought to tremble most are those who live and work and vainly try to run the world from Washington," the Shia cleric sneered. "To President Clarke—leader of the Great Satan—I warn: The day of your doom is fast approaching."

As Annie listened to the words, her eyes scanned the text scrolling across the bottom of the screen.

Israel invades Lebanon. . . . Lebanese president pleads for the world to come to his country's aid. . . . Kremlin denounces Israel's "unwarranted provocation." . . . Beijing urges U.N. to condemn Israel, impose "the harshest of sanctions." . . . Security Council to convene Monday in emergency session. . . .

Annie was astonished. She had lived and worked in Washington for nearly two decades. She had seen crises blow up out of nowhere. But this was unreal. When she had woken up that morning, the world seemed quiet. How had things gone so bad so quickly? She glanced at her watch. It was nearly noon. That made it almost seven in the evening in Beirut and almost 8:30 p.m. in Tehran.

"Judgment is coming, Mr. Clarke," said al-Hussaini, his eyes growing wild behind those thick lenses. "The Great Day of Judgment for you and your people is fast approaching. The stench of your corruption—so vile, so profane—has risen to the heavens. It has reached the nostrils of the Holy One. It has turned his stomach as it has turned ours. Do you think you can escape from the fires? Do you fancy you can somehow avoid the destruction that awaits you? Don't fool yourself. Our victory is certain, as is your utter and cataclysmic defeat."

Grabbing her mobile phone from its charging unit on the kitchen counter, she discovered she had thirteen missed messages. Nine were from her boss, Senator Robert Dayton, the Iowa Democrat. Annie winced. She had known the man since the day he had hired her fresh out of graduate school at Georgetown University's School of Foreign Service, where she had earned a master's in international relations. She didn't agree with the senator on every issue. Certainly not social and economic issues. But she deeply respected his patriotism and his commitment to U.S. national security. And she knew he was a man with a precious low tolerance for being unable to reach his staff.

She was just about to return the senator's calls when the Sheikh said something that stopped her cold.

"This morning, Mr. President, Allah delivered three of your cowardly fighters into our hands. All of them work for your State Department. All of them were captured along the border. They did not even resist my men. They surrendered instantly—weeping, bowing, crawling, begging for their lives. Today they are alive. But I will not guarantee they will be so for long. I told you, Mr. President. Judgment is coming. Once Allah delivers his decree, all three will be executed. One by one. Live on television, for all the world to see."

Annie knew instantly that Marcus was one of them. It wasn't instinct or intuition. Marcus had told her in confidence that he and Kailea were heading to Israel ahead of Secretary Whitney's visit. He'd said they would be doing an advance trip on the Lebanon border. It was all routine, Marcus had insisted. He'd be back in a few days. Still, he'd wanted her to know and asked her to pray for them. And she had.

The Sheikh then read out the names. Sure enough, the first was Special Agent Kailea Curtis.

Annie felt sick to her stomach. She knew Kailea. She liked and respected the woman. They had first met on Air Force One on the flight from Ben Gurion International back to Andrews after the peace summit in Jerusalem. That was nearly eighteen months ago. Since then, they had done countless things together, usually with Marcus, often with Pete Hwang, and sometimes with Geoff Stone. This could not be happening.

Annie braced herself for Marcus's name, but it never came. The next two names, in fact, she had never heard before, though al-Hussaini said that they, too, worked for the State Department's unit for the protection of diplomats.

Thomas Millner?

Daniel Case?

Who were they? Why had Annie never heard of them? And regardless, where was Marcus? If Kailea had been taken, why hadn't he? Had Marcus been killed in the raid? She was tempted to call Pete. He had to know what was going on. But she stopped herself, deciding it was more important for the moment to hear the rest of al-Hussaini's speech.

"President Clarke, I ask you: is there any price that you could possibly pay, any sacrifice that you could ever make, that would compel Allah—holy and righteous is he—to command me to release and return these three Americans to you and to their families?" the Sheikh taunted. "I cannot imagine so, but I will say this: if you choose to aid and abet the Zionist criminals— if you help the Jews shed a single drop of our blood or make even one of our warriors a martyr—then all hope for your people will be lost. And not only for these three, but for the entire American nation. Do not test us, Mr. President. We are ready to strike a lethal blow at the heart of your country. More than ready. We are hungry. Our mouths are watering."

Annie pulled up Pete's number on her iPhone and stared at it for several moments but then thought better of it. Instead, she speed-dialed the senator, who picked up on the second ring. "Where is he?" she asked, not mentioning Marcus's name or needing to.

"Annie, I'm sorry; I can't talk right now—not on an open line," Dayton replied. "I'm boarding a flight back to National. I'll call you when I land. We'll meet in my office, and I'll tell you what I know."

53

SOMEWHERE IN SOUTHERN LEBANON

The moment the broadcast ended, the prisoners were taken back to the freezer.

Kailea and Yigal were dragged, as they were barely able to stand. Marcus, on the other hand, was forced to walk on his own, the barrel of a Kalashnikov pressing into the small of his back. What surprised and somewhat confused him was that neither he nor his colleagues were blindfolded. The Hezbollah fighters were masked, as they had always been. Marcus had never once seen any of their faces, only the Egyptian's. Even now, al-Masri remained unmasked, eyeing them warily while standing in a doorway on the other side of the courtyard, somewhat aloof from his cheering and enthusiastic men.

Though Marcus had no idea why he had not been blindfolded, he had used every moment to absorb as much information as he could. For starters, the sun was setting. From the shadows, he guessed it was maybe seven or seven thirty. And given that al-Masri and his men were all wearing the same filthy uniforms they'd had on earlier and clearly had not taken showers, Marcus concluded that it was still the same day. From the palm trees surrounding the courtyard and the camouflage netting he noticed overhead, he decided they were still in Lebanon. The sounds of the gulls and the salt breezes meant they were near the coast. He could neither see nor hear any fighter jets or military activity of any kind, which suggested they had been moved well north of the Israeli border. But where?

From the courtyard, they were taken through what appeared to have once been a dormitory on the eastern side of the compound, through a dining hall filled with old wooden tables and chairs scattered across a floor covered with broken glass, and finally into a filthy and long-unused industrial kitchen. The freezer was located in the back. Marcus noticed two tall wooden stools—likely the perches of two of the three fighters who had just returned them to the freezer.

Once inside, they were again chained to the remains of the compressor unit. This time, the lights inside the freezer were shut off, and the door was slammed behind them. Marcus had noticed a padlock on the outside handle as they were being brought from the courtyard, and sure enough, he heard it being snapped back in place and double-checked to make certain it was truly secure. The three of them, however, were not sitting in pitch-darkness. Some light from the kitchen was seeping through the grid of the two exhaust fans.

For a long while, though all three of them were awake, no one spoke. They now knew there were at least two guards right outside the door, possibly three, and none of them wanted to risk drawing their attention or their ire.

Marcus used the time to chew on several things that were bothering him. The first was the fact that while he had recognized the voice of Sheikh Ja'far ibn al-Hussaini, he had not understood a word of what the man was saying. It had obviously electrified al-Masri's men. And Marcus had heard the Sheikh read the names of the three captives. But that was it. There were clues in that speech. There had to be. And it galled him not to know what they were.

There was something. Why were they being held in facilities that clearly had not been used in years? Why hadn't al-Masri taken them straight to

Beirut? Why hadn't they been handed over to Sheikh al-Hussaini and the Hezbollah leadership? Why hadn't they been paraded before the cameras to accompany what had to be the Sheikh's victory speech? Marcus was grateful they had not. The moment his face was seen on TV, it would not take long for Iranian and Hezbollah intelligence to figure out whom they had. So Marcus could only conclude that at this point they still did not know who he was. Or Yigal, for that matter.

But how much longer could that last? Would they not soon be heading for Beirut's Rafic Hariri International Airport? Would they not be loaded onto a plane bound for Tehran? Once there, he was a dead man.

In the silence, Marcus turned the questions over in his head again and again. Something was not adding up. Even if they were not being taken to Beirut, why hadn't al-Masri taken them to a legit Hezbollah base? Bringing them here, to facilities abandoned so long ago, made no sense.

And yet there was a reason, Marcus knew. There had to be. Al-Masri was evil, but he was not an idiot. He had just pulled off a daring border raid. He had taken three prisoners alive. He and his boss were utterly humiliating Washington and Jerusalem by telling the world they had captured three Americans—U.S. federal agents, no less—from Israeli soil. His men were well trained and highly disciplined. He was clearly a shrewd and skilled tactician. That meant he had a plan. So what was it? Marcus understood why al-Masri was hiding from the Israelis. But why did it seem like he was hiding from his fellow Hezbollah commanders as well?

54

"Hey," Yigal suddenly whispered.

Startled, both Marcus and Kailea turned toward him. Neither had heard the Israeli say anything since being taken prisoner. Marcus was not comfortable with him saying anything now, either. But Yigal motioned them to lean closer, and they both did.

"That speech," he said so quietly they barely could hear him. "That was the leader of Hezbollah."

"Yeah," Marcus whispered back. "We know."

"Know what he said?" Yigal asked.

They both shook their heads.

"You know, if you two plan on spending more time in the neighborhood, you really might considering learning some Arabic."

Yigal almost laughed at his own joke, then caught himself. Still, he smiled for the first time. His mouth was covered with blood, and two of his teeth were broken. Marcus recalled that Yigal had told them he was fluent in Arabic and French, as well as Hebrew and English.

In a voice barely above a whisper himself, Marcus cautioned the Israeli not to say more than he needed to as they could not afford to draw the attention of the guards.

The smile faded. A wave of annoyance washed over Yigal's countenance. Apparently he had things to say, and he was going to say them whether Marcus liked it or not.

Yigal made it clear that he had no intention of giving them a play-by-play of the speech. His point was simply that while Sheikh Ja'far ibn al-Hussaini had taken credit for their capture, Yigal wasn't buying it.

"Why not?" asked Kailea.

"Something's wrong," the Israeli whispered back. "There's no way this is a Hezbollah operation."

"What are you talking about?" she pressed. "You saw the guys out there. They were ecstatic when al-Hussaini spoke."

"That wasn't happiness; it was relief."

"Meaning what?"

"Look, the guards have no idea that I speak Arabic. Plus, they think I'm just a kid. So they've been talking, whispering—griping, really—around me from the moment they grabbed us. Okay, I've been unconscious at times, I admit. But not always. Mostly I'm just pretending to be out of it. And I hear things."

"What things?"

"They keep saying al-Masri is only the *deputy* commander of this unit, and that he's Egyptian, not Lebanese. They want to know where their commander is. *'Where's General Ali?'* they keep asking. *'When's General Ali coming back? Why would he not be here for such a critical mission?'* Then they ask why al-Masri ordered them to bring us here. Apparently we're on an old Hezbollah base along the coast, about ten klicks north of Tyre, that was abandoned after the 2006 war. They keep saying al-Masri should have taken them to Beirut by now. And there's something else."

"What?" Kailea asked.

"Al-Masri might be Egyptian, but his accent isn't."

"You're saying he didn't grow up in Lebanon? How in the world did he become a senior operative inside Hezbollah?"

"I'm sure he grew up here," Yigal clarified. "Most of the time he speaks Arabic with a colloquial Beiruti dialect. But I keep hearing him say words and phrases that are distinctively Libyan."

"How would you know?"

"Our family has lots of Libyan friends."

"Jews or Arabs?"

"Jews, but the dialects are the same," Yigal insisted. "When al-Masri curses—you know, when he goes on those tirades, those rants—he's often using language that's native to Libyan tribes, and not those along the border of Egypt, but those who live along the border of Algeria. And it's not just me. At least two of his men have picked up on it. I heard them talking about it. They were also complaining about al-Masri ordering them to hand in their mobile phones and not letting them be in touch with their families. They don't come right out and say it clearly, but they think something isn't right with this whole operation."

"You know, now that you say that, I heard some of them complaining about their cell phones too," Kailea added.

"Wait a minute," Yigal said. "When we were driving up to Haifa from the airport, you told me you don't speak Arabic."

"I don't."

"Then they were speaking English?"

"No, Russian—that's what really caught my attention."

"Russian?"

"Weird, huh?"

"Very."

Now Marcus asked a question for the first time. "Yigal, you said the men were relieved by the Sheikh's speech—what did you mean?"

"Like I said, all day I was picking up so much unease," Yigal explained. "Yes, when they heard the speech, they erupted in applause, but I was watching the men who had been guarding me. They were whooping and hollering, but they were also glancing at each other. It was subtle. Nonverbal. But it was like they were shrugging their shoulders and saying, *'Guess we were wrong.'*"

"Maybe they *were* wrong," said Kailea.

Yigal said nothing. But after a moment, Marcus did.

"No, they weren't wrong," he told them. "This can't be a Hezbollah operation. If it were, we wouldn't simply have been mentioned on that broadcast. The Sheikh would have paraded us out before the cameras."

"You think al-Masri has gone rogue?" Kailea asked.

"Yes, but not his men," Marcus replied.

"So who's al-Masri working for, if not the Sheikh?"

Marcus shook his head. "I don't know," he conceded. "But we'd better find out quick."

"And how exactly do you propose we do that?" Kailea asked, glancing down at their chains.

Again Marcus shook his head. "I have no idea."

55

Suddenly the freezer door burst open.

The chamber was flooded with light, making it impossible for Marcus to see what was happening. Someone began shouting commands, and Marcus soon found himself grabbed, blindfolded, unchained from the compressor, and shoved at gunpoint out of the freezer, then through the kitchen and the rest of the dormitory.

Though he had no idea where he was, it was clear that he was outside. The temperature had dropped a bit, and he could once again feel a breeze coming in off the Mediterranean and hear seagulls screeching overhead. He was chained to a metal pole—one of the flagpoles, he assumed—and smashed in the stomach with the butt of a rifle. Doubling over in pain, he fought to catch his breath, but a moment later, someone grabbed his hair, yanked his head back up, and slammed it against the pole. Then he felt the barrel of a pistol jammed into his left temple.

"You lied to me—*why?*" someone growled in his ear.

With a scarf or bandanna or kaffiyeh or whatever it was tied around his head and covering his eyes, Marcus couldn't see who it was. But he didn't need to. It was al-Masri, and the man was livid.

Marcus said nothing, still trying to assess what in the world was going on.

"You told me you worked for the State Department, but that was a lie, wasn't it?"

Marcus focused on breathing normally again.

"You don't work for DSS, do you, Mr. Millner?" al-Masri continued, pushing the barrel of the pistol deeper into Marcus's temple. "You work for the CIA."

Marcus was grateful his eyes were covered. There was no chance the Egyptian could see how stunned he felt. *The video.* Several hours earlier, al-Masri had forced Marcus at gunpoint to say his name, title, and badge number while being recorded on a smartphone. Marcus had fully expected him to send it to someone and have the image analyzed. He'd just hoped it would take longer—much longer—to come back with an answer.

"Tell me I'm right," al-Masri insisted.

Marcus refused.

"Admit it," al-Masri pressed. "Make a full confession and I will let you live. But if you continue to lie to me . . ."

Marcus heard the hammer being cocked. It wasn't an automatic pistol being held to his head. It was a revolver. Yet rather than feel his adrenaline spike and his heart rate soar, Marcus felt his breathing coming back. His pulse was slowing. The pain in his stomach was not subsiding, but he was slowly regaining control.

Why? he wondered.

Yes, he was ready to die. Not that he wanted to—not yet, anyway. There was too much to do, starting with rescuing his colleagues and getting them to safety. He still had no plan except one—resist, deflect, stall, and evade al-Masri's questions long enough to buy more time. How much time? He could not say. Whatever it took to give his country or the Israelis what they needed to come get them.

Yet that wasn't what was creating a calming effect, Marcus realized. As al-Masri's barrage of questions degenerated into another tirade, the answer came. The Egyptian was bluffing. If he knew Marcus was an officer with the Central Intelligence Agency, that information had to have come from Iran. Why, then, wasn't al-Masri asking him specific questions about the oil tanker, the East China Sea, the warheads, and the fate of Alireza al-Zanjani, the deputy commander of the Iranian Revolutionary Guard Corps?

Had there been enough time for someone to analyze that video and figure out who he was? Marcus had to say yes. But the more al-Masri demanded confirmation that he was with the CIA and not DSS, the more Marcus realized the man really did not know. Besides, al-Masri had just called him "Mr. Millner." If the Egyptian had known the truth about him, Marcus realized, then he would have known Marcus's real name.

Al-Masri was fishing, and Marcus wasn't going to bite.

"*Last chance,*" al-Masri shouted. "*Tell me what I want to know, or the boy is going to die.*"

Marcus had expected an ultimatum and was even prepared for it. He had not, however, expected the last six words. He was willing to give his own life for this cause. He could not bear the thought of sacrificing Yigal's. What a fool he had been not to have seen this coming. This was exactly how al-Masri had forced him to speak the first time—by threatening the life of the prime minister's nephew. Why would he not do it again?

"Mr. Millner, I'm going to start recording again," al-Masri explained. "Then I'm going to count to five. And if I don't hear a confession by the time I get there, I'm going to blow Mr. Case's head off and send that video to Al-Sawt to broadcast to the world. Are we clear?"

Marcus's jaw tightened. His stomach clenched. His wrists strained against the chains that had been wrapped so tightly around them that they were digging into his flesh and drawing blood. Suddenly the barrel of the revolver was removed from his temple, and Marcus could hear al-Masri's boots on the move.

"One," said the Egyptian from several yards away.

Marcus's thoughts reeled.

"Two."

Everyone broke. *Everyone.* Wasn't that what he had been taught? Wasn't that what he had taught so many others?

"Three."

Was this it? Marcus asked himself. Was this the point he had to give in? Or the line he had sworn not to cross?

"Four," al-Masri continued.

Marcus said nothing.

"Five."

There was a pause. Marcus did not use it. So al-Masri pulled the trigger and the explosion echoed throughout the camp.

56

"Thank you for coming in on such short notice."

CIA director Richard Stephens entered the conference room adjacent to his office and took his seat at the head of the table. Martha Dell, sitting to his right, slid him a three-ring binder containing bios, photographs, and service records for each person seated around the table. Stephens, however, never opened it. He knew them all and had hand-chosen them for this mission.

"I'm sure you're all wondering why you're here," Stephens continued. "Let me cut to the chase. We've got a new war underway that threatens to engulf the whole of the Middle East. We've got Americans held by enemy forces who show no desire for negotiations. And we have a commander in chief who has tasked this agency with getting them back—quickly and unharmed."

Stephens looked each man and woman in the eye.

"Over at the Pentagon, General Meyers and the other Joint Chiefs are developing options. But you know as well as I do that the United States is not about to invade Lebanon. We're not doing regime change. We're not engaging in a war of liberation. I see no scenario in which the Joint Chiefs are going to get the green light from the president for a military operation. That's why POTUS asked me to develop options for getting our people out quietly. Very quietly. No American fingerprints. No American casualties. That's why I've asked you to come in. If you sign on to this team, you'll have the full resources of the entirety of the American intelligence community. They won't know you're there, but trust me when I tell you they will be giving you their full support. Now let's get into some specifics."

Stephens directed their attention to wall monitors at the far end of the room. He put up a graphic that one of his analysts had made, comprising screen-captured images from CNN, MSNBC, Fox, BBC, Sky News, Al Jazeera, and Al-Sawt stating that Hezbollah had kidnapped three Americans.

"The first thing I need you to do is forget everything you've heard on the news," he explained. "We're not missing three Americans. That's fake news, though admittedly it's fake news of our own making. The truth is, two Americans and one Israeli have been captured, though for reasons you'll see very quickly, we want Hezbollah and the world to think that all the hostages are American."

Using a remote, Stephens put up a photo of the Israeli.

"As you heard in Sheikh al-Hussaini's speech, he stated that he is holding a DSS agent named Daniel Case. In fact, there is no such person. This is an alias. Unfortunately, it belongs to a young man named Yigal Mizrachi. In the briefing books that Dr. Dell is about to hand out, you'll get all the information you'll need on Mr. Mizrachi and our two Americans. But here's the thing you need to know right now. Mr. Mizrachi is the nephew of Israeli prime minister Reuven Eitan."

There were audible gasps around the room.

"Exactly—this is an incredibly dangerous situation whose implications go from very bad to very much worse if Hezbollah realizes who they have. The good news, however, is that we know several things from the Sheikh's speech. We know that Mr. Mizrachi is alive. We know he's successfully using the alias. We know his American colleagues are alive and backing up his story. And we know that neither the Sheikh nor his men realize that they have an Israeli, nor who he's related to. That's somewhat of a silver lining in an otherwise-horrific situation, though as we all know, it may not last. That's one of the reasons we need to move very, very quickly."

Stephens posted another photo on the screens.

"The one accurate thing the Sheikh said was that they are holding a DSS special agent named Kailea Curtis. Unfortunately, that is true. And she, like the others, needs not only the prayers of the American people but your best efforts to get her back. Now I need to draw your attention to the second American being held."

Everyone looked to the screens, but Stephens did not yet post a new picture.

"The Sheikh said he was holding another DSS special agent by the name of Thomas Millner. That is also fake news. There is no such person. Millner is a code name, another alias. Unfortunately, it's someone we all know."

Stephens punched a button, and a photo of Marcus Ryker went up on the screens. The director waited several moments for the nascent team to process the information.

"Again, the good news is that we can be certain Agent Ryker is alive and coherent, because he's using that alias. And Agent Curtis and Lieutenant Mizrachi are confirming to Hezbollah that that's his name. That's good. It buys us time, but again, not much. It's bad enough that Ryker and Curtis are being held by enemy combatants. But there's something else you need to know. We have reason to believe the Iranian Revolutionary Guard Corps has put a $10 million bounty on Ryker's head. The details are in the briefing book. The point is this: at the moment, neither Hezbollah nor the Iranians realize they have Ryker. If they did, they'd be using his real name. But again, whatever comfort that may give us, the clock is ticking. They're going to figure out who Ryker is and probably a lot faster than figuring out who Mizrachi is. That's why I need you people to go into harm's way, find these three, and bring them home. Before that, however, I'm sending you to Tel Aviv. A Gulfstream is fueling up at Andrews as we speak. You'll link up with Mossad director Asher Gilad and Shin Bet deputy director Tomer Ben Ami. They'll brief you on all the latest intelligence they have, including their interrogations of a Hezbollah operative they captured. But first I need to know, are you in or out?"

57

Stephens turned to his immediate left.

There sat Geoff Stone.

As a special agent with the Diplomatic Security Service and head of Meg Whitney's detail, Stone was supposed to be flying in a few hours with the secretary of state and her entourage to Riyadh, the first of eight Arab capitals they would be visiting in the next six days. Stephens had called him for two reasons.

First, he wanted someone from DSS who had combat experience. A Philly native, West Point grad, and Army Ranger, Stone had done multiple combat tours in both the Afghan and Iraqi theaters before leaving the service, joining DSS, and rapidly rising through the ranks. Stone had also been an intelligence specialist and was conversational, if not quite fluent, in Arabic.

Second, Stephens needed someone who knew Ryker and Curtis personally. Stone, now thirty-nine, fit the bill. He'd become acquainted with Marcus Ryker when Ryker was on the Presidential Protective Detail at the White

House and Stone was on the detail of a previous secretary of state. More recently, Stone had worked with Ryker and even more closely with Curtis in the run-up to the U.S.–Israeli–Saudi peace summit in Jerusalem. He knew their files. More importantly, he knew their faces.

"All in, sir," Stone said without hesitation.

"Good. And the secretary?

"You might want to give her a call, sir, but I think she'll be just fine without me."

"Fair enough." Stephens nodded and looked down the line.

Seated to Stone's left was Donny Callaghan. The former commander of SEAL Team Six, Callaghan was huge—six feet three inches tall and a muscular 220 pounds. He was also one of the best snipers in any branch of the U.S. Armed Services. Born and raised in south Boston, the son of a three-star Army general, he had closely cropped red hair and a bushy red beard, though both had been dyed black for this operation. He was married, had two young children, and had just celebrated his thirty-sixth birthday. For nearly the last two years following the operation in Tanch'ŏn, North Korea, where he'd first met Ryker, Callaghan had been detailed to the CIA, training young paramilitary operators by day and learning Arabic by night.

"It would be an honor, sir," Callaghan told the DCI.

"Good. Welcome aboard."

Stephens turned to his right. Sitting directly across from Callaghan was Noah Daniels. Now thirty-five, Daniels had ostensibly been working on the staff of the White House Communications Agency for the last four years, responsible for ensuring that the president and his senior aides had safe and secure phone lines and data links whether they were in the West Wing, the Residence, Air Force One, or on a road trip. In fact, however, he had always worked for the CIA, having first joined the Agency at the age of twenty-three after earning his bachelor's from MIT and both a master's and PhD from Stanford. Daniels was a whiz kid who still looked like he was in high school, but there was no system he couldn't hack or crash. What's more, he had known Ryker for years and had met Curtis in Jerusalem during the peace summit.

"Absolutely, sir—whatever you need," Daniels replied.

Only one person remained.

Sitting to the right of Daniels, this one had not been on Stephens's original list. It had been Dell's suggestion. Stephens had initially rejected it out of hand. Dell, however, had pressed hard. Eventually she had called in a favor from the national security advisor. Stephens had endured a lengthy and heated call with Bill McDermott, who had insisted that this person not only be on the team but lead it. McDermott had also made it clear that President Clarke wanted to see the person lead the team, as well, and Stephens had finally relented.

To say that the director of Central Intelligence was not happy about being overruled was to put it mildly. Yet he was nothing if not a master poker player and gave no hint to anyone in the room how much he had opposed this decision.

58

Jennifer Morris had once been a rising star in the Agency.

Now in her midthirties, she was ideal for this assignment.

On paper, at least.

A graduate of Cornell with an MBA from Wharton, Morris was fluent in Russian, Arabic, and Farsi. She had served in Army intelligence in Afghanistan and Iraq during the darkest days of the fighting, though she had never run across either Ryker or Stone back then. Upon Morris's return to the States, Martha Dell had personally recruited her to join the CIA and had overseen her training at the Farm. From there, Morris had been assigned to the Commerce Department. Her cover was that she was an economic attaché serving in U.S. embassies in some of the most sensitive countries in the world. In fact, she was a consummate Langley case officer—one of the most impressive Dell had ever seen—and had even been promoted to serve as the CIA's station chief in Moscow. She'd been the youngest station chief in the Agency's history before her ignominious fall from grace.

Morris had never met Kailea Curtis. But she certainly knew Marcus Ryker. And therein lay the problem.

It was Morris, after all, who had helped Ryker and a Kremlin mole known as the Raven pull off a daring escape from Russia. At the time, Morris had insisted she hadn't known the two men had just masterminded the assassination of the Russian president and the head of Russia's premier intelligence service. And in the subsequent lengthy investigation, both Ryker and the Raven had steadfastly backed her story, maintaining that they had never told Morris of their plans to take out the Russians but had simply employed her services to get out of the country. Given they had just prevented a NATO war with the Russian Federation, brought out of Moscow a treasure trove of the Kremlin's most closely guarded secrets, and gone on to defuse a crisis involving Iran and North Korean nuclear warheads, President Clarke had granted all three of them full pardons. He had secretly given the Raven political asylum in the U.S. and tasked him with assisting the CIA in making sense of all the computer files he had brought out with him. The president had also drafted Ryker into the employ of the Central Intelligence Agency, though his cover was that he worked for DSS.

Morris, however, had been left out in the cold. Though she had been seriously wounded in the Russia operations—and in fact had nearly died—when she finally came back to Washington, Stephens made certain she was assigned to a desk job at the Commerce Department, had absolutely no contact with either Ryker or the Raven, and would never set foot in CIA headquarters again. The reason was simple. She had lost Stephens's trust. Unlike Ryker, she had not developed a personal relationship with President Clarke. Dell had gone to bat for her, but none of her entreaties had worked. Stephens couldn't stand Ryker, had little use for the Raven, and utterly disagreed with Clarke's decisions with regard to all of them. Jenny Morris was the only one whose fate Stephens controlled. Thus, her banishment from all contact with Langley.

Until today.

★

All eyes were on her, waiting for her answer.

The ones that most interested her, however, were Stephens's.

Jenny Morris knew he didn't want her there. One didn't come in from the cold only to be tasked with an operation this sensitive and this complex. Dell had to have advocated for her, she concluded. But if Dell's opinion had been sufficient, she would have been welcomed back into Langley long before now.

Jenny stared into the eyes of the director. She had made her peace with her banishment. It was unfair, but so what? That was life. She wasn't going to complain and moan about it. Fully healed of her wounds and in peak physical fitness—she'd run both the Boston and New York marathons in recent months—she went into the Commerce Department every day and did her job, mind-numbingly boring though it was. She was not campaigning to come back. She had not called in favors or cajoled her network of heavy hitters. She had been tempted to in the beginning but concluded it was not worth it. She knew what she had done. She knew she had been right. If Stephens didn't like it, that was tough.

The look in the director's eyes was almost certainly imperceptible to the others. But she saw it. The disdain. The contempt. It was almost as if he wanted her to say no. To make a scene. To storm out. Anything but say yes.

So she smiled. "How soon do we leave?"

59

The silver Saab 9-5 Turbo roared up to the guard post.

Screeching to a halt, Peter Hwang showed his ID to the guards, ignoring their admonition not to drive so fast on Agency property. He had no idea why he had been summoned. All he'd been told was that it was an emergency.

Pete cursed under his breath and tapped his right palm on the stick shift as he waited for the steel barriers to be lowered and the gate to be raised. It seemed to take forever, but when the way was finally clear, he hit the accelerator. By the time he had found a place to park and cleared an extension security check, it was nearly 1:30 p.m.

8:30 p.m. in Jerusalem and Beirut.

10 p.m. in Tehran.

The armed female security officer who apparently had been assigned to wait for him gave him a once-over but said nothing about the Bermuda shorts, polo shirt, and penny loafers he was wearing. It was hardly the dress code for someone heading to the seventh floor. But Pete could not have cared less. He had not planned on being here nor wanted to come.

The officer escorted him to a bank of elevators and rode up with him in silence. Once the door reopened, he was handed over to two armed officers, both men this time, who guided him through yet another layer of security. Finally he was ushered into the director's spacious corner office.

Despite having been in the employ of the CIA for the better part of eighteen months, Pete had only been to the seventh floor once before, though never to Stephens's office. Indeed, he had only met the man once and had not particularly cared to do so again. On the other hand, the director was one of only a handful of people on the planet who knew that he worked for the Agency. And ultimately the man was his boss.

Stephens was on a call, so Pete stood there awkwardly, waiting for the director to acknowledge him. He had not been told the reason for his summons to Langley. Nor had he listened to anything but the Stones on the way back from Annapolis. So only when he glanced at the four television monitors on the far wall did he learn for the first time that the Supreme Leader of Iran had died and that a serious battle was underway on the Israel-Lebanon border.

★

MONUMENT, COLORADO

Marjorie Ryker had just finished her daily two-mile walk when her phone rang.

Stepping up onto her front porch, she took a seat in her favorite rocking chair looking out over her beloved Rocky Mountains, wiped her brow with a handkerchief, and looked at her phone. The number was blocked. Probably a sales call, she thought, and on a beautiful Saturday at that. *Didn't these people have anything better to do?* She answered and was about to scold whoever was interrupting her day when she heard a familiar voice.

"Hello, Marj? It's me."

"Maya?"

"Yeah."

"Maya Emerson?"

"Do you know another Maya?"

Marjorie could not help but laugh. "Not at all; I just can't remember the last time I heard from you."

"Well, I'm sorry about that. Got myself in a terrible funk after Carter passed. Stopped talkin' to most people. And was just plain mean to the rest. Includin' your son. Which is why I'm callin' now."

"Well, don't you worry about that. It was a loss no one should have to go through. And believe me, Maya, I've never stopped praying for you. You were there when Marcus was in trouble, and I know—"

But Maya suddenly interrupted. "Marj, are you not watching the news?"

"No, I've been out for a walk. Marcus told me I need to do a better job taking care of myself, so I started a daily constitutional and—"

"Listen to me," Maya said, interrupting again. "Go turn on the news."

"Why? What is it?"

"Wasn't Marcus supposed to be in Israel this weekend?"

"Yeah, but . . . how did you know about that?"

"Never you mind that."

"Maya, what's going on?"

"Somethin' terrible has happened on the border. I've got an awful feelin' that boy of yours is right in the middle of it. And I just thought I'd better stop everythin' and call you and pray together."

★

LANGLEY, VIRGINIA

Martha Dell entered from a side door.

"How's the arm?" she whispered as she motioned for Pete to take a seat at a small, round conference table near the windows.

"Fine," said Pete, in no mood for small talk.

Stephens ended his call, took off his headset, and tossed it on his desk. Then he put on his reading glasses and opened a folder while Dell sipped piping hot coffee from a CIA mug.

"Dr. Hwang," Stephens began as he scanned the file. "We haven't had much time to get to know each other since you came aboard."

"None, actually," Pete replied in a tone so cold that Dell looked up from her notebook as Stephens looked up from the file.

The two men stared at each other for several moments.

"Do you have something you need to tell me, Dr. Hwang?" Stephens asked.

"No, sir."

"Are you under the impression that the director of Central Intelligence has the time to hang out and befriend each of the twenty-one-thousand-plus employees in his charge?"

"Not at all."

"Or maybe you think you and your buddy Mr. Ryker are special," Stephens continued, "or that you two deserve VIP treatment."

"No, sir."

Stephens removed his reading glasses before continuing. "Tell me, Dr. Hwang, why does a renowned cardiologist with no previous experience in espionage give up a lucrative practice to join the CIA?"

"Sir?"

"What are you doing here, son?"

"I was summoned."

"What I mean is, why are you working for us—for me?"

"There are days I wonder about that myself, sir."

"I ask, Dr. Hwang, because not so very many years ago, you were making a seven-figure salary and living in Manhattan. Now you're making, what, ninety thousand and change, and living in an efficiency apartment in Anacostia. So I can't help but be curious—why is that?"

"Are you kidding?" Pete deadpanned. "Who wouldn't give up a once-in-a-lifetime opportunity to save lives in order to kill people and steal things?"

60

The tension in the room was palpable.

Martha Dell wondered when Stephens was going to get to the point.

Suddenly Pete Hwang stood up, walked over to the windows, and gazed out over the forest that enveloped the CIA campus.

"Tanch'ŏn was the only mission you've been part of, and frankly, that was a disaster," Stephens continued, clearly unamused. "You guys didn't get the files. Didn't get the mole. And lost good men, including Nicholas Vinetti, who I understand was one of your closest friends going back to your first days with the Corps. On top of that, you were injured. Rather seriously. Multiple surgeries. Now you're confined to a desk job. Hardly seems worth it. Or am I missing something?"

"I'm not sure what you want me to say, sir."

"Tell me the truth, Doctor—why are you here?"

There was a long pause. "You've got the whole story in that file, sir. I'm not sure what I can add."

"Context."

"Sir?"

"You heard me, Dr. Hwang—I'd like some context."

"Context?"

"Yes."

"What kind of—?"

Dell watched Pete stop himself midsentence. Then he looked at her and back at the director.

"What can I tell you, sir?" he said. "I've always been a patriot."

"Meaning what, exactly?"

"My parents came to this country from Korea. They arrived just after the war. I had the privilege of being born here, and I love this country, sir. It's given me everything. When we were attacked on 9/11, I decided to join the Armed Forces. Ended up becoming a Fleet Marine Force Navy Corpsman embedded with a Marine unit. The Navy eventually sent me to medical school. I became a surgeon. Once I'd paid my dues, I mustered out and tried my hand in the private sector."

"Where you did quite well."

"Professionally, perhaps," Pete conceded.

"Not personally?"

Dell noticed Pete stiffen.

"Let's just say my life with the girl next door didn't exactly go as I'd hoped."

"I understand your ex-wife had an affair with one of the partners in your medical practice."

Pete winced, and Dell could see the immense effort he was making to stay calm.

"She did, sir."

"And cleared you out."

"Yes, sir. Took everything, including my kids."

"I'm sorry about that."

"How did Hobbes put it, sir? Life is nasty, brutish, and short."

"So you packed up and moved to D.C." It was not a question.

"Senator Dayton's an old friend, sir," Pete replied. "He called and offered me a position doing domestic policy for his PAC. Sounded like interesting work. A chance to start over. Plus, there was a beautiful girl who worked on his staff. So I figured, why not?"

"Then everything went sideways."

Pete said nothing as Dell continued to study him intently.

"Ryker got in trouble," Stephens continued. "Asked you for help. You agreed, and the rest is history."

"Not to mention the girl wasn't exactly interested," Pete added.

"Sorry to hear that."

"Par for the course apparently."

Stephens took a sip of coffee as he measured his next words. "Look, Dr. Hwang, I'm sympathetic to the curveballs you've been thrown. Truly I am. But right now, I need a little less attitude and a little more team spirit. Understood?"

"This thing on the Israeli-Lebanese border?" Pete asked.

"It's bad," Stephens said, getting up, coming around his desk, and pulling up a chair at the conference table. "I'm sorry to have to tell you this, but Marcus Ryker and two of his colleagues have been taken hostage."

Pete looked stunned. "Where? How?"

Stephens glanced at Dell.

"As you know, they were doing a recon trip along the border," said the DDI.

"Advance for Secretary Whitney."

"Exactly. And there was an ambush," Dell said. "Ryker and his team fought back valiantly. But they were overrun, seized, and taken deep into Lebanon."

"Agent Curtis too?"

"Yes, and an Israeli as well."

"Who?"

"I can't say," she replied.

"Why not?"

"It's classified."

"I'm cleared."

"Not for that," said Stephens. "We've told you what we can for now, but I asked you to come in because we need your help."

"Of course," Pete said. "Anything."

"Good. For starters, we need you to contact Ryker's mom. POTUS wants someone who knows the family well. McDermott recommended you."

"Done," said Pete. "Just let me know what I'm allowed to tell her, and I'll fly out there immediately."

Stephens shook his head. "That won't be necessary. A call will suffice for the moment, because there's something else we need from you."

"Name it."

"I'm assembling a crisis management team, and I want you on it. You know Ryker better than any of us. We need to know how he's going to react, how he's going to handle himself under tremendous pressure, how long he might be able to go before giving up highly classified information, etc. And you know his family better than any of us too. We need to know how they're going to react, how best to take care of them, and how to keep them quiet. We absolutely cannot afford them going to the media. Hezbollah doesn't know they have Ryker. He's operating under an alias, but one comment to the press, and this thing is going to go from bad to terrible in no time flat. I don't have to tell you, Dr. Hwang, how badly the Iranians would love to get their hands on your friend. It's your job to help us make sure that never happens. So can we count on your help?"

"It would be my honor, sir."

61

SOUTHERN LEBANON—MAY 3

It was pitch-black when Amin al-Masri awoke with a start.

He grabbed the pistol from under his pillow and scanned the office that was doubling as his bedroom. He saw nothing amiss, so he got up and moved to the hole in the wall that was once a window. Peering into the moonlight, he saw no people, no movement, no obvious cause for alarm. Yet his instincts warned him something was wrong, so he stood there listening, straining to hear even the slightest sound beyond the waves and the gulls. The Egyptian waited for two minutes. Then five. After ten minutes had elapsed, he began to breathe easily again. He was not often wrong about these things. Maybe he was this time.

It was only 4:42 in the morning. The sun would not be up for another hour. But al-Masri could not sleep. He checked his satellite phone but found no text messages from his Kairos contact. He was awaiting instructions on when and how to transfer the prisoners, yet these had not yet come.

Snagging one of the bottles of water on the floor beside him, he poured some into his hands to wash them and his face. Then he grabbed his backpack, pulled out an electric razor, and proceeded to shave his head. It was time to change his look.

When he was finished with the razor, he finally stripped off the filthy T-shirt, undershorts, and military fatigues he had been wearing since the raid and tossed them aside. Next he pulled a fresh shirt from his pack and put it on. No longer could he wear a pair of Hezbollah-issued fatigues. It was time to look like a civilian—a local, in fact—so he put on a pair of faded, ripped blue jeans instead. His watch, too, he removed and tossed onto the pile of other clothes. It had been a gift from the commander of the Radwan Unit and was engraved on the back with a verse from the Qur'an. It was not something any of the farmers who lived in Lebanon's southern tier would own, much less wear. Like the rest of his past, it had to go.

Just before five, al-Masri reached into his backpack and took out the small, battery-operated transistor radio they had used the night before to listen to the Sheikh's speech as well as the one a bit earlier by the Iranian president announcing the death of the Supreme Leader. Turning on the power but keeping the volume low, he tuned to Al-Nour, the official radio station of Hezbollah, broadcasting from Beirut. At the top of the hour, the newscaster went on at length about the dramatic capture of "three American spies," giving their names and explaining their jobs with the Diplomatic Security Service and what the DSS was in the first place. Most of the details were completely made up, including biographical details of the three that al-Masri had never heard and was almost certain weren't true. The rest of the newscast was also pure propaganda, denouncing the "criminal Zionists" in Israel and making it sound as if the Jews had started the war. The announcer provided a litany of quotes from foreign governments from Ramallah to Moscow and from Beijing to Tehran condemning Israel and calling for the U.N. Security Council to impose "the most punitive sanctions possible."

There was no mention, of course, of the fact that the Sheikh had no idea where the three Americans were located. Nor, to al-Masri's relief, was there any mention of a nationwide manhunt for rogue elements who had conducted the border raid without authorization. The reason was simple. The Sheikh wanted credit for the attack instead of looking like the feckless, cowardly moron that he really was. Yet al-Masri had no doubt: the manhunt was underway, and he had become Hezbollah's highest-value target.

Al-Masri's thoughts were suddenly interrupted by the roar of two approaching Israeli fighter jets. Grabbing his AK-47, al-Masri raced out of his office and into the courtyard, startling the men on the night watch. He leaped onto a table, then onto the roof of a storage shed, and looked over the stone wall surrounding the compound and out toward the sea. The sun was just coming up behind him. He saw nothing. Turning south, he saw nothing there either. They were F-35s, he concluded. They had to be. Stealth fighters. The most advanced aircraft in the Zionists' arsenal.

Just then, a series of massive explosions erupted behind him. The ground shook. Night turned to day. Al-Masri whipped around as the rest of his men poured out of the bunks, weapons at the ready. The Egyptian stared north. His eyes narrowed as one fireball after another blazed across the horizon.

He knew instantly what the Zionists had hit. It was a fuel depot on the banks of the Litani River, not three kilometers away.

The men scrambled to the roofs of the buildings.

They all had to see the inferno for themselves.

As they did, al-Masri began to recalculate. He had planned to stay here for at least two more days or until he received instructions from Kairos. No one could have known or suspected they were there. He had personally stocked the camp and stocked it well. The men had food, water, medical supplies, and plenty of ammo. What they did not have was any way to communicate with the rest of Lebanon or the world beyond.

But the bombings changed everything. The Zionists were getting too close. Their drones and satellites would start doing damage assessments of the fuel depot in the hours ahead. If they widened their search, there was a real possibility someone's eye would be drawn to this supposedly abandoned Hezbollah camp. Al-Masri had ordered his men not to light fires or even use flashlights outdoors. Nothing to signal to the prying eyes of the world's intelligence communities that the camp was once again active. So far, he was confident they had followed his orders. But they still needed to move.

"*Get down,*" he shouted. "*Everyone down—off the roofs.*"

Al-Masri was the first to climb back down to the ground. The others quickly followed. He gathered them in the courtyard, under the camouflage netting.

"Men, it's time—we're going to Beirut," he told them. "Ali—you, Daoud, and Ismail will take the truck. Zayan and I will take the car. We will divide up the prisoners between us. Abdel, you are in charge of the remaining team. You will stay here and load up the vans with the rest of our equipment, ammo, and supplies. Wipe everything down. Make certain we have left no trace that we have ever been here. And wait until I call you and tell you it is safe to begin traveling. Am I clear?"

Al-Masri then surprised the young fighter by pulling from his pocket the man's mobile phone.

"You must make no calls nor take any except mine," the Egyptian instructed. "In fact, Abdel, I want you to put it in your pocket. Don't even take it out—for any reason—until you hear my ringtone. You must resist all temptation. Our lives depend upon it. Do you understand?"

The young man nodded.

"Do I have your word, Abdel?"

"You do indeed, Colonel."

Al-Masri stared him in the eye as everyone else looked on. Then he handed the young man the phone and watched as he shoved it into his pocket. The young man smiled, evidently proud that he had been entrusted with a position of leadership. He had no idea that the phone had no SIM card in it and thus could neither send nor receive any calls or text messages.

Al-Masri now lowered his voice and motioned his men to come in closer.

"Men, you have all performed with great courage and skill, and I am proud to call you jihadists. But make no mistake. You must not lower your guard now. The Zionists are invading our beloved Lebanon from the south. And we will face other threats as we move north. Our mission is to deliver these prisoners safely to Sheikh al-Hussaini. When we do, as I promised from the beginning, each of you will earn a significant cash reward. *Very* significant. Unfortunately, all of our brothers in arms throughout the country know that three Americans have been captured. Most of them are honest men and loyal to the Sheikh and would do everything in their power to assist in getting these prisoners to him without delay. But there are no doubt some who would wish us ill. They would not hesitate to strip the Americans from us and claim the credit and the reward for themselves. So we must be on our guard. Until we reach the Sheikh, we must take special precautions not to let anyone know that we are transporting the Americans. We must not even let anyone know that we are fighters with Hezbollah, much less part of the Radwan Unit. Our movement northward toward the capital would draw too much suspicion and put our mission and even our lives in jeopardy. No uniforms. Casual clothes only. Nothing flashy. Nothing that stands out. Personal IDs only. Destroy anything else. And no heavy weapons. You'll get what you need in Beirut. Handguns only, for personal protection. Am I clear?"

"Yes," they said in unison.

"*Am I clear?*"

"*Yes, sir,*" they replied, snapping to attention and saluting their leader.

"Good. Now get the vehicles and make the prisoners ready to move. Zayan, we're leaving in ten minutes."

63

Marcus had been badly shaken by the events of the previous night.

Rarely did he second-guess himself on an operation. Casualties happened. Nobody liked it. But you dealt with it and moved on. Becoming paralyzed by regret wasn't part of the warrior's code. It dulled one's senses. It slowed one's reflexes. It could get a man killed.

Still, Yigal Mizrachi was not just the beloved nephew of the prime minister of a key American ally. He was a member of Marcus's team. It had been Marcus's responsibility to keep the kid safe, and he had failed. Not that he could see how admitting to being an officer of the Central Intelligence Agency would have saved Yigal's life.

Marcus had certainly had plenty of time and quiet to think. After his interrogation and Yigal's summary execution, al-Masri's men had not taken him back to the freezer. Instead, they had taken him to the Egyptian's makeshift office and locked him in a latrine. Given the wretched stench, he had been awake much of the night, replaying the event from every possible angle.

Still, he had not come up with a way he could have handled things differently. The writings of Solomon echoed in his head. There was a time to be born. And a time to die. Apparently it had just been Yigal's time.

Now, it seemed, it was his.

Someone ripped open the door of the latrine. Three enormous men grabbed him, dragged him into the office, and forced him to the floor, on his stomach, facedown. Then, with the barrel of an automatic rifle jammed in the small of his back, they removed his manacles, pulled his hands behind his back, and wrapped them together with so much duct tape that he could not move them at all. After this, they wrapped his feet together with duct tape as well. Al-Masri barked an order in Arabic. The man named Zayan pulled a plastic case from his pocket. He proceeded to remove a syringe, then stuck the needle into a small vial of liquid and drew the plunger back. He squirted some of the liquid out of the needle and tapped the syringe several times, presumably to remove any air bubbles.

Wonderful, Marcus thought. *The Egyptian plans to put me down—but doesn't want me to die of an embolism.*

There was no way Marcus was going to take this without a fight. He struggled with the men to wrest himself free. Zayan tried to jab him in the neck, yet at the last moment Marcus shifted his position just enough that the needle missed its mark, scraping the edge of his neck. Al-Masri let fly a torrent of what had to be Arabic obscenities, then slammed his boot down on Marcus's head, preventing him from moving any further. This time Zayan found what he was looking for. He drove the needle into a vein in Marcus's neck and injected him with some sort of narcotic. Marcus could feel something oozing down his neck. He was not sure if it was blood or some of the agent meant to put him to sleep. Probably both, he figured. He certainly hoped so. That had, after all, been his objective. There was at least a chance now, however slim, that he would be waking up again before they intended him to.

As the men pulled him back to his feet, Marcus felt his body go limp. Whatever they had just given him, it was working faster than he had expected.

★

"Bring up the cars," al-Masri ordered. "I'll be right there."

Zayan and others dragged Marcus out of the office, and for a moment, the Egyptian was alone. He lit a cigarette, probably the last he would enjoy for a good while. Then he used his lighter to set his pile of dirty clothes—and the hair he had shaved from his head—on fire. It was, of course, a violation of the orders he had given his men. But the fire was small, and he could not afford to leave a trail behind him. The hardest part was watching the flames melt the watch. Yet he consoled himself with the knowledge that the money Kairos was paying him would cover a hundred others to replace it.

He checked his satellite phone but still found no text messages from Kairos. So he stood there for several minutes, staring into the flames. Then, hearing Zayan call for him, he took one last drag on his cigarette, tossed the butt into the flames, and stamped out the fire with his boot, taking special care to crush every ember. Next he finally transmitted the proof-of-life video to the secure email account the aide at Hezbollah's headquarters had given him.

There was only one more thing to do. He opened the desk drawer, reached inside, and found the mobile phone belonging to his brother Tanzeel. Reinserting the SIM card, he powered up the phone, tossed it back into the drawer, and headed to the courtyard. The "homing beacon" was on. It was now just a matter of time.

64

They dragged Marcus into the courtyard as a taxicab arrived in a cloud of dust.

It was old and rusted and yellow—a Mercedes-Benz circa the early 1980s. Marcus was confused for a moment, yet when he saw the Egyptian's assistant, Zayan, at the wheel, he realized they had not actually called for a cab. It had to be a ruse, some part of al-Masri's plan for transporting his prisoners to Beirut. For some bizarre reason, the backseat was packed to the roof with crates full of fruit—watermelons, as best Marcus could tell from this distance—but he could not imagine why. There was certainly no room left in the backseat for him. Yet these thoughts, along with his vision, were growing more and more fuzzy by the minute.

Suddenly a truck roared up and screeched to a halt a few yards from the cab. It was a modified pickup and reminded Marcus, even in his haze, of an old army jeep from the Korean or Vietnam Wars—something they might have used in the *M*A*S*H* reruns he'd seen on TV—with ratty, frayed green canvas tarps covering the sides and top of the truck bed. Stacked all around were dozens more crates of fruit. Watermelons for sure. Something else green—apples, perhaps. And something yellowy-orange—kumquats or loquats or some such things.

Zayan got out of the taxi, came around to the back, and unlocked and opened the trunk. Now things made more sense, as Marcus found himself being picked up and shoved inside the trunk and pushed as far to the back as possible. Zayan and his men then began loading several boxes of fruit in front of him and around him, filling what little space was left. As they did, Marcus caught a glimpse of Kailea and . . . Yigal? It was brief and hazy, but both were being led into the courtyard. Both were being forced to lie down on their stomachs and given shots of something.

Marcus wondered if he was hallucinating. Was that really Yigal? Was he really alive? How was that possible? Hadn't—?

And then Zayan slammed the trunk shut, and everything went dark.

★

Kailea couldn't believe her eyes.

As she was dragged across the courtyard, she caught a glimpse of Marcus being shoved into the trunk of a cab. Though it was only for an instant, Kailea had no doubt it was him. That stupid mustache and beard were the giveaways. Marcus had begun growing them several months earlier, presumably to cover up the scars on his neck and face—scars he had sustained in Jerusalem and the East China Sea. Yet the beard looked ridiculous. She had mocked him mercilessly for it. So had Pete, Geoff Stone, and the others at DSS. Nevertheless, the more they had teased him, the more stubbornly he had refused to shave it off. And now . . .

She was forced to the ground. Then someone jabbed her in the neck with a hypodermic needle. She winced in pain as she watched al-Masri's aide slam the trunk shut. She watched the man double-check it, making sure it was really closed and locked, just as al-Masri came out of one of the buildings on the far side of the courtyard. He shouted some orders and got into the front passenger seat of the taxi.

Kailea could barely process what she had seen. *Was Marcus really still alive? How was that possible?* Even from the confines of the freezer, she and Yigal had heard the gunshot. Marcus had never been brought back to them. She had, therefore, assumed—they both had—that the Egyptian had shot and killed Marcus, and for the rest of the night, Kailea had barely slept, grieving his death and beginning to lose all hope that either she or Yigal would ever get out of this thing alive. She had never been so relieved to be wrong.

Why, then, the gunshot? Kailea wondered as the world began to spin. Her vision was blurring. She attempted to speak to Yigal but could not. Still, she racked her increasingly fuzzy brain to figure out what was happening. *If Marcus had not been killed, who had been? Who was missing?* She tried to take a new count of al-Masri's team. Yesterday she had counted fourteen. Now, however, too many people were moving in too many directions.

And then she blacked out.

65

Zayan thought they were moving fast, but apparently not fast enough for the colonel.

"*Yalla, yalla—let's go, let's go,*" al-Masri shouted through the window of the cab.

Zayan cursed the team and demanded that they pick up the pace.

Having drugged both remaining prisoners, they gagged them, removed their manacles, and bound their hands and feet with duct tape. They lifted Kailea's limp body, set her into a large wooden shipping crate, and covered her with hundreds of the sour green plums known as *jenericks* that were presently being harvested all over southern Lebanon. When she was completely covered and not visible at all, Zayan ordered that they close the crate and nail the top down tightly. This they did. With the help of six men, they lifted the crate and shoved it into the back of the truck. After they had done the same with Yigal, they filled the rest of the truck bed with the remaining crates of fruit, then closed and locked the back hatch and made sure all the tarps were tied down and secure.

Armed guards now unlocked and opened the steel gates at the back of the compound, and the two-vehicle convoy began to roll.

At al-Masri's insistence, the truck took the lead. They traveled together at first, taking the coastal road—Highway 51—the north-south thorough-fare that was the most direct route to Beirut. On a normal day, the eighty-kilometer journey should only take an hour and a quarter, if that. This, however, was no normal day. With Israeli air strikes ongoing and buildings burning all around them, al-Masri knew there would be checkpoints—lots of them—some manned by the Lebanon regular army, others by Hezbollah fighters.

Zayan anticipated that the first would be at the crossing of the Litani River, and sure enough, the Egyptian ordered him to get off 51 as they approached the town of Mazraat Bsaileh. Zayan protested, noting that the truck was continuing onward without them, but al-Masri insisted.

"Silence," he ordered. "Turn now and stay sharp."

Confused, the young man nevertheless did as he was told. They were doubling back, headed south-southeast. They passed a restaurant and a mosque, then came to the town of Ain Abou Abdullah. There, al-Masri ordered Zayan to take a left. Now they were heading north again, on a road that ran parallel to 51.

"Get off up there, on the right," al-Masri said.

Zayan did, turning into the nearly empty parking lot of a small coffee shop known as Café bo Abboud.

"Turn off the engine," al-Masri instructed.

Even more perplexed since they had just gotten on the road, Zayan hesi-tated. Finally, however, he shut down the engine and watched in astonish-ment as al-Masri got out of the vehicle and began to stretch as though they had been on a long journey.

"Come," said the deputy commander. "You must be hungry."

Zayan stared at the man for a moment and was struck by several things. First, it was strange to see al-Masri not wearing a uniform. Zayan had known the man for almost three years and had never seen him in civilian clothes. Now he was wearing jeans and a white T-shirt that was clean though badly wrinkled. Second, Zayan had never seen the man wearing anything but a maroon beret on his head. This morning al-Masri was wearing a dirty green army cap that looked like something Castro or Che Guevara would have worn. When he removed it and tossed it back into the car, Zayan realized that his boss had shaved his head that morning. Gone was his thick black hair. The man was completely bald.

Zayan pulled the keys out of the ignition and looked back at the trunk but thought better of saying anything. He followed al-Masri inside. Three elderly men sat in a booth near the front, drinking coffee, reading newspapers, and talking in hushed tones, no doubt discussing the new war they found themselves in. A veiled older woman, probably in her sixties and most likely the wife of the owner, led them to a table by the back windows, overlooking the river. She gave them menus and promised to return in a moment.

On al-Masri's insistence, Zayan switched places with him. By the time the waitress returned, Zayan was gazing back at the entrance to the restaurant, the old men, and the windows looking out to the car. The Egyptian had a clear view of the river, and with it both the bridge and the checkpoint.

66

Pete sat alone in the office.

Staring at the phone, he still could not believe this was happening. He and Marcus had been best friends for as long as he could remember. They had been there for each other through the darkest of times—through his own brutal divorce, through the murders of Marcus's wife, Elena, and their son, Lars, through Marcus's resignation from the Secret Service, and through the deaths of Nick Vinetti and so many other friends and colleagues. Now he was supposed to tell his best friend's mother her son was missing in action?

Better him than someone who didn't know the Rykers, Pete told himself. Still, he wished he could be there to tell Mrs. Ryker in person.

He could picture the house in Monument that Marcus had grown up in. The home Mrs. Ryker had paid off using the insurance money she had received after her husband—an Air Force fighter pilot—was shot down and killed over Iraq. The home where Marcus had saved his mother's life when he was twenty-one. Pete knew all the family stories. He had been to that house countless times before. He had memories with these people that went back two decades, and it made this call all the more difficult.

Pete grabbed the receiver and dialed the home number. No one answered. He called again, but there was still no answer. No machine picked up; Pete knew Marcus's mom despised them. So he called her mobile number.

Marjorie Ryker answered immediately.

"Hello?"

"Mrs. Ryker?"

"Yes?"

"It's Pete Hwang. How are you?"

There was a pause. Pete heard her take a deep breath. But when the woman finally spoke, she did not seem surprised to hear his voice.

"To be honest, I've been better, Pete. But how are you?"

"About the same, ma'am. Look, you've no doubt heard the news, the ambush on the Lebanon border."

"I have."

"Then maybe you know why I'm calling."

"Just tell me if he's alive, Pete."

"He is, ma'am—we know that for certain."

"Praise God," she exhaled.

"I'm calling you from DSS headquarters. I've been assigned to the crisis management task force, and I can tell you we are doing everything we possibly can to get Marcus and his team back home safe and sound."

For the next few minutes, Pete walked through the notes that had been approved by Director Stephens, Secretary Whitney, and the head of the Diplomatic Security Service. The script was light on details and heavy on procedure—what to say and not say, why it was so important not to talk to the media, and so forth. Pete had been briefed that Tehran had put an enormous bounty on Marcus's head. He did not, of course, pass that along to Mrs. Ryker.

The call only lasted about ten minutes. What impressed him most was how calm Marcus's mother was. She did not burst into tears or collapse into hysterics. She did not ask a thousand questions she knew Pete could not or would not answer. The woman was a rock. Pete was not exactly surprised. He had seen her faith steady her through many a storm. Still, it moved him. Especially when she asked at the end of the call how his kids were doing and then if she could pray for him.

"Yes, ma'am," Pete said. "I'd like that."

67

Over a meal of hard-boiled eggs, chopped salad, and coffee, al-Masri watched.

For the benefit of anyone who might be eavesdropping on them, he spoke with Zayan about their crops, how much they could get for them at the open-air markets in Beirut, how good it would be to get away from the fighting, and their hopes that the Zionists didn't begin bombing cities north of the river. In fact, however, al-Masri kept his eye on the checkpoint, even as bombs kept falling not too many kilometers behind them, rattling the windows and the silverware and Zayan's already-frayed nerves.

A long and growing line of cars and trucks waited to be cleared. Some were families who had clearly packed as many of their possessions as they possibly could and now fled the fighting for safer ground. Others were trucks variously teeming with sheep and goats, chickens, or crates of eggs or fruits and vegetables or even tobacco. Agriculture was not a big percentage of the overall Lebanese economy. It was, however, upwards of 70 percent of the economy in the southern tier. There were no factories here, after all. No heavy industry. Few office buildings. No high-tech industries. No one wanted to invest in anything so close to a border so often ravaged by war. Agriculture, therefore, was almost all they had.

The longer they took to eat, the longer it would take to get over the bridge and on their way. Still, it could not be helped. He had to know what he was up against. By the time the bill came, he did know, and his stomach was in knots. The checkpoint was not being run by the Lebanese Armed Forces. It was being run by Hezbollah. He didn't recognize any of the men. Not from this distance. But the uniforms were distinct enough.

"Come," he told Zayan. "It's time to go."

Exiting the café, Zayan headed to the driver's side, got in, and started the engine. Al-Masri opened the back passenger-side door, moved aside a crate of watermelons, and pulled out a backpack he had stuffed under it. This he brought with him to the front passenger seat.

Once inside the car, he closed and locked the door, then unzipped the backpack, making sure to keep it low enough that none of its contents could be seen by anyone inside the café. He withdrew a loaded 9mm automatic pistol, a premade plaster cast, and a cloth sling. The cast had been made wide enough—though just barely so—for al-Masri to slide it over the pistol, now in his right hand, and over his right forearm. Having secured the cast in place, he proceeded to use his left hand to wrap the sling around his neck and over his right shoulder. Satisfied, he used his left hand to take the Cuban-looking cap and put it back on his freshly shaved head. Then he turned to Zayan and spoke in a near whisper.

"You know what you must do if I have to shoot, correct?" he asked.

"Hit the accelerator and don't look back," his aide replied.

The Egyptian nodded. "Let's hope it does not come to that."

"*Inshallah*," Zayan said.

"*Inshallah*." Al-Masri nodded again, and Zayan pulled out of the parking lot. If they had to run, they would not likely make it far, the deputy commander of the Radwan Unit knew. Though a 1984 model, the Mercedes-Benz W123 was an excellent car, and al-Masri knew Zayan's brother had kept it in pristine condition. But if something happened at the checkpoint, they would most likely be riddled with automatic rifle fire. Even if by some miracle they were able to break through the checkpoint and survive the first terrifying minutes, where could they go that Hezbollah or the LAF wouldn't find them? This was not a busy stretch of highway. Nor was it heavily populated. The nearest city, Sidon, was on the coast. The road they were on was well inland. There were some small towns and villages ahead, but no place they could hide for long. What's more, there were probably another six or eight checkpoints ahead, no matter which route they took.

No, al-Masri thought as they got in the line of cars and trucks, waiting their turn to be searched. The only place to hide was in Beirut. And the only way to get to Beirut was not to run. They were going to have to stay calm and take their time, though time was hardly on their side.

68

Zayan ibn Habib had long craved to live a life of danger and significance.

Now that he was getting his chance, he was having second thoughts.

Only twenty-six years old, Zayan was the eldest son of a prominent Lebanese industrialist. Yet he had never desired his father's wealth or public profile. A child prodigy, he had graduated from high school at the age of fifteen yet resisted his father's demands that he attend the American University in Beirut to earn his undergraduate degree in business and an MBA. Throughout high school, Zayan and his closest friends had become increasingly religious—far more so than any in their immediate or extended families. Together they had begun to memorize the Qur'an. Together they had read and endlessly discussed the sacred writings of the leading Shia imams throughout history. And together, and in defiance of their fathers, they had enrolled at *al-Hawza al-Ilmiyya*, one of the most prestigious and influential Shia seminaries in the world.

Nothing had electrified Zayan more than traveling to Iraq, to the city of Najaf, where the seminary was located. Najaf, after all, was the third holiest city for Shia Muslims—the burial place of the first imam, Ali ibn Abi Talib, cousin of the Prophet Muhammad and husband of the Prophet's daughter

Fatimah. The place was so rich with Islamic history, art, and culture. It was in Najaf that Zayan had discovered the legends of the Twelfth Imam, also known as the Hidden Imam and the Promised One, and the prophecies of his soon-coming return to earth to reestablish the Caliphate and bring judgment to every infidel kingdom. It was in Najaf that he had become entranced by the teachings of Hossein Ansari, the Grand Ayatollah of Iran, and enthralled by all he had done to prepare the way for the Mahdi's arrival. It was there, too, that Zayan had first heard of Sheikh Ja'far ibn al-Hussaini and decided that upon returning to Lebanon he would join Hezbollah.

Zayan had zero interest in an academic life. Neither teaching nor writing captured his imagination in the slightest. He was big. He was strong. He was just over six feet tall and two hundred pounds of lean muscle. Allah had made him this way for a reason, he told himself. Not to be hidden away in a class-room. But to be on the front lines. To wage jihad against the Little Satan—the Zionists just across the border—and against the Great Satan across the ocean.

This, however, was the first actual operation that Zayan had ever been part of. He felt disoriented and confused. Taking another man's life—even that of an avowed enemy—was not what he had imagined. Seeing a man bleed out was nothing he had ever considered before. Watching his leader strip and beat and torture a woman and nearly drown a boy not much younger than him had rattled Zayan to his core. He could not sleep. He was famished but could not keep down food. Colonel al-Masri had been too consumed with himself and his own thoughts to notice that Zayan had only picked at his breakfast and had twice gone to the restroom to vomit what little was left in his system.

Now his face and arms were covered with sweat. It wasn't just his nerves, however. The temperature had to be approaching forty degrees Celsius—nearly a hundred degrees Fahrenheit—and the Mercedes's air-conditioning, while functional, left much to be desired. The clock on the dashboard read 9:27 a.m. It had been nearly two hours since they had left the café. More than three since they had left the compound. They still had not crossed the bridge. They were, however, next in line.

Finally a heavily armed soldier waved them forward. Zayan took a deep breath and inched the car ahead until he was ordered to stop.

"Papers," the soldier demanded from behind rather stylish sunglasses.

Zayan handed over his ID, then al-Masri's. Both were fake, of course. They indicated that the men were sons of the same father, Shia Muslims, and residents of a town called Mansouri, located along the coast about twenty-five kilometers south of their present location. A half-dozen soldiers, equally well armed, eyed them warily while the first one reviewed the documents.

Zayan wondered if the soldier could hear his heart pounding in his chest. He still struggled with the notion of lying to fellow members of Hezbollah, to fellow citizens of Lebanon, especially in the midst of a war and one they had started. He certainly wanted the reward the Sheikh was offering, the one Colonel al-Masri kept telling them about. He did not want others to get the money, especially those who had not taken the risks he had. Still, such subterfuge was even more nerve-racking to the young Radwan fighter than the border raid had been. Then, he had had a clearly defined mission, a clearly defined enemy, and clearly defined rules of engagement. What did he have now?

The IDs were expertly done. And he knew his cover story backward and forward. These were not what concerned Zayan. The man in the trunk was. What if he began moving? What if he started shouting or making enough noise to draw the attention of the soldiers? Then again, what if he died back there? He could easily suffocate. Or cook to death. Even if they got all the way to Beirut, what could they possibly say to the Sheikh that would exonerate them for delivering an American corpse instead of the live federal agent that al-Masri had no doubt promised?

Tempted to wipe away the drips of sweat streaking down his cheeks, Zayan nevertheless kept still. No sudden movements. Nothing that would draw any attention. It would all be over soon enough, he told himself. Except that the soldier scrutinizing their IDs now leaned in the window and ordered al-Masri to remove his cap.

Al-Masri did as he was told. The man studied his face.

It was all Zayan could do not to glance down at the fake cast on the Egyptian's arm. In his peripheral vision, he could see the cast resting on al-Masri's lap, tilted upward at just the right angle. One wrong move and al-Masri would fire the pistol. One bullet to the face would be all it took. Then it would be up to him, Zayan told himself, to jam the car into drive and hit the gas. Could he do that with blood and gore all over his face and spattering the windshield? They were about to find out.

"Your nose," said the soldier, gesturing toward al-Masri. "What happened to it?"

The Egyptian laughed. "It's stupid," he said.

"Tell me anyway."

"I was milking a cow, but I wasn't paying attention, and she kicked me right in the face."

"That was stupid."

"That's why my wife tells me to stick to growing fruit," al-Masri quipped, then nodded to the crates in the backseat. "Safer."

Zayan noticed that the soldier did not crack a smile. He just glared at al-Masri. The woman had probably done him a favor by breaking his nose. The Egyptian's face was a contorted mess. Swollen. Black-and-blue. Still crusted with bits of dried blood. He barely looked like the photo on the ID, even though the photo really was of him. Zayan just silently prayed they were not asked to get out of the vehicle.

They weren't.

Instead, the soldier asked him to pop the trunk. Zayan forced himself to nod and not freak out. He reached down and pulled the latch on the floor, unlocking the trunk. The lead soldier, flanked by two others, walked around to the back of the car, peering into the windows of the backseat as they did.

Zayan forced himself not to glance back in the rearview mirror. Though he was tempted, al-Masri's left hand suddenly touched his right and patted him gently.

Stay calm, my boy. Stay calm.

The words were not spoken aloud. But Zayan got the message.

"All right, you're clear," the soldier finally said as he handed back their IDs and another soldier closed the trunk. "Drive on."

"Thank you," Zayan said, though his mouth was bone-dry. "God be with you."

69

"Did I not say the hand of Allah is upon us?" al-Masri asked as they drove north.

"Forgive me, Colonel; my faith is not like yours," the young man replied.

"You have much to learn, Zayan, but you have the makings of a great leader."

When they reached a junction that would put them back on Highway 51, Zayan asked if he should take it. Al-Masri told him to turn right instead. That put them on the Nabatiyeh-Tyre Road, heading east. Convinced the most elaborate roadblocks and most sophisticated intelligence officials would be guarding the country's most important thoroughfare, al-Masri preferred to stay away from the coast. They would take back roads and snake their way northward through the interior. It would cost them time he did not have, al-Masri knew, but it was far better than being caught. And they were now beyond the self-imposed limit of Israeli bombers.

Windows down and enjoying the gorgeous if stifling hot afternoon, al-Masri turned the radio on and found a station out of Beirut that recited the Qur'an twenty-four hours a day. They drove in silence, listening to each sura and meditating on its meaning.

They reached the next checkpoint just outside the city of Nabatiyeh. It was also backed up with dozens of cars and trucks—more than al-Masri had anticipated. He could see that Zayan was still anxious. The words of the Prophet, peace be upon him, did much to calm both their souls.

By 2 p.m., they had finally been cleared. They drove into the city and stopped to use the restroom and buy cold bottles of water. They did not stay long, however. They certainly did not have lunch. It wasn't worth the risk, so they pressed onward, heading north through the mountains and along the western shores of Lake Qaraoun.

★

BEIRUT, LEBANON

Kareem bin Mubarak was on the phone when an aide handed him a message.

The general quickly wrapped up the call and logged on to the secure account. Sure enough, the email was there. Logging out, he left his office and headed directly to the conference room where the Sheikh was receiving a briefing on the latest movement of Israeli troops and mechanized forces, now just ten kilometers from the Litani River.

"Your Holiness?"

"What is it?" asked the Sheikh.

"It's here."

"What is?"

"The email."

"From al-Masri?"

"Apparently."

"And?"

"I haven't opened it yet," said Mubarak. "I thought you would want to be the first to see it."

"Absolutely—put it on the main screen."

In the room were six of Hezbollah's highest-ranking generals. They began to gather up their maps and briefing books, but the Sheikh told them to stay. He told them he wanted them to see whether the highest-ranking traitor in the organization's history really had the Americans in his possession, whether they were actually alive, and if so, what kind of condition they were in.

One of Mubarak's colleagues offered him the use of his laptop, as it was already wired into the video screens in the conference room. Mubarak thanked him and logged into the account. He quickly double-clicked the email at the head of the queue and turned his eyes to the main screen, as did they all.

The video came up immediately. Shot on someone's phone, it was of poor quality, but three prisoners were clearly visible. Two men. One woman. Each was alive and capable of speaking—they each gave their name, rank, and ID numbers—yet all had been beaten severely. Two of them looked as if they had broken noses. The woman was not capable of standing. None of the prisoners appeared to be in the same room. The three videos had been strung together into a single ninety-second clip, and the date and time stamps confirmed that the shots had been taken on Saturday, May 2, all within minutes of each other.

Mubarak snuck a peek at the Sheikh, whose conflicted, contorted expression suggested both rage and relief. Yet there was more. At the end of the video was a shot of a yellow Hezbollah flag being set on fire. No face was visible. Certainly not al-Masri's. Just gloved hands. Nor was there a narrator or any distinct geographic markings. The shot was a close-up, and as the flag continued burning, the Sheikh shot to his feet, his face beet red, and demanded Mubarak stop the playback. Before he could do so, however, a final image of a skull and crossbones flashed repeatedly with a strobe-like effect, and then the screen went black. All the computers in the conference room shut down. Then all the lights were cut as well.

Emergency generators kicked in. But the damage had been done. The email had contained a Trojan horse. A lethal virus was sweeping through Hezbollah's computer systems, cutting off their ability to manage the war or even communicate with their troops in the field.

70

By 3 p.m., the Boeing 757 had touched down in the kingdom's second largest city.

Nestled on the eastern shores of the glistening Red Sea, King Abdulaziz International Airport was the gateway to Mecca, Islam's most sacred jewel, the destination of millions of pilgrims every year, only an hour's drive away. The sky was blue. The temperature was eighty-six degrees Fahrenheit, and there was a lovely breeze coming in off the water. It was no wonder, then, that the crown prince had already moved his family and staff here and taken up residence in his summer palace. Back in Riyadh, it was a sizzling 107 degrees in the shade with no breeze whatsoever.

The American secretary of state, however, paid scant attention to the weather or the view as she stepped onto the tarmac and was whisked into the backseat of a black bulletproof Lincoln Navigator by her security detail. She was only going to be on the ground in Jeddah a mere two hours. By nightfall, she would be dining with the king of Bahrain in downtown Manama. By breakfast the following morning, she would be in Abu Dhabi, and then it was off to Cairo and Amman.

The motorcade of four identical American-made SUVs was flanked by police cars, a phalanx of motorcycles, and several vehicles from the Office of Royal Protocol. They roared off the airport grounds and in short order arrived at the Al-Salam Royal Palace and entered through the western gate.

Meg Whitney had spent the drive buried in her briefing book. Now, however, she looked up, removed her reading glasses, and remembered what Special Agent Geoff Stone had told her over the phone before she had taken off. It was on this spot, just a few years before, that a twenty-eight-year-old homegrown Saudi terrorist by the name of Mansour al-Amri had launched a brazen attack, jumping out of a Hyundai and opening fire with a Kalashnikov, killing two palace guards and wounding three others before being cut down himself in a hail of gunfire. Whitney had not exactly understood why the head of her detail was telling her this, especially since Stone wasn't coming with her, and she told him as much.

"I'm telling you, Madam Secretary, because you need to understand something about the crown prince," Stone had replied.

"And what's that?" she had asked.

"Well, let me say up front that I'm making no assessment of his politics or even his policies," Stone had replied. "I just think it's critical that you understand what drives the man."

"Fair enough," Whitney had said. "What does?"

"I've studied His Royal Highness very closely since the mess in Jerusalem not so long ago," Stone had explained. "And I've come to believe he wakes up every morning asking himself three questions. The first is—*How do I not die?* The first Arab leader to make peace with Israel was Anwar Sadat, and he was assassinated by Egyptian radicals in 1981. Israeli prime minister Yitzhak Rabin made peace with Jordan and signed the Oslo Accords with Yasser Arafat, and then he was assassinated by an Israeli radical in 1995. Is the Saudi crown prince really ready to finalize a deal with Israel? He hasn't yet. Maybe he will. But the incident at the western gate of the very palace you're going to be visiting is a reminder. The radicals will never accept peace with Israel, and they are gunning for anyone who moves in that direction."

Agent Stone had paused a moment to let that point sink in, then moved on.

"Second, the crown prince asks himself, *How can I protect myself and my kingdom from external threats like Iran, the Muslim Brotherhood, al Qaeda, ISIS, and a list of others that goes on and on?* Obviously he's deeply concerned about Iran getting the Bomb and the long-range missiles to deliver them as far as the United States. And just as obviously he's worried about Iran funding, training, arming, and directing proxy forces like Hezbollah, Hamas, and the Houthis. Ideally, he would love to dramatically strengthen and solidify his strategic alliance with us. Signing a peace deal with the Israelis would go a long way in helping achieve that. But as you well know, there are grave risks that even engaging in peace talks with the Israelis will cause his external enemies to become even more hostile, more aggressive, more willing to use their missile forces to decimate the Saudi oil fields and refineries. Are there benefits to the kingdom to making peace with Jerusalem? Yes. But there are very serious risks as well, and you can be sure that the crown prince—and his father—are weighing them all."

"And the third?" Whitney had asked.

"Every day the crown prince wakes up asking himself, *How do I fundamentally transform the Saudi economy before the oil runs out?* He's got a very ambitious plan to wean the kingdom off its dependence on oil revenue. But to get it done, he desperately needs foreign direct investment, foreign technology, foreign trade, and a flood of foreign tourists from all over the world. Peace and stability help him achieve his goals. Another war in the region does not."

As the motorcade pulled onto the grounds, Whitney found herself once again pondering these three questions. Geoff Stone was not one of her undersecretaries or even an assistant secretary. He was not an ambassador or part of her Bureau of Intelligence and Research or even on her Policy Planning Staff. He was a member of the Diplomatic Security Service, typically seen and not heard and rarely noticed even if he was seen. Yet in a single phone call, Stone had given her more insight into the future king of Saudi Arabia than anyone on her staff. How was that possible? And why wasn't he with her now?

71

The meeting did not exactly get off to an auspicious start.

In fact, more than forty minutes after she had arrived, it had still not begun. The king was ill. The crown prince was on a call. The foreign minister's plane had engine troubles, so he had only just landed at the airport and was still on his way. All the while, the chief of royal protocol kept apologizing and bringing more mint tea.

At first Whitney was annoyed. She had a schedule to keep, and this was not helping. Then she grew furious. For all the strains in the bilateral relationship over the years, the Saudis had no better friend or closer ally than the United States. This was particularly true of the Clarke administration, which had vigorously protected the alliance from the wolves on Capitol Hill and the visionless bureaucrats in Brussels. How dare the Saudis stand her up, given all that was at stake?

Yet as the minutes ticked by, such thoughts and emotions eventually morphed again, this time into worry. The eldest son of the Saudi monarch was not on a call, Whitney surmised. He was sending a message. He and his father were furious at the Israelis and were making their displeasure known by disrespecting Israel's best friends. The royals really were looking for a way out of the peace process. The summit in Jerusalem had made front-page headlines from Tehran to Tucson. Hope of a new, peaceful, stable Middle East had soared, and with it stock markets the world around. Yet that was all well over a year ago. Since then, no treaty had been signed. The Saudis kept asking more questions, requesting more clarifications, and finding new reasons for new delays.

There were plenty of possible reasons for the royals' frosty feet, even in the midst of the sweltering Arabian desert. Fear of assassination had to top the list. But insurrection, waves of terror, and a missile war with Iran were likely runners-up.

Fifty-three minutes after Whitney had arrived, Crown Prince Abdulaziz bin Faisal Al Saud finally made an entrance. Alone. No foreign minister. No aides. Not even a notetaker, a translator, or a member of the Royal Guard. The thirty-eight-year-old heir to the throne apologized for his delay, but he did not look happy and did not greet her warmly, and this only stoked Whitney's fears.

"We have a problem," the crown prince said.

Apparently, she thought but for the moment said nothing.

"Whom does your CIA believe will replace the Supreme Leader?"

Whitney had expected the question, but not right out of the gate. "I'm sorry?"

"When the Assembly of Experts meets, whom do your people think will be tapped to be Iran's next Grand Ayatollah?"

Confused as to what this could possibly have to do with the crown prince being so late, much less the peace treaty or the missile war underway in Lebanon, the secretary of state nevertheless set down her glass of tea—her third since arriving—and tried to recall the names they had been bandying about. This was the very essence of diplomacy, she reminded herself—sounding thoughtful and helpful even when one was fit to be tied.

"Well, I suppose the front-runner would be Abdolhasan Farahani," she began. "But then again, Daryush Ebrahimi is probably a strong contender as well."

"Why these two?" Abdulaziz asked with an expression that was at once severe and inscrutable.

Whitney took a moment to compose her thoughts, then replied, "Well, both men are highly trained, highly respected clerics. They're both former students of Ansari. Both are hard-liners, though maybe not as crazy as he was."

"And?"

"And both are certainly long-serving members of the assembly themselves. They know everyone. Everyone knows them. And I guess I'd add that there has been a great deal of speculation about both men in the media— well, the media outside of Iran—ever since the health of Ansari was known to be in decline."

"Why do you suspect Farahani would be more likely than Ebrahimi?"

"Did I say that?"

"You implied it."

"Yes, I guess I did," Whitney said. "For one thing, Farahani is younger. His health is fine, so far as we know . . ."

"And?"

"And what?" she asked. "Do you not agree?"

"Actually, I do," the crown prince replied. "You're absolutely right. Both are very strong contenders. And they have both been on the top of our lists as well. I have leaned toward thinking Ebrahimi had the edge on Farahani. My father has believed just the opposite."

"How is your father?"

"Not well," the crown prince confessed. "And he apologizes for not being with us today."

"It's that bad?" Whitney asked.

The crown prince was silent for a long while.

"I don't mean to be nosy," Whitney said gently. "But with one succession in motion, I have to ask. Are we about to have another?"

This produced another awkward silence.

"Perhaps," Abdulaziz finally replied. "He is battling pneumonia. It is his second bout this year. My brothers and I are concerned. But with all that is going on in the news, we don't want this to get out, and I would ask that you keep this between us."

"I ought to tell the president."

"Of course, and the vice president also," said the crown prince. "Director Stephens I will talk to personally. But beyond this, we must ask for your discretion."

"You have it."

"Thank you," he said. "We can discuss this more in a moment, but right now I have some troubling news."

Whitney braced herself. She knew what he was going to say. She just did not want to hear it.

72

The Saudis were going to abandon the peace process.

And the prince was about to give her an earful about Israeli "aggression" in southern Lebanon.

Whitney knew what was coming. But it hurt all the same. She and the president and their team had invested so much in helping forge the first new full-fledged Arab-Israeli peace treaty in over a quarter of a century. She could not bear to see everything fall apart now, and all because of an obvious Iranian plot to sabotage the talks.

"What kind of news?" she asked, as calmly as she could.

"It's from one of our sources."

Whitney was confused. "Your sources?"

"Yes."

"In Tehran?"

"Yes."

"Inside the palace?"

"Close enough."

"And?"

"And our source says the balance of power has just shifted."

The prince was delaying the inevitable. Still, the secretary went with it for now. "Shifted?"

"Dramatically."

"How so?"

"The commander of the Revolutionary Guards—"

"General Entezam."

"Yes."

"What about him?"

"Apparently he has secretly thrown his support behind a new contender."

"Who?"

"Afshar."

"Yadollah Afshar?"

"Yes."

"The president of Iran?"

"Yes."

"Are you certain?"

"I'm afraid so," said the crown prince. "It won't be known publicly for several weeks while the country mourns. But when it is announced, when it actually comes to pass, it will be a disaster for you and for us."

The two were silent for some time. Whitney was trying to take in the full measure of the catastrophe and comprehend just how deeply Saudi intelligence had penetrated the highest echelons of the Iranian regime.

"Yadollah Afshar is not just a hard-liner," the crown prince continued. "He's a genuine Twelver—and that doesn't even begin to explain the full situation. He's a fanatic, really. He talks all the time about preparing for the arrival of Imam al-Mahdi. He is leading the effort to build Iran's nuclear arsenal and the missiles to deliver them against your country and mine, to say nothing of the Israelis. He doesn't simply believe the Hidden Imam is about to reveal himself or that the Caliphate is about to rise. He can't think or talk about anything else. We have recordings of him. Intercepted phone calls. Text messages. Letters. Speeches. Afshar speaks not just of conquering Christendom and Israel and our kingdom. He speaks of annihilating us all. *Annihilation.* That's the word he uses again and again."

"That's crazy—that will never happen," Whitney protested. "The assembly would never choose him."

"Why not?"

"Because they have never chosen a politician to be Supreme Leader."

"Ah, but Afshar is a cleric," the crown prince said. "He, too, was trained in a seminary—in Qom, by Ansari—and it makes perfect sense. Ansari treated him like a son, like a prince."

"A crown prince?" Whitney asked.

The Saudi nodded, then grew even more somber. This was it, Whitney realized. She took a sip of tea, wiped her mouth with a linen napkin, folded her hands on her lap, and waited for the bomb to drop.

Yet to her amazement, it did not.

"We're ready," said the prince.

"For what?"

"To sign the treaty."

"With Israel?"

"Of course."

"I don't understand," Whitney said. "Why? And why now, after all your delays?"

"We only delayed in order to further lay the groundwork, to prepare our people," Abdulaziz replied. "We could hardly be seen by our citizens or the Muslim world as rushing into this. We needed to be thoughtful and deliberative and appear that way. And we wanted to squeeze some more concessions from Mr. Eitan. Now we've done all that. Now the Terrible Tyrant of Tehran is dead and soon to be buried. And now the Iranians have once again launched a horrible war of aggression against Israel and against the people and leaders of the United States. They think we are going to be frightened off because of this. But just the opposite is true. Hezbollah's action—at Iran's direction—has emboldened us. It has shown the Saudi people—indeed, all the Arabs in the region—that unless we band together in an alliance of strength and unity, we will never stop Iran, and what they are doing to Israel they will then try to do to us. Madam Secretary, we have a window—a brief window—to define our future and that of the new Middle East, and we are ready to seize it. And we will."

Whitney was so stunned, she said nothing.

"Do you think the president would be willing to host a signing ceremony on the South Lawn of the White House?" the prince asked.

The secretary pulled herself together. "I believe he would," she replied. "How soon are you thinking?"

"How does next week sound to you?"

"Next week?"

"Next week."

"Carpe diem?" She smiled.

"Carpe diem," he said and smiled back.

73

SOMEWHERE IN LEBANON

The drugs were wearing off.

Marcus was fading in and out of consciousness and trying to remember where he was. He was once again drenched with sweat, and as he came to, he was finding it hard to breathe. It was brutally hot. He could barely move. This was not the freezer. Nor the latrine. He caught a whiff of sour fruit, and that was when he remembered.

His first task was not to panic, he told himself. But that was easier said than done. He was trapped in the trunk of a Mercedes-Benz. And being cooked alive. The narcotics, he realized, had been a blessing. He had no idea how long he had been asleep, but he was tempted to wish he had never woken up.

Marcus forced such thoughts away. He was awake now. And there was no going back. He could feel the car moving. He could hear the road beneath him. There was no telling how much longer they would be driving. He had no idea where they were going. He assumed Beirut, and likely to the airport, to be transferred to Tehran. There were only two things he was certain of now. For the first time since his capture almost two days earlier, he was not being watched. That meant this might be the only chance he had to escape. And he had to escape.

The trunk was pitch-black. But it would not be for long. He was barefoot. He remembered that his boots and socks had been stripped from him in the earliest minutes of his capture. There was, therefore, the real risk that he would cut himself and be unable to stop the bleeding. But it could not be helped. To escape, he needed at least some light, and to get it, he had only one option. So he began to kick furiously at the left taillight, the only one he could reach. The lights were plastic, not glass. It should not be that hard, he decided, and he was right. Before long, Marcus had his first success. The light popped out, and day flooded the trunk of the cab.

Now he needed some room to maneuver. He had never been claustrophobic, but the combination of the tight space and the immense heat was rapidly getting to him. He could feel his heart rate spiking. His breathing was becoming more intense. There was not much time. Either he was going to break free, or he was going to go crazy. He began counting down from fifty. That had always worked for him in the past. But this time it did not. So he abandoned the effort and silently begged God for mercy.

His hands were bound behind his back. Without their use, he knew he had no chance. He pressed his torso against the wood crates and pushed them as far toward the front of the trunk as he possibly could. It wasn't much, but it gave him a couple of additional inches.

Next he curled himself up in a ball and forced his bound hands downward until—with enormous effort—he was able to get them under his legs. Now they were in front of him. Part of his SERE training in the Corps had been how to break free from a range of makeshift handcuffs, from flexicuffs and zip ties to duct tape and rope. If he had a little more room, he knew he could tear the duct tape in a flash. He just needed to raise his hands above his head and bring them down onto a sharp object in a sudden, swift motion while pulling his wrists apart. If it did not work the first time, a few more tries would strain and then rip the tape, and he would be free. But there was not nearly enough room to try it now.

And Marcus felt the panic beginning to overtake him.

★

The closer they got to Beirut, the more checkpoints they encountered.

Al-Masri knew entering the capital was going to be difficult, especially if they tried to enter from the south. He therefore directed Zayan to head to the city of Jounieh but not enter it. Jounieh was a city of well over a hundred thousand people. The broader metropolitan area comprised more than four hundred thousand. It might be a good place to hide, but as it was not their destination, there was no point risking additional checkpoints.

Instead, al-Masri ordered Zayan to hook around Jounieh's eastern suburbs and take Highway 51 heading south. This route would finally take them to Beirut. It would also cost them precious hours.

The clock on the dashboard already read 7:16 p.m. The sun would soon be going down. And they still had hours to go before they were safe.

★

Marcus felt around in the shadows for the wooden crates surrounding him.

The ones in the backseat of the taxi had been filled with watermelons, he recalled. They were likely built of far sturdier boards than these crates, which were filled with smaller fruits—loquats, he thought—not nearly as heavy as the watermelons. These crates were built of thinner boards, and from the feel of them they had seen a lot of sun and a lot of rain. They were old and weathered, and Marcus had an idea. Grabbing hold of the middle slat of the closest crate, he yanked on it, trying to break it off. Instead he simply pulled the whole crate toward him.

He shoved the crate back against the front of the trunk with his torso and tried again. He pulled up his knees and placed them against the box to create some resistance. Then he took hold of the slat and yanked again. The crate didn't move, but neither did the slat break off.

Again Marcus shifted his position. He curled himself up in a ball, used his legs to push against the crate with all the force he could muster, and yanked the slat with opposite force. This time the slat did break free. Sour plums tumbled out all around him, and he felt a jolt of pain as the sharp wood drove into his left forearm.

74

Marcus winced as he removed the jagged edge of the slat from his flesh.

Immediately he felt blood trickling down his arm, but knowing he had not hit an artery, he paid the wound no mind. Rather, he took the broken slat between his knees and with all his might drove his hands onto it so that the sharp edge bit into the center of the duct tape, in the narrow gap between his wrists. This, too, was a risk. Done wrong, he could jam the wood directly into one of his wrists and truly unleash a bloodbath. In this case, however, he did it just right, creating enough of a hole in the fabric of the tape that he could, with additional pressure, pull his wrists apart.

In another few seconds, he had completely removed the remains of the tape from both wrists. Before long, he had ripped the tape from his feet as well. At once, he began rubbing his wrists, then his ankles, to get the blood flowing through them again. As he did, he could feel the panic beginning to subside. That was, until he felt the Mercedes slowing to a stop.

★

They approached the last checkpoint.

They were now just outside the neighborhood of Zalqa.

It had taken them far longer than al-Masri had planned, but they were finally on the outskirts of Beirut. This was the jewel in the Lebanese crown—her capital and her largest city, with a population of more than two million souls.

On their drive along the coast from Jounieh, they had watched the fiery red ball of the sun slip beneath the waves on the horizon. It had, for a moment, taken their minds off their troubles, so beautiful was the handiwork of the Creator and Sustainer, but not for long.

Night had now fallen. The lights of the city were coming on, beckoning them forward. In a city of millions, they could disappear. For a while, anyway.

Al-Masri found himself more anxious than he had been on enemy territory, just two days earlier, but he dared not show it to the young man sitting to his left. "Relax, Zayan," he insisted. "Everything is going to be fine."

The Egyptian hoped it was true. Yet he braced for the worst, still gripping the pistol hidden in the fake cast on his arm.

There were only a dozen cars ahead of them. This surprised him, given the far longer lines at most of the other roadblocks they had come to. Then again, who in their right mind would be trying to enter Beirut today of all days if they did not have to?

"Are you hungry, Zayan?" al-Masri asked, seeing the younger man's anxiety and trying to distract him.

Zayan shrugged.

Al-Masri interpreted that as modesty and slapped him on the back.

"Me, too," the Egyptian replied. "Once we clear this, we will top off our gas, find a good place to eat, and celebrate Allah's kindness upon us."

Two soldiers approached the passenger side. Two more approached the driver's side and motioned for Zayan to lower the window. The lead officer asked for their IDs and for the registration of the vehicle. It was the first time anyone at these checkpoints had asked for that. Fortunately, al-Masri had remembered to get that forged as well. He fished it out of the glove compartment and gave it to Zayan, who handed it over.

"Where are you coming from?" the officer asked.

As he had all day, al-Masri did the talking. He talked about their village, about the horrible bombing, about their need to bring their fruit to market and make at least some money to pay their workers and put bread on their table.

★

The car was merely idling now.

Marcus could hear every word al-Masri said. Not that he understood the Arabic. Just the tone. It was calm. Uncharacteristically soothing.

But why?

Marcus remembered that al-Masri had gotten into the front passenger seat. While it was possible that he had switched along the way and was now driving, it was more likely that the man's aide was still driving. And the aide was nervous. In need of reassurance. They must not be entering a Hezbollah stronghold. If al-Masri really had gone rogue, then neither were they about to enter whatever safe house he had arranged. They were approaching some-place dangerous. Men they did not know. Men who clearly were armed.

Marcus could hear dogs barking. He could hear someone speaking on a walkie-talkie. Through the broken taillight, he could tell that the sun had gone down. That meant they had been traveling for more than twelve hours.

Where could they possibly have gone that would take so long? Highway 51 to Beirut would not take much more than an hour.

Unless checkpoints had been set up to find the Americans and those who were holding them. If al-Masri was trying to avoid all or most of those checkpoints, he would have to have taken a circuitous route—east for a good while, and then north, perhaps through the Bekaa Valley or perhaps . . .

Marcus stopped himself. He did not have the time to waste on imagining al-Masri's route. The man was heading to Beirut. There was no other way to get his prisoners out of the country. The exact route he and his aide had taken didn't matter. What was important was that the driver was nervous. That suggested they were coming into the capital and were now stopped at a major military roadblock.

75

Marcus pulled himself deeper into the trunk.

As quietly as he could, he repositioned the crates around him to block anyone's view if—and, more likely, when—they opened the trunk. He scooped up the plums that had tumbled out of the crate he had broken into and stuffed them back into the crate and covered the hole with his body to keep them from falling out again.

The taillight he had kicked out could not be helped. It might draw attention. But then again, the Mercedes was old. From the brief glimpse he had gotten, Marcus pegged it as a model from the early eighties—of course one of its lights was missing. It was amazing the rusty bucket of bolts still ran at all.

He remonstrated himself for not finding a way to have escaped earlier. In a matter of minutes, he would likely be found out. Then again, with the sun having gone down, the temperature outside was dropping. He could even feel a cool breeze coming in from the Med. He could smell the salt air. These were small blessings, but blessings nonetheless, and he was grateful.

As the minutes ticked by, Marcus felt the car accelerate, then brake. The engine stopped. Then it started again, and they moved forward. Then the car halted, and once again the engine was cut. Marcus counted twelve rounds of this. He heard soldiers talking. They were close. They were right beside him. And al-Masri was the only one who replied. The young aide never said a word.

The trunk opened. Marcus held his breath. A beam from a flashlight swept over him. He could see through the cracks that a soldier was about to remove one of the crates. But just then he heard the screeching of tires. Men began shouting. Marcus heard the sound of automatic weapons fire erupting. He saw the soldier turn and run off. Dogs barked furiously. More gunfire. More yelling. More commotion. Then someone slammed the trunk shut. Someone else—someone close by—yelled something in Arabic, presumably at al-Masri and his aide. Suddenly the engine of the Mercedes roared to life. They were moving again. Marcus had no idea what had just unfolded. Nor did he care. All that mattered was that they had cleared the checkpoint, and—for the moment, at least—he was still alive.

Marcus felt himself breathing again. There was not, however, any time to relax. He got to work. The first thing he did was kick out the other taillight. The streetlamps whizzing by did not provide much illumination inside the trunk. The new opening did, however, draw in a bit more fresh air. More importantly, it gave him a second hole through which he could get rid of all this fruit. For the next several minutes he was shoving fruit out of the holes as fast as he could. Yes, there was a risk that someone would see him. But again, it could not be helped. He desperately needed to create more space to maneuver, and this was the only way.

Once most of the fruit had been dispensed with, Marcus began ripping apart the crates, shoving pieces of wood out the holes and onto the city streets. He was not worried about the noise he was making. He could barely hear himself think over the roar of the engine and the tires on the pavement. There was no chance al-Masri or Zayan could hear what he was doing.

With more space to maneuver in, Marcus tore back the carpet on the floor of the trunk. Though he could barely see, he could now feel the spare tire, a jack, and some other tools. These, however, were not his objectives. Feeling around with hands, including the arm that was still bleeding, he searched around to his right, which, since he was facing backward, was the driver's side of the car. Finally he felt the cable he was looking for. Following it forward, he confirmed that it was attached to a mechanism on the inside of the trunk. This, he knew, was the trunk release cable. He yanked it, but nothing happened. He yanked it again, harder this time, but the trunk still did not pop open as it was supposed to. He positioned his feet against the back wall of the car to give him more leverage and yanked the cable as hard as he could. Not only did the trunk fail to open, but the cable came completely out of the mechanism.

Marcus gritted his teeth and balled up his fists and fought to resist the immense temptation to hit something or shout out in frustration. He lay there in the darkness for several moments trying to catch his breath and figure out his next move. Exacerbating the situation was the fact that something sharp was driving into his back. He shifted positions and felt around and realized it was the jack. As he held the warm metal in his hands, he had an idea.

Working quickly, Marcus set up the jack in the back of the trunk. He glanced out one of the holes where the brake lights had once been and saw only one car on the street behind them. Several blocks later, the car turned off on a side street. At that instant, Marcus started cranking up the jack. In less than thirty seconds, the force of the extended jack strained the locking mechanism to its limit, and the trunk door finally popped. Marcus grabbed its lower edge, lest the wind catch it and force the trunk completely open. He was not yet ready for that. The car was still going at least thirty or forty miles an hour. These were city streets. It might not be suicide to jump now, but it was close. And what if al-Masri or his aide saw him jump?

Still, Marcus discounted that possibility. He remembered that the backseat of the Mercedes had been filled to the roof with crates of watermelons. The chance of the men in the taxi seeing anything behind them was remote unless they happened to glance in the rearview mirror at exactly the wrong moment. That was a chance he was going to have to take, and fast. There was no more time.

For the moment, Marcus could see no cars behind them. This was it. He pushed the trunk completely open. Then he ripped out the rest of the carpet and wrapped his upper body in it. Finally he hefted the spare tire and moved to the edge of the trunk.

Just then, he felt the Mercedes slow. Fearing al-Masri had seen him, he glanced back but realized that they were only taking a turn. This was ideal, though not something he had even considered. To make the turn successfully without rolling the car, the driver had to brake. At that moment, the taxi was doing only fifteen or twenty miles an hour, if that. Marcus did not hesitate.

He leaped out of the trunk, tossing himself onto the pavement. The spare tire cushioned his fall. He was wearing only boxer shorts, but the carpet protected his upper body. Still, the landing was hard—harder than he had expected—and knocked the wind clean out of him. When he finally stopped rolling and caught his breath, he found that his bare legs and feet were badly scraped up. They were bleeding. But his bones were not broken. The Mercedes was gone. He was alone. Alive. And free.

76

Scrambling to his feet, Marcus spotted a darkened alleyway.

He grabbed the tire and the carpet and dashed off the main boulevard they had been traveling down and into the shadows. A few cars whizzed by, going in the opposite direction. None of them stopped. Their drivers had probably not even seen what had happened, but even if they did, were they really likely to stop, turn around, and come find the madman who had jumped from the trunk of a moving vehicle? Only if they were cops. Or soldiers. And they were neither.

In the alleyway, Marcus found a dumpster. He tossed the tire and carpet inside but found nothing he could use. No clothing. No shoes. Not even rags to wrap his wounds. He did spot an outdoor water faucet and an old bucket. He kicked the bucket aside, turned on the nozzle, and proceeded to wash the filth off his hands. Then he began cupping water into his mouth, but this method hardly sufficed. Marcus had had nothing to eat or drink for at least the past day and a half, and he felt like he had sweat out most of the liquid in his body. So he got down on his knees, put his mouth under the spigot, and drank until he could not drink any more.

He was about to clean his wounds and do his best to remove some of the stench that had built up on him but thought better of it. Instead, he turned the water off, plunged his hands into the shallow pool of dirty water in the gutter, stirred a bit to make some mud, then slathered it all over his legs, arms, chest, and face. Infection and gangrene were distinct possibilities, he knew, but not his immediate concerns. Looking like a homeless person— a *crazy* person—was his new objective. The layers of filth helped, as did all the scars and bruising on his face and torso.

Mission accomplished, Marcus spotted a door across the alley. Glancing both ways and seeing no one, he moved to it and tried the knob. It was locked, but he saw another door a few yards away and tried it as well. It, too, was locked. He looked up the side of the building, hoping to see a fire escape. He did not. This wasn't Brooklyn or the Bronx or Denver. Marcus was a long way from buildings constructed according to U.S. fire codes. Indeed, the apartments on both sides of the alley looked like they had been built back in the early 1900s. To describe them as decrepit or dilapidated was charitable. Most had been damaged, some severely, in Lebanon's civil war back in the seventies. Others by Israel's bombing of Beirut in the eighties. In the States, these buildings would have been condemned, torn down, and—given their proximity to the waterfront—sold to wealthy developers to create multimillion-dollar penthouses. Here, they were simply rickety, rat-infested homes for those too poor to move.

Marcus did not, therefore, see any means by which he could easily get to the top of the building. What he did see, however, six floors above street level, was a clothesline and a combination of men's and women's laundry hanging from it. With a new target in sight, he again tried the handle of the door in front of him. It was most definitely locked, but it was also loose. Looking around and finding the coast clear, Marcus took a step back, then rammed the door with his shoulder. The lock immediately ripped apart. Splinters of wood went flying. He had made more noise than intended. But he was in.

The hallway was dimly lit. It stank of urine and was filled with trash. Marcus moved quickly, worried less at this point about making noise than getting out of sight before someone opened their door to see what all the commotion was about. He saw no one in the stairwell, so he bounded up the steps two at a time. By the third-floor landing, he had to stop and lean against a wall, needing a moment to catch his breath. He had not realized just how little energy he had left after the events of the past thirty-six hours. But he did not dare rest for long, knowing that the moment al-Masri discovered he was missing, he and his assistant would retrace their steps and no doubt bring reinforcements.

By the time Marcus had reached the sixth floor, he was winded again. So far, he still had not spotted a soul. But he could hear televisions and radios on inside the flats. He could hear families talking and laughing behind the doors and the bark of an occasional dog. He now realized there was no way he could break into someone's apartment. It wasn't simply the fact that he was planning to steal some poor family's clothing that bothered him so much, though even in his exhausted state he knew it should have. It was the fact that he was simply not prepared to do harm to someone in the safety of their own home.

Just then, a door opened somewhere on the fifth floor—the one right below him. He heard two women's voices chatting and laughing but could not tell if they were coming up or going down. He rapidly made his way up the rest of the stairwell until he burst through a door and onto the roof. To his surprise, he found row upon row of clotheslines strung between water tanks and satellite dishes. Most were empty. Two were covered with towels, sheets, and other linens. One was just women's undergarments. There was, however, one that drew attention. Hanging from it were several pairs of men's blue jeans, some T-shirts, and various other articles. Leaving aside the underwear—he was desperate, all right, but not *that* desperate—Marcus grabbed a gray T-shirt. He started to put it on only to realize it was far too small. The jeans were too small as well, he soon discovered.

Frustrated, he carefully attached them back to the line, just as he had found them. That's when he spotted a set of items he absolutely needed.

Socks. There were several pairs hanging there. The ones he chose were black sports socks, each with a white Nike swoosh on the ankle. They were damp, but they were clean. As he put them on, Marcus felt a twinge of guilt about taking them, but he did it anyway. This wasn't about comfort. It was about not leaving a trail of bloody footprints wherever he went. He winced, suddenly realizing he had left Colonel al-Masri and his minions more than enough visual clues to track him down. He was horrified, knowing his SERE instructor would have certainly failed him by now.

Marcus grabbed a damp towel from the line and began wiping away his footprints as best he could. Then he climbed onto a water tank, removed the top, dropped the dirty towel inside the tank, and replaced the lid. It was not enough. He knew he had left footprints all the way up the stairs. There was nothing he could do about that just now. But he had to get more serious.

And that meant he had to keep moving.

PART
THREE

77

President Ahmet Mustafa had barely slept at all.

He prayed five times a day for Allah to bring down the corrupt, debauched, pagan empire based in Washington, and he had done so for years. He had no doubt that just as the Soviet empire had imploded, so would the American one. And soon.

The question was whether he was ready for a direct confrontation, and the answer was simple: not yet.

Hamdi Yaşar was a faithful Turk and a good man, and he was right. The objective had been to capture Israelis. Their man had grabbed three Americans instead. The only thing to do now was to trust that Allah in his beneficence had given them just what they needed, if not what they wanted, and to complete the extraction plan they had already set into motion.

Mustafa stepped into his personal study, opened his wall safe, and removed the satellite phone Yaşar had once given him during one of their "interviews." Then he sent the man a simple text.

Buy the tickets. Get them out.

★

THE KIRYA, TEL AVIV, ISRAEL

"Miss Morris, gentlemen, welcome to Israel," said Asher Gilad.

Israel's revered spy chief, now in his midsixties, looked exhausted, like he hadn't slept for days—and he probably hadn't, Jenny Morris thought as she stepped off the elevator on the top floor of the IDF headquarters, a massive skyscraper located in the heart of Israel's commercial capital. She shook hands with the Mossad director, who promptly introduced her to Lieutenant General Yoni Golan, the IDF chief of staff, and Tomer Ben Ami, deputy director of the Shin Bet.

Jenny, in turn, introduced her team—Geoff Stone of DSS, former SEAL commander Donny Callaghan, and Noah Daniels from the CIA. After some pleasantries that were not really so pleasant, given the situation, Gilad led them into a secure, windowless conference room. They were served coffee and bottles of water and asked if they wanted anything to eat. Jenny was famished after the long flight, but she declined, as did the men. Their friends were being held, and probably tortured, by the worst of humanity. It was time to get down to business. It was time to get them home.

"I must tell you," Gilad began, "that while you were in the air, a great deal has happened."

"Please tell me you've found them," Jenny said.

"Not exactly, but we have found something."

"What is it?" Jenny asked. "Tell us everything you know."

Gilad glanced at his Shin Bet colleague and nodded, and Tomer Ben Ami continued the briefing by directing their attention to a large screen mounted on the wall. Using a remote, he brought up two images, one after the other. Both were of the same young Arab man. In one, he was in handcuffs and wearing a Hezbollah uniform. In the other, he was wearing prison garb and sitting in an interrogation room.

"As you know, we have a prisoner," Tomer began. "His name is Tanzeel al-Masri. Unfortunately, he's a pretty small fish. Only seventeen. Has been training with the Radwan Unit for less than a year. Insists he knows nothing. Not the plan. Not where the prisoners are now. Not any of the safe houses that the team is likely using."

Geoff Stone stared at the screen, then back at Tomer.

"But . . . ?"

"But his brother is another story," the Israeli replied.

"Who's his brother?"

Tomer flashed another picture up on the screen. "Amin al-Masri," he explained. "Twenty-eight. Born and raised in Beirut, though he lived in Libya for a time. Mother is Lebanese. His father was Egyptian. Both father and son worked in the Libyan oil fields before Amin moved back to Beirut, joined Hezbollah, and started steadily rising through the ranks."

"Thus the surname," said Jenny. "Al-Masri—the Egyptian."

"Exactly."

"And why is he important?"

"Because Amin al-Masri is the man who led the raid."

All eyes turned back to the screen.

"Amin is not just a member of Hezbollah," Tomer continued. "He's the deputy commander of the Radwan Unit, the most elite of all of Hezbollah's special forces."

"So—a big fish," said Noah.

"Very big," Tomer continued. "Now I've been the one interrogating Tanzeel, and I have to give him credit. Despite his youth and inexperience, he is not as talkative as we had hoped. Won't talk about his brother. Or the unit. Or his colleagues. Or the mission. But a little while ago, he made a serious mistake."

"What kind of mistake?" Jenny asked.

"For six hours last night, I asked him every conceivable question about his family, the operation, everything you would want me to ask. Tanzeel held his ground. Gave me nothing. But he was getting tired. And hungry. And thirsty. And I kept going. Past midnight. Until around 3 a.m. Then I let him have a bottle of cold water and told him to get some rest and we would try again in the morning. We put him in a cell by himself with a cot, a blanket, and a decent pillow. He fell asleep immediately. But an hour later, we woke him up again. Gave him a freezing cold shower. And then began the conversation all over again. He kept begging me for something to eat and more time to sleep. We went three and a half hours; then I finally let him go back to his cell. Again, he fell fast asleep. But a half hour later, we woke him up once again. Another cold shower. But this time I offered him a plate of hummus and freshly baked pita and even some grilled lamb, but only if he would give something I could verify. I told him to forget about the mission or his brother, to just tell me a little about himself. You know, just some basic biographical information I could put in his file. Date of birth. What hospital he was born in. Where he went to school. What's his mobile number. What's his ID number. Does he have his driver's license yet. You know the drill."

"And?" Jenny pressed again, eager to get to the bottom line.

"And he finally gave me something we can use."

78

Tomer smiled.

"He gave me his mobile number. I made it sound all boring and routine and unimportant and just something I needed so I could persuade my superiors to let me give him a little food, a little more rest. That kind of thing. And because of his youth and inexperience—and his feeling that he had successfully resisted all of my important questions—he talked. I think the smell of the lamb and the fresh coffee may have clinched the deal. But regardless, when we finished, I let him eat and then go back to his cell to get some real sleep while my team and I verified that he was telling me the truth."

"Well, was he?" Geoff Stone asked.

"He was," said Tomer. "I asked my guys to study all the calls made to and from Tanzeel's mobile phone over the past six months. I was hoping this might lead me to his brother's number and to others on the team. It did not. He'd been much more careful than I'd hoped. But then, to my shock, my guys told me that Tanzeel's number is still active. The phone is still on. And we know exactly where it is."

"Where?" Jenny asked.

Tomer picked up the remote again, and all eyes turned back to the screen. A map of Lebanon appeared, and the IDF chief of staff spoke again.

"That red dot near the coast is Tanzeel's phone," General Golan explained.

The Google Earth image zoomed in from thirty thousand feet down to just five hundred feet.

"The signal is coming from this building on the left," Golan continued, "which is part of what we thought was an old abandoned Hezbollah training camp just north of the city of Tyre."

Tomer punched more buttons. Several still images—all black-and-white—appeared in succession. These were no longer generic images from a Google satellite. These were classified photos that had been taken just ninety minutes earlier by an Israeli reconnaissance drone. And each showed the activity inside the camp.

"As you can see in this first photo, those are fresh tire tracks inside the compound," the *Ramatkal* noted. "And not just one set, but two. These tracks on the left were made by a car—midsize, probably four-door, and judging by the tires either a Mercedes or an Audi. These other tracks here, on the right of the screen, were made by a truck, possibly by a jeep."

Tomer clicked to another image.

"This photo shows the rear gate to the compound," the general continued. "You can see clearly the dusty trail made by both vehicles as they exited the compound and turned right. The cloud disintegrates quickly, but they were clearly heading north. Best guess, they were heading to Highway 51, which would be the fastest route to Sidon, or more likely, Beirut."

"So they're gone," Geoff said. "We missed them."

"Not necessarily," said the general.

Another image flashed up on the screen. This time it was a video clip showing two men walking around the camp. The video zoomed in, and it became clear the men were armed. When the clip ended, Tomer ran another. This had been taken on the other end of the compound, but it also showed two men walking, and they, too, were armed.

The Mossad chief spoke again. "We've been surveilling this place for the last ninety minutes. So far, we've seen eight men. All military age. All armed. They're all wearing Hezbollah uniforms. They're clearly doing patrols. They're guarding something or someone. And Tanzeel's phone is on and nearby."

"That doesn't make sense," said Jenny. "Why take prisoners to an abandoned camp? And why so few men?"

"I don't know," Gilad admitted. "You're right—it doesn't make sense. If Tanzeel al-Masri was good enough, even at his young age, to qualify to be a Radwan operative, he ought to be smart enough not to leave his mobile phone on. Or even leave his SIM card in the phone. Certainly his brother taught him that."

"It could be a trap," Geoff said.

"It could," Gilad agreed.

"Or a break," said Noah.

"Look," said the general, "in any other scenario, I'd simply send a pair of F-16s over the camp and take it out. But if there's a chance—however remote—that our people are in that camp . . ."

Golan didn't finish the thought.

Jenny Morris was about to finish it for him.

But Donny Callaghan beat her to it. "How soon can we leave?"

79

BEIRUT, LEBANON

There were only two ways off this roof.

And Marcus was not going back down the stairs.

Which meant he was going to have to jump.

But first he had to get a sense of where he was and what his next objective should be. Moving toward the roof's edge, he surveyed his surroundings. It was night, of course, but the moon was nearly full. What was more, all the lights of the city were on, and visibility was good. Better yet, the temperature was dropping, and there was a steady breeze coming off the water.

What struck Marcus immediately was the plethora of mosques and minarets all around him. That he was in a Muslim neighborhood was clear. What was not so clear was whether he was in Shia territory or Sunni. Three blocks to his right, however, he spotted two crosses atop two church steeples, side by side, adorning a massive church building with a red tile roof. That, he knew, had to be a Maronite Christian neighborhood, probably the one known as Mar Maroun. Getting there was his new objective.

The only problem—well, the first problem, anyway—was not that he was nearly stark naked. Nor that his entire body was bloodied and bruised. Or even that his face was so beat up that he was nearly unrecognizable. They were all challenges, to be sure. But he would have to deal with those later.

The immediate problem before him was that the next apartment building was a bit farther away than he had realized. When he reached the edge of the roof, he checked the distance and guessed it was about twenty feet. The world record for a running jump was maybe thirty feet, give or take. But that was the Olympics. Marcus had never run track and field. Even if he had, his feet had been repeatedly subjected to electric shocks. They were burned, bloody, and killing him. And he was shoeless. Yet what other choice did he have? There was no way he could spend the night on this rooftop. It was either jump or . . .

Marcus reconsidered his options for a moment and concluded he had been too hasty. Yes, heading back into the stairwell and working his way down through the building was a risk. But jumping was even more of one. True, there were still hours to go before most people went to sleep, and he could hardly afford to be spotted. But how could he possibly track down Kailea and Yigal if he tried to jump, missed the mark, and splattered all over the alleyway?

He heard sirens in the distance. Glancing over the front edge of the building, he spotted three police cars coming up the boulevard. They were at least a half mile away, but they were heading in his direction. Lights flashing. Sirens blaring. They might not be for him, of course, but he was not going to wait around to find out.

The decision made for him, he removed the socks lest he slip. With nowhere else to put them, he stuffed them into the waistband of his boxers. Then he backed up to the far end of the roof. There was no time to do a test. So he broke out in a sprint. It was all or nothing. Do or die.

Hitting full speed and trying to ignore the pain, Marcus reached the edge of the roof. He planted his right foot, pushed off as hard as he could, and swung his arms forward, reaching for the edge of the next building. With a burst of adrenaline, he sailed over the alley. But he had way overshot. He reached the other side, all right, but did not exactly stick the landing. Rather, he stumbled badly and skidded to a stop on his knees. More blood. More evidence. And he had lost the socks.

He found more clotheslines with no clothes, but he at least grabbed a clean, dry sheet from one of them. Tearing it into strips with his teeth, he proceeded to wrap several sections around his knees, not as tight as a tourniquet but snug enough to stop the bleeding. With the sirens growing louder, Marcus once again broke out into a sprint. He again reached the end of the building, planted his right foot, and pushed off. Again, he found himself flying over an alley, and by the grace of God he cleared it.

There was no alley on the other side of this building but an entire boulevard. Still finding nothing on any clotheslines that he could wear—nothing but women's garments and linens—there was no reason to stop. He caught his breath, but only for a moment. Then he eased open the door into the stairwell and listened. More music. More laughter. More families. More dogs. But the sirens were even closer now, so there was no point waiting. Nor any point inching his way down the stairs. Instead, he ran down them, blowing past a few startled ladies congregating on the third-floor landing.

Only when he reached the ground floor did he come to a complete stop near a side door. He quietly, carefully turned the knob, opened the door an inch or so, and peered out. Just then, the three police cars raced past him. All other traffic stopped to let them pass, then continued as normal. Marcus watched and waited for a lull, and when he found one, he sprinted across the boulevard and into another alleyway. He had no idea whether he had been spotted or not. Nor did he have time to worry about it. His mission at this point was to keep moving. So that's what he did, darting between buildings, behind trees, behind parked cars, and through whatever alleys he could find.

Ten minutes later, he found himself hiding in the shadows behind a church building on a corner. It had a sign in both Arabic and English that read *St. Joseph's Church.* This was not the one he had spotted from the rooftop. It had one steeple, not two. Marcus decided to give it a try. Using the shadows cast in the moonlight for cover, he crept up the back stairs and tried the door. It was locked. He retraced his steps and moved around to a side door, but it, too, was locked. Breaking in did not seem like a wise move, especially not as he heard more sirens approaching. Hiding behind a dumpster, Marcus waited for the additional police cars to pass, then moved deeper into the Maronite neighborhood.

He wove through one alleyway after another, past several bistros, several more apartment buildings, a pharmacy, and numerous private flats, until he finally reached the St. Maroun Maronite Catholic Church. This was the one he had seen—an enormous structure with a red tile roof and two cross-topped steeples towering overhead. Marcus scanned the environment in all directions but saw no one on the streets. No couples strolling. No old men walking their dogs. No teenagers courting or plotting mischief. Every door he found was locked. But he spotted a basement window ajar. There were no lights on inside. No voices. No music. No evidence that anyone was nearby. So he crept toward it, yanked it all the way open, and slipped inside and shut and locked the window behind him.

Marcus found himself in what looked like a small Sunday school classroom filled with toys. Children's drawings of Jesus and the apostles adorned the walls. He tiptoed forward, listening for any signs of life on the other side of the door. Hearing none, he slowly turned the knob, opened the door slightly, and peered out into a dark hallway. It was clear, so he began moving forward.

Everything was going well until he reached the end of the hallway and turned the corner. That was when Marcus found himself looking into the eyes of a very startled priest.

80

The two men stared at each other for what seemed like an eternity.

The priest wore a black skullcap and a traditional black ankle-length robe with red buttons known as a *cassock* or a *jibbee*, though Marcus was not sure which term applied. Around the man's waist was a dark-red sash known as a *fascia*, and a large metal cross hung around his neck.

From behind his round, wire-rimmed glasses, the stunned priest tried to size the intruder up. Marcus had not seen himself in a mirror, but he could only imagine how disastrous he looked. Mind racing, he decided he should capitalize on his appearance. He began speaking in gibberish, making wide, sweeping gestures with his hands and stumbling toward the man as if he were drunk.

It seemed to work. The man took a whiff of him and winced immediately. Marcus knew he was not smelling alcohol. The odor the priest was picking up on was from the fact that Marcus had not had a shower in nearly two days. For good measure, Marcus began coughing up a lung and let saliva drip down his beard.

The priest—a slight, bookish man—backed away. Yet, choosing to press the offensive, Marcus continued toward him, grasping his stomach as if trying to make it clear just how hungry and thirsty he was. It was no act. And it worked. Once the priest realized that Marcus was not a threat, just another person desperate for the church's help, his anxiety seemed to vanish, and his compassion kicked in. The man began going on and on about something. The words were in Arabic and thus of little help to Marcus, but the tone was soothing. Then the man took him by the arm and led him up a flight of stairs and down several hallways to an industrial-size kitchen.

Once the priest turned on the lights, Marcus could see how immaculately clean the place was. What a contrast, he thought, to the Hezbollah compound. The priest sat him down on a stool beside a large stainless steel island in the center of the kitchen. He opened the door to a massive refrigerator and pulled out a big bowl of chopped salad and some things to make a sandwich. Moments later, Marcus was wolfing it all down, enjoying every morsel. To the food, the priest added a large glass of ice-cold lemonade, which Marcus chugged down in about three seconds flat. He did the same with a second glass. And then the man put a bowl of soup in the microwave, warmed it up, and set it before Marcus with a spoon and several napkins. Staying in character, Marcus did not even glance at the napkins, much less touch or use them. But he slurped up the soup in short order. When he was done, he pushed the bowl away and let out a hearty burp.

The priest did not seem to know whether to be offended or amused but in the end let out a chuckle and started speaking to him once more in Arabic. It was not hard for Marcus to act like he had no idea what the man was saying. Rather than look confused, however, Marcus acted like he could not even hear the words. Instead, he just stared at the empty bowl, then looked absent-mindedly around the room and fixated on a mixing bowl resting up on a shelf.

When the priest realized he was still not getting through, he again took Marcus by the arm and led him up several flights of stairs. As they headed down this hall, the priest motioned for Marcus to be very quiet. All the doors were closed, and Marcus guessed that this might be a dormitory for priests. When they reached the last door on the left, the priest opened it and led Marcus inside to a room with several empty bunk beds, each of which had a towel and washcloth folded and sitting on the pillow. Through an open side door, Marcus glimpsed the sight of many men sleeping on bunk beds in a spacious adjoining room. They must be homeless, he thought. Many looked as disheveled and lost as he did. But they were all clean. Clothed. Tucked in. And snoring up a storm.

The priest motioned for Marcus to remain quiet, then pointed to a bunk that he could use. Next he rummaged through the drawers of a wooden dresser until he found a fresh T-shirt that would fit Marcus and a pair of tan khaki trousers that—though well used and a bit tattered—were clean and likely to fit him as well. From another drawer, the priest fished out a pair of socks and an unopened package of men's briefs. All these the priest set on the bunk. Then he opened an antique wooden wardrobe, picked out a dark-blue polo shirt that seemed about Marcus's size and a well-worn pair of brown shoes—slip-ons, without any laces.

Once he had set these, too, on the bed, the priest led Marcus to an adjoining washroom, complete with a sink, a toilet, and a shower stall with no curtain. This could not be what all the men used; it was too clean and too small. But he was not about to start asking questions, so he feigned a look of near-complete lack of understanding, then dropped down on the floor, cross-legged, and leaned his head against the wall.

Marcus could feel the astonishment of the cleric, the man's eyes boring into him. But he knew his only chance of this guy not picking up the phone and calling the police was maintaining the act of a man deeply troubled yet unlikely to do harm. So Marcus stayed in that position and did not look up.

Eventually he heard the man sigh, mutter something in Arabic, and then leave the room and close the door behind him. Through the bathroom door, Marcus could still see the sleeping men in the adjoining room. For good measure, in case any of them had woken up and were now looking at him, Marcus did not move for another ten minutes. Then he slowly toppled over onto his left side, curled up in a fetal position, and stared blankly into the bunkroom. This position he held for a good while longer, until he had scrutinized the face of every man that was visible through the doorway and became convinced that they were all truly asleep.

81

After a few minutes, Marcus finally rose to his feet.

Creeping to the door to the next room, he slowly—*silently*—closed and locked it. Then he moved to the hallway door and locked it, too. Only then did he head to the bathroom. When he had closed and locked that door behind him, the first thing he did was rifle through the drawers of the vanity until he found a new toothbrush and a tube of toothpaste. He ripped the package open, squeezed some toothpaste onto the end of the brush, ran it under a spritz of cold water, and proceeded to brush his teeth. It was strange just how good something so simple, so routine, felt to him at that moment.

As he spit and rinsed, he debated whether or not to take a shower. He was dying to, but would doing so spoil the illusion he was trying to create? Probably. And yet, the rest of the men, for all their myriad troubles, had obviously cleaned themselves up from the filth of the streets. They did not stink. And they were wearing the clean, if used, clothes that the church had provided them. If Marcus did not do the same by the following morning, did he risk drawing attention and generating questions he could not answer?

In any case, Marcus knew there was a far more urgent priority than a shower just then. He had to find a phone. As part of their contingency planning, he and Kailea had memorized various phone numbers that they could call in case of an emergency. The higher-ups in Washington—from DSS to Langley to the White House—were already aware that he, Kailea, and Yigal were alive because the Sheikh had used their names and aliases in his broadcast. That was good. It meant the American military and intelligence community—along with the IDF, Mossad, and Shin Bet—were already actively hunting for them. Now Marcus needed to provide them a location so they could come pick him up. Only then could they turn their attention to finding and rescuing Kailea and Yigal.

This could not wait for a shower. It certainly could not wait until tomorrow. Al-Masri and his men were already hunting for him. If they really had gone rogue, then Hezbollah was hunting for him too. He could not take the risk of waiting until morning to find and use a phone. In his world, tomorrow might never come. He needed to let Washington know where he was. Only then could he let himself enjoy a shower and maybe even a few hours of sleep.

Nevertheless, he grabbed the handle in the shower and turned the water on full blast and as hot as it could go. That might buy him some time. If someone came looking for him, hopefully they would think he was taking a shower after all. With steam filling the room, Marcus unlocked the bathroom door, moved to the door to the hallway, and listened for a full minute. He heard no one out there, though there was always the possibility the priest was standing guard. Or that the church had a closed-circuit television system to monitor any movement in the hallways. Those were risks he was going to have to take. Just in case, Marcus decided to pretend he was sleepwalking. He carefully unlocked the door, opened it, and headed into the hallway in a seemingly catatonic state. He knew it was highly unlikely there would be a phone on a floor filled with homeless men. So he drifted to the stairwell and stumbled his way up to the next floor.

At the top of the stairs, he stood in the center of a hallway for a good minute or two, staring into space, listening intently, and waiting for someone to come retrieve him and take him back to his room. No one did. Nor had he spotted any cameras, though the lights were off and the hallways were rather dark. Maybe the church couldn't afford a CCTV system. Maybe it was broken. Maybe it was working, but they could not afford a night watchman. Then again, maybe they could, and whoever was watching the feed had fallen asleep or more likely was watching television or browsing social media.

Marcus knew he had to keep moving. He continued his trancelike progress down the hall. There were signs on each closed door. They were all in Arabic. But Marcus doubted they were Sunday school classrooms. These, somehow, seemed to him like offices. Picking one, he pretended to bump into a wall, then into the doorjamb. Then he turned the handle and stumbled inside before closing and locking the door behind him.

Marcus smiled. His instincts had not failed him. The room he had just entered was not a single priest's office but appeared to be a bullpen of cubicles that were probably used by the church's secretaries. The doors to adjoining rooms, one to the left and one to the right, were locked. But it did not really matter. Each of the desks around him had a phone. He picked up one and heard a dial tone.

82

Marcus knew he needed to move quickly.

He proceeded to punch in one of the set of numbers Langley had given him. As expected, the call went straight to voice mail. Marcus recited his personal, onetime authorization code, then spoke briefly and quietly. Keeping his eye on the second hand of the clock on the wall, he made sure he stayed on the line long enough for a trace to be executed. At precisely ninety seconds, he hung up, then wiped down the receiver with a tissue he pulled from a box on the desk and tossed the tissue into a trash basket.

It was now 11:19 p.m. Marcus moved to the door and strained once again for any evidence that someone was coming. He heard none. No shoes coming down the freshly mopped hallway. No keys jangling. No hushed voices. No squawking portable radios. Marcus could almost hear his SERE training officer telling him to double-time it back to the bunkroom. He had taken all the risks he needed to for one night. It was time to wait for the cavalry to arrive. But Marcus had never been one to play it safe. So he decided to explore a little.

Not sure exactly what he was looking for, though a mobile phone would be handy—not to mention a Glock 9mm—Marcus began with the file cabinets. Most of what he found was of no value to him. Personnel files. Financial ledgers. Folders filled with receipts of various kinds. Datebooks filled with apparent scheduling notes. Almost nothing was in English. He shifted to the desk drawers. Here, too, he found little of value. More files. Office supplies. Snack foods he had no interest in trying. And a tangle of wires related to phone chargers, laptops, and other electronic devices. But no phone.

In the bottom of one drawer, however, he hit pay dirt—a metal box with a small steel padlock on it. This looked promising, so Marcus rooted around in the nearby drawers for a key. Finding none, he settled for a paper clip. He unbent it, then snapped it in half. Taking one L-shaped piece in each hand, he inserted them in the key slot on the underside of the padlock and began jiggling them both, applying pressure in a clockwise direction. A moment later, the lock clicked open.

He opened the box and found five stacks of crisp 1,000-pound Lebanese notes in their distinctive teal color with the sketch of a cedar tree on each side. Each stack was bound by a rubber band. In addition, there was a handful of loose bills, plus some change. Marcus made a quick count. In each stack there were two hundred 1,000-pound notes. That put the total at over one million Lebanese pounds.

It was not as much as it sounded—worth about seven hundred U.S. dollars—but given that he had nothing, it seemed like a gift from heaven. With this, he could easily buy a burner phone, allowing him to stay connected with Langley as he avoided the forces that al-Masri and the Sheikh had deployed to find him and then linked up with whoever the Agency had sent to rescue him. Or maybe he could use the money to simply hire a cab to take him to the U.S. Embassy or to the Swiss or British Embassies. Maybe that was the best way—the fastest and the simplest route to safety in a city crawling with people bound and determined to kill him.

Marcus stared at the money, hesitating. He needed it, to be sure, but could he really justify taking money from a church? Perhaps. He flashed back to his childhood and all the stories his mother had taught him from the Scriptures. Hadn't she taught him that God loved him and would always take care of him? Hadn't she taught him that the Lord in his mercy could provide for his every need? And wasn't that exactly what was happening now? How else could he explain stumbling on so much cash, right when he needed it most?

83

Hesitation was a mistake, Marcus reminded himself.

It could get you captured.

It could get you killed.

And yet the more Marcus tried to justify what he was doing, the more uncomfortable he became. He recalled a Bible story about David, on the run for his life from the wicked King Saul. When he had been hungry and alone, David had taken and eaten the sacred bread that was supposed to be set on the altar, a sacrifice to the Lord, forbidden for mere mortals. Yet David had not actually stolen the bread. The priest, a man named Ahimelech, had given it to him. The same was true when David had been desperately in need of a weapon to defend himself. Yes, David had taken from the house of the priest the very sword he had once used to kill the giant Goliath because there was nothing else available to him. Yet, again, David had not robbed the priest. He had asked Ahimelech for help, and the man had willingly given him the sword.

Marcus shook his head and put the money back in the box. He promptly closed it, put the padlock on it, and returned the box to the drawer, just as he had found it. Then he wiped it down with tissues and threw these and the broken pieces of the paper clip into the garbage pail. There were always going to be hard choices in this line of work, he told himself. This was not one of them. Socks off a clothesline were one thing. Stealing money that a church probably used to care for homeless men was another. And after all, the Lord had provided for him—a meal, clean clothes, a roof over his head, and—lest he forget—a phone. It was time to be grateful, not greedy.

He heard someone coming. It was the jangling keys he heard first. Then a garbled voice over a portable radio. A night watchman was doing his rounds, and he was close. Glancing to his left and right, Marcus remembered that the doors to both adjoining offices were locked. The door to the hallway was the only way out. Except for the windows.

He turned quickly, pushed back the drapes, unlocked the window, and opened it. There was a narrow ledge outside, and he crawled out onto it. He closed the window behind him and moved to his right along the ledge just as the door to the secretary pool opened and a flashlight swept the area.

There was a four-foot gap between the end of the ledge he was on and the start of the next one, outside the window of one of the locked offices. There was no point looking down. Marcus knew he was four floors up and would not likely survive a fall. Still, he could not take the risk that the watchman had heard him raising or lowering the window. Without thinking, he leaped to the next ledge and nearly slipped off. Gripping the side of the building with everything he had, he regained his footing, then dug his fingernails under the sash and forced the window open. The moment he got it open and slipped inside, he could hear the watchman raising the sash two offices away. There was no way he could now lower the window he had just come through without alerting the watchman to his presence. So Marcus left it open, headed for the door to this office, unlocked it, opened it, peeked into the hallway, and made a dash for it.

Two minutes later, he was back in his bunkroom. He left the door to the hallway unlocked in case someone came to check on him. Then he stepped into the bathroom and was immediately enveloped by a cloud of steam. He closed and relocked the bathroom door and readjusted the water temperature so as not to scald himself. Then he stepped under the cascade and let it wash away the blood and the dirt and the grime, if not the memories of the past two days.

When he was done, he turned off the water, toweled down, ripped open the package of men's briefs, and put on a pair, along with the clean T-shirt the priest had given him. Then he tossed his towel down on the bathroom floor to soak up as much of the water as he could, threw the filthy boxer shorts he had been wearing in the trash, and climbed into bed.

The symphony of snoring in the adjacent room was still underway. But Marcus barely noticed. He had done all he could to alert his team to his location. There was nothing more he could do for now. And he fell fast asleep almost as soon as his head hit the pillow.

84

Five blocks away, a half-dozen squad cars screeched to a halt.

Police officers moved quickly to set up a perimeter around the apartment building, cutting off traffic on the street in front of the building, as well as the street at the other end of the alley, on the building's back side. A moment later, an unmarked car pulled up. General Mubarak stepped out and surveyed the scene. He was alone, but only until two trucks pulled in behind him and two dozen Hezbollah commandos in full battle gear began to deploy.

Mubarak directed a pair of snipers to take up positions on the roof of one of the buildings across the street, then ordered a dozen of his men to assist the police in reinforcing the perimeter. The rest he led into the alleyway, where they were met by the building manager, a spindly, balding gentleman who looked to be in his early fifties.

"It was my son who saw him, or thinks he did," the man said after giving his name to Mubarak. "He's a cook."

"Where?"

"At a restaurant downtown."

"No," said Mubarak. "I mean, where is your son now?"

"Inside, with my wife."

"I want to hear it from him."

"Follow me," the man said.

They passed through the side door, and Mubarak was already on alert. He could see the lock had been ripped off the door, and there were wood splinters in the alleyway. The man led them down a dim hallway, turned right, and invited the general into his flat.

Before entering, Mubarak turned to his men. "You, stay with me. You two, wake up the neighbors on this floor. Find out if anyone else saw or heard anything. The rest of you head up the stairs and let me know what you find."

When they complied, Mubarak entered, his right hand resting on his holster, a commando guarding the door and watching his back. The building manager introduced his twenty-six-year-old son. Mubarak sized him up and asked to see his ID, then asked the boy why he had told his father to call the police.

"I was coming back from my shift and had just gotten off the bus when—"

"Where?" Mubarak asked.

"About a block up that way," said the young man, pointing. "Near the little French bistro."

"L'Artisan du Liban?"

"Yes, that's the one."

"Go on."

"I got off the bus and was about to walk home when I suddenly saw some guy jump out the back of a car."

"What kind of car?"

"A taxi."

"Color?"

"Yellow."

"Make?"

"What?"

"What was the make and model of the car?"

"It was a Mercedes, for sure, but I don't know much about cars. I just—"

"Old or new?"

"Old."

"How old?"

"Again, I don't really know—I don't really—"

"Guess."

"Old. Maybe from the eighties—early nineties?"

"Go on."

"Well, I mean, suddenly the trunk pops open and this guy jumped out," the young man explained. "It startled me, so I just froze and stared at him. And it was weird because he was wrapped in something."

"What?"

"I don't—like a rug or something."

"A rug?"

"I think so. And he had a tire—the spare tire—he jumped out of the taxi and landed on the tire, like he was trying to cushion his fall or something. And there was something else weird about him too."

"What?"

"He was naked—well, not completely naked—but he wasn't wearing a shirt. Or pants. Only boxer shorts."

"I thought you said he was wrapped in a rug."

"He was."

"Then how could you see what he was wearing?"

"Because once he stopped rolling and came to a stop—bloodied and all scratched up and everything—and he wasn't wearing shoes either—"

"No shoes."

"None—but once he came to a stop, after jumping, he took off the rug, gathered it up with the tire, and went running into the alley."

"The one we just walked through."

"Yes."

"And then?"

"I don't—it was all so sudden, and all so weird, that I told my father."

"And you think this man is in the building?"

"Yes."

"Why?"

"Because when I came into the alley, I noticed bloody handprints on the dumpster."

"Wasn't it dark?"

"Yes."

"Then why were you noticing the dumpster?"

"I had brought home food from the restaurant where I work. I ate it on the bus ride home. I was about to throw the bag in the dumpster when I noticed the handprints."

"And then?"

"Then I noticed the door had been busted into."

"Go on."

The young man talked for several more minutes. Mubarak got the basic contours of his account, then doubled back to the beginning to press for more details. His radio crackled to life. His men had found bloody footprints leading to the roof. Several of them were up there now, and they urged the general to come right away.

Mubarak excused himself, left the manager's apartment, and followed the footprints up to the roof. There, his men pointed him to new clues. They began with a bloodstained pair of socks. Next, they showed him more bloody footprints, some that led to a clothesline, others that led from the left side of the building directly across to the right. There was also a smudge of dried blood on the very edge of the roof.

Mubarak examined everything, then pointed his flashlight across the alley to the adjacent roof but could see nothing. Radioing back to head-quarters, he requested a hundred more men. They were going to have to search both buildings, and possibly several more, room by room.

Next, he speed-dialed the chief of the Beirut police force. Though not a member of Hezbollah, the man's two sons were, and the chief himself had always proven helpful to the cause. Indeed, it was the chief who had called

Mubarak the moment he was informed that his officers were responding to such a bizarre call after the APB had gone out for al-Masri.

The chief answered on the second ring. "What have you got?"

"A blood trail," said Mubarak. "And it's fresh."

"Al-Masri?"

"I doubt it."

"Then who?"

"I'd say one of his prisoners escaped."

"Escaped?"

"The eyewitness says he saw some guy bailing out of the trunk of a taxi."

"You're kidding."

"No, and he was wearing nothing but boxer shorts. He was wounded and covered in blood. Came up to the roof; then something spooked him—jumped to the next building. I've got reinforcements on the way."

"Do you need more police?"

"No—my guys will do," said Mubarak. "But we're looking for a yellow taxicab."

"That narrows it down."

"A Mercedes. Old. Maybe something from the eighties or early nineties."

"General, you're talking about most of the fleet at work in this city."

"This one's special."

"How so?"

"Both of the taillights have been smashed out."

"Okay, that's a start. I'll get my men right on it."

85

On the south side of the city, al-Masri told Zayan to take a right.

Then a left.

Then to pull into a public parking garage underneath a supermarket in Laylaki, a Shia community immediately adjacent to the Beirut airport.

The market, Zayan knew, was not far from where al-Masri had grown up. It was closed. There was no one out on the streets at this hour. And every level of the garage was empty. Except the last. Three floors down, al-Masri ordered Zayan to pull into a spot next to a rusty blue Dodge van. He did as he was told, then shut down the engine.

"We need to move fast," the Egyptian instructed as he jumped out of the passenger side, pulled a set of keys from his pocket, and unlocked and opened the back doors of the van. "Help me get this guy into the van; then we'll wipe down the taxi and move the rest of our bags over."

Zayan complied. He got out of the driver's side and came around the back of the van, then saw confusion on the commander's face. Following al-Masri's gaze, Zayan became confused as well. Both of the taillights were gone. Not broken. Not cracked. Gone. And the trunk lid was unlatched and slightly ajar.

"*Open it,*" al-Masri ordered.

Rattled by the sudden anger in the man's voice, Zayan raised the trunk lid. But it was empty. Not only was their prisoner gone, so was all the fruit. All that was left were a few splinters of wood. Even the carpet that lined the trunk floor was gone, as was the spare tire. The two men just stared into the empty space. Zayan braced himself for the tirade that was coming. But it did not come. Al-Masri merely stood there, mouth open, unable to speak, unable even to move for what seemed like an eternity.

"It's not possible," the colonel finally said, more to himself than to Zayan.

Zayan knew better than to reply. He was scared. More than that, he was terrified at what al-Masri might do to him.

"We . . . no . . . we can't . . . ," al-Masri mumbled, though he was barely audible. "How can we go back?"

Zayan kept quiet.

Al-Masri tried to speak again but was struggling to form words. "I guess we . . ."

The words trailed off. Al-Masri turned and stared at the empty parking garage.

"But where? I don't . . . I can't . . ."

Again, the words trailed off.

And Zayan could only stand there, frozen in place.

★

It was if all the circuit breakers in al-Masri's head had suddenly blown.

He simply could not process what his eyes were telling him.

The implications were unimaginable.

Until now, things had been going so well. Yes, the raid had been messy. And yes, he had lost his brother, probably forever. But those were costs he was willing to pay. The mission was still on track. And it was nearly complete. Al-Masri had spent the entire drive from the east side of Beirut praying that they would not be stopped by the local police or Hezbollah patrols. Those prayers had been answered. How, then, could Allah have allowed this to happen, especially when he was so close to achieving victory?

Interspersed between his prayers, al-Masri had also been making a mental checklist of all that he needed to do when they reached the safe house and the storage facility. And then, just moments ago, he had finally received the text from his Kairos contact, the text he had been waiting for. The new passport, credit cards, and other papers he had demanded had been produced. The route had been booked. The tickets had been purchased. They were taking Turkish Airlines flight 831. It was scheduled to depart Beirut at 9:10 in the morning and land in Istanbul just two hours later. From there, the exchange would be made. The prisoners would no longer be his concern. He would be rich. And he would be free to melt away into the crowds.

Now what? he asked himself. *How in the world was he supposed to find Thomas Millner? The man must have escaped sometime after they had cleared the last checkpoint. That was back near Zalqa, eighteen kilometers away. At this hour, even with little or no traffic, it would take them thirty minutes to get back there. In theory, of course, he and Zayan could retrace their steps. But so what? How could they possibly find him? How long might it take? In a few hours, the sun would be up. The morning rush hour would begin. The roads would be gridlocked. And what then?*

86

It simply wasn't possible.

Millner was gone, al-Masri concluded, and there was not a thing he could do about it. There was no point trying to come up with a plan. There was no way he could risk being stopped and caught as he tried to move back and forth across a city that was hunting him.

The Egyptian began pacing around the empty garage. Zayan was staring at him, waiting for orders, but al-Masri ignored him. This was a disaster. His heart rate was spiking. He was struggling to breathe. Everything he had planned, all that he had promised . . .

His hand slowly started to reach for his sidearm. *This was Zayan's fault. How could this fool have let this happen? First, he had left Tanzeel behind at the border, and now this? The first was bad enough. This was unpardonable.*

Yet he stopped and forced himself to take several deep breaths. There would be time enough for vengeance. For now, he reminded himself, there was still much to do. For the next few hours, at least, he needed Zayan. Then he could be dispatched.

What was more, he told himself, he still had two hostages. They were still worth a great deal of money. More than enough to relocate and set up a new life. Perhaps in the Far East someplace. Or the rain forests of Brazil. It did not matter to him where. With that kind of money, he could be comfortable anywhere. So long as he remained invisible to the long arm of Hezbollah. He was going to have to tell them, of course. Kairos was not going to be happy. But there was nothing more to be done.

"Leave it," al-Masri finally told Zayan. "We're going to the safe house. But there is something I must do first."

Abandoning the taxi, they jumped in the blue van and peeled out of the parking garage. As the Egyptian barked out directions, Zayan drove south six blocks until they reached a storefront housing the facilities of a private delivery service. Al-Masri told Zayan not to stop. Not yet. Rather, he wanted him to circle the block. Was anything out of place? Was anyone watching them? Following them? When he was confident the coast was clear, he ordered Zayan to pull up out front. The van was not stolen. Nor were the plates. He had purchased the vehicle several weeks earlier from a trusted friend, paid cash, and had no worries that it should attract any attention from the police.

While Zayan kept the engine running, al-Masri used his passkey to enter the building. He found the PO box that he had recently rented and used another key to open it. Sure enough, inside was a large envelope that had been sent by airmail from Istanbul. Al-Masri glanced around, confirmed that there were no security cameras monitoring him, and then ripped open the package. Inside was a Turkish passport in his name, airline tickets, credit cards, a bank card, and everything else he had demanded. He exhaled, thanked Allah, and pocketed it all. Then he stuffed the remains of the package back in the PO box, closed and locked it, and headed back to the van.

"Okay," he said, "the safe house."

Five minutes later, they had parked in front of a high-rise, luxury apartment building just blocks from the airport, taken an elevator to the twentieth floor, and entered the penthouse suite. The rest of their team was waiting. Everyone embraced. Though al-Masri insisted they keep their voices down—the last thing they could afford to do was draw the attention of their neighbors—there was nevertheless a palpable sense of relief in the air. They brought out food and cold drinks and briefed each other on the harrowing adventures they had been through since they were last together, and then al-Masri asked about the condition of their prisoners.

"They're fine," one of the men replied. "We washed their wounds and gave them the antibiotics, just as you instructed."

"Here?"

"No, no, in the container at the cargo terminal."

"How did you get them past security?"

"We dressed them in the abayas you gave us, pretended they were our sisters, and told the guards they were asleep."

"And you weren't asked any questions?"

"None—we flashed our IDs and they waved us right through."

"And Jamal is with them?"

"He is."

"Any signs of heightened security?"

"None."

"Good," said al-Masri. "Now get some rest. Then pack up and wipe the place down. We need to be back at the airport by six."

"Excuse me, Colonel—permission to speak freely?" said another one of the men.

"What is it?" al-Masri asked.

"I don't understand," the man said. "Why are you asking us about the prisoners? Didn't you see them when you went?"

"We haven't been to the airport yet."

"Why not? Where is your prisoner?"

Al-Masri tensed. *Should he tell them the truth? It was humiliating. And they had no right to it. He was their commander. They were his subordinates, his servants. They did not need to know anything more than he told them. Yet what if he lied to them, and Zayan later told them the truth?*

He shot a glance at his aide and saw the fear in his eyes.

Good, thought al-Masri. *The idiot would not talk. He knew better.*

"We turned him over to the Sheikh already," he told them.

Zayan swallowed hard but said nothing.

"Then why are we not handing these two over to the Sheikh, as well?" one of his men now asked.

"If you must know, the Sheikh is keeping one and sending the others to Tehran."

He scanned the men's faces. He saw confusion, but no one dared ask another question. So he bade them a good sleep and told them to be ready to depart at six. He waited for them all to go to their bedrooms or retreat to their air mattresses. Then he turned out the lights, headed for the master bedroom, and closed and locked the door behind him.

Stepping out on to the balcony, he gazed out at the sea and the lights of the airport. There were not many flights taking off or landing at this hour. Indeed, the area's usual hum was rather subdued. Al-Masri spotted the Turkish Airlines cargo terminal. Its distinctive red-and-white sign was clearly visible from this location and especially this height—one of the reasons he had rented this particular flat. He thought about the two prisoners. They were his tickets to freedom. But what was he going to tell Kairos?

For the moment, he decided, there was no reason to make contact. In just a few hours, they were going to know the truth.

87

"No, not yet—shut it and get back to your posts."

Abdel Rahman was furious. When he had news for them, the twenty-four-year-old Radwan fighter told the other men in the compound, they would be the first to know. Until then, he was sick of hearing them ask. No, the phone in his pocket had not rung. No, it had not vibrated. No, it had not chirped. And true to his word, he had resisted the temptation to call or text anyone.

Their mission was simple: wait for instructions and do not move until they got them. *Why, then, had so much time passed?*

They had all expected to get the word to move out within hours of the rest of the team's departure, which had been just before breakfast early the previous morning. By lunchtime, the men in his charge had been growing antsy. By dinner, they had become worried. Now it was well past midnight.

Abdel could not believe it was already Monday morning. There still had been no word, and the men, unable to sleep, were about to go ballistic. Since they dared not blame al-Masri, they were aiming their attacks at Abdel, outright accusing him of either screwing up or refusing to share with them critical operational details. The problem was compounded by the fact that while Colonel al-Masri had put him in charge of these men, Abdel did not actually outrank them. Thus, he really had no authority over them, and they knew it. As the hours ticked by, Abdel feared a mutiny was building.

For the moment, his outburst had quieted them. But they would be back, and he needed answers. Had something gone wrong? Had al-Masri and Zayan been captured? Killed? Had the others? If so, by whom? He had no answers. The taxi and the jeep had not headed south, closer to enemy territory, deeper into the war zone. They had been heading north, into the arms of friendly forces.

None of it made sense, but suddenly Abdel heard explosions. Then machine-gun fire. As he and his men tried to pinpoint the direction it was coming from, one thing became clear—whoever was doing the shooting was getting closer. Taking a page from al-Masri's playbook, Abdel grabbed a pair of binoculars, sprinted through the courtyard, and leaped up onto a table and then onto the roof of a storage shed. This was the highest vantage point in the compound and allowed him to look over the stone wall and out toward the Med. The rest of his team quickly joined him.

With no lights on in the compound, a full moon, clear skies, and calm seas, Abdel spotted two speedboats, maybe a kilometer south of them, in a high-speed chase toward the shore. In the lead was a small rubber craft with a half-dozen or so Hezbollah commandos aboard. Behind it was an Israeli *Shaldag*-class fast patrol boat. Abdel estimated their speed at close to fifty knots on the open water, and the Israelis were rapidly gaining ground. They were also unleashing their 20mm cannon on their prey. Whoever was in the lead craft was returning fire, but they were in grave danger of being blown entirely out of the water.

Abdel adjusted the focus on the binoculars and zeroed in on the commandos. They were all wearing black masks. Black scuba gear. Doing their best to stay low. And putting up a good fight. But they needed help, and they needed it now. Abdel knew his orders. They were supposed to stay quiet and out of sight until they received word from al-Masri to move north to the safe house. But there was no way he and his men could stand by and watch while the criminal Zionists slaughtered their Hezbollah brothers who were obviously retreating from some operation near the border, probably in or around the Israeli port of Haifa, or perhaps the city of Nahariya.

Abdel had to make a split-second decision. If he ordered his colleagues to train their mortars on the Israeli Navy vessel and open fire, they would undoubtedly draw an air strike. But there was nothing sacred about staying in this compound. They could be in their trucks and on the move in less than a minute, well before the IDF Northern Command could give their F-16s the proper coordinates. And if Abdel could buy his fellow warriors some precious time, it would all be worth it.

He gave the order. His colleagues were under no compulsion to comply, but they erupted in cheers. He was finally giving them something to do, and they moved like lightning. A moment later, mortar rounds began erupting from the courtyard. Abdel stayed on the roof, watching through the binoculars where the rounds landed and calling out adjustments on the fly. One by one, the rounds were exploding closer and closer to the Israeli craft. Abdel was just about to call out another adjustment when a massive explosion rocked their world.

The force of the blast threw Abdel off the roof, and he landed hard in the dust. Then came a second explosion, followed almost immediately by a third. By the time he caught his breath and climbed to his feet, he could see the buildings on the other side of the courtyard consumed by fire. The dormitory was gone. So was the industrial kitchen and the walk-in freezer where their prisoners had once been held. Abdel stumbled forward amid the leaping flames and the billowing smoke. He was calling out to his friends by name, hoping some of them—any of them—were still alive.

88

Of the nine men al-Masri had left behind, Abdel feared he was the only one still alive.

No one was responding to his calls, though it was hard to hear anything over the roar of the inferno that was now engulfing nearly the whole of the compound.

Abdel had already found the severed head of one of his men, though the face was burned beyond all recognition. Picking through the rubble, he soon came across more body parts but could not determine if these went with the head he had just found or if they belonged to someone else.

He heard someone shrieking in pain and sprinted through the flames into what was left of the garage. He found one of his men alive, though barely. His left leg had been blown off, and he was bleeding out. Abdel removed his belt and tied it around the man's upper thigh as a tourniquet, pulling it as tight as he possibly could. But to no avail. The man's eyes soon rolled up into his head. Abdel felt for his pulse, but he was gone.

Grabbing his Kalashnikov rifle, he began working his way around the out-side of the camp, doing a perimeter check, looking for bodies, and praying to find survivors. He quickly discovered that the front gate had been blown to pieces. So, too, had the back gate, along with large sections of the surround-ing wall. The only structures still standing were the one al-Masri had used as an office and the shed Abdel had been standing on when the Zionists had fired their missiles.

Covered in blood, soot, and dust, Abdel staggered about in shock. He had been so certain that they would have enough time to fire on the Israeli craft and still evacuate the premises. How could he have been so wrong? How could the Israelis have struck so hard and so fast?

There was no time to process the questions. Abdel suddenly heard another one of his men shouting. Two, actually. Whoever they were, the men were not crying out in pain. They were calling him to come quickly. Electrified, Abdel sprinted around to the far side of the shed, in the direction of the voices. When he came around the corner, he was thrilled to see two faces he recognized. But then he saw the pain in their expressions. They were both burned, but they were breathing and on their feet. And they were not worried about themselves. They were standing over a body. As Abdel raced up to them, he found himself staring down at the lifeless, glassy eyes of the youngest member of their team—at least the youngest now that Tanzeel was no longer with them.

They stood there for several moments, just staring at their fallen com-rade, not sure what to say and therefore saying nothing. They were so rattled by all that had befallen them in the last few minutes that they did not even notice the commandos who now approached them from behind.

"Hey, you guys okay?" said the leader.

Startled, Abdel turned around, as did his colleagues, weapons at the ready. To his astonishment, Abdel was staring into the fiery, battle-weary eyes of five Hezbollah operatives—the very ones the Israelis had been shoot-ing at. They were no longer wearing wet suits and scuba gear. They were all wearing black- and white-checkered kaffiyehs that covered most of their faces and olive-green uniforms that were as filthy as they were drenched with sweat and seawater. When Abdel spotted the yellow Hezbollah flags sewn onto their sleeves and the special forces pins on their lapels, he lowered his weapon and began to breathe again, though he wasn't sure whether he should laugh or cry. "Who are you guys?" he asked.

"Radwan, like you," the leader replied. "The Sheikh sent us to infiltrate Nahariya. We were supposed to hit one of their schools, take everyone out, strike fear into the hearts of the Zionists. Unfortunately, we got turned back."

One of the men behind the leader spoke up as he ejected a magazine from his AK-47 and replaced it with a fresh one. "Thanks for the help. You really saved us."

"Yes," said the leader. "We're just sorry it cost you so much."

Abdel nodded, then wiped the sweat from his face and motioned for his colleagues to lower their weapons. Reluctantly both men did. "My name is Abdel," he said, shifting his weapon to his left hand and reaching out with his right. "Abdel Rahman."

"You're Abdel?" the leader said with surprise. "So you know Colonel al-Masri, right? I can't believe we found you."

"Of course we know him," Abdel replied. "We're on the colonel's personal staff."

"Then praise Allah—we've come to the right place."

The man stepped forward to shake Abdel's hand. The moment he grabbed it, however, he twisted Abdel's arm behind his back and put a .45 to his head. Both of Abdel's men started to raise their weapons. One was double-tapped to the forehead and died instantly. The other was shot once in the knee and once in the shoulder. He dropped to the ground, writhing in pain.

Then the kaffiyehs came off, and Abdel's face became as pale as a ghost.

89

"Good job, gentlemen," Jenny Morris said as she unveiled her face.

She brushed past her colleagues until she was staring into the stunned, haunted eyes of Abdel Rahman. Then she raised the silenced Glock in her right hand, put it to his forehead, and asked in flawless Arabic, "Where is the Egyptian?"

Rahman said nothing.

His eyes darted from face to face, then back to Jenny's. The man was as bewildered as he was scared. A moment earlier, he had thought he was in the presence of friends, comrades, not simply fellow jihadists but Radwan Unit warriors who had come to help him. Now he had been blindsided and could barely process the notion of having been captured and interrogated by an American, much less a woman.

Jenny used this to her advantage while Donny Callaghan held the man, Geoff Stone handcuffed him, Tomer Ben Ami handcuffed and bandaged the wounded terrorist on the ground, and Noah Daniels watched their backs.

"Where is the Egyptian?" Jenny asked again.

Once again, Rahman said nothing, a look of defiance spreading across his face, replacing the fear, or trying to, anyway.

Jenny lowered the pistol from the man's forehead. This single act caused Rahman to sag in relief. He exhaled loudly, then began sucking in deep breaths of air. But Jenny was not giving up. She was changing tactics. She aimed the Glock at his left foot and squeezed the trigger. The silenced 9mm bullet that spat out made barely a sound. But Rahman did. He screamed in pain, and Jenny aimed at his right foot.

"I have all night," Jenny said. "You don't."

"I don't know," Rahman shrieked. *"Truly—I have no idea where he is. You have to believe me."*

Jenny laughed. "But I don't, *habibi*," she told him. "And there are no points for lying to me."

She squeezed the trigger again. Rahman collapsed, and Callaghan let him fall to the ground. The man's hands were locked behind him. He certainly could not run. Not anymore. The only question was whether he was going to talk.

Jenny turned to Noah and asked him to find the phone—the one belonging to Tanzeel. She told Tomer to drag his prisoner off and find out what he knew. She then asked Geoff to head over to what was left of the garage, see if there were any vehicles in working order, and if so, pull them into the courtyard. The men all nodded and scrambled off to complete their assignments. As they did, Callaghan raised his M4 and scanned the area to make sure the three of them were truly alone and safe. When he was satisfied, he pulled the injured prisoner into a seated position.

"Look, Abdel, we know al-Masri was here with the rest of your squad," Jenny explained. "We know he was headed north. We know he took the prisoners with him. Now we need to know where."

"But I've already told you," Rahman said through gritted teeth. *"I have absolutely no idea where he is."*

"Don't play games with me, Abdel. You know full well what I'm asking.

Where is he heading? Where were you supposed to link up with him?" Jenny pointed her pistol at his left knee.

The threat worked, even faster than she had hoped.

"Beirut," he said.

"Obviously," Jenny reply. "But *where*?"

When Rahman hesitated, Jenny asked him another question.

"You understand, don't you, that al-Masri betrayed you all?"

"That's not true."

She smiled. "Of course it is. Why do you think you are here while your boss and the three prisoners are safe in Beirut?"

Rahman said nothing. Jenny waited. Then the man finally blurted out, "The colonel told us to wait here until he called."

"Where's your phone?"

"In my pocket."

"Has it rung?"

"Not yet."

"Has it buzzed? Has he sent you a text?"

"No, not yet."

"When did he leave?"

"Yesterday morning."

"What time?"

"Just after sunrise."

"How long does it take to get to Beirut, even with checkpoints—ninety minutes? Two hours?"

"Maybe."

"Then why hasn't he called?"

"What are you saying?" Rahman pushed back.

"I'm saying he double-crossed you. He was never going to call. The phone he gave you doesn't even work."

"That's ridiculous," snapped Rahman. "Of course it does."

"Have you used it?"

"No."

"You haven't made any calls?"

"He ordered me not to."

"Texts?"

"No."

"None at all?"

"I just told you—he told me to put the phone in my pocket and to wait. So that's what I did."

Jenny shook her head. "The phone doesn't even work," she told him. "It has no SIM card in it. He was never going to call you. He was never going to give you the green light to come to Beirut to be with him or to get your money. Think about that, Abdel. He cut you loose."

"That's a lie," Rahman shouted. *"You have no idea what you're talking about."*

Jenny asked Callaghan to extract the phone from the man's pocket. Callaghan did and handed it to Jenny. She glanced at it, then showed it to Rahman.

"See, Abdel?" she said. "No signal. No SIM card. Al-Masri was never going to call." She tossed Rahman's phone on the ground, and the man stared at it dumbly.

"But there is a phone here that works perfectly," she continued.

"What are you talking about?"

"What I'm talking about, *habibi,* is the phone belonging to Tanzeel al-Masri. Remember him? In your haste to get back to Lebanon, you guys left him behind. The Israelis captured him, but don't worry. He's fine. Eating well. Sleeping in a cell by himself. Satellite television. A fitness room. He couldn't be happier, and he's been singing like a canary."

Rahman winced.

"But that's not really the point," Jenny continued. "Tanzeel isn't the problem. His brother is. His brother—your boss—left his in the little office over there. With a SIM card. With a signal. That's how we found you. My colleague is over there right now retrieving it. But the colonel didn't expect us to come in person. He expected the Israelis to find the signal and drop a couple of five-hundred-pound bombs on this place, blowing it to kingdom come and all of you men with it."

Jenny let that thought sink in for a moment, then continued.

"There's more, Abdel—the colonel didn't just leave you to die; this whole operation has been one giant betrayal. You and your colleagues are loyal Shias. Loyal Lebanese. Faithful members of Hezbollah. But the Egyptian is not. This operation was not planned or sanctioned by the Sheikh. Oh, sure, the Sheikh is taking credit for it now. That's because he doesn't want to look foolish. The fact is, your boss planned this raid on his own. He's working for someone else. Not the Sheikh. Not Hezbollah. Not the Radwan Unit. He's got another agenda. He's working for someone outside the country. We don't know who yet. But we're going to find out. And if you help us get our people back and capture the Egyptian, we'll make it worth your while."

90

Jenny did not explain how.

Not yet.

She still had to convince the man that al-Masri really had gone rogue and was, in fact, playing them for fools. To do so, she pulled a small digital voice recorder from her pocket and pressed Play. What Abdel Rahman heard next were a series of intercepted telephone calls between senior Hezbollah leaders and some of their commanders in the field. In one recording after another, Amin al-Masri was declared an "enemy of the movement" who had "betrayed the cause" and must be "hunted down and killed immediately." The last was actually a conversation between the Sheikh himself and Mahmoud Entezam, head of the IRGC.

"What do you mean you don't have the prisoners?"

"General, this wasn't my operation. It's still not clear to us who authorized the attack, but I assure you it wasn't me."

"Then why didn't you say this when we first spoke?"

"I don't know. I was still in shock. It was all happening so quickly. I thought it was possible—unlikely, highly unlikely, but possible—that one of my men had ordered it. If that were the case, I was prepared to be held accountable, to take responsibility myself. But we're now certain. All of my generals were as blindsided as I was."

"You should have told me this immediately."

"I know, and—"

"We ordered you to fire your missiles because we thought—"

"Yes, I realize that, and I'm—"

"This is a disaster. Do you know how much damage you have—?"

The recording was cut off there, but it was clear from the look on his face that Rahman knew the voices. He could not, of course, have any idea how the Americans had intercepted the calls, nor that it was in fact Unit 8200—Israel's equivalent of the NSA—who had done it. But there was no doubt in his mind that the recordings were authentic and that Jenny was telling him the truth.

"The airport," Rahman said, pain thick in his voice. "One of the cargo terminals."

"Which one?"

"Turkish."

"Turkish Airlines?"

"Well, Turkish Cargo, but yes."

"Not Iran Air?"

"No."

"Why not?"

Rahman shrugged.

"Doesn't that seem strange?"

"What?"

"Using the Turks instead of Iran?"

"I guess," Rahman said. "I didn't really think about it."

"How do you know?"

"Know what?"

"That al-Masri is using Turkish Air?"

"Because we went there."

"Who?"

"The colonel and me and his aide."

"His aide?" Jenny asked. "Who's that?"

"His name is Zayan."

"What's his full name?"

"Zayan ibn Habib."

"Who is he?"

"He's on our team. He's young. But I think he's being groomed for a more senior role."

"How old is he?"

"I don't know. Twenty-six—maybe twenty-seven—I never asked him."

"And the three of you went there together?"

"Yes."

"Why you?"

"I'm the colonel's driver. He trusts me."

"Why aren't you driving him now?"

"I told you—he said to wait here and come when he called."

"When did you go?"

"Where?"

"To the airport, to the cargo terminal."

"Last week."

"Why?"

"What do you mean, why? To prep everything—you know."

"No—tell me."

"Please," said Rahman. "I need some painkillers. I can't—"

But Jenny cut him off. "Shut up and answer my questions."

Rahman shook his head but then thought better of such defiance and kept talking. "We went to the office."

"The Turkish Cargo office?"

"Yes."

"Where is that?"

"Just past the taxi stand, on the south side of the airport—next to UPS."

"Okay, and?"

"And the colonel went inside."

"Not you?"

"No."

"Zayan?"

"No, he told us to stay in the car. He went in alone."

"How long?"

"Five minutes."

"That's it?"

"Maybe ten—but no longer."

"And then?"

"Then he came out with a manager and told us to follow them. We went into the cargo terminal. The man led us to a storage area, gave us the keys, showed us the layout, and that was that. The colonel thanked him, and we left."

"Cameras?"

"What?"

"Were there security cameras?"

"Of course."

"Inside and out?"

"Yes."

"Are there guards out front?"

"Yes."

"How many?"

"Just one, in a booth—he's the one authorized to open the big garage doors so you can move your containers or boxes or whatever in and out."

"Is there any other way into the terminal?"

"In the back—that's where all the forklifts and other equipment move the cargo from the terminal to the planes."

"What about the sides of the building? Are there entrances?"

"On the north side, yes."

"With a guard?"

"No, just a keypad—you swipe the card they give you, and the door opens electronically."

"How far is that entrance from the storage area the colonel rented?"

"I don't know—forty meters, fifty maybe."

Jenny pulled out a notepad and pen from the pocket of her flak jacket and tossed them onto the man's lap. She nodded to Callaghan to remove his handcuffs.

"Draw me a map," she ordered, then took a step back and aimed her pistol at Rahman's head, just in case.

91

There was no time to be clever.

With all the fireworks they and the Israelis had just set off, men bearing arms—probably lots of them—would be arriving any minute. If they were going to make it out alive, not to mention get to Beirut before morning, they needed to do their work and hightail it out of there, pronto.

Noah Daniels pulled out his Agency phone and dialed Tanzeel al-Masri's number. The ring was faint at first, but as Noah moved inside the last standing structure in the compound, he could hear it growing louder. By the time he reached the back room, which looked like it had once been someone's office, the ringing was crystal clear. Spotting an old wooden desk, he rummaged through the drawers, found Tanzeel's phone tucked deep inside one of them, and silenced it.

Immediately checking the contacts, he was disappointed to find no names or numbers listed. The phone was new, he realized—perhaps only a couple of weeks old. It had made no calls and had received only a handful and only from three numbers. One was his, of course. The other two were clearly phone numbers based in Lebanon and, he was pretty sure, centered in Beirut. Using his own phone again, he texted both numbers to the watch commander at the CIA's Global Operations Center at Langley and asked her to run them through all of their databases as well as the NSA's and get back to him as quickly as possible. An instant later, the watch commander wrote back to say she was on it.

Noah now found something else in one of the drawers. A box for an Iridium 9555 satellite phone. It was empty, but on the back were three stickers, each containing UPC bar codes as well as a range of other letters and numbers. One of the stickers noted Thailand as the phone's country of origin. This, too, was a very recent purchase. Noah carefully looked through the box and then through the drawers, searching for a receipt. Finding none, he snapped a picture of the bar codes with his phone and texted it to the watch commander with the same request.

The room was a mess. All the windows had been shattered. There was glass all over the floor. There was an air mattress. It was deflated but looked new. The combination of Tanzeel's phone, the satphone box, and the mattress comprised strong circumstantial evidence that Amin al-Masri had used this as both his office and bedroom. Who else but a senior commander was likely to have quarters for himself?

In the corner, in the shadows, Noah suddenly spotted something else. Using the flashlight on his phone, he moved closer and found a pile of ashes. He squatted down for a closer look, set down his backpack, pulled out a pen, and used it to sift through the soot. The ashes were cool but fresh. The smell of smoke was still in the air, and Noah was disappointed with himself for not noticing it sooner. What struck him was that these ashes were not remains of paper. Someone, almost certainly al-Masri, had been burning clothes. Digging deeper, he uncovered bits of burnt army fatigues. He also found scorched pieces of cotton that might have come from a T-shirt, and to his astonishment, one of the pieces was drenched in blood.

A delicious thought came to Noah at that moment. Had al-Masri been injured in the firefight on the border? Had a round from Ryker's weapon, or

Curtis's, actually struck the man? That would be beautiful, but it was, he had to admit, just as possible that it was Ryker's blood, or Curtis's or the Israeli's, that somehow had gotten on al-Masri's shirt.

There was a way to find out. Noah quickly unzipped his backpack and pulled out a rubber pouch. Opening it, he withdrew a device known as a PCR thermocycler. Used to amplify and analyze segments of DNA, such machines were typically much larger and housed in laboratories, hospitals, and the like. This one, however, was handheld and could be linked to Noah's smartphone. Noah next pulled out a test kit, which included a bunch of fresh cotton swabs. There in the darkness, Noah went right to work, taking samples, loading them into the thermocycler, and simultaneously uploading the genetic information via satellite back to Langley so the results could be double-checked on their far more sophisticated machines and run through the Agency's DNA databases. The whole process could take an hour or so, but hopefully around the time they got to Beirut, they could at least rule in or out whether the blood belonged to Ryker, Curtis, or Mizrachi. Whether they could definitely prove it was al-Masri's was yet to be seen, but it was certainly worth a try.

Just before Noah was about to pack up everything and get back to the group, he took once last look with the help of the flashlight on his phone. That's when he spotted the mounds and mounds of burnt hair.

92

Rahman had not made one map.

He had made two.

One laid out the grounds of the airport, where exactly the terminal was located, what was around it, where the doors were, and the location of the guards and the cameras. The other sketched out the terminal's floorplan, what section the rented storage compartment was in, where the exits were, and where the cameras, restrooms, and stairwells were. As Jenny kept asking more questions, the man kept adding more details. When she was satisfied that she had all that she needed—or, at least, all that he remembered—she told Callaghan to put the handcuffs back on. Abdel Rahman might have been shot in both feet. He was in no position to run, but he was, after all, still a trained killer, and this was no time to take chances.

Once the cuffs were on, Jenny moved fast. Before Rahman realized what was happening, she had shoved a needle in his neck. The drugs kicked in quickly, and the man was soon out cold.

"Tomer, talk to me," she said into her headset. "How's your guy doing?"

"I just put him out," the Israeli radioed back.

"Did he talk first?"

"A little."

"What did you get?" Jenny pressed.

"Name, rank, ID number—the basics."

"That's it?"

"Well, he did tell me there were thirty men in their platoon when they set out Saturday morning."

"How many did Ryker and Curtis take out on the border?"

"We found fifteen bodies plus the guy we captured."

"Tanzeel."

"Right."

"So they lost half their guys in the initial attack?"

"Exactly," Tomer confirmed.

"And how many are headed to Beirut?"

"He said six."

"So aside from him and this Rahman guy, there should be six more bodies in this compound—am I getting that right?"

"I believe you are."

"Okay, hold on," Jenny said. "Stone, you there?"

"Roger that."

"Find us any wheels?"

"There's a cargo van here—a Mazda Bongo—that I managed to get running. I found a Toyota and a Ford, as well, but they are pretty much KIA."

"Can we make it to Beirut in the Mazda?"

"I think so."

"How much fuel does it have?"

"Half a tank."

"That should be fine—stand by," Jenny said, then radioed Noah to get a sitrep.

Noah filled her in, along with the rest of the team who were listening, on what he had found. When he was finished, there was dead silence.

"Hair?" Jenny finally asked.

"Yeah, hair—lots of it—all jet-black."

"I don't understand."

"By the looks of it, and the amount, someone shaved their head."

"Al-Masri?"

"That's my guess."

"But why?"

"I have no idea," Noah said.

"I do," Donny Callaghan said over the headset, even though he was standing right next to her. "To improve his chances at bluffing his way through the checkpoints."

Jenny nodded and even smiled. "You might be right."

"Yeah," said Geoff Stone. "Which raises a good question—how are *we* getting through checkpoints? Or are we heading back out to sea?"

"No, going by water will take too long," Jenny said. "Meet me in the courtyard, all of you—I have an idea."

★

Ten minutes later, they were all in the van.

They quickly pulled away from the compound, heading for the junction to Route 51. No sooner had they gotten on the highway than Geoff Stone heard a pair of Israeli fighter jets approaching from the west. Then he heard the telltale high-pitched whistles, if only for a split second. The pilots had fired. The missiles were inbound. Geoff covered his ears and braced for impact.

Suddenly the entirety of the compound was obliterated in a massive fireball. The shock waves made the van shudder and weave. Despite the protection from his hands, the concussion nearly blew out Geoff's eardrums. And then came the second wave and then a third.

The entire team, except for Tomer, who was driving, craned their necks to watch the spectacle behind them, roaring flames shooting forty, fifty, sixty feet into the night sky. Geoff couldn't help but watch as well. It had been years since he had been on the battlefield, and he marveled at both the split-second timing and the simple rationale of the strike. The Israeli leadership back at the Kirya had obviously been watching them via a live drone feed. Once Tomer had given General Golan and his team the word, the F-16s were on the scene almost instantly. Three strikes might have seemed like overkill. But that was the point. Any Hezbollah forces who were on their way there would find nothing left. Not them. Not their prisoners. Not even the remains of Tanzeel's phone.

93

Abu Nakba could not sleep.

He lay in his bed for a while, staring at the motionless ceiling fan. It was far too chilly to use a fan, at least at night. It was only in the midsixties. If anything, he reasoned, it was time to turn on his space heater. Kicking off the single wool blanket he was using, he swung his legs over the side of the bed, slipped on his sandals, reached for his cane to steady himself, and with a great deal of effort, got himself to his feet.

He padded over to the wall in his light cotton robe, plugged in the space heater, and turned it on. Then he worked his way over to his wardrobe and found a shawl to put over his shoulders. He thought about going into his study to watch the latest news. The images of the ongoing missile war between the Zionists and Hezbollah were a great comfort to him—especially the scenes of wounded children, crying, pleading for their mothers, searching desperately for their fathers. And this was just the beginning. So much more was coming.

He was a son of the desert, and its vast expanse now drew him out onto the balcony. Bundling up under the shawl, he took a seat in his favorite chair and looked out at the shifting, swirling sands bathed in the bluish tint of the nearly full moon. The pain from the catastrophe in Jerusalem—his beloved al-Quds—was still fresh. That operation had taken so much planning and had offered so much promise. The leaders of the United States, Israel, and Saudi Arabia. In one place. At the same time. With a Kairos operative in position to take them all out. Yet the mission had failed. He still could not accept it. Yes, the money was still flowing. Yes, the Iranians and the Turks and even the Russians were still pleased with all his success. Hamdi Yaşar kept insisting that they had accomplished much to be proud of. But Hamdi was wrong. Al Qaeda had taken down two American skyscrapers. The Taliban had bogged down the Americans in Afghanistan for two decades. The Islamic State had waged outright genocide and, however briefly, had established a fully operational caliphate. What had Abu Nakba and his men achieved in comparison?

Sabotaging the Saudi peace treaty with the Zionists would be progress. But there was so much more he had in his heart to do. Why, then, was he being thwarted at every turn? How had the Americans and the Zionists repeatedly turned the tables on Kairos? True, they had suffered losses, but not nearly enough. And time and time again, the trail led back to one man. One American. One special agent.

Marcus Johannes Ryker.

The Russians suspected him of taking out their president, prime minister, and FSB chief. The Iranians were convinced he had prevented them from successfully transferring North Korean nuclear warheads to their shores. And then, of course, he had shown up on the Haram al-Sharif during the peace summit.

Abu Nakba found himself shivering in the cool night air. Yet he delighted in the news that Hamdi Yaşar had given him just before bed. It seemed too good to be true. The pictures were clear. The video images did not lie. The man calling himself Thomas Millner was, Hamdi insisted, actually Marcus Ryker.

Abu Nakba had not believed him at first. But a careful comparison of the proof-of-life images that their man in Lebanon had provided with images of Ryker on the Temple Mount and in numerous newspaper and magazine accounts afterward was unmistakable. The Kairos leader had no qualms about paying millions to have this man in his hands. He would readily have paid a hundred times more than al-Masri was demanding.

And yet something was wrong. Abu Nakba could not put his finger on it. But something was nagging at him, robbing him of his sleep.

Rising back to his feet, he reentered his bedroom and headed for his study in the room next door, where he took a seat behind his desk and dialed Hamdi Yaşar in Doha.

Despite the hour, the man answered immediately. "What's wrong?"

"I don't know. But something is troubling my spirit."

"What is it, Father?"

"When was the last time you talked to our friend in Lebanon?"

There was a slight pause. "Why?"

"I'm not sure, but I have an uneasy feeling."

"Yes?"

"Call him."

"Now?"

"Yes."

"And say what?"

"Ask him about our packages. Make sure they are ready for delivery."

94

They sped north and soon reached the first checkpoint.

It was located just ahead of the bridge spanning the Litani River.

As the cargo van slowed, Geoff found himself impressed with the plan Jenny Morris had laid out for them. Until that meeting at Langley, he had never met the woman before. He had heard her name, knew she was CIA and that she had been the Agency's station chief in Moscow. Geoff had even heard a few rumors from time to time about her possible involvement in the extraction of a high-level mole the Agency had code-named the Raven. But that was it. He had no idea how or when she had first met Marcus Ryker.

Whatever her exploits in the past, Jenny's CIA training was being put to good use now. Back in the courtyard, she had ordered them to find as many of the fallen Hezbollah terrorists as they could. They did their best in the five minutes she allotted and brought her four bodies and some additional body parts. These she wanted loaded into body bags they had brought with them and set in the back of the Mazda Bongo. With that done, she had them zip Abdel Rahman and the other prisoner into body bags and load them into the back of the van as well, underneath the bodies of the others. Rahman and his colleague were not dead, of course. But as drugged as they were, they certainly looked like corpses, especially when Jenny smeared dirt, blood, and soot on their faces and hands to accentuate the effect. For good measure, she had ordered Geoff to remove the boots of one of the bodies and put those boots on Rahman, so that if someone looked carefully, he would not be wearing boots with a bullet hole in each foot.

When the van reached the front of the line at the roadblock, the Hezbollah soldiers told them to stop the vehicle, turn off the engine, and step out slowly. They did, playing the parts that Jenny had assigned them. The men were all wearing their filthy, bloodstained Hezbollah uniforms and kaffiyehs over their faces. Their cover was that they were returning to Beirut from the front with the bodies of their fallen comrades.

Jenny, however, was no longer wearing a uniform. She had, instead, changed into a black abaya and black hood that covered her from head to toe. Only her brown eyes were visible through the small rectangular slit in the front of the hood. Though this was more typical of Shia women in Saudi Arabia than southern Lebanon, it was certainly not unusual in Lebanese cities farther north. The role that she had assigned herself was that of a tearful sister, traveling with her brother—Tomer, the leader of the group, and the most proficient Arabic speaker—back to Beirut for the funerals of all these men, including, ostensibly, her and Tomer's youngest brother.

Noah, meanwhile, was to feign having been severely shell-shocked—unable to hear, unable to speak, and barely able to stand on his own two feet. Geoff was tasked with holding him up and praying that neither of them was asked a question, since Noah didn't speak Arabic and Geoff's accent would give them away.

Callaghan was the last and most reluctant to exit, but he finally did from the front right passenger seat. His job was to look tough and exhausted and annoyed by the whole "been there, done that" process. Jenny was not worried about him at all. He had learned Arabic during his four combat tours in Iraq and had sharpened it quite a bit during his recent studies. With his dyed hair and beard, he looked the part well enough, despite his light skin.

Nearly twenty Hezbollah operatives swarmed around them. The leader, wearing a black hood, barked a series of questions at them. Tomer answered for the group. The leader demanded they remove their kaffiyehs, then checked each person's face against photos he had on his smartphone. When the commander in charge of the checkpoint came over to him, Geoff caught a glimpse of the photos he was scrolling through. Not surprisingly, they were pictures of Ryker, Curtis, and Mizrachi. But there were also pictures of al-Masri and members of his team.

Geoff tensed, though he tried not to show it. Did the commander have photos of all of al-Masri's men? More to the point, did they have a shot of Abdel Rahman or the other still-living prisoner in the back of the van? He was about to find out.

While the commander continued talking to Tomer, other operatives moved to the rear of the cargo van and opened the hatch. Keeping Noah close to him, Geoff drifted back a bit, trying to see if the men were going to check the body bags.

They did. The first one, fortunately, was filled with bloody body parts, including not one severed head but two. The faces had largely been blown off, making visual identification impossible. The men quickly zipped that one back up and opened another. This bag contained an entire intact body, but it too had been so badly burned—not just the torso and limbs but the face, as well—as to prevent a positive ID.

One of the men began to vomit. Others were looking away, repulsed by what they were seeing, especially since the uniforms—however bloodied and burnt—made it clear that these truly were fellow Hezbollah warriors. Still, one of the men seemed determined to go through all the body bags—then someone started yelling.

95

Not just yelling.

Someone was shouting at the top of his lungs.

As Geoff turned, he was stunned to see that it was Tomer. It was all in Arabic, but it became quickly obvious what he was saying. The commander of the checkpoint was about to remove the hood of Jenny's abaya, and Tomer was trying to stop him. When the commander ignored him and actually touched Jenny's arm, Tomer raced for him, shot a right jab to the man's jaw, and knocked him out cold.

At this, every gun went up—not just those of the Hezbollah forces but those held by the Americans, Geoff and Tomer included. They all stood there for at least a minute, guns pointing at each other, everyone but Geoff and Noah screaming at the top of their lungs. Finally Tomer raised his left hand in surrender and slowly lowered the Kalashnikov that was in his right. The rest of the team followed his lead. Geoff was last. If he was going down, he wanted to take these guys with him. But when Tomer turned and spoke to him in calm, steady Arabic, Geoff decided the man knew what he was doing. He bent down and set his own AK-47 on the ground, then stood again and raised his hands over his head.

One by one, each man began to breathe. Tomer said something to the deputy commander. To Geoff, it did not sound like an apology but more of an explanation. Tomer was saying he was simply trying to protect the honor of his sister and that in his place the deputy would have done the same. It worked. The deputy ordered his men to stand down. Then he came over to Tomer, started laughing, and gave the Israeli a hug. *If he only knew,* thought Geoff.

While the unconscious soldier was given smelling salts and pulled off the road, Tomer motioned the team to get back in the vehicle. Jenny got in first. The rest followed. And a moment later, they were on their way.

★

Jenny was silent as they drove northward.

And she was not alone.

Though everyone in the Mazda was a combat or intelligence veteran, the incident on the bridge had shaken them. Tomer's tactics had been a serious gamble, and for several minutes there, Jenny had doubted they were going to make it out alive. But she had to admit the gamble had paid off. It had worked because Tomer was not thinking like an Israeli, like a commando or a spy. He was truly playing the part of a radicalized Shia Muslim man and a battle-hardened Hezbollah commander. He had defended his "sister's" honor, and he had probably saved their lives. Yet it was a sobering reminder of just how out of their element they were.

When the Mossad director, Asher Gilad, had told her that Tomer would be joining them on the mission, Jenny had not thought it wise and had said so. She had been overruled. As Gilad put it, Israel was not going to outsource the rescue of the prime minister's nephew. They were happy to work closely with an American team, but they wanted their own man involved, and Tomer was the guy. He had, after all, spent nearly thirty years working for the Shin Bet. Before that, during his years in the IDF, he had been a sniper and later a member of a highly secretive unit known as Kidon, directly involved in the targeted killings of some of the most dangerous terrorists Israel had ever faced. He was a native-born Israeli from a Jewish family that had emigrated from Syria. He had, therefore, grown up not only speaking Arabic but several dialects native to Syria and neighboring Lebanon as well.

Sitting in the center backseat, Jenny remained quiet but leaned forward and patted the Israeli on the arm. Tomer glanced into the rearview mirror and nodded his appreciation for the gesture, then put his eyes back on the road.

The clock on the dashboard said it was 2:47 a.m.

At 3:04, they reached another checkpoint. Jenny could feel the anxiety rising as they did—her own as well as her team's. There were no other vehicles ahead of them and only four soldiers, only one of whom seemed fully awake. By 3:14, they were moving again. No drama this time. But according to the intel they had been given, there were still three more checkpoints to go before they reached the outskirts of Beirut, and still another at the entrance to the airport grounds.

They continued driving in silence, the passengers cleaning their weapons and checking their equipment, until Noah piped up from the back row.

"Hey, hey, I've got something—wow, unbelievable," he said, electricity in his voice.

"Let me guess, DNA results," said Jenny.

"No, no," he replied. "This is really something."

"What?" she pressed.

"It's Ryker," he said. "He called the safe house. I just checked the messages. It's him. Ryker escaped—he's free."

96

DOHA, QATAR

Hamdi Yaşar hung up the phone.

Not wanting to wake his wife and children, he stepped out onto his balcony. As he looked out over the sleeping Qatari capital and the moonlight dancing on the waves of the Gulf amid all the sailboats moored in the marina, he tried to make sense of that call. Just hours earlier, Abu Nakba had been skeptical and then euphoric. What could possibly have changed in so short a time?

Bleary-eyed, yet ever faithful to the founder and spiritual leader of Kairos, Yaşar dialed the number for his man in Lebanon. The man, however, did not pick up. Eight rings. Then a ninth. After a tenth, he hung up.

Something was wrong.

★

BEIRUT, LEBANON

Amin al-Masri stared at the phone in his hands.

It had stopped ringing, but that only made things worse.

He had to tell them. If he did not own up to what he had done, he would not get paid. And then what? The noose was tightening. Al-Masri could not see them—not yet. But he could feel the Sheikh's forces converging upon him. He knew who was heading up the operation. There was only one man it could be. The chief of *Amn al-Muddad*—Kareem bin Mubarak. The two had a long history together. The Radwan Unit was often engaged by the counter-intelligence unit to hunt down and capture or kill Zionist spies and infiltrators. Unlike so many in the high command, Mubarak was hardly a yes-man, nor was he a sycophant of the Sheikh. To the contrary, he was one of the smartest and most clever in the senior ranks of Hezbollah, and the man was coming for him. Of this, al-Masri had no doubt.

That made his mission clear. Al-Masri had to be on that 9 a.m. flight. He had to have his prisoners with him. Even if there were only two. He had to collect his money from Kairos. Or else he would be out of options and out of time. The Egyptian got up, went into the bathroom, and vomited into the toilet. When he was finished, he wiped his mouth, flushed, washed his hands and face, and took a swig from the small bottle of mouthwash on the counter. Then he took a deep breath, went back into the bedroom, and hit Call Back.

"Sorry I missed you," he said when his call was answered on the first ring. "It's been a very busy night."

"And all is well?"

"No. I've lost a lot of men. The rest of us are injured and exhausted."

"I couldn't care less how you and your men are doing," came the quick reply. "How are the gifts you promised me? Are they wrapped and ready for delivery?"

"Of course."

"All of them?"

Al-Masri was stunned by the question. "Why do you ask?"

"Never mind my reasons—answer the question."

Al-Masri hesitated, and his contact pounced.

"Answer my question, or I cancel your ticket and dispatch a team to hunt you down and gut you like an animal—that is, if your own people don't find you first."

"Okay, look," al-Masri said. "We split up the prisoners in multiple vehicles, like you requested."

"Three?"

"No, just two—that's all we had," al-Masri lied.

"And?"

"And one of the vehicles made it to the safe house just fine, but . . ."

"But what?"

"But there was an incident at one of the checkpoints."

"What kind of incident?"

"The details aren't important," al-Masri insisted, making this up on the fly. "But there was a shoot-out. Things got out of hand. My bodyguard and I were able to kill all of the soldiers at the checkpoint. But Mr. Millner . . ."

"What?"

"Well, he was killed in the cross fire."

"Then bring me the body."

"We couldn't take the body. We had to run. We had to leave it there."

"You're telling me Millner is dead?"

There was a long pause. "Yes, that's what I'm telling you—Thomas Millner is gone."

"And Hezbollah has him."

"I don't know. I told you, we had to run. How else was I supposed to get you the other two? And remember, you only asked for one—and an Israeli, at that. I'm delivering you two Americans. That's better than you asked for. The thing with Millner couldn't be helped. But in a matter of hours, you will have two American federal agents in your hands. Again, that's more than you asked for and well worth the money."

There was a long silence on the other end of the line.

"Hello? Hello?" al-Masri pressed.

"Do you know what you've done?" asked the man whose name al-Masri had never known nor asked to know. "Do you have any idea whom you have lost?"

"Thomas Millner. DSS agent. So what? You have two more just like him."

"No, there's no one like him. His name is not Thomas Millner. That was an alias. A lie. To fool an idiot like yourself. And it worked. But it did not fool us. The man you lost is Marcus Johannes Ryker. He is wanted by the Iranian Revolutionary Guard Corps. He is wanted by the Kremlin. By the Dear Leader in Pyongyang. A man worth a hundred times what we were paying you. And now you tell me you have lost him?"

97

It was almost nine o'clock at night in the nation's capital.

Pete was still at DSS headquarters but needed a break from the crisis management team. It was long past dinnertime, but he could not eat. He certainly could not bear to watch the news any longer. The war was raging on. Untold thousands were dying. The biggest crowds he had ever seen were dancing in the streets of Beirut over the abduction of the three Americans.

A colleague found him in the hallway and tried to engage him in conversation, but he barely responded. He asked about Pete's kids, asked if he had any vacation plans for the summer, asked what he was reading these days, whether he missed his life in medicine—anything, that was, other than Marcus, DSS, and the crisis at hand. Yet Pete only mumbled a response.

Pete Hwang was a deeply private person. He was not about to tell this guy that he had not seen his kids in months. That he was in a bitter new fight with his ex-wife. That he had no plans for a vacation. That even his ridiculous attempt to get away with friends to do some sailing had promptly been scuttled. That he would never go back to medicine. Or that he had no idea what to do with his life. He was stuck. He was scared. And the last people he intended to share such things with were his colleagues at DSS. He barely knew them—not personally, anyway—and he liked it that way.

Excusing himself, he headed down to the cafeteria alone. He bought a cup of coffee, found a table in a quiet corner, and sat by himself, emotionally and physically spent and thinking about how few friends he had left in the world. Vinetti was dead. McDermott was a workaholic. Marcus and Kailea were captives somewhere in Lebanon. Senator Dayton was a good man, but they had never been close. Annie Stewart was as kind and polite and beautiful as ever, but as much time as they had spent together, she had never seemed to reciprocate his feelings. He had never pressed the issue. Never asked her out. Never tried to define their relationship. And now . . .

Pete reminded himself that he had decided to let that all go. She was not interested in him, not that way, and she was in fact interested in someone else. There was no point being a jerk about it. And certainly no point dwelling on it.

It underscored, however, just how alone he felt. He was estranged from the church. Estranged from his parents. Never went back to Houston. Didn't stay in touch with the kids he had grown up with. Never been to a high school reunion. And he despised social media. Who, then, was left but Marcus? And now this.

Pete's phone rang. It was Dell at Langley. There was news. He braced himself for the worst but was stunned by what the DDI proceeded to tell him.

"Marcus has escaped," she said.

"You're serious?"

"I am."

"So he's safe?"

"I wouldn't say that," Dell clarified. "He left a brief message on the answering machine at one of our safe houses. We know he's escaped. We know he's injured. We know he's on the run in Beirut and that he's got a lot of bad actors hunting for him. *Safe* is not a word I would use. But he is free."

Pete exhaled. "That's great news," he said. "I'll call Mrs. Ryker."

"No—not yet," Dell insisted. "We can't afford a leak."

"Mrs. Ryker is an Air Force widow. I think you can trust her."

"It's not my call. The gag order comes straight from POTUS. Things could still go sideways. McDermott will brief the crisis management team shortly. But as a courtesy, I wanted you to be the first to know."

"I appreciate it. Thanks. Keep me posted."

"Don't worry. I will."

Pete set down his phone, finished his coffee, and was about to head back upstairs. But he paused a moment, trying to imagine what Marcus was going through, and for the first time in years, he bowed his head and said a prayer for his friend.

98

Marcus sat bolt upright.

Sweat pouring down his face. Heart racing. Hands shaking. Images of Yigal's and Kailea's mangled, twisted, battered, shattered faces firing like a strobe light in his mind's eye. For a moment, he had no idea where he was. He certainly had no idea where they were. But he had to find them. He had to. He would never be able to look their families in the eye if he did not. It was his job, his mission, his sworn duty to protect them.

But how?

For several minutes, Marcus sat there in the shadows, lights off, moonlight streaming through the open windows, curtains fluttering in the breezes coming off the sea. He was no longer hungry, but he was drained. Physically. Spiritually. Emotionally. He had nothing left. It had been all he could do to survive. To break free. To find shelter. But now what? Even if he were rescued, and that was by no means certain, how was he going to find two needles in a haystack of two million people? And even if by some miracle he could locate them, he could barely walk. Every inch of his body was in pain. His feet were no longer bleeding, but that was only because he had wrapped them in gauze from a first aid kit he'd found in the bathroom cabinet.

Marcus abruptly darted out of bed and into the bathroom. He went right for the toilet but not in time. Everything he had eaten before sleeping came up like a volcano. It was only a minute, but it seemed like forever. Sharp pains ripped through his stomach and chest. Then came another wave of vomit. Followed by another. Until he lost count. Until he passed out on the floor.

When he came to, he was covered in filth. As was the toilet bowl and the floor all around him. Forcing himself to his knees, he grabbed a towel and began mopping up the mess. In a closet he found a mop and some cleaning fluids and went to work. Tossing the used towels in a laundry basket, he stripped down and got back in the shower. But there was no more hot water, so he stood there in the cold until his fingers were wrinkled and blue.

Stepping out, he used the last towel he could find to dry off. He brushed his teeth several times, trying to get rid of the taste of bile, then went back into the bunkroom, found another pair of clothes, pulled them on, and climbed under the covers. He was shivering with a fever. His stomach still ached, though there was nothing left in it. His throat was raw. His eyes were bloodshot and moist. And he still could not sleep.

But he did.

He had no awareness of drifting off. He did not even recall his eyelids moving to half-mast. But suddenly he was no longer in Beirut but on the flight from Dulles to Tel Aviv a few nights before, in the last row of economy, his knees on his chest, sitting next to Kailea, getting grilled on a topic he had no wish to discuss.

"Hey, Romeo, why didn't you tell me?" she had teased.

"Ki, drop it—I really don't want to—"

"You know, Pete is not exactly happy with you these days."

"Kailea, seriously."

"McDermott says you asked her out when you knew—you *knew*—he had been in love with her for so long."

"Ki, there is nothing in that sentence that is true—not a single word."

"You didn't ask Annie out?"

"No—she asked me."

"What?"

"That's right. And for the record, Pete hasn't been in love with her. A crush? Sure. An infatuation? Maybe. But I called him the moment I got off the phone with her. I told him she'd asked me to the White House correspondents' dinner. And I made it clear I'd say no if he wanted me to. But he said he was cool with it, said if he had really been in love with her, he would have done something about it, but he never did."

"Wait, wait, wait—*she* asked *you* out?"

"What are you, deaf?"

Kailea smirked. "Maybe. But I just want to get my facts right."

"Finally."

"So she . . . ?"

"Yes, she asked me. Why is that so hard to believe?"

"Uh, partly because McDermott told me the exact opposite."

"Well, he wasn't there, was he?"

"So what happened?"

"What do you mean, 'what happened?'"

"I mean, *what happened?* When did she call you? And why?"

"What do you care, anyway?"

"I don't, old man. I just have a twelve-hour flight to kill, and I've seen all the movies on this plane. So spill."

"I need a drink," Marcus had said.

"Tell me about it," Kailea laughed.

"Water, you idiot. Come to the galley with me. My legs are killing me."

The two climbed out of their seats and headed to the back of the plane—not a long walk—where they asked a flight attendant for bottles of water and then picked up their conversation in a whisper since most of the rest of their fellow passengers were sound asleep.

"Look, it wasn't a big deal," Marcus began. "A friend of Annie's from her Georgetown days covers the president for Reuters. She invited Annie to be her guest at the correspondents' dinner last Saturday. Annie had never been. Thought it sounded fun. Went out and bought herself a new dress. And then the reporter wakes up Saturday morning sick as a dog and can't go."

"And?"

"And she gave her ticket to Annie and encouraged her to take someone else."

"So she bypassed St. Pete and called you."

"Not even close."

"What do you mean?"

"She called Maya Emerson."

"Really? Why?"

"After Carter's death, Annie and Maya became close. Annie's been going to the church pretty regularly and—"

"Same service as you?"

"No, she goes to the early one."

"And you like to sleep in."

"And you don't?"

"Point taken. Go on."

"Maya hardly ever goes out of the house anymore. No one really noticed during the pandemic, but Annie's been worried about her. So she thought it might be fun to give her a big night out."

"But?"

"Actually, Maya wanted to do it—but she had her grandkids in town that weekend and had to pass."

"So Annie called you."

"Wrong again."

"Come on."

"I'm just telling you what happened. You said you wanted to know."

"I do, I do. Go on."

"Fine—so she called Senator Dayton's wife."

"Esther."

"Right."

"And?"

"And Esther was back in Iowa visiting family."

"You're killing me with the suspense."

"It was Esther who suggested Annie call me."

"Really?"

"Yeah."

"Why?"

"She was worried about me. Thought I needed to get out of the house more."

"That's true."

"I get out plenty."

"Yeah, right. Going out on the town with Pete and me and the guys from DSS doesn't count. I'm talking about dates, geezer. When was the last time you left your retirement home, got out of your wheelchair, and actually took a woman on a real date?"

"No comment."

Kailea laughed again. "Exactly. So, anyway, she just called you up?"

"Yeah, about 10:30 in the morning. I'd just come in from running. I'm soaked with sweat. The phone rings. I see her number and I immediately think something bad has happened in the world."

"Was she shy?"

"*Shy* doesn't even begin to describe it."

"But she asked you."

"Yeah."

"And you said yes."

"She said she was desperate."

"She'd have to be."

"You're hilarious."

"True, but irrelevant. Come on, Ryker, what happened at the dinner?"

99

Marcus's eyes shot open.

Thinking he had heard something in the hallway, he grabbed the mop handle he had snapped off and brought from the bathroom and moved to the door. It was quiet. Slowly he turned the handle, opened the door, took a quick look, and then pulled his head back in. The hallway was empty. He waited several minutes, then looked out again. Still empty. He closed the hallway door and moved to the door to the adjoining room, opened it, and found all the men still sleeping in their beds, snoring as loudly as before, but one of the bunks was empty. Had someone been sleeping there before? Marcus couldn't remember.

He kept watching for a full minute. Finally, convinced it was only his fever talking, he closed the door again, went back to the bathroom, and splashed water on his face and neck. Then he toweled off and climbed back into the bottom bunk.

Soon enough he found himself again transported to Washington. He could see himself standing on the steps of a brownstone walk-up in Northeast, just a few blocks from the Capitol, wearing the classic Armani black tux he had bought back in his Secret Service days. Even now he could feel the rush of adrenaline he had felt that night, the perspiration on his palms, the jitters in his stomach, his heart pounding as he waited for the door to open. And when it did, Annie Stewart took his breath away.

She wore a sleeveless, floor-length black gown with a glittering silver bodice and a matching silver purse. Her gingery-blonde hair was pulled back, revealing stunning diamond earrings that matched her equally stunning diamond choker necklace. Her lipstick was a soft pink, as were her nails, and when she smiled her adorable, shy smile, Marcus thought he was going to melt.

"Wow, you look . . . I mean—wow" was all he could manage.

"You clean up pretty well yourself, Mr. Ryker."

"I just—I've never—wow."

She laughed and locked the door behind her. When he offered his arm, she took it, and he led her to the black Mercedes Uber he had ordered for the night.

"Nice," she said as they settled into plush leather seats for the twenty-minute drive to the Washington Hilton.

"Well, you know, parking's going to be a madhouse over there, and I didn't suppose you were up for hoofing it so far in high heels."

"Good call," she said with a smile, and he could barely think straight. "I hear you're heading back over to Israel."

"You've got good sources."

"You think we're going to get this peace deal thing done anytime soon?"

For the rest of the drive, they talked about the advance trip he was taking for Secretary Whitney and why the Saudis seemed to be dragging their feet on a peace treaty that was their idea in the first place. But the closer they got to the hotel, the more uncomfortable Marcus became, and Annie could see it in his eyes.

"Second thoughts, huh?"

"Not about you—not at all."

"Then what?"

"Honestly, I just . . ."

"What is it?" Annie pressed.

"It's just that, well, the correspondents' dinner is not exactly my crowd."

"Tell me about it," Annie confessed. "I'm terrified to go in there."

"Believe me, I worked a lot of these back in the day," Marcus said. "It's all cabinet secretaries and senators and the Hollywood A-list and, of course, every reporter who makes my life . . ."

"Miserable?"

Marcus laughed. "Yeah."

"Why did you say yes?"

"Because it was you."

There was a long, awkward silence, and then Marcus made a suggestion. "Hey, have you ever been to that restaurant at the top of the Key Bridge Marriott?"

"The one that's supposed to have that spectacular view of the city?"

"Yeah."

"Nope—never have."

"Me neither," said Marcus. "Any chance you want to bail on this thing and give that a try?"

Annie exhaled, the relief in her eyes palpable. "Love to."

Marcus took her hand and squeezed it, then turned to the driver and called an audible. Marcus pulled out his phone to make a reservation. "Really, only table left? Great. We'll take it."

Fifteen minutes later, they were sitting at a candlelit table for two in the corner. The lights were set low, giving patrons the optimum view through enormous plate-glass windows of the Potomac River, the Washington Monument, the Lincoln Memorial, and the rest of the extraordinary cityscape. Annie asked about Marcus's mom and sisters, whom she had met and even had dinner with a year and a half earlier along with Senator Dayton. It had been a lovely event, Annie recalled, even if it was, she joked, a "special op" designed to keep the Ryker family in the dark about his "extracurricular activities," referring to his clandestine work in Russia, North Korea, and eventually the East China Sea.

The conversation was both playful and discreet. Though they had never done anything social like this, and certainly not alone, Marcus began to realize that Annie was familiar with more details about his life than almost anyone he knew. In part that was because she was a staffer for a member of the Senate Intelligence Committee. She had clearance above top secret and was read in on some of the most sensitive operations the CIA and other agencies were running. And in part it was simply because they had known each other for nearly twenty years, from the time they first met on a helicopter in Kabul, Afghanistan. It was precisely for these reasons that Marcus never felt any concern that she might inadvertently mention something classified or even get close to the line, even if they were speaking softly and leaning into one another. Annie Stewart was one of the smartest and classiest women he knew, and she was nothing if not a consummate professional.

He was surprised to find himself dying to ask why she had never been married. She was certainly dedicated to her work, and yet in all the years that Marcus had known her, she had never struck him as wed to Washington or a classic workaholic. Type A? Certainly. No one survived in the nation's capital without being one. But consumed? No. Hostile toward the concept of marriage? He doubted it. Unattractive? Not even close. Then how could a woman like this still be available?

The very question embarrassed him. He covered up his mounting curiosity by asking her what it was like to grow up in Charleston, South Carolina, why she had chosen to go to American University and later to Georgetown when she had been accepted to so many other good schools, what her favorite part of the country was, and what was on her bucket list.

It took all of Marcus's concentration to stay focused on her answers.

100

Annie's emerald-green eyes were stunning, almost hypnotizing.

Marcus found he often had to look down at his meal or out across the river and the city not to betray the intense, if conflicting, emotions he was feeling throughout the night.

He learned that Annie's father had gone to American University and that her mother had not only been the first woman in her family to go to college but had gotten a full scholarship to Georgetown. He learned about her love for Charleston and her even deeper love for the Outer Banks of North Carolina, where her family went every summer. Her aunt and uncle owned a huge home there in Corolla, right on the beach, and though they rented it out for July and August—covering the entire year's mortgage in just eight weeks—in June the whole extended family came to stay and play. They were, she told him, the sweetest memories of her childhood, though after her parents were killed in a plane crash about ten years earlier, she had never gone back.

Marcus was stunned. He had no idea her parents had passed. *How was that possible?* he wondered as she reminisced about their summers together. Then again, he realized, while they were acquaintances and even colleagues, he and Annie had never been close. They were not even really friends. She knew a great deal about him. They had traveled together for work. She had met his mom and sisters. She had been to Lars and Elena's memorial service. But he did not really know her. He had never met her family. Apparently he had never even asked about them. Not in the last decade, at least. Of course, he had also been a married man, a father, and a Secret Service agent on the Presidential Protective Detail—a life that barely afforded him the time to visit his own family out on the Front Range, much less forge deep, personal friendships with people outside his immediate orbit. And whether he had had time or not, he'd never been in the habit of forging such friendships with attractive, single women.

And then, of course, there had been Pete.

"Marcus? Helloooo? You still with me?" Annie had asked, trying to get his attention.

Embarrassed, Marcus suddenly realized he had zoned out. "Yeah, sorry, I . . ."

"That boring, eh?"

"No, no—please, no—I was just . . ."

"It's okay; you don't have to . . ."

"No, really, it's not you; it's—"

"If you give me the 'It's not you, it's me' line, I'm really going to have to deck you."

Marcus laughed. "No, it's not you or me; I'm just thinking about Pete."

"Pete who?"

"What do you mean, 'Pete who?' Pete Hwang. Who else?"

Annie looked quizzical. "What does Pete have to do with any of this?"

Marcus stared back at her. "Uh, he's been kind of crazy about you for, you know, forever," he finally replied.

"Really?"

"You didn't know?"

"I mean, we're friends—good friends—and of course we worked together for a while, but . . ."

"You never saw it?"

She shrugged, trying to think back over her years of knowing Pete.

"And you call yourself an intelligence professional?" Marcus teased, drawing a laugh from her.

"I guess I suspected he might have a little crush," she conceded. "But he never said anything. So I didn't think it was serious."

"Why do you think he moved here?"

"To work for Senator Dayton."

"No."

"No?"

"Not even close."

Stunned, Annie sat back in her chair and stared out the window.

"Look, it's not really a big deal," Marcus said. "I called him. I told him we were going to this thing together. And he was fine with it. Really. But . . ."

"Should I say something to him?" Annie asked.

"No way," Marcus replied. "He'd die. Actually, he would kill me first and then die. Really, it's not a thing. It's just . . ."

A waiter came over to take their dessert orders.

"Can we have a minute?" Marcus asked him.

The waiter nodded and stepped away.

"I love Pete," Marcus said.

"Obviously."

"We've always been close, but after Elena and Lars were killed, he helped me a ton, and after Nick died, Pete became the closest friend I have in the world."

Annie nodded.

"And I feel bad for the guy, you know? He's alone, and it's eating at him, and I want him to find someone who is head over heels for him."

"Absolutely," said Annie, taking his hand across the table. "I'm a pretty good matchmaker."

Marcus laughed. "Well, that may be a little quick. I don't think he's ready to have you, of all people, try to hook him up with someone. But . . ."

"What?"

"After tonight I am going to have a longer talk with him."

"About?"

"Us."

Annie looked taken aback. "Us?"

"Yeah."

"What are you saying, Marcus?"

"I'm saying one date isn't going to be enough, Annie. I'd really like to see you again."

101

The sun was beginning to peek up over Mount Lebanon and the Bekaa Valley.

Kareem bin Mubarak was hungry, exhausted, and snapping at his men.

They had already cleared twenty-six apartment buildings, thirteen restaurants, and a smattering of other shops and cafés up and down the boulevard. Their perimeter kept expanding. Now they were combing every square meter of a Catholic hospital, yet they still had not found either the man they were searching for or even any new clues that he had been anywhere in the area. It was as if the man had jumped off the first roof and disappeared into thin air. Nor had Mubarak's forces, or the whole of the Beirut police force, found a yellow taxicab with missing taillights.

If that were not bad enough, the Sheikh was demanding hourly updates, regardless of whether there was anything to report. The general wanted to go public and had advised al-Hussaini as much. They should release to the media everything they had on al-Masri, his men, and his prisoners, he had argued. That would turn everyone in the capital into their eyes and ears. Yes, they would be flooded with tips, many of which would not pan out at all, but there was no way the traitor and his team could stay hidden for long. The Sheikh, however, had vehemently disagreed. To go public would be to admit that Hezbollah had never had the prisoners and would invite ridicule and humiliation, most of all from the Zionists. No, Mubarak was told, they would get no help from the media or the public. Too many people knew as it was.

It was, therefore, all the general could do not to explode when his mobile phone began ringing yet again.

"Excuse me, is this General Mubarak?" said the voice on the other end of the line.

"Who's asking?" the general shot back.

"Uh, right, sorry to bother you, General," the man stammered. "You don't know me. And my name is of no importance. But I may have information that could be of use to you."

"What kind of information?" Mubarak replied.

"I'm a guest at a church in the Mar Maroun district, not far from where you are now."

"How do you know where I am?"

"Well, from my window, I can see up the boulevard, and I can see all the police cars and military vehicles and all the commotion."

"And? Get to the point."

"And I asked one of the officers near the church and . . ."

"Spit it out—I don't have time for this."

"Yes, yes. I'm so sorry—I understand you are looking for a man."

"Yes."

"A badly injured man, maybe one who had very little clothes on when—"

"How do you know this?"

"Like I said, I'm staying at the church. I've been here for several weeks. My wife kicked me out of the house, and the priest here was kind enough to take me in. But anyway, tonight I could not sleep. So I crept downstairs and went for a walk. Everyone in the neighborhood is talking about it and . . ."

"And what? Do you know something about this man?"

"Well, yes, I might. You see, a man came to the church tonight—a man none of us had ever seen before . . ."

★

Marcus sat up, instantly on high alert.

It was the boots.

He could hear them coming down the hall, and they were moving fast. He sprang out of bed and moved to lock the door to the hallway, but just then the side door burst open. Suddenly a flashbang detonated beside him. Marcus dropped to his hands and knees, blinded, unable to hear a thing. The next thing he knew, there was a boot on his back, shoving him to his stomach.

Instinctively Marcus turned over and drove his right fist into the back of someone's kneecap. Whoever it was stumbled away, and Marcus scrambled to his feet. He still could not see, but there were more hands on him now. Lashing out wildly, he shot an elbow hard into someone's ribs, then delivered a roundhouse punch to someone trying to grab him from behind.

Free again, at least for an instant, Marcus kept his eyes closed and struck out wherever he sensed movement. He connected with one man's neck and another's stomach. Picturing the room in his mind's eye, he felt for the bunk bed, then used it as a foil. Diving onto the lower bed, he rolled right and came out on his feet on the other side. He stood erect and grabbed for the top level of the bunk and pushed it forward with every ounce of his strength. He could hear several people grunt—two, at least—then yanked the bed to his left, hoping to take out more.

It didn't work. Someone now tried to tackle him from behind. Rather than go down immediately, however, Marcus glanced off the bedframe and against a wall, then was able to turn in time to lift his right leg and drive it deep into his attacker's solar plexus.

More men kept coming at him. As he fought viciously to fend them off, his hearing began to come back. His vision began to clear. Not that it was helping much. It was too little and too late. All he could see were flashes of uniforms, boots, fists, and truncheons. Then someone threw a sucker punch to his face and sent him crashing to the floor. Before he knew it, the barrel of an AK-47 was driving into his back. A hood was thrown over his head. There were at least four men on him now. Despite all his thrashing about, they were pulling his arms behind him. They were putting his wrists in flexicuffs and zipping them down so tightly he was sure they would draw blood. He was still trying to kick the crap out of whoever was stupid enough to go for his legs, but within another few seconds someone had secured his ankles and zip-tied him up like a steer in a rodeo.

All he could do was shout at the top of his lungs, so he did, pleading with the priests to help him, to have mercy on him. But in the blur of the moment he was shouting in English. Even if the priests and the men in the room next door heard him—and they could hardly miss the commotion—he had blown his cover. He was not Lebanese. Nor was he French. He was an American, and now he was caught.

102

Father Pierre Fauchet and the others stared on as the American was dragged away.

They had never seen a Hezbollah commando unit up close. Certainly none had ever entered the church. The man was not going without a fight, and the soldiers were having a terrible time dragging him down the hall, down the stairs, and to the parking lot out back. Fauchet and the men followed the action from a distance. But no one had told them they could not watch, and they were not going to miss it. This was the most excitement any of them had experienced in years.

Pouring out the back door, the priest in the lead, they watched the masked, heavily armed soldiers strip their prisoner down and put an orange jumpsuit on him. Then they injected a hypodermic needle into his neck and threw him in the back of a cargo van, though he was still twisting and writhing and trying in vain to break free. And then, as quickly as they came, the soldiers were gone. The van peeled away, its tires squealing with every turn, and all was quiet again.

Still, the homeless men just stood there. All of them. So did the priest.

It was only a few minutes past 6 a.m., and already the temperature was beginning to rise. It was going to be another scorcher, thought Fauchet. They had better get moving.

"Come, everyone—back inside," he told the gawking crowd. "What do you say we get you gentlemen cleaned up for the day and make some *petit déjeuner?*"

The word *breakfast* got their attention, and everyone piled back inside.

Fauchet led the men back up to their bunkrooms, then encouraged half of them to use the showers, while the other half made their beds and waited for a shower stall to become available. Rather than head straight down to the kitchen, however, the priest entered the bunkroom where the American had been staying. It was a disaster. Broken furniture. Pillows, blankets, and clothes strewn about. Streaks of fresh blood on the floor.

For the next several minutes, he picked up and straightened up what he could, threw away what he must, and then headed to the custodian's closet down the hall to get a mop. Fauchet was stunned to see at least two dozen more commandos dressed in full battle gear approaching him from all directions, pointing automatic weapons at him. A tall man in a black uniform with red trim and a black beret put his finger over his lips.

Fauchet froze in his tracks.

"I'm General Mubarak," said the tall one in a hushed voice as he approached the priest and directed his men to take up positions farther down the hall. "Where is he?"

"Who?"

"Are you Father Fauchet?" Mubarak said in French.

"I am."

"Someone from this church called me, said there was a person of interest hiding in this place."

"I don't understand," said Fauchet.

"Where is the new man, the one who arrived last night?" Mubarak whispered. "We're here for him."

"But your men were just here."

"I'm sorry?"

"Not ten minutes ago," said the priest.

"Who was here?" Mubarak asked, clearly not understanding what Fauchet was trying to tell him.

"Your soldiers," said the priest.

"You mean these ones with me?"

"No, no—they were dressed simpler—guns and helmets and regular green uniforms. Not like these. They came and took the man. Tied him up. Put him in an orange jumpsuit. Threw him in the back of a van, and like that, they were gone."

Mubarak looked as stunned as the priest. Finally, however, he ordered his men to search the floor and the rest of the building. To his deputy he assigned the task of taking a full statement from the priest. Then he speed-dialed the Sheikh.

"*Do you have him?*" al-Hussaini asked immediately.

"No, I'm afraid we don't."

"Tell me he did not escape, General Mubarak. Please tell me that."

"No, Your Holiness, he did not escape," Mubarak replied, heading back downstairs to his car.

"Then what? Where did he go?" pressed the Sheikh.

"Colonel al-Masri got to him first."

103

The van barreled out of Mar Maroun, then took 51 south toward the airport.

They were careful to keep their speed just under the legal limit. The last thing they needed was to get pulled over. But when they reached the Salim Salam Mosque, they suddenly veered off the highway and into the parking lot and circled for a moment. The sunrise prayers had taken place at 5:45 that morning, and most of the faithful were gone. There were not many vehicles in the lot, but one of them was ideal. A Toyota HiAce utility van. White but filthy. At least a decade old but still looked dependable. And no windows in the rear or sides.

As they pulled to a stop next to it, Marcus unleashed. *"Get off of me—now."*

As everyone else bolted out the front and side doors, Geoff Stone climbed off Marcus's back. Then he cut the plastic restraints from Marcus's wrists and ankles. The moment he did, Marcus ripped off the hood. His head and face were drenched with sweat. He was breathing heavy and fighting mad. But he was alive. And astonishingly, he was free.

"Good grief, Ryker, you look terrible," Jenny Morris said as she looked into the back of the Mazda Bongo at her severely wounded friend.

Marcus couldn't believe his eyes. "You? I thought . . . How did you . . . ?"

"You left a message at the safe house, remember? You didn't think we would come get you?"

"I thought someone would, eventually, but how . . . ?" Marcus was having trouble reconciling the sight of his friends with the fear and rage he had felt moments before.

"We were in the neighborhood," Jenny said. "We figured it was time you stopped playing hostage and started doing some actual work for a change."

Marcus shook his head. "Then why the attack? I could have killed some-one. I tried to, in fact. You stuck a needle in my neck. What . . . ?"

"Relax," said Stone. "Just saline. We had to make it look authentic, didn't we? It's no good if the locals think you were rescued by friendlies."

"Honestly, we didn't expect you to put up such a fight," Jenny said. "Are you all right?"

Marcus was finally starting to put the pieces together. "Just a few flesh wounds," he said. "Now quit your gawking."

She smiled. "Good to see you, too. And you're welcome."

She tossed him a burnt, ripped, and bloodstained Hezbollah uniform they had taken off one of the bodies back at the compound.

"These the latest fashions?" he asked.

"You got it—all the kids are wearing them."

Jenny looked away as Marcus stripped to his briefs and gave the orange monstrosity to Geoff, who tossed it aside.

"The jumpsuit was a nice touch if you were going for authenticity," Marcus said. "But isn't that al Qaeda's MO—ISIS, too—not Hezbollah?"

"Shut up, ingrate," said Jenny, her back to him.

Geoff gave Marcus a package of disinfectant wipes, a tube of antibiotic ointment, and a bunch of gauze and bandages. As Marcus patched himself up, Geoff proceeded to give him a series of shots to boost his immunity and stave off infection.

"I suppose it must have added to the spectacle," Marcus said.

"Certainly did," Jenny assured him. "You should have seen the look on that priest's face. Not to mention yours."

"And those homeless guys," said Noah as he smashed the driver's-side window of the Toyota parked right next to them, then set about hot-wiring the engine. "They were in total shock."

Callaghan, meanwhile, began rubbing dirt on Marcus's face and slathering blood from a plastic bag over his hands and feet and face.

"Is that real?" Marcus asked.

"'Course it's real," said Callaghan.

"It smells real."

"Because it is."

"Where'd you get it?"

"It's mine."

"Yours?"

"Yeah—Jenny drew it while we were coming to get you."

"That's disgusting."

"Shut it, Ryker, and let me finish."

Noah couldn't suppress his laughter. Nor could Jenny.

Now it was Tomer's time to weigh in. "Hey, I just got off the phone with the Kirya. They had a drone over the church. Watched the whole thing, and you won't believe it."

"What?" Jenny asked.

"Six minutes after we pulled out, two dozen Hezbollah commandos stormed the church."

"Why?" asked Noah, coming back over to them now that the Toyota's engine was purring.

"They have no idea," Tomer said.

"Do you?" Marcus asked.

"Maybe the priest reported to the police what happened," said the Israeli.

"No, that doesn't make sense," said Marcus. "Could one of the homeless guys have—?"

But Jenny, glancing at her watch, cut them off. "Enough of the chitchat, gentlemen—everybody finish up, and let's hit the road. We're sitting ducks out here."

The men did as they were told. Noah smashed out the window on the passenger's side, to give his work on the driver's side a little symmetry. Fewer questions that way. Then he brushed out all the glass from both sides into the parking lot, taking care not to leave a single shard inside the Toyota.

Meanwhile, Callaghan, Tomer, and Geoff transferred all their weapons and gear into the Toyota. Marcus put on the camouflage shirt Jenny had given him, then climbed into the back of the Toyota and into a fresh body bag Geoff had laid out for him. Noah gave him a small radio receiver to put in his ear and attached a tiny microphone under his collar. Jenny handed him a loaded Glock 9mm pistol, and Geoff gave him his bowie survival knife.

"Just in case," Stone deadpanned.

Marcus smiled, then poked several small, discreet air holes into the bag—just along the zipper line and near his neck. Once this was done, he disappeared into the bag. Geoff zipped it up over his face, then worked with the others to position the bag toward the side and back of the Toyota. Next, they proceeded to transfer all the rest of the body bags from the Mazda to the Toyota, positioning them on and around Marcus so that he would be the last bag anyone would be able to check.

Finally Geoff checked on Abdel Rahman and the other live prisoner. Like Ryker, they were potential liabilities as the team tried to clear security at the airport, and it certainly would not do to have them wake up in the middle of an inspection. Geoff unzipped their bags and was relieved to see they were unconscious yet still breathing. He checked their pulses and other vital signs. Then, with Jenny's approval, he gave them each an additional injection of narcotics, not enough to kill them—not quite—just enough to keep them comatose for another six hours.

When he was done, he slammed the back doors of the Toyota shut, they all piled in the front, and they got on their way.

104

Inside the bag, Marcus silently began counting.

He needed to slow his breathing and his heart rate. He felt a bit better when the Toyota began moving, but he continued counting down from fifty.

Then he did it again.

Marcus had never struggled with claustrophobia and wasn't now. Darkness had always been his friend; he used to joke with Elena that his favorite verse of Scripture was John chapter 3, verse 19: *"Men loved the darkness."* The very thought of being zipped up in a body bag, surrounded by dead bodies and body parts, would have freaked her out. But not him. That was not what was causing his heart rate to spike well above normal.

What was? As he lay there, feeling every bump in the road, he tried not just to slow his pulse but his mind, to sift things through and make sense of the intensity of the past few days. For one thing, every part of his body was in pain. The burns on his chest and feet and groin felt worse today than yesterday. His face had been mangled. He had gashes and contusions all over his arms and legs. The only thing he had eaten in days was what that priest had graciously served him back at the church.

It was not just physical, though. What he had seen and heard of al-Masri and his men was nothing short of demonic. Marcus could still see the burning bodies of the IDF soldiers in those vehicles along the border road. He could see the ones who had fought back so hard and so well yet had not made it. Then there was the senseless missile war raging between Israel and Hezbollah, all of it driven by Iran. So many people were being killed on both sides of the border. So many homes and businesses were being damaged and destroyed. Hadn't the people of Israel and Lebanon suffered enough? Wasn't there already more than enough bitterness and bile to last several generations? What good could come from all of this?

Lebanon once had been the "Switzerland of the Middle East," an oasis nestled along the gorgeous, glistening Mediterranean. Peaceful. Prosperous. Fun. Multicultural. Multireligious. Tolerant. Respectful. Sweet. Quiet. Yet now, after decades of war and terror, it was a basket case. The country was bankrupt. The currency was in freefall. The political leadership was paralyzed and corrupt. Why did the good people of Lebanon accept all this? Didn't they want more? Didn't they want something better? Why didn't they rise up against Sheikh al-Hussaini and say, "Enough"? Why didn't they drive Hezbollah out of their beautiful, extraordinary country the way Jordan's King Hussein had driven the PLO out of his?

Then again, Marcus thought, what were the people really supposed to do? They did not have a strong, decisive monarch, a man of peace and moderation like King Hussein and his son, King Abdullah. Maybe they could have cut out Hezbollah like a cancer early on, back in the eighties or nineties. Now it was probably too late. The Sheikh and his forces were too strong, too entrenched, and somewhere along the way Lebanon had ceased to be a sovereign, independent nation-state. It was now, for all intents and purposes, a province of the mullahs of Iran.

Yet even all this, as wrenching and unjust as it was, was not the main thing fueling Marcus's anger and his fears. It was, he knew as he thought about it more, Kailea and Yigal. The historic, epic, ancient, intractable troubles of Lebanon and Iran and the entire region were way above his pay grade. He was not paid to fix the problems of the Levant. His job was to protect people like Kailea and Yigal. And he had failed. What was eating at him was not knowing where they were, not knowing if they were alive, not knowing if they were okay, and being pretty sure they were not.

Marcus felt the Glock in his right hand and the knife in his left. He was not growing calmer. He was getting angrier by the minute, and that was the problem. His rage might not have been an unjustified emotion, but it was not going to be helpful. When they arrived at their destination, he needed to be calm, focused, surgical, and ready for anything.

He took several breaths and tried to imagine what was happening up front. He could picture Tomer behind the wheel and Callaghan riding shotgun. Jenny was in the back, giving them directions. He could hear her. And Noah was updating the Global Operations Center back at Langley on the fact that they had him—aka "the package"—in their possession and were moving to the final stage of the operation. And Geoff? What was Mr. Stone doing? Marcus had not heard him say a word. But as he listened more closely, he heard magazines being ejected and reinserted. Geoff was triple-checking everyone's weapons.

Just in case.

Marcus was grateful for these guys. They had been through hell for him, and it was not over yet. As he lay there in the darkness, waiting for the battle to begin, the number *six* began echoing in his head. Six, as in minutes. That's what Tomer had said. If they had been just six minutes later, Marcus would not be with this team that he had come to love so much. He would instead be in the hands of the most formidable and feared terrorist organization on the planet.

How thin was the margin in the world he had chosen.

105

They pulled onto the airport grounds.

Jenny ordered everyone to keep quiet, let Tomer do the talking, and whatever they did, keep their weapons out of sight. It was hardly a necessary reminder for a team that had successfully cleared a half-dozen checkpoints already. But she was taking no chances.

They got in a line behind a dozen other cars. Each driver was being asked numerous questions about where they were going, what flight they were taking, where they had just come from, and so forth. Trunks were being checked. Occasionally luggage was being opened too. None of it boded well, but Jenny, boiling under her abaya even though she had asked Tomer to jack up the air-conditioning to full blast, did her best to stay calm. Under the black gown, she had a fully loaded Uzi submachine gun. She was the only member of the team who had her hands on her weapon. Everyone had theirs strategically hidden close but out of sight. If things went badly, she had to be the first to respond.

It took almost twenty minutes, but it was finally their turn. Tomer pulled forward, then came to a complete stop. As instructed, he put the Toyota in park and turned off the engine.

"Passports," the lead officer asked.

Tomer handed over five well-worn Lebanese passports.

"Destination?"

"Actually, none of us are traveling today, sir," he explained in Arabic. "We have business in the cargo terminal."

"What kind of business?"

"It is a bit sensitive."

"Do I look like I care?" asked the officer.

"No, sir, it's just that—never mind—we are meeting the owner of a casket company. He said he would meet us here. I'm afraid we have some . . ."

"Some what?"

"Well, sir, we have some bodies."

"Bodies?"

"Yes, sir—corpses that need to be put in coffins and shipped out."

"To where?"

"Tehran."

"Why Tehran?"

"Because they are all fighters, members of the Revolutionary Guard Corps."

"I see," said the officer. "And where are the bodies?"

Tomer nodded toward the rear of the van. "In the back."

"Show me."

"Of course."

With the guard's permission, and under the careful watch of several armed soldiers, Tomer got out and walked around to the back of the vehicle. He unlocked and opened the doors and saw the officer recoil.

"They are not refrigerated?"

"Not yet," said Tomer. "But they will be soon. Again, that is why we have come."

"From where?"

"The south. The fighting is very bad there."

The officer nodded. "Open one," he said.

"You're sure?" asked Tomer.

"Of course. I served as well. I have, unfortunately, seen my share over the years."

"Very well." Tomer went for the bag he knew was the most revolting, the one with the various heads, arms, and legs. The man instantly recoiled and fought to suppress his gag reflex.

"Enough," he said. "Proceed."

With that, the officer waved them through. His colleague lowered the steel barrier. Tomer got back in the van, retrieved their fake passports, and drove forward. Two minutes later, well out of sight of the checkpoint at the airport's front gate, they pulled up to the Turkish Airlines cargo terminal. Only Noah got out of the van, however, and headed straight for the guard-house. The Radwan uniform bought him the element of surprise, and he used it to great effect. Before the guard had finished asking him his business, Noah had tased him. Fifty thousand volts of electricity left the man paralyzed, and he dropped to the floor.

When Jenny was certain no one was watching, she radioed for Noah to enter the guardhouse. He did so, then ducked down out of view for about a minute. When he reappeared, Noah was sitting on the man's stool, wearing the guard's shirt, hat, and sunglasses. A moment later, he opened the main garage door and waved them forward.

Knowing that Noah had injected the guard with the same narcotics they were using on Abdel Rahman and could now monitor all the CCTV cameras in and around the building, Jenny ordered Tomer to get inside as quickly as possible. The moment they were in, Jenny radioed Noah to shut the door behind them. Tomer, however, did not stop. Weaving through shipping containers, various pallets of goods being readied for the next flight, and any number of workmen using forklifts and pallet jacks, he made his way to the far side of the enormous warehouse.

Meanwhile, Geoff and Noah were helping Marcus extract himself from the body bag and getting him cleaned off. By the time Tomer pulled to a stop and set the brake, Marcus's face and beard were clean. So were his hands. He had pulled on a pair of gloves and donned a black balaclava, as had the rest of the team. Jenny, too, had extricated herself from the abaya, suited up for combat, and was ready to go.

Bursting out the back and side doors of the van, every team member moved to the position to which Jenny had assigned them, while Tomer kept the engine running. Jenny sprinted to a prefabricated metal staircase located in the corner of the facility and bounded up the steps two at a time. When she reached the second floor, she raced around the steel-grating walkway that rimmed the facility, set up her sniper rifle, and hiding behind a stack of large crates, prepared to give her men cover.

Hefting a M60E4 light machine gun with a backpack full of additional ammo, Callaghan headed directly to a nearby men's room. He checked each stall to make certain there was no one inside, then positioned himself just inside the doorway. This gave him the clearest, least obstructed view of most of the men working on the warehouse floor and any threat that might approach.

Marcus and Geoff grabbed their M4 carbines and zigzagged down a series of double-wide hallways to the storage container al-Masri had rented, Geoff in the lead, Marcus covering their six. Given the early hour, there was no activity in this section of the warehouse. Noah was tracking their every move on the bank of monitors in the guardhouse and radioing them and the rest of the team about what was around each corner. That would have been exceptionally helpful in any other scenario.

There was only one problem. When Marcus and Geoff burst into the storage container, it was empty.

106

"Repeat—did not copy," Jenny insisted. "I say, again, repeat, Alpha One."

"Alpha One to High Top," Marcus replied. "I've got no one here."

"No one?"

"Affirmative."

"You're sure you're at the right one?"

"Affirmative—they're gone, High Top."

"Wait," Noah radioed. "I think I've got them."

"Where?" asked Marcus.

"I see a group of men around a forklift and a baggage tractor."

"Okay, but *where*?" Marcus pressed.

"Behind the terminal. Now the baggage tractor is pulling away. The men are getting into a . . ."

But Marcus had already stopped listening. Using their code names, he ordered Callaghan and Jenny back to the van. He and Geoff were heading out the back door. Noah was to keep them apprised of any new developments and meet Jenny and Callaghan at the plane.

★

Jenny began to protest but stopped herself.

This was her mission, but there was no point pulling rank. Ryker wasn't wrong, and he and Stone were closest to the exit and thus had the best chance of catching up to the baggage tractor.

Slinging her sniper rifle over her shoulder, she sprinted back to the metal staircase and down to the ground floor. By the time she got there, Tomer had pulled up the van. She and Callaghan jumped in, and soon they were moving, weaving through a maze of pallets and people who were crisscrossing their path and severely slowing their progress.

★

Marcus burst out the back door and was blinded by the blazing morning sun.

He threw on the sunglasses the team had given him and scanned the tarmac. He saw at least a dozen narrow-, medium-, and wide-bodied Airbus commercial passenger jets, all owned by Turkish Airlines, all being refueled and loaded with baggage and cargo.

"*There,*" Geoff shouted as he raced up behind him. "*Two o'clock.*"

Geoff pointed to a twin-engine A319 about two hundred meters away. It, too, was being serviced, but it was the only jet being approached by a baggage tractor pulling a line of trailers and dollies and a cargo loader on which sat a half-dozen well-armed men.

There was no way they could simply make a run for it. They would be spotted immediately and be an easy target for any fighter good enough to be in the Radwan Unit. With Jenny, Tomer, and Callaghan nowhere to be seen, Marcus glanced around to see what was available. Parked nearby was a potable water truck. Marcus ordered Geoff to take the driver's side while he would ride shotgun. But the truck was not running, and there was no key in the ignition.

They were running out of time. Al-Masri and his men were almost at the Airbus. A refueling truck pulled up. Marcus bolted from the water truck and raced up to the refueler. He should have taken Noah's Taser—it was the only one the team had—but he had not thought of that. Not wanting to do serious harm to the driver, Marcus nevertheless had no time to improvise. The moment the man opened his door, Marcus sucker punched him in the face, knocking him out cold. The angle of the truck blocked anyone in the cargo terminal or the flight line from seeing any of this. But that was the only consolation. There was nowhere in the cramped cab to put the man, so Marcus and Geoff had to lift him up, carry him back to the water truck, and put him in the driver's seat, slumped over the wheel.

Locking and closing that door, they now dashed back to the refueler—Geoff to the driver's side, Marcus to the passenger side. The truck was still running. Geoff hit the gas as Marcus lowered his window and readied his M4. He was about to take his first shot when Jenny came on the radio to remind him that they needed al-Masri and at least some of his men alive. There was no other way they could properly interrogate them and find out who was behind this whole operation. But that was not going to be easy. The tarmac had not been repaved in years. It was not exactly dotted with potholes, but at this speed and acceleration, and with the cab of the refueler shaking and rocking as they crossed all kinds of cracks and rivulets in the pavement, Marcus knew his shots were not going to be precise.

There was no time to overthink it. Jenny wasn't wrong, but she also wasn't there. He had no idea what was taking her and Callaghan so long to catch up with them, but Marcus refused to wait. With a prayer that none of his shots struck a container with Kailea or Yigal inside, he pointed the M4 out the window and opened fire at about sixty yards out. He was using a suppressor, so no one heard the shot. Certainly not over the whine of the jet engines and the roar of all the electric and diesel motors. When the first man dropped off the cargo loader, the rest of the men were stunned. They had just reached the Airbus, and the loader came to a stop. Marcus could now see that all of the cargo had already been loaded into the fuselage of the plane.

That's when he took the second shot. That went wide, so Marcus switched to semiautomatic and let loose one burst and then another. A second man dropped to the tarmac. Everyone else got the message. Scurrying for cover, they began returning fire. Both Marcus and Geoff ducked, but Marcus kept firing, and as he did, he ordered Geoff to floor it.

"Into them?" he asked in disbelief.

"No other option," Marcus shouted over the gunfire.

They could hear rounds pinging off the engine block and even the storage tank they were pulling. Given that it was filled with hundreds of gallons of aviation fuel, Marcus couldn't help but wonder if they had made the right choice. But there was nothing they could do about it now.

"*Hit it, Geoff—now,*" Marcus repeated. "*Or we're both going to die.*"

The front windshield was being riddled by rounds from four AK-47s all being fired at them simultaneously. It exploded an instant later. Shards of glass rained down on them. Both men lowered their heads even further to shield their faces and eyes. They felt the impact. They heard the crunch of metal. And then came the screams of men being run over.

As Geoff slammed on the brakes, Marcus could feel the big truck blasting through the cargo trailers and trollies and skidding across the tarmac. The moment they lurched to a halt, Marcus kicked open his bullet-ridden door and jumped to the ground. The carnage was unbelievable. Blood and broken bodies were everywhere. But Marcus didn't stop to check on them. Kailea and Yigal were in the fuselage. Marcus had to get to them before the cargo bay doors closed and the plane started moving.

107

He was about to make a dash for it when gunfire erupted from inside the cargo hold.

Marcus crouched down and positioned himself behind the left-rear wheel of the refueling truck. Another burst of gunfire. Then a third. And now a fourth. With this burst, Marcus realized that whoever was doing the shooting was not really aiming at him. He was aiming for the storage tank. If he could puncture it and ignite the fumes, it would all be over. Not only for Marcus and Geoff, but for the 130 or so passengers on board the plane and for Kailea and Yigal as well.

Jenny's voice came over the radio. She and Tomer were finally out of the warehouse and were racing across the tarmac to link up with them. She could see what Marcus and Geoff had just done and ordered them to hold their positions and wait for backup. But Marcus neither waited nor replied. There were lives to save, and every second counted.

Pivoting around the back of the tanker, Marcus fired a quick burst from the M4. Then he sprinted across open ground until he reached the mangled, twisted wreckage of the baggage tractor. His movement drew fire from whoever was hiding inside the jet. That was expected and exactly what Marcus wanted. It alerted Geoff to the shooter's precise position. And sure enough, Geoff returned fire.

Marcus eyed the elevator truck used to hoist containers and baggage into the cargo hold. It was ten, maybe twelve yards away, but he thought he could make it. Sprinting forward, he again drew the shooter's attention and fire. But Geoff emptied an entire magazine into the fuselage, forcing the shooter to retreat from the cargo bay doors. Marcus surveyed the bodies around him. He counted five at least, all facedown. As best he could tell, there was only one to go. He hoped it was al-Masri.

Marcus could also see the Toyota racing across the tarmac. What he did not see or hear were any lights or sirens of emergency vehicles approaching. Not yet, but it would not be long. If he was going to move, it had to be now.

Suddenly, however, as Geoff reloaded, the shooter reappeared, unleashing one burst at Marcus, another at Geoff, then emptying the rest of his magazine into the side of the fuel tank. Whoever he was, his plan was succeeding. He might not have blown the truck, himself, and the plane to kingdom come. But his rounds had finally penetrated the reinforced tank. Fuel was spilling down the side of the truck and pooling under it.

Marcus popped up, took aim, and fired. The man snapped back and yelled out in pain. Marcus doubted he had done more than graze him, but it was a start and bought them precious time. Marcus crouched down, caught Geoff's eye, and signaled him to throw a flashbang into the cargo hold. Geoff responded immediately. The instant the device exploded, Marcus emerged from cover, scrambled up the side of the elevator truck, and raced inside the belly of the plane.

He found a pallet and took cover behind it. Then, risking a quick peek, he saw the shooter stumbling backward, temporarily blinded and searching wildly for cover. Marcus recognized him immediately. It was al-Masri. And even with Jenny's order to capture the man alive ringing in his ears, Marcus was not about to take chances with a killer of this caliber. He fired two bursts from the M4, then pulled behind the pallet again. Hearing the man drop to the ground, Marcus suspected that he had once again hit his mark. He ejected a spent magazine, reloaded, and came around the corner of the container ready to finish him off. But al-Masri was not there.

Geoff was.

He had followed Marcus's lead and climbed up into the plane and found himself a position of cover. Marcus pointed to a trail of blood, then signaled for Geoff to throw another flashbang. Geoff did, and the two of them immediately covered their eyes. The moment the device went off, they began their advance. Marcus took the left side of the plane. Geoff took the right. Outside, the rest of the team had arrived. Jenny was on the radio again, demanding a sitrep. Marcus told her only to make sure their escape hatch was ready. They would be out soon.

Jenny began talking again, but Marcus was not listening. He removed his earpiece, shoved it in his pocket, raised his weapon again, and kept advancing.

Slowly—knowing al-Masri was a wounded, cornered animal—Marcus and Geoff moved deeper into the plane. If Marcus could speak Arabic, he would have been shouting for any and all baggage handlers and other airline personnel to bail out immediately. But he could not. He had to trust that the flashbangs, automatic weapons fire, and the crash outside had already done the trick. Any movement he saw now, he figured, had to be al-Masri.

And then a single grenade came rolling down the center aisle of the cargo hold.

108

Marcus shouted for Geoff to take cover, while he did the same.

The explosion was catastrophic, blowing a gaping, fiery hole in the fuse-lage of the plane no more than ten meters behind them. Through the flames and the smoke, Marcus could see the tarmac and part of the plane's landing gear. Choking on fumes, Marcus called out to see if Geoff was okay. But the force of the concussion had completely deafened him. Not only could Marcus not hear if his colleague was responding, he could not even hear himself, only a high-pitched constant ringing.

Undeterred, Marcus knew he could not double back to check on Geoff with al-Masri still out there. He had to finish the job and had to do it quick. Advancing up the left aisle, Marcus wove his way around metal containers, wooden boxes, and shrink-wrapped pallets of all shapes and sizes. Not being able to hear was a problem. He was trying not to make any noise, determined not to give away his location, but he realized that al-Masri could be charging at him from behind and he would never know. Still, it was very likely, he realized, that the Egyptian could not hear him either.

As Marcus came around a corner, he spotted al-Masri just another five or six yards ahead. The man was crouching between two pallets and looking the other direction. As Marcus watched, al-Masri fired down the right aisle. Marcus hoped that was a good sign, that the man had seen a moving shadow. If so, it could only be Geoff, and that meant he was alive and still kicking.

The moment al-Masri stopped firing, Marcus shouted at the top of his lungs for him to put his weapon down and his hands up. For several seconds, the man did not move. Marcus again wondered if al-Masri could even hear him. He was about to shout his warning once more, but it was too late. The Egyptian did not set down his weapon. Instead, he jumped to his feet, pivoted hard, and brought his Kalashnikov around. But the man never got off another shot. Marcus put two bullets in his chest, and al-Masri collapsed to the floor.

Marcus watched him for a moment, looking for any sign, any twitch, any movement at all. Unconvinced that he was truly dead and not willing to take any chances, Marcus kept his weapon aimed at al-Masri's head and slowly moved toward him. When he was just a yard away, Marcus fired three more bullets into the man. Now he was sure.

A moment later, not only Geoff but Callaghan and Tomer raced up behind him. Using his foot, Geoff rolled the body over. There was no doubt who it was. Nor, however, was there time to celebrate. Marcus still could not hear. Nor, apparently, could Geoff. But Marcus shouted for the other two to search the body for intelligence and then get it down to the Toyota as quickly as possible. When they nodded and got to work, Marcus motioned for Geoff to help him find the container.

But how? The fuselage, or what was left of it, was jam-packed with hundreds of small and midsize shipping and storage containers, most of which looked the same.

Tomer slapped Marcus on the back. Startled, Marcus turned around and found a ring of keys and a set of bloodstained shipping documents the Israeli had pulled off al-Masri. All four men scanned the manifest quickly, memorized the code numbers, and fanned out to find the right container. It was Callaghan who hit the jackpot. Marcus took the keys from Tomer and, trembling with emotion, fumbled to unlock the container.

When he finally got it right and swung the door open, it was the stench that hit them first. Marcus reached inside and lifted Kailea out. She was unconscious. She was barely breathing. She looked terrible—bloodied, bruised, and covered in filth. Marcus set her down gently and quickly untied her hands, then her feet, then hoisted her up and put her over his shoulder in a fireman's carry. Moving aside, he made way for Geoff, who did the same for Yigal—also alive but unconscious.

Now the question was how to get out of the plane. Marcus's hearing was beginning to come back. Though it sounded faint, at least to him, he could hear sirens approaching. Yet there was no way to get back to the open cargo bay doors, for before them now was the enormous hole in the bottom of the plane.

109

Callaghan hoisted al-Masri's corpse over his shoulder.

As he did, Marcus shouted to Tomer over the roar of the growing fire to radio Jenny and have her pull the Toyota directly under the hole. The moment she did, Tomer jumped down onto its roof. Noah scrambled up onto the roof from below. Together they took Kailea as Marcus lowered her down to them. With Jenny's help, they got her to the tarmac and then onto the backseat.

They repeated the procedure with Yigal.

When it came to al-Masri, however, Jenny told them they had neither the time nor the room to take him. Instead, she instructed them to snap a picture of the man and leave him behind. Marcus began to protest, but Jenny was adamant. She was in no mood to have another order of hers disregarded, and fire trucks and ambulances were rapidly bearing down on them. Marcus relented and jumped to the roof of the van and then to the ground. Geoff did the same.

Callaghan was last. The fiery agent could not simply leave al-Masri behind without exacting some measure of revenge. So he simply let go of the body. It landed with a thud on the tarmac, legs and arms askew. As Callaghan jumped onto the roof, Tomer snapped pictures with his mobile phone.

The last thing to do was make room in the back of the van. While Jenny climbed into the driver's seat, the men dumped all the body bags onto the tarmac. As the others piled inside, Tomer remembered to unzip the bags containing Abdel Rahman and the other living prisoner. Then he climbed in as well. Even before he had shut the door behind him, Jenny had hit the accelerator, and they were off.

Minutes later, the team reached the private aviation section on the other side of the airport grounds. They quickly boarded a waiting Gulfstream V business jet—the "escape hatch" the extraction team had arranged—where they were greeted by none other than Mossad chief Asher Gilad and a team of the IDF's best combat medics. The moment Kailea and Yigal were hooked up to IVs, the Gulfstream taxied out to the flight lines, and before they knew it, they were airborne.

As they streaked into the cloudless blue sky and banked westward, no one said a word. Marcus, for one, needed time to let the adrenaline stop pumping and his system to stabilize, and he was certain the rest of the team needed it too. When they reached their cruising altitude, however, Gilad unbuckled his seat belt and rose to his feet.

"I just want to say a word of congratulations to each and every one of you for a job very well done," he began, his eyes uncharacteristically red and moist, his face beaming with pride. "Thank you. I mean it. This was rapidly shaping up into the worst hostage crisis that either of our countries has faced in years. And while I realize there are a great deal of people on both of our teams who played critical behind-the-scenes roles, I could not have asked for more from you guys."

Gilad turned to Marcus. "Mr. Ryker, I don't even have the right words to express how good it is to have you and your colleagues back."

Everyone cheered, even the doctors in the rear of the plane, and Marcus nodded his appreciation to them all.

"And, Miss Morris, I don't care what they say about you at Langley, you were absolutely stellar—every step of the way—and if you ever want to jump ship, I would be honored to have you come work for me and the Mossad any day."

The cabin erupted in laughter as Jenny shot Marcus a look that suggested she was just as embarrassed and uncomfortable as he. They were not ones to seek or want attention, even from their colleagues. But this was clearly Gilad's show, not either of theirs.

The Mossad chief went on for several minutes, making specific comments on the impressive performances of Tomer, Callaghan, and Noah and the roles each of them had played in the stunning success of the operation he had code-named the Beirut Protocol. It was, he told them, a bit of an inside joke, a spin on the Hannibal Protocol, a policy the IDF had long before discontinued and yet had so disastrously tried to reinstitute in recent days.

Then he popped the cork on some very expensive champagne. "To better days," he said.

"To better days," they all replied.

After they had all taken their first sip, Geoff asked if they were really headed back to Israel, since that would seem terribly suspicious to everyone monitoring flight paths in the region, including reporters.

"You're right," Gilad replied. "We're headed for Rome. There, we'll change planes—and thus tail numbers—then fly to Cairo, where we'll change planes again and fly back to Tel Aviv. Director Stephens and Deputy Director Dell should be on the ground by then and will be waiting for us. As you can imagine, they're eager to debrief you and celebrate with you. And then, of course, the prime minister would like to host you all for a private, off-the-record dinner at his home. Hopefully Yigal and Special Agent Curtis will be well enough to join us."

At this, Marcus cleared his throat and Gilad readily gave him the floor.

"Mr. Gilad—"

"Please, call me Asher. We Israelis are not so formal as you."

"Fair enough," Marcus replied. "And I certainly want to thank you—each of you and all the others who worked to get us out. But I have to say I think this celebration is all a bit premature."

Everyone was caught off guard by the remark, and a hush settled over the cabin.

"Don't get me wrong—I truly am grateful to be free. And yes, we took out al-Masri and his cell. But I think it should be clear to all of us by now that Hezbollah was not responsible for Saturday's attack on the border. Al-Masri was working for someone else. The question we all need to be asking ourselves is, Who?"

110

Marcus was not finished, Jenny realized.

"Sir," he said to Gilad, "you said a moment ago that there was nothing more you could have asked of us. But actually we have something more to give to you."

"Oh?" Gilad asked. "And what would that be?"

"I know you had hoped we could bring back Amin al-Masri alive so you could interrogate him and get to the bottom of all this," Marcus continued. "I'm afraid under the circumstances that simply wasn't possible. He was about to fire on me. I had no other choice but to take him out first."

Gilad nodded soberly. "Understood, Agent Ryker—I would never have expected you to—"

But Marcus raised his hand to interrupt. "I'm sorry, sir, but I wasn't quite finished."

Jenny raised an eyebrow. Marcus certainly had a unique way of speaking to power. She had seen it in Moscow. She had seen it while they were on the run across Russia. And she was seeing it again.

"Please, sir, I mean no disrespect," Marcus added, seeing the eyebrow and getting the point. "I just wanted you to know that while we could not deliver al-Masri to you, we may have the next best thing."

"What's that?"

"His satellite phone."

Marcus turned to Callaghan, who produced the Iridium 9555 he had stripped off al-Masri's body back on the plane.

"If you don't mind, sir, I'd like to ask our tech whiz here—Noah Daniels—to get inside this thing and see what he can find."

The Mossad chief grinned. "By all means."

★

General Mubarak stepped out of his car.

Surrounded by bodyguards, he approached the crime scene just as most of the firefighters and other first responders were wrapping up their work. The fire was out. There was foam all over the site. To be cautious, the fuel was being pumped out of both the plane and the bullet-riddled tanker into a fleet of other refueling trucks. The passengers had been evacuated. Those who had been seated in the section directly above where the grenade had exploded and had received various injuries had been transported to nearby hospitals. Most were suffering shock.

Nothing else had been moved. The mangled, twisted, charred vehicles and equipment were still in place. Even through all the foam, Mubarak could see hundreds of shell casings strewn about. And then there was the pale, lifeless body of Amin al-Masri, lying faceup on the tarmac in a pool of his own blood, his eyes still open and glassy.

Mubarak stopped walking. Putting on a pair of latex gloves, he knelt down and examined the body. No papers. No wallet. No phone. Not even a weapon. Just multiple entry wounds in his chest. He examined al-Masri's face. It was immediately apparent to the Hezbollah counterintelligence chief that the man's nose had been broken. Not by a bullet. The wound was more than a day old. Could one of the Americans have done this?

Mubarak walked around the rest of the site, examining each of the other bodies. Then he was driven to the cargo terminal, where his colleagues were interviewing witnesses. His deputy briefed him on what they had learned so far.

"This was Hezbollah," Mubarak was told. "Worse, it was Radwan."

"You're saying this was an inside job?" Mubarak asked, incredulous.

"Everyone I've talked to says the same thing—the attackers were all young, military age, and wearing Hezbollah uniforms with Radwan insignia. They were masked. They were fast. And they were thorough."

Mubarak's phone rang. It was another one of his investigators, on the other side of the airport.

"I've got two witnesses who say they saw at least a half-dozen Hezbollah fighters board a Gulfstream V," Mubarak heard the man say. "And get this— they carried not one but two other adults onto the plane. The witnesses said it was all very odd. They tried to notify security, but every line was busy. The timing matches up with when the mess on the tarmac was ending."

There was more. Much more. But Mubarak had heard enough. He thanked his man and walked out of the terminal, out the back door, and onto the tarmac. There, alone, he speed-dialed the Sheikh.

"They're gone."

"The Americans?"

"Yes."

"All of them?"

"Yes, and despite eyewitness accounts, it wasn't us who carried out the attack."

"Then who?"

"The Americans? The Israelis? Both? Who knows? Who cares? They took off on an unmarked Gulfstream about an hour ago. I'll track it, but I guarantee you it'll be a ghost. We'll never find it."

"And that traitor, al-Masri, any sign of him?"

"Got him."

"Tell me he's alive."

"Not even close."

Mubarak had to take the phone away from his ear. The Sheikh was scream-ing loudly and apparently smashing things in his office. The tantrum lasted at least a minute or two; then the Hezbollah leader came back on the line.

"So what do we do next?" he asked.

"Simple," said Mubarak. "Go on television again and say that you have uncovered a joint Zionist-American spy ring trying to penetrate Hezbollah, but all those involved have been exposed, tracked down, shot on sight, and killed on your command."

"This is a disaster, and you want me to take credit for it?"

"I do, and fast, before the Zionists do—or the Americans."

"What about the prisoners?"

"What about them?"

"How will we explain their escape?"

"We'll deal with that later, sir. For now, you need to get a jump on the story. That's why you need to go on television now, in the next five min-utes, announcing a major counterintelligence victory over the Mossad and the CIA. That will be the big news for today. Tomorrow we'll deal with tomorrow."

111

The flight time from Beirut to Rome was three hours and thirty-five minutes.

While Noah worked on bypassing the phone's password, the rest of the group compared notes on what they had learned about al-Masri and the myriad reasons why they all agreed with Marcus's assessment that the man had gone rogue. They disagreed, however, on whom he was working for.

Jenny argued the most likely suspect was Iran. Her reasons were simple. They had known their Supreme Leader was dying. A succession process could get messy. As a result of American-led sanctions, Iran's economy had been tanking before the pandemic and the collapse in oil prices. Now it was in the toilet. The regime needed to distract people's attention from the country's mounting internal problems. Plus they were itching to throw a monkey wrench into the Israeli-Saudi peace process. What better way than to instigate a war between Israel and the Arabs?

Tomer, however, was not convinced. To be sure, they had conclusive evidence that the commander of the Revolutionary Guard Corps had ordered

Sheikh al-Hussaini to launch his missiles at Israel once the hostages were taken and once the head of Israel's Northern Command took it upon himself to initiate the Hannibal Protocol. But they also had strong circumstantial evidence that both the Sheikh and the powers that be in Tehran were caught off guard by the border raid.

"Besides," he noted, "if Iran had wanted the Sheikh to launch such a raid, all they had to do was ask."

"Perhaps they were trying to go around the Sheikh," Jenny suggested.

"Okay, but why?"

To this, she had no answer.

Tomer had his own theory. To him, it was far more likely that this was a Kairos operation, an attempt both to retaliate against Marcus for having thwarted their suicide bomber plot on the Temple Mount during the Israeli-Saudi summit and to drive a nail in the coffin of the peace process once and for all.

"Just look at the pattern," he said as they soared over the Med at thirty-four thousand feet. "The most daring terror attacks against Israel and the U.S. in the last few years—bar none—have been the work of Kairos."

"True," said Marcus, "but maybe not this time."

"Why not? Besides Iran, who wants you dead more than Kairos?"

"Actually, the list is getting rather long," Geoff quipped.

"Unfortunately, he's right," said Marcus. "But in this case, there was no way either Iran or Kairos could know I was going to be in that convoy at that moment. They couldn't have even known I was in Israel. The trip wasn't publicized, and my role certainly wasn't."

"Maybe they're tracking you," said Tomer.

"Maybe, but then they should have hit me in Washington, which would be far easier than on the Lebanese border. No, I don't buy it."

"Then who do you think al-Masri was working for?" Tomer asked.

"I don't know," Marcus said. "And that's what worries me."

Geoff Stone chimed in. "What about the Turks?"

"What about them?" asked Jenny.

"I'm prepping for a trip I'm supposed to take with Secretary Whitney next month. I've been getting read in on everything Langley and DIA and NSA have gathered on the Turks, and I don't like what I'm seeing."

"Go on," said Marcus.

"Have any of you guys taken a good, close look at Ahmet Mustafa?" Geoff asked.

"The Turkish president?" Jenny asked.

"Exactly," Geoff said.

Gilad said nothing. The others shook their heads.

"This is one spooky dude—sees himself as a sultan, rebuilding the glories of the old Ottoman Empire—wants to make Istanbul the epicenter of the next Caliphate, the vortex of all Sunni radicals around the world. He's totally capable of pulling off something like this. He's got tons of ambition. Tons of money. A huge population . . ."

"How many?" Jenny asked.

"About 82 million," Geoff replied. "Plus he's got the second-biggest military in NATO behind the U.S. Huge spy service. Hates us. Hates you all in Israel. So why not?"

Jenny took that one. "Well, you just said it—he's a Sunni. Yes, he's pulling together the Brotherhood, Hamas, and other radicals under his roof, but they're all Sunni. Hezbollah is Shia."

"But where were we an hour ago?" Geoff asked. "The Turkish Air cargo terminal in Hezbollah-controlled Beirut. On a Turkish Airbus. In the belly of a plane heading to the largest city in Turkey. You don't think there's a connection there?"

Marcus was intrigued. It was an interesting argument and one he had not thought of himself. But he still was not sure who had kidnapped him or why, and he was determined to find out. He turned back to Asher Gilad. "Sir, what about you?"

Israel's legendary spy chief did not respond right away. Rather, he got up and stretched in the aisle for a moment, then poured himself another glass of champagne, having finished his first.

"I certainly agree with you, Miss Morris, that Iran has the most to gain here," Gilad began. "Your logic is sound, but Agent Ryker is correct—there are far easier ways to get at him, and it would have been all but impossible to know he would be at that exact spot on the border at that exact moment. No, I don't think al-Masri was targeting Marcus. And besides, if he was, then he would have known who he was dealing with and never would have let him escape. Nor would he have fed the name Thomas Millner to the Sheikh. It's clear to me al-Masri was going for Israelis. The fact that he bagged two Americans—and thought he had three—was purely serendipitous."

"Then who?" asked Jenny.

"Well, the Turkish theory is imaginative," Gilad conceded. "But I have seen no evidence that 'the Sultan,' as you call him, Agent Stone, is ready to take direct action against us. He's too clever for that. He would use a proxy, a cutout, but even then it would be awfully risky."

"You're saying it's inconceivable?" asked Geoff, a touch defensive.

"No, but maybe a bit premature," Gilad replied. "Under Ahmet Mustafa, Turkey is definitely swinging to the dark side. I grant you that. But I don't see him taking this level of action against us. It's just too soon."

"So," said Jenny, "you think it's Kairos."

112

Gilad shrugged.

"I don't know, but Tomer makes the strongest case," he said.

"You're just biased because he's Israeli," Geoff said, smiling.

"Probably. But look, does Iran have more to gain? Absolutely. But they also have more to lose. A war between their main proxy and us is not, in fact, in their best interest right now. Soon, yes, but not on the day of Ansari's death. They are doing their best to take full advantage of what al-Masri has done, but they were blindsided by this. Kairos, on the other hand, has been laying low for the past year or so. They had big, showy, spectacular operational successes in your capital and in London and very nearly in ours. And this does fit their profile. They recruit smart, savvy, disgruntled mid-level operatives in key cities and then give them a great deal of money and a plan to execute. Somewhere, somehow, they found al-Masri. They learned he wasn't happy with the Hezbollah leadership, or at least that he wanted or needed a great deal of money, and they recruited him to do their bidding."

"Maybe you're right, but all that just leads back to Marcus's question," Jenny said. "Whether it's Iran or Kairos or someone else, we can't make a move until we know exactly who recruited al-Masri and who was handling him."

"Actually, I may be able to shed some light on that," said a voice behind them.

Everyone turned to find Noah coming up the aisle.

"What've you got?" asked Marcus.

"Al-Masri only took or made calls to two numbers on this phone," Noah replied. "Want to guess where?"

"Tehran," said Jenny.

"Survey says . . . no."

"Ankara," said Geoff.

"Survey says . . . no again—but you're close on one of them."

"Istanbul."

"Bingo."

Geoff threw his hands up in the air in victory.

"And the other?" Marcus asked.

"You tell me," Noah said.

"Beirut," said Callaghan, piping up for the first time.

"No."

"Somewhere else in Lebanon?" Callaghan asked again.

"Sorry, no."

"Athens," said Tomer.

"No."

"Anywhere in Greece?" Tomer pressed.

"No."

"Just tell us, Noah," Marcus insisted, in no mood for a game.

"Fine—be that way," said Noah. "The other number is in Doha."

"Doha?" Jenny asked. "As in the capital of Qatar?"

"Is there another?"

"Not that I'm aware of."

"This is where most of the calls are to and from," Noah explained. "There are only three calls to Istanbul, but thirteen to Doha."

"That's where his handler is," Gilad said.

"Then that's where we need to go," said Marcus.

★

HEZBOLLAH HEADQUARTERS, BEIRUT, LEBANON

Sheikh Ja'far ibn al-Hussaini locked himself in his office.

He ordered his chief of staff and personal secretary to clear his schedule, keep everyone away, and put no calls through to him until he told them otherwise. He desperately needed time to think, time to come up with a way out of this self-inflicted catastrophe.

How in the world could this have happened? he asked himself over and over again. *How could his men have let this happen?* Against every instinct in his body, he had listened to the fools around him who had insisted he go on live television to tell the world that Hezbollah had captured three American spics. Worse, he had let himself be pressured by that traitor Amin al-Masri to speak to the nation even before al-Masri had turned over the prisoners to him. For what? None of it was true. And now the Americans had escaped.

Mubarak's advice had a certain logic that was compelling. Getting out in front of the story of the prisoners' escape by announcing that Hezbollah had uncovered and eliminated a joint Mossad/CIA spy ring had an unmistakable appeal. But how long would it be before the Americans showed up on their own television networks to give their version of what happened? Hours? Days? And what would he tell his forces, much less the world, then? The prisoners would very likely sound far more credible than he when they went public. They, after all, knew what happened to them. He still had no idea.

No, he decided, he could not do another broadcast. Not yet. Not until he knew more. And certainly not until he had spoken to General Entezam. Or better yet, until he had spoken to President Afshar. But what was he going to tell them? How was he going to explain the utter incompetence of what was supposed to be the most feared terrorist organization in the world—what the Americans had once called "the A-Team" of international terror?

Tehran, however, was not his only problem. There was still the war with the Zionists. He had upwards of forty thousand IDF troops occupying the entire south of Lebanon, up to the Litani River. As a result of devastating air strikes, millions of Lebanese no longer had power to run their lights or air-conditioning or refrigerators or any of their appliances. They could no longer even watch a televised broadcast if he gave one. At the moment, all their anger was directed at the Zionists. But once they found out the Americans had escaped, would that change? Would their anger be directed at him? At Hezbollah? At the regime in Tehran?

He had to stop this war, the Sheikh suddenly realized. He had to find a way to declare victory and de-escalate. But how?

113

By the time the G5 landed, Noah had a new lead.

"NSA says the satellite phone account that al-Masri was calling so often in Doha is paid for by Al-Sawt," he told the team as they transferred to a different plane, in this case a Dassault Falcon 900 business jet.

"The news channel?" Jenny asked. "The so-called 'Voice of the Arabs'?"

"Exactly," Noah confirmed. "Now don't quote me on this—it's early yet, and Langley is trying to verify—but they believe this specific phone number is used by one of their producers, a man named Hamdi Yaşar."

"Does that name ring a bell with you, sir?" Marcus asked the Mossad chief.

"No, it doesn't, but I'll have my people get to work on it," said Gilad, immediately pulling out his secure mobile phone and drafting a text.

"What's Dell saying?" Jenny asked.

"At the moment, she's unavailable," said Noah. "She's en route to Tel

Aviv. But the watch officer at the Global Ops Center says Yaşar is a thirty-one-year-old Turkish national, a highly respected, award-winning field producer for Al-Sawt. He's a globe-trotter, focuses on foreign policy and national security stories, and has arranged interviews for his anchors and correspondents with most of the leaders throughout the Middle East, North Africa, and Europe."

"A Turkish national, you say?" Geoff asked.

"Yeah, why?"

"Oh, no reason," Geoff replied, winking at Marcus. "Go on."

"Anyway, Langley has no file on him," Noah continued. "There's no record of Yaşar being involved in terrorism or criminal activity of any kind."

"Then he would be perfect for this," said Tomer. "He's got the ideal cover as a middleman."

"For whom?" Jenny asked. "General Entezam?"

"Maybe," said Tomer.

"Or Ahmet Mustafa?" Geoff asked.

Tomer nodded. "Perhaps. Or maybe . . . Abu Nakba."

"We need to find out fast," said Marcus. "If this Hamdi guy is linked to this, we need to grab him before he realizes that his man in Lebanon is dead."

"And we have his phone number and al-Masri's phone," said Noah.

Marcus turned back to Asher Gilad, who had finished sending his text. "Refile the flight plan," he said. "We need to go to Doha."

Gilad shook his head. "Mr. Ryker, that's not how it's going to work. First of all, I don't work for you. Second of all, this is a Mossad jet, not the CIA's. It's registered to a high-tech start-up company in Tel Aviv. We can't just fly to Qatar. So that's the bad news. The good news is we're heading to Cairo as planned, and I'm going to put you on the phone with Director Stephens and Dr. Dell. You can make your case, and maybe they'll let you go to Doha on an Agency plane. Best I can do."

Marcus bristled at the insinuation that now that the Israelis had their guy back, they were bowing out. Catching the look in Jenny's eyes to watch his step, however, he tacked to a different course. "You're right, sir; sorry to presume," he said.

"That's okay, son. If it were up to me, I'd go grab this guy myself. But I've got a war to manage back home."

"Understood—but look, I'm not the best guy to brief Stephens and Dell."

"Why not?"

"It's a long story—way too long to get into here—but trust me when I say it would be far better coming from you."

"What exactly do you propose I tell them?"

"Call Stephens from your comms deck back there—very nice, by the way, state-of-the-art—and tell him we're out, we're safe, but we've uncovered a hot lead that needs to be acted on immediately. You can't do it. Tomer can't do it. But you recommend the rest of us go get this guy and see what he knows before he disappears off the grid, only to plot another attack. Meanwhile, in Cairo, we jump off and link up with our station chief. You guys head back to Tel Aviv with Agent Curtis and Mr. Mizrachi, make sure they get the care they need, and then you and your guys pursue whoever is in Istanbul that al-Masri was talking to."

Gilad looked Marcus in the eye, then around the cabin at the other Americans. "Happy to," he said. He walked to the rear of the plane, past the medics, to the communications center.

Fifteen minutes later, Gilad was back. The deal was done. Stephens and Dell were on board. A plane in Cairo was being readied, along with new passports and cover stories.

Within an hour, they would be headed to Qatar.

114

It was late in the evening when they finally touched down at Al Udeid Air Base.

Home of the forward headquarters for the U.S. Central Command, the air base was run jointly by the U.S. Air Force and the Qataris but also housed forces from the RAF and various other NATO countries, all involved in counterterrorism operations throughout the region. The team's cover story upon arriving was that they were American military advisors who had been wounded while assisting Egyptian forces combating al Qaeda, ISIS, and other insurgents operating in the northern Sinai. While they had been in the air, both the Egyptian Foreign Ministry and the U.S. State Department had issued brief statements to the media regarding a new terror attack near Egypt's border with the Gaza Strip resulting in a number of casualties. None of it was true, but it helped reinforce their cover in case the Qataris started asking questions. Fortunately, they did not.

When they left the air base in a black armor-plated Chevy Suburban, each member of the team had new passports and supporting documents with totally new identities and cover stories. All of them had been provided by the CIA's station in Cairo with assistance from a CIA field office on the base. They knew the stories would not hold up well under close scrutiny, but the plan Marcus and Jenny had mapped out called for them to be in the country for only a few hours.

It was 1:23 in the morning when they reached the luxury high-rise building where Hamdi Yaşar owned an apartment. They found a place to park on the street out front, grabbed their backpacks and duffel bags of equipment, jimmied a lock to a side door, and headed inside. Fanning out to three different elevators, they rode up to the twenty-third floor, regrouped, checked their weapons, and moved quickly to apartment 2319. Noah picked the lock. Marcus then eased the door open and led the team inside.

The vestibule was pitch-black. So were the living room and dining room. The lights in the kitchen were off too except for a night-light over the stovetop. Each team member now moved to their preassigned positions. Noah closed and locked the door behind them and guarded it. No one was getting in or out except through him. As he waited for the others to creep forward, he also quietly removed a device from his pocket and activated it. This jammed the Wi-Fi and all phones and electronic devices in the flat so that no one could call in or out. No one in such a fancy VIP building used landlines anymore, so that was of no concern.

Marcus gave the signal. Geoff and Jenny quietly slipped into the children's room, where a boy and a girl both under the age of six were sleeping soundly. Geoff stood over the boy, Jenny over the girl. On a silent count of three, they quickly put strips of duct tape over the children's mouths, then bound their hands and feet with tape as well. Jenny told them in fluent Arabic that they needed to be quiet and assured them that everything was going to be over soon, and no one would hurt them. Then she left Geoff to keep watch over them, returned to the hallway, and closed the door behind her.

With Marcus in the lead, they burst into the master bedroom. Marcus and Callaghan moved for Hamdi. Jenny took care of the terrified wife. Within seconds, the wife had been drugged, her mouth covered with tape, and her hands and feet tied up. It took a few more seconds to subdue her husband, but though he struggled wildly, he was never able to make a sound. Then he, too, was drugged and fell silent.

As Callaghan bound the Turk's hands and feet, Marcus searched the bedroom. He found a loaded pistol under a pillow and breathed a silent prayer of thanks that Yaşar had not been given the opportunity to grab and use it. A thorough search of the rest of the bedroom turned up nothing, so Marcus went hunting. A spare bedroom next door turned out to be Yaşar's private office, and this proved a treasure trove. Marcus found three laptops, multiple satellite phones, two sets of file cabinets, and a wall safe.

After loading up as much as he could in the two duffel bags they had brought, Marcus relieved Noah and sent the young man to go crack the safe. Three minutes later, Noah returned with both duffel bags in hand. The job was done. The safe was open. All the contents had been removed. They were good to go.

Marcus returned to the master bedroom. He nodded to Jenny to go help Noah get everything down to the car and for Callaghan to do the same with Yaşar. The wife he left in her bed, sleeping soundly. Marcus checked her pulse before he left. She was fine. He saw the woman's purse on the dresser. Inside, he found her mobile phone. He took it out and set it on the bed beside her. In a few hours, she would wake up. She would get the tape off her mouth and call the police. She would tell them she did not remember anything and she and her children were fine, but her husband was missing. By then they would be on a plane heading for a black site with their prisoner and two bags full of evidence.

As he headed down the hallway to leave, he stopped at the children's room. Both were propped up in their beds, a look of terror in their eyes. Marcus felt a pang of compassion for them. But there was nothing he could do. Their father had put them in this situation, not him. He motioned for Geoff to catch up with the others. Then he noticed a television and DVD player on the side table. He turned it on, found a bootleg version of *Toy Story* in Arabic, put it on with the volume set low, and gestured for the kids to stay quiet and not to move. Then he closed the door and set a chair in front of it so they could not easily get out until their mother came for them. And with that, the team slipped away as quickly and quietly as they had come.

115

"Your Excellency, they are here."

"Very well," Yadollah Afshar told his aide, looking up from his briefing papers and removing his reading glasses. "Let them in."

A moment later, the troika was back together—the president of the Islamic Republic, the commander of Revolutionary Guard Corps, and the director of the country's ballistic missile program—huddled in Afshar's private study with strict orders that they not be disturbed.

"I understand you have news, General," the president began.

"I'm afraid I do, and none of it is good," replied Mahmoud Entezam. "I just received a call from the Sheikh in Beirut. For starters, all the computers in their war room have been shut down by a computer virus."

"The Zionists?"

"No."

"The Americans?"

"No—al-Masri."

"What?"

"The virus was embedded in the proof-of-life video al-Masri sent the Sheikh. For reasons that are beyond me, they didn't run a virus check before they opened it. Now everything is fried. They're working from a backup system, but it's complicating everything. Furthermore, the war is turning very decidedly against them. The Sheikh admitted to me that his forces have sustained immense casualties, and—"

"How many?"

"Hezbollah has lost almost thirty-five hundred, to say nothing of their wounded."

"*Thirty-five hundred?*" Afshar said in disbelief.

"I'm afraid so."

"That's, what? Seven or eight times what they lost in '06?"

"Give or take, yes, Your Excellency," Entezam replied.

"The numbers in the news reports have been much lower—barely over two hundred."

"Well, sir, they're telling the press that most of these are civilian casualties, but the bitter truth is the Zionists have had far better intelligence this time around, far more precise missiles, and are exacting a far higher price. Not only that, but the Zionists have intercepted roughly 75 percent of Hezbollah's rockets, limiting their dead to 157 at the moment and their wounded to around 600 or so."

Afshar was furious.

"How is this possible, Haydar? You assured us that Hezbollah's rockets and missiles had our most advanced guidance systems."

Dr. Haydar Abbasi looked pale. It was obvious he had no idea how to respond, but Entezam didn't give him the chance.

"Your Excellency, this is not the worst part," said the IRGC commander.

Afshar's face was flushed as he turned back to Entezam. "No?"

"No."

"What now?"

"Your Excellency, I must inform you that the main reason the Sheikh was calling was to tell us that . . ."

"That what?"

"It's the prisoners, sir."

"What about them?"

"They have escaped."

"What? All of them? That's impossible."

"Actually, sir, *rescued* might be the better word for it," Entezam clarified. "Yesterday morning, around eight o'clock local time, a team of special forces operators—all disguised as Hezbollah commandos from the Radwan Unit—conducted a raid on a cargo terminal at the Beirut airport. It is not clear at this time whether they were Americans or Zionists. Possibly both. Likely both. But anyway, what is clear is that they rescued all three hostages and took out the Hezbollah cell that had captured them."

Now it was Afshar who looked pale. He sat there behind his desk for the longest time, unable to speak. Entezam could not help but note that the man was no longer dressed in a $3,000 suit from Savile Row, silk tie, French cuffs, and hand-tooled Italian shoes. Ever since his address to the nation on Saturday night, Afshar had begun wearing the black robes and turban of the clerics. He said it was to honor his mentor and spiritual father, the late Hossein Ansari. But Entezam knew better. The man was positioning himself to become the next Supreme Leader, and this was a none-too-subtle reminder to every member of the Assembly of Experts that, in fact, he was one of them.

With every passing day, it was becoming more unbearable for Entezam even to be in the presence of this man he so deeply despised. Yet this was not the time to make his move. The nation was in mourning. The assembly did not want a messy succession battle. If Afshar wanted the role, and there was no question that he did, then Entezam's read was that the assembly was prepared to anoint him and to do it quickly. That was why Entezam knew he had to watch his step. He had to embrace Afshar, pledge his support, convince him of his loyalty. For now, anyway. Otherwise, Afshar would soon be in a position to remove Entezam from his post and banish him to the outer reaches of the Republic.

"Your Excellency, if I may," he said, trying to reengage the increasingly despondent chief executive.

Afshar nodded his consent.

"Your Excellency, I believe the time has come to cut our losses," Entezam explained. "Al-Hussaini was not your choice to lead Hezbollah. Nor was he mine. He was, as you well know, chosen by our dearly departed friend, peace be upon him. But he is clearly in over his head. He has made one decision after another that has put our entire strategic plan in jeopardy."

"What are you saying, Mahmoud?" Afshar asked.

"I'm saying it's time to tell the Sheikh enough is enough. End the war. Stop the missiles. Appeal to the U.N. to pressure the Zionists to pull back. Quiet things down. Let's focus on making you our next Supreme Leader. And once that's done—once you have what is rightfully yours—then we can make decisions about whether the Sheikh is fit to lead or whether it is time to install a man more worthy of the task and more loyal to you and the future of the revolution."

Afshar nodded almost imperceptibly. But he said nothing. So Entezam continued, turning to his right, to the short, wiry, balding man in his late fifties with his thick wire-rimmed glasses and trim salt-and-pepper beard.

"The time has come for a clean slate and a fresh start, has it not, Dr. Abbasi?"

"Yes, of course—I could not agree more."

"Those unable or unworthy must be rooted out, wherever they are—true?"

Abbasi, white as a ghost, nodded, and Entezam saw the man's hands trembling. Without taking his eyes off the missile chief, Entezam pressed the offensive.

"Your Excellency, this man is a traitor. I have conclusive and overwhelming proof that he has been passing our most intimate secrets and plans to the head of Saudi intelligence. Video and audio recordings from cameras and microphones hidden in his apartment. Transcripts of the calls. Dates. Times. Like Amin al-Masri, this man has betrayed us to the worst of our enemies. I recommend we put him on trial and hang him immediately."

Afshar's emotions shifted yet again, from shock to rage. "Is this true,

Haydar? Have you sold out the revolution, and to the House of Saud, of all infidels?"

"No . . . I . . . It's not . . . But how . . . ?"

Afshar suddenly shot to his feet. Instinctively, Entezam did as well. Abbasi, however, could not move.

"In the name of Allah, I command you to tell me the truth," the president demanded.

Abbasi tried but could say nothing, his face covered with perspiration.

"There will be no trial," Afshar sneered. "The last thing we need, especially in the face of such incompetence by the Sheikh, is to give our enemies one more reason to gloat. You will burn for this, Haydar. You will burn today."

The president nodded to the IRGC commander.

Entezam drew the nickel-plated pistol from his holster. He aimed into Abbasi's terror-filled eyes. And then he squeezed the trigger.

116

Marine One landed at the mountain retreat center just before 9 a.m.

Soon President Andrew Clarke pulled up on a golf cart in front of Laurel Lodge, flanked by his Secret Service detail. When he spotted Marcus and Jenny, the commander in chief gave them each a bear hug and asked how they were doing.

"We're fine, sir," Jenny replied. "Thanks for asking."

"And you, Ryker? You trying to give me an ulcer? It's always something with you."

"Yes, sir—I mean no, sir," Marcus replied.

Clarke slapped him on the back. "How about Agent Curtis? How's she holding up?"

"She apologizes for not being here," Marcus said. "She's going to need a bit more time, but she'll be back on her feet and giving me grief soon enough."

"Good," Clarke said. "Talk to your mom yet?"

"Briefly, by phone."

"And that girlfriend of yours?"

Marcus was blindsided. "Sir?"

"You know, that one you brought to the correspondents' dinner—or started to and then bailed. Works for Dayton, right?"

Marcus could see the look in his colleagues' eyes. They knew none of this, but they were going to have a field day ribbing him the first chance they got.

"Annie," Marcus said.

"Right, right, Annie Stewart—not bad, Ryker, not bad at all."

"Uh, thank you, sir, but how did you—?"

Clarke chuckled. "Are you kidding, Ryker? I know *everything* about you."

"Apparently—more than my mom."

"You haven't told your mom?"

"It was only dinner, sir."

"Well, for crying out loud, Ryker, what are you waiting for?"

Marcus was dying, but the president was hardly finished. "She's in the Springs, right?"

"I'm sorry?"

"Your mom—she lives out in Colorado, right, in the Springs?"

"Well, Monument, sir, but close enough."

"When do you head out there?"

"As soon as we get this thing wrapped up, Mr. President."

"Are you taking Annie?"

"Sir, really, it was just dinner," Marcus insisted, in no mood to talk about his private life with the president of the United States or these jokers from the Secret Service. He would never hear the end of it.

Clarke laughed. "You're a terrible liar, Ryker—I don't know why we let you do what you do. But very well, let's get started."

When the president turned and took Jenny into the conference room, Marcus's Secret Service buddies erupted in laughter.

"Annie Stewart, huh?" one agent quipped, punching Marcus on the arm. "Nice."

"Shut up, Tom," Marcus said, mortified but hardly angry.

With all the agents ribbing him—their way, he knew, of welcoming him home—Marcus headed into the conference room as well. The entire National Security Council was present, and everyone was standing. When the president took his seat at the table, they all took theirs. Marcus spotted Jenny and sat next to her against the wall with several mid-level NSC staffers.

Marcus was not seated for long, however. After the president opened the meeting and introduced their two "special guests," he asked the director of Central Intelligence to bring them all up to speed. Almost immediately Stephens turned the floor over to Marcus. Marcus stood and walked around the table to a set of large flat-screen monitors mounted on one of the wood-paneled walls. It had been five days since he, Kailea, and Yigal had been rescued. There was no need to recap any of that. Nor did he need to cover the snatching and imprisonment of Hamdi Yaşar. All the principals had been given daily briefings by Stephens and National Security Advisor Bill McDermott.

"Mr. President, Mr. Vice President, General Meyers, ladies and gentlemen, first of all I want to say thank you for everything you did to rescue Agent Curtis and me, and of course the prime minister's nephew," Marcus began. "I've only been back on American soil for a couple of hours. I landed at Andrews this morning after spending most of the week at Gitmo. But I can't even begin to express my gratitude, and Kailea's, to you all. We're proud to be Americans and proud to have the honor of serving our country."

The room erupted in applause and then a standing ovation. Marcus blushed for the second time in as many minutes. That was not what he had expected or intended. He just had to start at the beginning.

"We can now say conclusively that the raid on the Israeli border patrol one week ago today was solely the act of the terrorist organization we have come to know as Kairos," Marcus said when everyone settled down. "Did Hezbollah and the Iranians seize the moment and take advantage of it? Absolutely. But the evidence is overwhelming that this was not a plan hatched by them. It was hatched by this man."

A grainy black-and-white photo came up on the screen.

"This is Walid Abdel-Shafi," Marcus explained. "Born in the Gaza Strip in 1936, he is better known to all of you as Abu Nakba—'Father of the Disaster'—and is the founder and spiritual leader of the terrorist organization we have come to know as Kairos."

Marcus put another photo on the screen. It was in color, though faded a bit, taken sometime in the late 2000s.

"On the left, you'll see Abu Nakba again. On the right is Hamdi Yaşar, now thirty-one years old, born and raised in Istanbul, a celebrated producer for the Al-Sawt satellite news network. As you know, we have him in custody. But you may not know that he is in fact Abu Nakba's closest and most trusted advisor."

117

Marcus now showed a series of disturbing photos.

Each showed the carnage from a different Kairos attack over the past eighteen months. Some were from the church shooting in Washington, and the subsequent car bombing in D.C. that took the life of Ambassador Tyler Reed. Others showed the suicide bombing at Number 10 Downing Street that killed former National Security Advisor Barry Evans and the suicide bombing on the Temple Mount during the peace summit. Marcus said nothing as he worked his way through the photos. There was no need to go through the particulars of each event. The looks on everyone's faces were proof enough of how deeply and forever etched in their psyches these attacks were.

"Hamdi Yaşar may not be talking to us—yet—but believe me, his hard drives are," Marcus finally said. "His phones are. His files are. The videos of each attack we found in his possession are. Yes, grabbing him in the capital of an ally we had not informed we were coming was a risk. And I know that some of you have questioned the wisdom of that tactic. But it has paid off in spades, and I'm grateful to Director Stephens, Dr. Dell, and most of all to the president for the decision to give us the green light."

At this, Marcus introduced Jenny, who spent several minutes briefing the group in more detail on what they had gleaned from the files and equipment they had taken from the apartment of Hamdi Yaşar. When she was done, she showed slides documenting the number of phone calls Yaşar had made to al-Masri and Abu Nakba, often within minutes of each other. Next, she showed details of wire transfers from a bank in Athens to banks in Switzerland, accounts belonging to—or at least controlled by—Yaşar, according to records found in his safe.

"We were told the name of the organization was Kairos, but that's not the real name, and the organization is not Greek," Jenny explained. "The reason neither we nor any of our allies, including the Greek government, have ever found any solid evidence that Abu Nakba and his team are operating in Greece is because they aren't. The name, the press releases, and the other assorted breadcrumbs we've picked up in Athens and Corinth were all designed by Abu Nakba and his operatives to send us and other intelligence agencies on a wild-goose chase."

Finally she put up satellite reconnaissance photos of a desert compound.

"This is the real home and base of operations for Abu Nakba," she continued. "This is where he lives and works and plots his wicked schemes. The compound is located just outside a godforsaken town in the western desert of Libya known as Ghat. It's not far from the Algerian border. Abu Nakba was born in Gaza, but he was actually raised in the oil fields of Libya, and that's where he settled. We have receipts of nine flights that Hamdi Yaşar has made to Libya—mostly Tripoli, but also Benghazi—from Doha or other cities around the Mideast and Europe over the last several years. We have no hard evidence linking Yaşar to the compound in Ghat. But NSA has reconfirmed—less than an hour ago, in fact—that the satellite phone Yaşar has been calling so often is still active and is currently located inside that compound."

When she was done, the president asked the question on everyone's mind.

"Where are we going with this, Miss Morris? What are you and Ryker recommending?"

At this, Jenny deferred to Marcus.

"Sir, we are both nonofficial cover officers for the Central Intelligence Agency," he replied. "It is not our role to make recommendations, simply to bring you actionable intelligence."

"So you want me to take action?" asked Clarke.

"Again, that's not my place, sir."

"But you want me to order General Meyers here to bomb that compound to kingdom come, right?"

All eyes were on Marcus. He was being asked a direct question by the commander in chief of the United States. Marcus had no intention of glancing over at Director Stephens, though he could see the man was about to cut him off. So Marcus just looked the president in the eye and said, "Well, sir, that sounds about right to me."

There was a discussion, but it was brief. The president polled the room. The result was unanimous. Everyone wanted him to strike, even Secretary of State Meg Whitney, fresh back from the region.

"Mr. President," Whitney said, "I'm happy to report that Hezbollah is de-escalating. The Israelis are ready to pull their troops back to the Blue Line once the rockets stop flying. And believe it or not, we're all set to host the Israelis and the Saudis for a signing on the South Lawn of the White House on Tuesday. I can't think of any better message to send to the radical jihadists of the world that their day is done and a new era of Middle East peace and prosperity has dawned."

POTUS nodded and scanned the room, then looked back at Marcus and Jenny. "So be it—let's get it done."

★

Thirty-seven minutes later, a squad of F-35 fighter jets took off from the deck of the USS *Nimitz*, which was presently steaming across the Mediterranean Sea. As the president and his national security team watched on the monitors, the jets swooped low, hard, and fast across the Libyan desert to avoid detection, then shot up into the blazing afternoon sky and fired their missiles.

The compound was obliterated in a blinding fireball in a matter of seconds, and the satellite phone signal they were all watching on the monitors suddenly went silent.

The room erupted in cheers. Everyone leaped to their feet, shaking hands, slapping each other on the back, and celebrating the total annihilation of the group that had terrorized them and taken too many of their friends.

Everyone, that was, except Marcus.

"You okay?" Jenny asked.

"No," he said, fighting back his emotions. "But I will be."

She bent down and gave him a gentle kiss on the cheek.

"I know," she said. "I know."

EPILOGUE

United flight 212 landed just before 8 p.m. Mountain time.

Marcus Ryker had not checked any luggage, so he grabbed his carry-on from the overhead compartment, passed through the terminal, and caught a cab. As he made the short drive to Monument, gazing out at the snowcapped Rocky Mountains, Marcus finally let himself breathe a sigh of relief. His mom still did not know he was back in the country, much less heading her way. Stephens and Dell had insisted he not tell anyone, even her, that he was coming. They had even booked his ticket under an alias, so determined were they to keep the Ryker name out of the media.

As the taxi pulled up in front of his childhood home, a storm of conflicting emotions was building inside him. On the one hand, when he thought about everything he had been through over the past week, it was surreal to be back here, of all places. Yet the joy of it was offset somewhat by the pain and worry he had once again put his mother through. And then there was Oleg Kraskin, aka the Raven. He was living—and working for the Agency now—up near Aspen, only a few hours away. Marcus needed to catch up with him, and soon. But there was no way he could see his Russian friend on this particular trip.

Marcus paid the driver and walked up the driveway and onto the front porch. Spotting his mom's rocking chair, he also heard her voice inside. She was talking to someone on the phone. Hoping to maximize the surprise, he did not walk right in. Rather, he rang the doorbell and waited with anticipation.

When his mom came to the door, it took her a moment to register what she was seeing. But then, rather than burst into tears, she burst out laughing.

Marcus, caught off guard, started laughing too.

Then she opened the screen door and put her arms around him. "Wow— it's really you—welcome home, sweetheart."

"Thanks, Mom," he said, his eyes filling a bit. "I didn't die, but I guess I did get arrested."

"I suppose I'll let it slide this time," she whispered.

They stood there for several minutes, just holding each other and not saying another word. This woman was incredible, Marcus thought. He had always assumed that he had inherited his father's courage and grit. But he was beginning to think it was just as much an inheritance from his mother. Yes, she had missed him. And yes, like any mother, she had worried about him every day. But she had not gone to pieces. She was a fighter pilot's widow. And the mother of a Marine. She did not fret, and she did not gush. And he loved her for it all the more.

"You hungry?" she finally asked.

"Famished."

They headed inside, and Mrs. Ryker made them a late dinner of steak, asparagus, and potatoes. And broke out a nice bottle of merlot. Marcus shared a little about his adventures, but not much. Most of it was classified, but that was not really it. There were some things you just did not tell your mother.

What he did tell her was they had tickets to head right back to Washington the following day.

"Washington? Good heavens, whatever for?"

Marcus explained that he wanted her to be his guest at the signing ceremony at the White House on Tuesday afternoon when history was set to be made. The Saudi crown prince would be there without his father, as the king, sadly, was apparently too ill to make the journey. The Israeli prime minister would also be present. And of course the president and vice president of the United States.

"It's really happening?" Mrs. Ryker asked.

"Yeah," Marcus replied. "It really is."

"I can't believe it."

"I know—it's crazy. This is the first new official peace treaty to be signed between Israel and an Arab neighbor since October of 1994."

"That was with Jordan, right?"

"That's right—signed by King Hussein and Yitzhak Rabin."

"Has it really been that long?"

"Other than the agreement with the UAE, yes. I was just a teenager."

"And you really want me to be there?" Mrs. Ryker asked, still incredulous. "That all seems too grand for me."

"If you say no, you'll have to take that up with the president."

"Whatever for?"

"Because he's the one who insisted that I come get you."

Marcus's mom sat there for a moment, her plate of food barely touched. Then she finally asked her son a question. "Sweetheart?"

"Yeah?"

"Maybe I shouldn't ask this, but . . ."

"What?"

"I was just wondering . . ."

"Spit it out, Mom. What's on your mind?"

"I was just wondering if there was any chance that you could get one more ticket."

"Probably. Why?"

"Because there's someone who would like to see you, and I thought that maybe you should ask her to come with you to the ceremony as well."

Marcus could not believe what he was hearing. How did she even know about this? They had only gone on one date. And yet it seemed that everyone knew.

"Mom, I'm not going with Annie. It's not exactly the kind of event you take a date to. And besides, she'll already be there with Senator Dayton."

"Annie? Annie who?"

"Annie Stewart."

"Now why would I want you to go with Annie Stewart? Lovely girl. Don't get me wrong. But what does she have to do with this?"

Marcus just sat there bewildered. Some spy he was.

"No, no—don't be ridiculous," his mother continued.

"Okay, then who?" asked Marcus.

"Maya."

"Maya Emerson?"

"Of course."

"Uh, I don't think she—"

"You're wrong, Marcus."

"Am I?"

"Yes, you are. Maya and I have been talking all week, praying for you and catching up, and I'm telling you she feels terrible about how she left things with you, but she doesn't know quite how to broach the subject. So I just thought . . ."

Marcus leaned over and gave her a kiss on the forehead. "Happy to— thanks."

★

WASHINGTON, D.C.—MAY 12

The two of them took a Washington Flyer cab to the White House. It was a stunning spring day. Blue sky. Bright sun. Vivid-green lawns. Brilliant-red roses. And dozens of American, Israeli, and Saudi flags snapping in the refreshing afternoon breeze.

Everyone who was anyone in the Washington elite was there. At a private, off-the-record meet and greet in the Oval Office, President Clarke offered to seat Marcus and his mom near the front. Indeed, Prime Minister Eitan and Asher Gilad insisted upon it, as did the Saudi crown prince. Marcus, however, thanked them but politely declined. "It's your day, gentlemen."

"But this is history, Ryker," the president declared. "It wouldn't be possible without you, and you should be honored for your role."

"With respect, sir, it is history, and I'm so glad you all have gotten to this point. But you know as well as I do that I'm the one who is going to be history if the Iranians catch a glimpse of me anywhere in this crowd."

They laughed and agreed, and Marcus and his mom said their goodbyes to take their place on the lawn. As they headed through the West Wing, they ran into Pete Hwang and Bill McDermott. There were hugs all around, an impromptu reunion of the last survivors of their Marine Expeditionary Unit from so long before.

"We good?" Marcus whispered as he hugged Pete.

"Yeah," Pete whispered in reply, slapping Marcus on the back twice. "We're good."

McDermott excused himself, needing to get back to the side of the principals. Marcus, his mother, and Pete headed out to the South Lawn and found a row of empty seats—the absolute last row, in fact. Far from the congressional leadership. Far from the diplomats and the Joint Chiefs. Far from the media and the rest of the Washington glitterati.

Unfortunately, Kailea was going to be in the hospital for some time. She was expected to make a full recovery, but she was in no condition to join them that beautiful spring afternoon. Likewise, Yigal Mizrachi was not well enough to make the trip with his uncle, the prime minister. He was in stable condition at Hadassah hospital in Jerusalem and had a long road of recovery ahead of him.

As the Marine Corps band began to warm up, preparing to play the national anthems of all three countries, Marcus was surprised to see Senator Robert Dayton and his wife coming up the aisle toward them. With them was Jenny Morris. And Annie Stewart.

"Ryker, I see you've got a few seats left there," said Dayton. "May we join you?"

Marcus immediately rose to his feet. "Sir, you're more than welcome, of course, but I think all the seats for prominent Democrats who don't completely hate the president are up front."

"Yeah, yeah, yeah—but we thought it might be more fun to sit back here in the cheap seats with all of you. Mind?"

"Not at all, sir. We'd be honored."

The senator beamed, then reintroduced his wife to Mrs. Ryker. Marcus introduced Jenny to everyone but felt strangely awkward with Annie. His mother, though, gave her a warm hug and asked Annie to sit next to her. Marcus suddenly regretted that he had not yet told his mother of his romantic interest in her. Everyone shook hands and chitchatted. Then Marcus noticed that Pete gave Annie a hug. With the Marine band's warm-up session growing louder, he could not actually hear what the two were saying, but it looked amiable enough, and Marcus felt himself relax.

At the last moment, as everyone was beginning to take their seats, Maya Emerson found them. She looked warm and flustered, and she apologized repeatedly for being late. She also gave Marcus a kiss on the cheek and whispered, "Can we talk after the ceremony?"

"We can," Marcus whispered back. "But there's no need, Maya. Consider it all forgiven and forgotten. Water under the bridge."

"Bless you, child," she replied, giving him another hug. "You're a good boy."

Marcus gave her his seat. The only space that remained was next to Annie, on the other side of Marcus's mom, and that was where Pete was about to sit. Instead, Pete silently but most adamantly insisted that Marcus take it, while he headed for a seat at the far end of the row.

Reluctantly Marcus accepted it, sitting down next to Annie. Jenny leaned back, caught his eye, and winked mischievously, but before anyone could say anything, the ceremony mercifully began. The anthems were probably quite stirring. The speeches were almost certainly moving and historic. But Marcus would never remember any of it. It occurred to him how much Elena would have enjoyed being here and seeing this, and all at once he found himself missing her terribly. But in the end that thought, too, faded.

Later he realized he could not remember the cheers, the music, the standing ovation. He did not even remember watching the prime minister and the crown prince sign the treaty.

All he could remember was holding Annie's hand.

ACKNOWLEDGMENTS

It is surreal to me that I actually get to write novels for a living.

How is that even possible?

I'm so grateful for this dream come true and so grateful to each and every person who helps make this dream a reality.

Scott Miller has been my rock-star literary agent and dear friend from the very beginning of my career—he and the Trident Media Group are absolutely fantastic.

Tyndale House has been my rock-star publishing team for all but two of my books and they are equally fantastic—Mark Taylor, Jeff Johnson, Ron Beers, Karen Watson, Jan Stob, Andrea Garcia, Maria Eriksen, Danika King, the entire sales force, and all the remarkable professionals who make Tyndale an industry leader. Thanks to copy editor Erin Smith. And very special thanks to Jeremy Taylor, the best editor in the business, and to Dean Renninger, who keeps designing one gorgeous book cover after another.

Nancy Pierce and June Meyers are my rock-star personal assistants, taking care of all of my logistical needs, from scheduling and correspondence to flights and finances and so much more—always with good cheer, grace, and faithful prayer. I couldn't be more thankful for them both.

A big shout-out to my parents, Leonard and Mary Jo Rosenberg, and to all of my extended family and Lynn's. I can always count on all of them for wise and patient counsel, prayer, and much-needed encouragement, and to make me laugh and keep perspective, even in a crazy and cruel year like 2020.

I could not be prouder of, or more thankful for, our four dear sons: Caleb—and his lovely wife, Rachel—Jacob, Jonah, and Noah. The more they grow in wisdom and stature and in favor with God and with men, the more I relax and smile and know that they will do just fine in this hard world. And the more I miss them when they head off for new schools, new jobs, and new missions. I love you guys so much.

To my beautiful, brilliant, and courageous wife, Lynn, thank you for marrying me and making me the happiest and most satisfied man on earth. I have treasured each and every moment that God has given us together over these thirty-plus years, even the hard ones. I never want them to end. There is nothing I fear more than losing you. May the God who gave us to each other in the first place keep us close and safe to the finish line. For my part, I will stick to you like glue.

ABOUT THE AUTHOR

Joel C. Rosenberg is a *New York Times* bestselling author of sixteen novels and five nonfiction books with nearly 5 million copies in print.

Rosenberg's career as a political thriller writer was born out of his filmmaking studies at Syracuse University, where he graduated with a BFA in film drama in 1989. He also studied for nearly six months at Tel Aviv University during his junior year. Following graduation from Syracuse, he moved to Washington, D.C., where he worked for a range of U.S. and Israeli leaders and nonprofit organizations, serving variously as a policy analyst and communications strategist.

He has been profiled by the *New York Times*, the *Washington Times*, and the *Jerusalem Post* and has appeared on hundreds of radio and TV programs in the U.S., Canada, and around the world. As a sought-after speaker, he has addressed audiences at the White House, the Pentagon, the U.S. Capitol, the Israeli president's residence, the European Union parliament in Brussels, and business and faith conferences in North America and around the world.

The grandson of Orthodox Jews who escaped out of czarist Russia in the early 1900s, Rosenberg comes from a Jewish background on his father's side and a Gentile background on his mother's side.

Rosenberg is the founder and chairman of The Joshua Fund, a nonprofit educational and humanitarian relief organization. He is also the founder and editor in chief of All Israel News (allisrael.com) and All Arab News (allarab.news).

He and his wife, Lynn, are dual U.S.-Israeli citizens. They made aliyah in 2014 and live in Jerusalem, Israel. They have four sons, Caleb, Jacob, Jonah, and Noah.

For more information, visit joelrosenberg.com and follow Joel on Twitter (@joelcrosenberg) and Facebook (facebook.com/JoelCRosenberg).

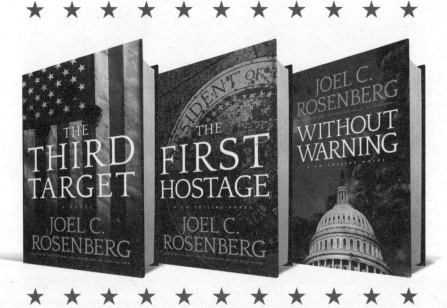